GUILDWARS®

EDGE OF
DESTINY

J. ROBERT KING

Based on the Acclaimed Video Game Series
from ArenaNet

POCKET STAR BOOKS

NEW YORK   LONDON   TORONTO   SYDNEY

Pocket Star Books
A Division of Simon & Schuster, Inc.
1230 Avenue of the Americas
New York, NY 10020

First Pocket Star Books paperback edition January 2011

POCKET STAR BOOKS and colophon are registered trademarks of Simon & Schuster, Inc.

For information about special discounts for bulk purchases, please contact Simon & Schuster Special Sales at 1-866-506-1949 or business@simonandschuster.com.

The Simon & Schuster Speakers Bureau can bring authors to your live event. For more information or to book an event contact the Simon & Schuster Speakers Bureau at 1-866-248-3049 or visit our website at www.simonspeakers.com.

Cover art by Kekai Kotaki
Cover design by AJ Thompson
Map cartography by Robert Lazzaretti

Manufactured in the United States of America

10   9   8   7   6   5

ISBN 978-1-4165-8960-0
ISBN 978-1-4391-5604-9 (ebook)

The moment before the axe-rifles fired, Logan Thackeray swept his hand out in a fan.

A blue aura bled from his fingertips into the air, solidifying it in a curved wall before the scouts.

"Fire!" the charr centurion roared.

The axe-rifles boomed and vomited smoke and lead. But the shots struck the ethereal membrane and sank into it and were eaten away. Bullets showered rust to the ground.

The leader of the charr stared, his jaw dropping. "You're full of surprises!"

"I'm Logan Thackeray. I protect those who are mine."

"I'm Rytlock Brimstone," the charr shot back. "I kill those who aren't."

"I recognize your blade. Did you say *Rurik* Brimstone?"

"Rytlock," the charr snarled.

Logan shrugged. "I just figured since you stole Prince Rurik's sword, you probably also stole his name."

Rytlock lashed the air with the burning blade. "The sword's mine now."

"After this fight," Logan said, whirling his war hammer in a figure eight, "Sohothin will once again be in the hands of a human."

"*During* this fight," Rytlock spat, "Sohothin will once again be in the *guts* of a human." He looked back at the charr around him. "Turn those damned rifles around and chop them to pieces!"

To Eli, the ardent player;

To Aidan, the ardent listener; and

To Gabe, who named his hamster Rytlock

Acknowledgments

Many thanks to everyone at ArenaNet, especially Will McDermott, Ree Soesbee, Jeff Grubb, James Phinney, Randy Price, Stephen Hwang, Colin Johanson, David Wilson, and Bobby Stein. A special thanks to Jeff Strain, Patrick Wyatt, and Mike O'Brien, the founders of ArenaNet and creators of *Guild Wars*.

Thanks also to Pocket Books and Ed Schlesinger, and to fellow authors Matt Forbeck and Jeff Grubb.

And thanks especially to Jennie and the boys, for putting up with me as I fight dragons.

Time Line

10,000 BE: Last of the Giganticus Lupicus, the Great Giants, disappear from the Tyrian continent.

205 BE: Humans appear on the Tyrian continent.

100 BE: Humans drive the charr out of Ascalon.

1 BE: The Human Gods give magic to the races of Tyria.

0 AE: The Exodus of the Human Gods.

2 AE: Orr becomes an independent nation.

300 AE: Kryta established as a colony of Elona.

358 AE: Kryta becomes an independent nation.

898 AE: The Great Northern Wall is erected.

1070 AE: The Charr Invasion of Ascalon. The Searing.

1071 AE: The Sinking of Orr.

1072 AE: Ascalonian refugees flee to Kryta.

1075 AE: Kormir ascends into godhood.

1078 AE: Primordus, the Elder Fire Dragon, stirs but does not awaken. The asura appear on the surface. The Transformation of the Dwarves.

1080 AE: King Adelbern of Ascalon recalls the Ebon Vanguard; Ebonhawke is established.

1088 AE: Kryta unifies behind Queen Salma.

1090 AE: The charr legions take Ascalon City. The Foefire.

1105 AE: Durmand Priory is established in the Shiverpeaks.

1112 AE: The charr erect the Black Citadel over the ruins of the city of Rin in Ascalon.

1116 AE: Kalla Scorchrazor leads the rebellion against the Flame Legion's shaman caste.

1120 AE: Primordus awakens.

1165 AE: Jormag, the Elder Ice Dragon, awakens. The norn flee south into the Shiverpeaks.

1180 AE: The centaur prophet Ventari dies by the Pale Tree, leaving behind the Ventari Tablet.

1219 AE: Zhaitan, the Elder Undead Dragon, awakens. Orr rises from the sea. Lion's Arch floods.

1220 AE: Divinity's Reach is founded in the Krytan province of Shaemoor.

1230 AE: Corsairs and other pirates occupy the slowly drying ruins of Lion's Arch.

1302 AE: The sylvari first appear along the Tarnished Coast, sprouting from the Pale Tree.

1319 AE: Eir Stegalkin forms a band of heroes known as Destiny's Edge.

EDGE OF
DESTINY

Prologue

DREAM AND NIGHTMARE

The flames were beautiful. They looked like autumn leaves—red and gold, rattling as the wind tore through them, breaking free and whirling into the sky.

The village was flying away. Thatch and wattle and rafters all were going up in ash.

Caithe watched the village and the villagers burn.

She was too late. Everything was fire.

Still, it was beautiful.

Caithe, sylvari of the Firstborn, dropped down from the boulder where she had crouched and stalked slowly into the burning village. Like all of her people, Caithe was slender and lithe, the child of a great tree in a sacred grove. She was one with the natural world. Even her travel leathers bore the vine motifs of her homeland. Caithe pushed silvery hair back from wide eyes, watching for signs of life in the burning village. Only the flames lived. She listened for voices, but only the fire spoke.

Caithe didn't fear the fire. She was young and strong,

voracious and indomitable and curious—just like fire. It had drawn her here. It was *interesting.*

Who had started it? How? Why? What had this village been called?

"I love a bonfire," came a voice—deep and dark, feminine and familiar.

Caithe turned to see a sylvari woman garbed in a black-orchid gown as if this were some fancy ball. Caithe's eyes narrowed. "What are you doing here, Faolain?"

Faolain gave the suffering smile of an addict. "The fires drew me."

"A moth to a flame."

"Just like you."

In fact, Faolain and Caithe were nothing alike. Faolain's hair was jet-black, as were her nails and her eyes. They had been that way from the moment the two women emerged together from the Pale Tree. Faolain had been all about questions, and Caithe had been all about answers. They were dear to each other and set out together to explore the world. But Caithe's spirit had grown straight and true like a young tree while Faolain's had grown twisted like a poison-ivy vine.

"Did you set this fire?" Caithe asked.

Faolain threw back her shock of black hair and breathed smoke through flared nostrils. "A nice idea, but no. It was destroyers—magma monsters."

Caithe shook her head grimly. "They boil up everywhere."

"The Elder Dragon Primordus is taking back the world."

A loud moan came from a burning barn nearby.

Caithe rushed to the door, hauled it open, and stared within. The hayloft boiled with black smoke, and the threshing floor was mantled in fire. Against the far wall lay a blackened figure that could hardly have been alive—except that it moaned.

Caithe wove among the flames to reach the man and dropped to her knees. His eyes were gone, his face, too— just cracked bark over oozy muscle. His lips were half-fused. "Burning beast . . . burning beast . . . burning . . ."

"I will help you," Caithe said.

"Such sweet words," Faolain whispered, kneeling on the other side of the man. "Hope is like oil on the fires of misery."

"Is my skin peeled off?" the man groaned. "Is it?"

"Yes," Caithe said gently.

Faolain laughed. "Oh, you're cruel."

"They came from underground," he muttered. "They scrambled up. Roaches. Black, with bodies of fire—"

"Destroyers," Faolain said.

"We'll get you to a chirurgeon."

"Chirurgeon?" Faolain gripped Caithe's arm and grinned. "You're doing this for me, aren't you?"

"What? No! It's for him."

"He's dead already. You're only tormenting him for *my* sake."

"No! I'm not."

Faolain's eyes blazed. "You want me to feel for him. You want me to feel *empathy*."

"No!" Caithe said. "I mean, yes, of course."

"Help me!" the man sputtered, his lip splitting.

"I will," Caithe said.

Faolain's eyes slid closed, and her jaw clenched. "You can't win me back."

"I'm not trying to win you back."

"Come with me, Caithe. Join the Nightmare Court."

"I'm saving him!" Caithe yelled, reaching beneath the blackened figure and hoisting him from the floor. Caithe strode toward the barn doors.

But Faolain rose in her path and set her hand on Caithe's chest. The touch of her palm blazed like fire. Then a different sort of heat bloomed across Caithe's chest. She pulled back to see the farmer's throat fountaining, severed by Faolain's dagger.

"What?" Caithe cried, staggering back and falling to her knees. "You killed him?"

"I *released* him. Come with me."

"I will never turn to Nightmare."

Faolain's eyes flashed. "My touch—and the sacrifice of this man—have awakened darkness in you." She turned away. "You will be mine again soon."

PART I

GATHERING HEROES

1

FOOLS AND FOLLOWERS

D
on't move!"

The huge wolf snapped his head upright, eyes blazing.

"Stay exactly like that."

No one else in the world could order Garm to sit still. He was, after all, a dire wolf—five feet tall at the shoulder and twenty stone, with jet-black hackles and fire-red eyes. He was made to lope and chase and drag down. Not to sit still. Not to listen. But he did.

For Eir Stegalkin, he did.

Garm flicked a glance toward the norn warrior. She was tall, too, her hand rising to the rafters twelve feet up and snagging a mallet that hung there and bringing the thing down in her brawny grip. Her eyes darted toward Garm, who glanced forward again and tried to look fierce.

It wasn't that he feared this woman and her big hammer, which she swung just then with terrific force, pounding a massive chisel and striking a wedge of granite from a huge block. Garm hazarded a look at that block, amorphous and pitted from chisel strokes. Soon, it would be a statue. A statue of him. But that wasn't why he sat still.

He sat still because she was the alpha.

The mallet fell again, the chisel bit, the block calved. More chunks of stone crashed to the floor, first in wedges and then shards and chips and finally a shower of grit.

Garm's figure was taking shape.

Eir stepped back from the sculpture and dragged an arm over her sweating brow. Her face was statuesque, her eyes moss green. She had drawn her mane of red hair back out of the way, bound by a leather thong. The leather work-apron she wore freed her arms but protected her chest and legs against stone shards. An intense look grew on her face, eyes etching out the shape in the stone. "This could be my masterpiece."

Garm looked around the log-hewn workshop at her other sculptures—a rearing ice-bear, a great elk with sixteen-foot antlers, a coiling snow serpent that stretched from floor to rafters, and of course her army of norn warriors captured in stone and wood. They hadn't started out as an army, but individuals who had come to be immortalized before going off to fight the Dragonspawn—the champion of the Elder Dragon Jormag.

Now only their statues remained.

"Hail, house of Stegalkin!" came a shout at the door. A norn warrior thrust his head in—long hair like a horse's tail and a face like what might be beneath. "By the Bear, the place is packed!"

Someone behind the man hissed, thumping his shoulder, "Them's statues!"

The warrior in the lead nodded, his hair flicking as if to shoo flies. "Course they are. Statues. That's why we're here." He paused to hiccup. "Soon, one of them will be me. I mean, I'll be one of them. I mean, I'll get my own. By the Raven, you brew it strong, Uri."

Eir stood there unmoving except for the vein that pulsed in her temple. "Patrons." With mallet and chisel in hand, she strode toward the door.

Garm broke from his pose to lope at her heels.

The man in the doorway nearly stumbled off the threshold.

Eir said, "You have come full of . . . courage, but it smells of hops."

"Yes!" the man enthused, glancing back at a group of twenty or so norn warriors swaying in the courtyard. "I am Sjord Frostfist."

"Sjord Foamfist?" she mispronounced, raising an eyebrow.

"Exactly. And I have come by Snow Leopard and Raven and Bear—by every living beast—to declare war on the Dragonspawn!"

Eir nodded. "You've come to the wrong place. I am not the Dragonspawn."

Sjord laughed. "Of course you aren't. You are norn, like me."

"Not quite like you."

"No! Of course not," Sjord said, suddenly earnest. "You're an artist. While I carve up monsters, you carve up rocks."

The warriors laughed.

Eir's fist flexed around the mallet handle as if she were about to carve Sjord himself.

"No offense meant, of course. Somebody has to make statues of us."

Garm looked to his master, wondering why she didn't just kill the man. She could. This man and all the others. Or Garm could. With just a word from her, he would tear the man's throat out, but Eir never gave the word.

"You want a statue in your image."

Sjord put his finger to his nose, indicating that she understood exactly.

"Pick any you wish," she said, gesturing to the statues behind her. "Brave young fools just like you, who gathered at the moot and drank and decided to save the world. I've met you before, a hundred times. Each of these men went to fight the Dragonspawn."

Sjord's grin only widened. "Then we understand each other." He thrust a bag of coins into her hand.

Eir stared levelly at him. "Take your money. Go rent a room. Go lie down and sleep. You cannot defeat the Dragonspawn."

Sjord stepped back, affronted, and the warriors behind him raised their eyebrows. "You are saying we should give up? You are saying that our people should get used to fleeing our homelands? Why do you oppose a man who would fight our foe?"

"I do not oppose you. I *warn* you."

"Warn me of what?"

"You cannot defeat the Dragonspawn. You will go to fight him but will end up fighting *for* him."

Sjord shook his head. "I will fight him and kill him, and you will commemorate what I do. There is your payment."

Eir slipped open the drawstring. The bag held a small fortune in silver. She sighed. "Come, Sjord Frostfist. Let us select the block of wood that will be your memorial."

"Monument," he corrected. "And, it will be stone, not wood."

"Silver buys wood. Gold buys stone."

Sjord scowled, hanging his head. "Wood, then."

Eir pressed past him and strode into the courtyard, with Garm loping behind. "Fir is better than stone, anyway," she said, passing a row of blocks and boles along one wall. "Fir is alive. It grows out of stone. Its roots break the stone into sand."

"Yes," Sjord said, the hopeless twinkle returning to his eyes. "Which of these great boles will become my statue?"

"This one." Eir stopped beside a fir trunk three feet wide and ten feet tall. "This one will immortalize you."

Sjord stared at it as if he could see his own figure trapped in the wood. He slowly nodded. "Good, then. Carve me."

Eir nodded grimly, hoisting the huge bole and planting it on the ground in the center of the courtyard. "You, stand over there."

Sjord moved into position and gestured excitedly to his comrades, who gathered around, quaffing from their flagons.

"Don't move!" she ordered.

Sjord snapped his head up, trying to look ferocious. Garm sympathized.

As the man posed, Eir returned to her workshop. A few moments later, she emerged, wearing a carving belt filled with dozens of blades, from axes and hatchets to knives and chisels. The band of warriors gazed in awe as Eir strode up before the fir bole.

"Spirit of Wolf, guide my work."

A few of the armsmen tittered, but their laughter tumbled to silence as Eir brought the first blades out—a great axe in either hand. Both weapons began to rotate in slow, deadly circles above Eir's head.

Garm sat down to watch the show.

These warriors had no idea what they had unleashed. Eir was no mere sculptor. That was no little prayer she'd spoken. It was an invocation, channeling the powers of the boreal forests to make her art.

And they did.

Out of that thunderhead of swinging steel, an axe dived down to shear away the bark from one edge of the bole. The other axe followed like a thunderstroke, stripping the opposite side. The blades rose again, spinning, and fell. The broad bole grew slender. Already, it was taking on the lines of the man.

Sjord no longer posed, but gaped.

Eir circled the fir bole, axes slicing down in rhythm, cleaving away all that was not Sjord Frostfist. Halfway through this ecstatic dance, the axes slid back into the belt, and the hatchets came out. They chopped at the form, flinging off chips and rounding the wood into the figure of the man.

"Straighten up!" she reminded without stopping.

Sjord jerked back into his noble pose.

And just in time, for the daggers and chisels were out now, fitted to sleeves on her fingers that brought them to bear with intricate care on the wooden form. Now it was down to shavings, curled ribbons of wood cascading around the rough figure.

"It's me," said Sjord breathlessly.

And so it seemed, the bole taking the shape of the man.

"Bear, guide my work."

And then it was not knives and chisels in her hands but living claws, long and sharp, sliding along every contour of the figure. And it was not the lashing brawn of a norn warrior beneath that apron but the ancient muscle of a grizzly. The artist had been transfigured in her art.

Then she stepped back from the figure, the bear aura melting away. She was Eir Stegalkin once more, artist and warrior, slumping on a nearby bench and staring at what she had made.

It was magnificent. The sculpture was the man—Sjord Frostfist in wood. Indeed, the man and the statue stared at each other with such unrelenting amazement that few could have told them apart.

The swaying brothers began to chant, "Sjord! Sjord! Sjord! Sjord!" They hoisted the man who would lead them into doom.

"Not me!" Sjord protested, laughing. "The statue! The statue!"

The men lowered their friend to the ground and snatched up the carving. "Off to the market! Off to the market!" they cried joyously. "Sjord will stand forever in the market!"

"And nowhere else," Eir murmured as Garm loped up beside her. She was spent. These ecstatic moments of creation always left her drained. She looked down at Garm and said bitterly, "He can't save us. He can't even save himself."

That night, Eir couldn't sleep. Garm had seen many such nights. The spinning in the bed, the pacing, the muttering, the sketching. She was imagining something, conceiving it as other women conceived children.

Garm rose from his blanket and trotted over to the workbench and looked down at the page where she drew.

It was an army of wood and stone.

For a week, she didn't carve but only sketched in her workshop or paced through the courtyard or stared past the bridges that joined Hoelbrak to the Shiverpeaks all around. Garm had seen this look before. Eir was waiting for something. He knew by the way she sharpened her blades and oiled her bow.

A fortnight later, as the cold sun descended into clouds, the sentries of Hoelbrak began to shout.

"Invasion! Invasion! Icebrood!"

Eir turned from a sketch and strode to the wall where her battle-gear hung. She dragged off her work tunic and strapped on a breastplate of bronze. She girded herself and threw on a cape of wool, strapped on boots, and slung a quiver charged with arrows. To these, she added also her carving belt.

She looked to Garm and said, "Today, I carve Sjord Frostfist—again." Lifting her great bow, Eir headed for the door. "Come."

Garm followed his alpha out into the courtyard, where the shout of sentries was joined by the thud of boots. Eir charged into the lane, Garm loping beside her. Bjorn the blacksmith spotted them and trotted from his smithy, iron armor clattering on his smoke-blackened figure. They passed the weaver's workshop, and Silas emerged with short bow and shafts. Olin the jeweler and Soren the carpenter formed up with them as well. They were the crafters of the settlement, and Eir was their leader.

"Some of these icebrood will seem to be norn," she advised as they rushed down the lane toward the northern bridge, "but they'll not be. They are newly turned, their minds stolen by the Dragonspawn. They'll still have flesh and blood within their frozen husks, and killing them will be like killing our own kin."

Bjorn shook his head in anger. "We send our fools north, and the Dragonspawn sends its armies south."

"There are other, more deadly icebrood, too," Eir reminded. "They're mindless beasts of ice. There's no reasoning with them. Only shattering them."

Beside her, Silas nodded. He was a thin norn in the twilight of his fighting days. "So, for the ones that look like norn, it's arrows then, yes?" he asked, hoisting his short bow.

"Yes. We must kill as many as possible on the tundra before they reach the forts, but if the horde is great, the battle will push past the forts and reach the bridges to the hunting hall." She glanced at the rest of her militia. "Then there'll be plenty of work for all of us."

There was no more time for words. The group ran onto a bridge that stretched from Hoelbrak out to the fields beyond. At the end of the bridge stood a wooden defense-work that already bristled with warriors, including Knut Whitebear and his handpicked warriors—the Wolfborn. More norn streamed in each moment.

Eir led her group past the cluster of fighters to a thinly defended ridge and gazed out on the darkening northern fields. Mottled moss and torn lichen stretched to the misty distance, beneath towering mountains of ice.

"I don't see anything," Silas said, squinting.

"There," Eir replied.

Out of the mist emerged a brutal horde. A dozen appeared at first, no match for the hundred norn along the ridge. But more came with each moment. Soon the icebrood were as many as the defenders, and then twice their number.

"Are they hardened yet or newly turned?" Silas asked. "My eyes are thick."

"Most look newly turned," Eir said. Indeed, the enemy were covered with a thin crust of rime, though their eyes were dead things.

"Arrows, then!" Silas said, hoisting his short bow and holding it somewhat shakily.

"Yes, Silas," replied Eir as she lifted two arrows and nocked them on her bow and drew back. "Wait until they reach the red lichen, so that you can see them and your bow can reach them." With that, Eir let fly, and both shafts soared out above the ridge and climbed the sky, seeming to sail forever. They vanished in the darkling air, but a moment later, two of the distant figures fell, pinned to the ground. Even as they dropped, she loosed two more shafts, and as they skimmed the sky, she unleashed two more.

Four down. Six. Eight. Then other archers began to fire. In their dozens, the icebrood were falling, but in their hundreds, the invaders bounded over the bodies and kept on coming. When they reached the red lichen, Silas shot his shaft, and it found its mark in the forehead of an ice-caked foe.

"Not hardened yet!" Silas shouted. "Bring them down!"

Now their foes were close enough to hear, and what a howling sound they made! They had been driven mad with the desire to serve their lord.

Eir had already sent fivescore arrows, and she drew the last two from her quiver and buried them in a pair of icebrood. The rest crashed on the ridge like a tidal wave.

"Wolf, guide my work," Eir murmured. Her eyes glowed with battle and her hands glowed with axes. She swung them overhead in a storm of steel.

An icebrood, newly turned, flung himself over the ridge and came down with a swinging axe. "Die!"

Eir leaped back from the blade and brought her own around to split the creature from shoulder to hip.

Another dead man leaped the ridge and bounded toward her.

Her other axe fell and broke the man like bread.

"Fall back!" Eir cried. "Give them room to land."

The crafters complied, stepping back while mauls and axes and swords rained down.

Eir was in the midst, her knives and chisels now slung on her fingers. They flew as if she were carving wood instead of frozen flesh. They flayed skin and muscle from bone.

Beside her, Garm leaped to latch onto throats and bring down more of the enemy.

Bjorn meanwhile pounded the icebrood as if they were iron.

Olin and Soren fought back-to-back, cudgel and pry bar wreaking havoc.

Which left only Silas, the weaver, who had felled two of the creatures before they reached the ridge.

Now two felled him. One ripped out his belly while the other smashed his face.

Eir heard Silas's scream and turned to ram her chisels into the back of Silas's attacker. The steel sank to her fingertips, and red foam bubbled hot from the wounds. The rime-covered norn, gasping, rolled from Silas. Garm clamped onto the neck of the other icebrood and shook him like a rag.

Eir looked down at the weaver, her old friend. It was too late. Silas was gone.

Face and belly—he was gone.

Eir roared, her blades flinging out to slash the throats of two more icebrood. They fell beside her as another came on—a man with hair like a horse's tail.

She knew this man, though his face was smashed, his nose canted to one side, his teeth gone where some great fist had struck him. His flesh was sealed in ice. His eyes were white, filled with the fury of the Dragonspawn.

"Bear, guide my hands," prayed Eir as she strode toward him.

It was just as it had been back in the sunlit courtyard. It was a storm of steel, slicing away what was not Sjord Frostfist. As she worked, she became the Bear—transforming so that the work of chisels became the work of claws. The only difference, this time, was that she carved flesh instead of wood.

Soon, the bloodied bear stepped back, and only pieces were on the ground before her.

That's how she fought the rest of the battle. That's how she avenged Silas and defended Hoelbrak.

When the battle was done, the defenders had prevailed. Even so, it seemed as if the Dragonspawn had won.

Back in her workshop that night, the bloodied woman stripped away her armor. She poured steaming kettles into her bath and washed the battle away. Dressed in a simple tunic, she used the water to bathe her wolf as well.

Wet and weary, Garm retreated to his blanket. He drifted into fitful sleep, haunted by the monsters he had fought.

Eir, though, was haunted by something else. She wandered among her army of statues, at last reaching the one where she always stopped. It was an aged norn male, his once-proud figure stooped a bit, his head bald, his eyes enfolded in rings. But a hopeful smile was on his lips.

"We stopped them, Father," Eir said simply, looking

down at the statue's feet. "I wish others had stopped them for you." Her hand strayed into his, carved of stone and cold. She had carved that hand, had known it so well from holding it just this way when she was a girl—before the icebrood came.

"I'm going to kill the Dragonspawn, Father. I'm going to kill the Dragonspawn and the Elder Dragons themselves."

CAT AND MOUSE

Logan Thackeray knelt beside a boulder and glanced back, motioning for the other scouts to vanish into the rubble field. They did. Logan smiled. With dun-colored leather armor, the scouts could move like ghosts through this blasted landscape. That was fortunate, since they were stalking a company of charr.

Logan cupped a hand to his ear and made out the distant thunder of clawed feet. Brown eyes flashing with anticipation, he slid to his stomach and crawled out across a shelf of stone. Just ahead, the shelf dropped away. Logan crept to the edge and peered down.

Below lay a deep, narrow canyon, a passage through this arm of the Blazeridge Mountains. About a mile to the east, the charr were on the march. They looked like beetles in their glinting black armor, scuttling along the base of the canyon.

Up close, though, charr were huge. Five-hundred-pound brutes. Muscle and fur and fang. They had faces like lions and horns like bulls, barrel bodies and bow-legs, clawed hands and feet. Ravenous. They'd already stolen all of Ascalon—all except for Ebonhawke—and they were determined to take that fortress, as well. They were marching to intercept a supply caravan from Divinity's Reach, but they hadn't figured on Logan and his scouts.

"Got to stop them." The stone shelf underneath Logan was crisscrossed with fractures. "A little more weight, and this would shatter like an egg." He glanced back up the boulder-strewn slope. "The right lever beneath the right stone at the right time . . ."

This was exactly the kind of job Logan loved—moving fast, striking hard, vanishing. His brother would call him a mercenary, but Logan preferred leather armor to polished steel.

Staying low, Logan drew back from the cliff's edge and motioned for his team to follow. They picked their way up the boulder-strewn slope. At last, near the peak, Logan found what he sought—a great round stone poised on a lip above the rest and hidden from the canyon by a fir tree.

In its shelter, he gathered his team. "Ready to strike a blow for humankind?"

Twelve pairs of eyes returned a look of eager resolve.

"We'll need a lever—a sapling, stripped of branches. And we'll need a fulcrum, flat on the bottom and angled on top. This stone, here, will start the rockslide."

"Close off the gap," said Wescott, "before the charr can march through."

"Exactly. We've got little time. Wescott, take Perkins and Fielding and get us a lever. Bring the tree down quietly, out of sight from the canyon. Everlee, work with Dawson and Tippett to position the fulcrum. Castor, take the rest of them to scout an escape over that ridge to the west. When we bring this rockslide down, this hill will be swarming with charr."

"We've never faced charr," said Everlee. "We're not Vanguard or Seraph."

"Thank the gods you're not. You'd be in a hundred pounds of plate mail." Logan grinned. "No, we're scouts—fast on our feet. Now, get going."

The young scouts went swiftly and silently.

While his teams worked, Logan climbed to a lookout point. He surveyed the scene—the keystone boulder, the rockslide slope, the choke point that would soon become a wall, the canyon . . .

From it rose a streaming banner of dust, kicked up by hundreds of claws on the march. Logan watched the ribbon of dust rise and stretch and coil, approaching the choke point. "Almost time." He withdrew, rejoining his team beside the trigger stone.

Already, they had a long bole poised atop a fulcrum, and the team had positioned themselves on either side of the lever.

"Hold," Logan said, lifting his hand. He peered down the slope to see the snake of dust approach the choke point. "Now!" The scouts heaved on the lever. It strained against the fulcrum, hoisting the great boulder. The huge rock creaked forward, tilted up on the lip of stone, and tottered. The scouts climbed onto the lever, and Logan put his hands on the rock: "Push, you sods!"

The boulder teetered beyond the lip and began to roll. It bounced once against the slope and bashed another boulder. The second rock rumbled down as well. These two struck more, setting off a chain reaction. Giant rocks leaped into motion, and the hillside became a thundering herd of stone.

The ground shook.

Logan and his comrades stared in awe.

The rockslide reached the cliff and poured over it, breaking loose more stone. Massive blocks hurled themselves into the canyon and funneled in to fill the gap. Dust and debris plumed above the cleft while more boulders cascaded down. They piled atop the charr, forming an impassable wall. "We've done it!" Logan called to his team, pounding Wescott's shoulder.

The last of the stones tumbled down, and the roar of rock gave way to the roar of the legion—a sound of fury.

Logan cringed. "Everyone, stay low and out of sight. Castor, take us over that ridge. And quickly!"

The young woman nodded, turning to lead them down a dry wash, through a cut of trees, and to a narrow pass over the ridge. They left the roar of the charr legion in the valley behind them and gazed out on a rugged but silent wilderness.

"Well done, everyone," Logan said. "We bought the caravan a day, maybe. Might've even crushed some of the vermin. Still, some of the charr'll track us, so we can't go back to the caravan. We've got to lead them as far away as possible before the sun quits us."

Centurion Korrak Blacksnout led three hundred charr soldiers through the Blazeridge Gap. The centurion lifted his grizzled face, snorting dust from lionlike nostrils and sneezing. The scars that crisscrossed his dewlaps seized up as if his face might fall apart. The old creature blinked cloudy eyes and ran a claw over his horns, broken from hard campaigning. He growled, "Can't wait to sink my claws into some fat human merchants."

"They say it's the last caravan," said Legionnaire Sever Sootclaw beside him. "They say Queen Jennah's going to get the asura gate in Ebonhawke repaired. It'll be a highway for troops."

"Let her try! We'll turn our siege to storm and tear down the walls and the damned gate," Blacksnout growled. "In the meantime, we've got to stop *this* caravan!"

"Got to get through the pass, first," muttered Rytlock Brimstone.

Korrak shot a hateful look at him. The dark-furred Brimstone wasn't even Iron Legion, just a Blood Legion cur who'd volunteered for this thankless duty. "What are you doing up here, Soldier Brimstone?" growled Korrak. "I sent you to the rear so I wouldn't have to listen to you."

"I came up to warn you."

"About what?"

Rytlock grunted his disbelief. He nodded horns

toward the steep canyon walls. "You're heading into a trap."

"To the animal mind, all is a trap," Korrak hissed, though he, too, scanned the upper canyon. "Where's your courage?"

"It doesn't take courage to march into a trap," Rytlock snorted, eyes narrowing beneath black brows. "It takes idiocy."

Korrak snapped, "Watch your mouth, soldier!"

"Don't you see the rubble fields up there?" Rytlock gestured with pointed claws. "If I were trying to stop a charr legion, that's where I'd be."

Korrak whirled on him. "Is that what you're trying to do, Brimstone—stop a charr legion? Trying to stop *me*!"

"Heh heh," Rytlock chuckled. "If I wanted to stop you, Centurion, you'd be stopped."

Korrak seized Rytlock's armor and planted the barrel of his axe-rifle in the upstart's throat. "What are you doing here, Brimstone?"

"I told you, warning you about the trap."

"No! I mean what are you doing *here,* a thousand miles from your own legion?"

"I go my own way!"

"Only because they wouldn't *have* you! They drove you off—your own legion—not because you couldn't fight. I've seen you fight. No, it's because they couldn't *stand* you!"

Brimstone's eyes blazed, and his nostrils flared as if he had heard this speech countless times. But a slow smile spread across his lips. "You've got it wrong. *I* couldn't stand *them.*"

"Or anyone else."

"I don't suffer fools."

"*Insufferable!*" Korrak roared, jabbing the barrel of his rifle deeper into Rytlock's jaw. "Why shouldn't I empty that hateful head of yours?"

Rytlock's eyes still blazed, unflinching. "You Iron Legion cowards are all alike, hiding behind your guns."

Korrak Blacksnout lowered the axe-rifle, and his voice became a deadly growl. "If this is a trap, Brimstone, you're going into it first." He waved his rifle toward the defile. "March!"

The Blood Legion rogue stared at him for a moment, then marched ahead of the column. He trudged into the narrowest section of the canyon.

Behind him, Blacksnout walked with the rifle aimed ahead, his dewlaps stretched in a smile. "Why do you fear humans, Soldier Brimstone? They're cowards in caravans. They've lost Ascalon, and they're losing Ebonhawke. You have nothing to fear from them."

"I don't *fear* them," Rytlock replied thoughtfully, looking up the rock wall. "I *know* them."

A few more steps brought Korrak and a dozen other charr through the choke point. "You even *think* like a human."

There came a boom like a mallet blow, and the crackle of rocks.

The charr looked up.

Sound lagged sight: A huge rockslide was scouring the slope above. The tumbling chaos of boulders poured over the edge of the cliff before the roar of it reached their ears.

Rytlock, Korrak, and the command corps turned around, shouting to the warriors behind them in the choke point. Their warnings were drowned out.

The first boulder smashed down atop a charr axeman. Another slab hammered a whole warband. Then stones pounded down in such numbers that the soldiers were lost in a crimson cloud of dust.

Korrak, Rytlock, and the command corps fell back as rocks cascaded into the canyon. Stones spun in clouds of dust and hurled out shrapnel. They mounded in the gap—thirty feet and sixty feet and ninety feet high, filling the canyon. At last, the final stones slid over the cliff's edge and clattered to a stop on the huge pile.

It was more than a pile. It was a cairn. Warbands lay interred there.

"A trap!" Rytlock shouted.

"Shut up!" Korrak snarled.

"I *told* you it was a trap!"

"I said shut up!" Korrak swung the axe end of his weapon in a wide arc.

Rytlock rolled away and came up in a crouch. A fierce smile ripped across his face. He grasped the hilt of his sword and drew it slowly from its stone scabbard. A fiery blade emerged, forged of two sharpened strands of twisted metal. Its name was Sohothin. Long ago it had belonged to a human prince of Ascalon. Now it was Rytlock's.

"You would raise your blade against me?" Korrak Blacksnout growled. "I will put an end to—"

The centurion's threat was cut short along with his neck, severed and cauterized. The head toppled, and the body crouched and fell.

Soldier Rytlock Brimstone turned to the dozen Iron Legion warriors standing with him on the near side of the rockfall and said, "Guess you're going to need a new leader."

One by one, they dropped to their knees and nodded their loyalty.

"We acknowledge you as our centurion—for the moment," snarled Sever Sootclaw. "Shall we clear the passage?"

"Let the charr behind the rocks clear it. We'll hunt down the humans who did this!"

Sootclaw's brow rose. "Humans? Here?"

"Yes. Here." Rytlock glared toward the cliff top. "They're cannier than you realize, but they're also cowards. They'll be fleeing now. We must be faster." Rytlock unclasped his breastplate and let it clank to the ground. "Take no needless thing. We have a long climb and a longer run and a battle afterward."

One by one, the kneeling warriors stood, their breastplates falling to the ground around them. They had given up their defenses. Now, they would fight to the death.

Day was dying as Logan Thackeray and his scouts reached a high pass above the timberline. They were about to descend into a new valley, but Logan lingered on a rocky overhang and peered back the way they had come, watching for movement. So far, only the shadows had moved, lengthening as the sun quit the world. The route they had taken would discourage any but the angriest pursuers.

Of course, *these* foes were furious.

At first, there was nothing. The mountain was silent, the air still. But then he glimpsed it. Five miles back and half a mile downslope, the saplings shivered with their passage.

The charr were coming.

Logan scrambled back from the overhang and went to his scouts. "They're closing on us. They're only five miles back."

The scouts stared at him, their faces white. They were light scouts trained for merchant caravans—not even part of the Ebon Vanguard. None of them had faced a single charr, let alone a dozen.

"The mountain and the darkness are our allies," Logan said. "We'll set traps as we retreat."

"Where? To the west? Those are ogre lands!" objected Wescott.

"Maybe we'll get past the ogres and the charr won't," Logan said simply. "Let's go!" He led the others down into a new valley.

Beneath a staring moon, Legionnaire Rytlock Brimstone bounded along a trail, dragging the air into his lungs. "They're close now. Can't you smell them?"

In the blackness, Sever Sootclaw crashed his foot on a stone. "Draw your sword. We need light."

"And show them where we are?" snarled Rytlock.

"We can't see. We've lost two already to their traps. How many more?"

"It wasn't the darkness that killed them. It was their

own stupidity, and the cleverness of these humans. Their leader knows this land. He knows how we fight."

Sootclaw's brow rumpled. "You sound as if you admire him."

"Yes, like the hound admires the fox," Rytlock said, his eyes flashing. "Fall in! After me! They went this way—south and west." He grinned in the darkness. "We'll catch them within the hour."

"This way!" Logan hissed in the darkness as he ran along the rocky bank of a mountain stream. It was the only sure path through the forest. On all sides, moonlight showed thickets of pine that they couldn't navigate. Behind them flashed glints of horn or fang or steel.

The charr were converging.

Logan and his scouts pelted along the stream, fighting to keep their footing on water-smoothed stones. They were bunched tight, prey running from predators.

The stream dropped away before him in a sudden waterfall.

"Hold up! Hold up!" warned Logan.

The other scouts halted behind him, stopping just on the brink.

"How far down?" asked Wescott.

Logan kicked a stone over the edge and counted to five before he heard it hit. "Too far."

"What now?"

Logan smiled grimly. "Now we wade the stream and find another way."

"They're closing," Everlee noted.

"Yes, they are," Logan replied. "We've killed two or three, but their leader is a wily one. We'll kill a few more before they corner us. Come on."

He stepped into the frigid stream. Water rose to his knees and hips before it grew shallower. Sodden and shivering, Logan and his team rushed up the far bank and away into the darkness.

But there was no stream to guide them now, and little moonlight. In minutes, they had blundered into a thicket. Swords came out to hack through. At last, they broke into a high glade and ran beneath the moon.

Behind them, charr blades battered through the thicket.

Logan and his team ran between two stands of pine and into a narrow valley striped with moon shadows. Blindly they rushed forward and into a steep stone wall.

"Find a way out!" growled Logan.

"There's no way out!" Wescott replied. "A box canyon."

"Try climbing! Find anything to grab hold of," commanded Logan.

The scouts fumbled in the darkness along the rock walls.

Then a light dawned—a fiery light. The scouts turned to see a flaming sword sliding from a stone scabbard. The light sketched out a lionish face, grinning with fangs and eyes that smiled red. The charr stalked forward, towering over the man, and thrust his flaming sword high.

Logan pulled his war hammer from his belt and stepped up. "Wedge formation behind me."

The scouts lifted their weapons and positioned themselves.

The charr with the burning sword spoke. "At last, the rats are cornered."

Logan flashed a cockeyed smile. "We took out a few of you."

"And now, we'll take out *all* of you," the charr growled. Around him, more charr warriors marched up, slinging their axe-rifles down and pointing them at the humans. Their leader shouted, "Fire!"

The rifles roared, hurling out a barrage of smoke and lead.

LITTLE PEOPLE, BIG PROJECTS

"Hel-looo? Hel-loooo?"

The black dire wolf raised his head from the warm blanket and blinked at the workshop doorway.

No one was there.

"Hel-looo? Heeeel-looooooo?"

Eir shifted on her bed, lifting a tangle of red hair to look toward the door. She didn't see anyone, either.

The voice spoke again. "Nobody's home."

Another voice answered, "Maybe they're sleeping in."

"Sleeping in? Are you crazy? The greatest norn artist of her generation isn't sleeping in."

"Well, she's probably working. Famous sculptor and all. She's probably off carving something."

"She's not working. *This* is her workshop, isn't it?"

"Yes, it is," said Eir Stegalkin, rolling out of bed and standing, "*and* her bedroom." She looked toward the door and blinked. "Oh, there you are."

Garm quirked his eyebrows and stood also, seeing at last two little people standing in the doorway. They came up only to the belt of a norn, and they were gray, with giant ears swept back from their childlike faces. One was male, dressed in a greatcoat over a buttoned-up vest and brown trousers. He wore two large gauntlets with gems hovering over the backs of them. The other figure was female, decked in bluish body armor that looked jury-rigged, as if she changed its dimensions constantly. Despite their strange voices, they looked intently serious.

"Oh, *there* you are," said the slightly taller creature. "Eir Stegalkin, I presume. I'm Master Snaff of Rata Sum, asura genius. I've been told you're the best."

"Told by whom?" Eir asked. Asura. Of course they would be asura. Short, smart, and irritating.

Snaff smiled, bowing. "I cannot reveal my sources." The younger asura shot him an annoyed look, as if he often revealed his sources. Unperturbed, Snaff continued, "This is my associate, Zojja, genius-in-training."

She also bowed, but her scowl only deepened.

"We've come for a commission," Snaff said.

"I'm not accepting commissions," Eir replied.

The little man wandered into the workshop, glancing sidelong at the statues that towered all around. "Really? What are all these, then?"

"I mean, I'm *no longer* accepting commissions."

Garm trotted up behind the male asura, who reached only his shoulders. The wolf snuffled the creature's greatcoat, which smelled of swamp water and fern spores.

Snaff seemed none too concerned with having a big

black wolf hounding his steps. "Well, that's a shame, an artist of your caliber no longer taking commissions. There are only three possible reasons: One, that you are retired, which clearly you cannot be, given your age and the bits of stone and wood all over your floor; two, that you've somehow gone haywire, which your hair does seem to indicate—"

"I just got up!"

"Or three, that you have found your subjects of late unworthy of your genius, which judging from this rogues' gallery of puffed-up posers, I would guess to be the reason."

"You have guessed well, little master." Eir stepped into a pair of trousers and drew them on beneath her night-shirt. "I am tired of watching fools go to their deaths."

Snaff smiled, spreading his hands. "We're not fools."

"But she just said she *liked* fools," said the apprentice.

"I didn't."

Zojja dragged a finger through a pile of shavings on the floor. "You said you are tired of watching fools go to their deaths. If you hated them, you would never tire of this. Ergo, you must *like* them."

"You may *have* something there," Eir conceded.

"Well, then I suppose," Snaff replied, looking askance at his apprentice, "I would be wise to say that we *are* fools. Except that fools aren't wise, in which case my apprentice's inquisitiveness has once again landed us in a conundrum."

"Once again," Zojja said almost pridefully.

A grin was fighting its way onto Eir's face. "Hypo-thetically speaking—"

"I *love* hypotheses!" Snaff broke in.

"—if I *were* taking commissions, whose image would you want?"

Snaff's grin grew from Eir's own. "My assistant's, of course."

Eir looked at the petulant young asura and asked, "Why?"

Snaff shrugged. "She's got a good head on her shoulders. And that's all I want. A head and shoulders."

"Well," Eir said, "that's a pretty small statue. I'm a pretty-big-statue maker. Maybe you'll want to find a smaller sculptor."

"Except that her head needs to be five times taller," Snaff said.

Zojja shot him a look of annoyance.

"I suppose that is a commission worthy of my talents, but it'll cost you. Twenty silver."

"A bargain," said Snaff, reaching beneath his greatcoat to grasp a bag on his belt. "This will be a bust in stone, of course."

"In wood, of course," Eir clarified. "It'd be twenty gold for stone."

"Ah," said Snaff, reaching to the other side of his belt. "Then gold it will be. Twenty, did you say?" He opened the bag, a pile of coins shimmering within the burlap.

Eir's eyes widened as she peered at the bag.

She snagged her leather apron, mallet, and chisel belt and led the way outside into the courtyard. The others followed. She guided them along her stock of boles and boulders. "This one is granite, which is very hard. This one is marble—too expensive in this case. Here we have columnar basalt. This is limestone. . . ."

"Basalt!" exclaimed Snaff. "That's volcanic rock, yes?"

"Yes," said Eir, standing beside a large gray chunk. "And this one is particularly dense."

"Perfect for depicting my student!"

Zojja hit him.

Eir cocked an eyebrow at Zojja. "You should show more respect for your master."

Snaff rubbed the spot she had hit and smiled tightly. "Most asura assistants get browbeaten by their masters. With Zojja, it's the other way around."

"Why do you put up with it?" Eir asked.

Zojja glared. "I'm not sure if that's your business, giantkin."

Eir stared back. "Your master might put up with your abuse, but I will not."

"Now, now," said Snaff, chuckling lightly. "It's quite flattering to have you two fight over me."

Both women gaped at him in amazement.

"I think I understand," said Eir to Zojja.

Snaff just beamed. "Well, good then. All things are mended. Let's get started. Zojja, why don't you stand over there in the light? . . . Yes. Excellent. And, of course, Eir, you know where to stand. And I'll step out of the way so that neither of you can hit me."

Eir stepped up before the block of basalt, drew a large chisel from her belt, set it to the stone, and lifted the mallet above her head. "Wolf, guide my hands." She brought the mallet down, shearing off a chunk of stone.

Basalt was a tricky medium, formed of cooled lava. The question was how it cooled—quickly beneath the ocean or slowly on land. Land was better. This particular stone had come from the throat of a long-dead volcano. It had cooled slowly, and it was amorphous, without striations. As Eir worked into the block, she sensed it had no hidden faults or fissures that could split her work. It was solid.

As was her model. This annoying little creature had a solid will. She held her nose up and remained still, seeming to sense the importance of this moment.

Eir worked the stone to bring forth Zojja's features. That lemon-shaped head, those great eyes, her button nose, her small, determined mouth, her perky chin . . . but hardest of all were those ears—shaped like a rabbit's, but swept back from her forehead so they seemed almost like small wings.

"How's it coming?" asked the apprentice.

Eir wished she hadn't moved. Her previous expression had been perfect—focused and slightly proud, willful and determined. Now the lines had shifted to dubious and frustrated. "Well," Eir replied, "could you try to get the old look back?"

"What old look?"

"The look that you are smarter than everyone else and that they will be shocked when they realize it." Suddenly, the look was back, and Eir shifted to a smaller chisel to capture it.

Nearby, Snaff idly sized up a floor-to-ceiling drake in

alabaster. "It's good to be immortalized, my dear. Most apprentices don't make it, you know." He turned toward Eir. "Maybe you didn't realize that, but they're always handling caustic substances, building precarious mechanisms. . . . Unless they're clever, they just don't make it."

"And Zojja, here, is clever?" Eir asked as she finished the little snarl beneath Zojja's right nostril.

"She's here," Snaff pointed out.

Eir stepped back from her sculpture. "Yes. I suppose she is. In both ways. The likeness is complete. Come see."

The two asura walked toward the sculpture with the numb air of people who cannot believe what they see. Though the statue was five times the actual height of Zojja, it was dead-on. Eir had captured not only the young asura's expression but also her personality.

Zojja's look of wonder slowly soured. "Why did you have to make me look so big?"

"It's five times actual height," Eir replied.

"Four times would have been enough," Zojja snapped. "It's fine. Fine."

"It's perfect," said Snaff. "Thank you very much! It was certainly worth the coin." He turned to his apprentice and said, "All right, now. Let's take this back with us."

Zojja scooted to the opposite side of the stone bust. She and her master set their fingers beneath the carving. "One, two, three!"

The two asura struggled, trying to lift the five-hundred-pound block, but not moving it an inch.

Eir stood above them, arms folded.

Snaff looked up at her and tittered nervously. "I wish I had more coin to pay you to carry this."

Eir smiled. "You *have* more coin. You were about to pay me in silver before I asked for gold."

Snaff blushed around a tight-lipped smile. "Oh, all right—"

"Never mind," interrupted Eir, stepping between the two asura and wrapping her arms around the huge statue and hoisting it off the ground. "Where do you want it?"

Snaff crooked a finger in her direction and said, "Follow me."

Garm looked up wonderingly at his alpha. She had never followed anyone. If ever she followed anyone, it would be a creature taller and more powerful and more clever than she, not some tiny thing. But Eir did follow him. Massive bust in hand, Eir followed, as did Zojja. Garm joined in, if only to see what this asura was up to.

They paraded out of the courtyard and into the lane. "Hey, everybody," called Snaff into the shops, "look at the new sculpture. Isn't it a masterpiece?"

"Where do you *want it*?" Eir repeated as she struggled to carry the bust.

"Just up here, my lady," Snaff said.

They passed into a plaza filled with market tents and tables loaded with fruits, scarves, iron implements, and goods of every other type. In the center of this trading den stood an ancient gate of gray stone, carved with strange runes. Just now, the arched gate flickered and, in that flicker, gave a vision of another marketplace in a port city.

"Not going to Lion's Arch today," Snaff said to the

gate attendant, another asura. Slipping him a coin, Snaff said, "Rata Sum, if you please."

The attendant crouched beside an array of powerstones, and a stone in his hand sent sparks leaping into the other crystals. The flickering scene in the arch changed to a rocky desert, a mountain lake, a golden meadow. At last, it showed a brief glimpse of what looked like three massive pyramids.

"Thanks," Snaff said, straightening up and stepping through the portal.

Eir shrugged and followed, carrying her huge load. Garm came at her heels.

Passing through the portal was like plunging into a hot bath. The cold air was ripped away from their skins, replaced by stinging, sticky heat. Instead of wintry skies, there was a blazing sun. Instead of permafrost, there were cut stones and giant leaves. The group stood on a platform that jutted from the side of a huge pyramid.

Eir staggered to a stop and looked around. "Whoa."

They stood in what seemed to be a plaza between three gigantic pyramids, except that, instead of a plaza, a chasm descended to unseeable depths. Above that chasm, giant stonework cubes seemed suspended on thin air. The lines of massive architecture were softened by palm trees planted in huge rectangular pots and pyramidal lanterns floating over the stone balustrades.

"Floating?" Eir gulped.

Snaff smiled. "Nice, eh?"

"How?"

Zojja piped up, "Even a genius-in-training knows

that. It's all held aloft by powerstone fields arrayed using the dodecaic equation of the Eternal Alchemy."

"Dough-decay-what?"

"The twelvefold equation. It's the most obvious expression of universal balance in base twelve."

"Base twelve?"

Zojja turned to Snaff and muttered, "She must still count on her fingers."

He nodded discreetly. "It's the temptation of having ten."

Eir hadn't understood a word. But she did understand that this was a magical place, with purplish plasma flaring up from columns here and there, and lightning sparking along arched bridges, and powerstones glowing everywhere.

"Isn't that bust getting heavy?" Snaff asked.

"Yes. . . . If we could just get to the spot."

"Of course! Of course!" Snaff strode out in front, his three-toed feet scampering along at a pace that was just a lumbering stroll for Eir. He led the group down a series of stairs, ever deeper into the city. Massive walls of stone rose all around them. "I live in the old city—down *below.*"

"Of course you do."

As they walked along one pyramid, an asura krewe swarmed the slanted side, hauling a huge dandelion puff up the incline. One asura shouted, "Nice statue, Master Snaff! A little idol worship, is it?"

Snaff laughed easily. "I appreciate my apprentice. I don't idolize her. Good luck with your test flight! Just let us pass before you launch."

Eir murmured, "Test flight?"

"Test crash, more likely. Master Klab's been working for two years on that puffball—made of milkweed dander and butterfly scales and a whole lot of hastily cobbled spells. Won't fly, I assure you. But the fellow knows how to glad-hand. He never lacks for a krewe or investors."

"On three!" came a shout from above. "One . . . two . . ."

"Let's run," Snaff advised, and he and Zojja did, which still amounted to only a fast walk for Eir and Garm.

"Three!"

A loud series of pops sounded on the stone slope, sending a blast wave of air across the dandelion puffball. Hundreds of silken sacks inflated, and the thing lifted off the stone slope. The puffball broke free, rising into the air like a floating balloon. At its center, Master Klab hooted excitedly in his harness.

"Heigh-ho, Master Snaff! Running from true genius, are we? Whenever there's something clever going on, you're always heading in the opposite direction!"

The little gray master was looking slightly green as he stopped to stare upward at the flying puffball. He muttered, "I'll never hear the end of it."

Just then, the puffball rose above the city, where a breeze dragged it suddenly away.

Master Klab shouted to his krewe, "Bring the skyhooks! The skyhooks!"

Eir sniffed, "Maybe you just *did* hear the end of it."

"You're a good lass."

Eir huffed. "Um, can we get on with setting this thing down?"

"Ah, yes, that. Well—see that small ziggurat down

there?" Snaff pointed toward the bowels of the city, at what looked like a temple missing its top. "Home, sweet home!"

They descended a series of switchback stairs and at last arrived at Snaff's ziggurat.

He piped happily, "Now it's just up the side, down some stairs, and we'll be in my laboratory."

"Good," Eir said with relief.

Except that the stairs were made for asuran feet. Eir struggled up them to reach the peak of the temple— or what used to be the peak. The top had apparently been blown off by a violent blast, with a single staircase descending into the heart of the ziggurat.

Panting, Eir paused at the brink of the crater and said, "An experiment gone awry?"

Snaff pursed his lips. "No. Why do you ask?"

"I mean, the crater."

He shrugged. "It's called a *skylight*. Saves on candles. Come along!" He scuttled down the stairs into the darkness, with Zojja close behind.

Even Garm pushed past Eir, apparently to make certain this wasn't a trap. He loped down into the shadows, plunging into a cool chamber with ornately carved walls, tiled floors, and trapezoidal stone tables arrayed across them. Much of the light in the space came through the "skylight," though some also came from magic lanterns that hung from great chains and sent a bluish glow down over everything. Light also leaked from great vials and beakers and tubes on the tabletops, and from strange mechanical contraptions all around.

"Oh, much cooler!" sighed Eir as she reached the floor. "Where should I put this?"

"Here," said Snaff, standing beside a table where one of the contraptions sprawled. "What an exciting day!"

Eir ambled over to the table and eased the heavy block down.

"No. Lay it down. . . . Yes. On its back. Right, but shove it up against this mechanism here. . . . Excellent!" he proclaimed, dragging a great red stone from his pocket and setting it on the forehead of the statue.

The stone sank into the forehead, embedding itself and pulsing to life.

"Wonderful! Wonderful!" Snaff cried.

Metal loops rose from the magical creation that lay there, clamping down on the shoulders of the bust and forming a collar. The machine groaned, pitched forward, and sat up—a towering golem with the head of Zojja.

THE ENEMY OF MY ENEMY

The moment before the axe-rifles fired, Logan Thackeray swept his hand out in a fan. A blue aura bled from his fingertips into the air, solidifying it in a curved wall before the scouts.

"Fire!" the charr centurion roared.

The axe-rifles boomed and vomited smoke and lead. But the shots struck the ethereal membrane and sank into it and were eaten away. Bullets showered rust to the ground.

The leader of the charr stared, his jaw dropping. "You're full of surprises!"

"I'm Logan Thackeray. I protect those who are mine."

"I'm Rytlock Brimstone," the charr shot back. "I kill those who aren't."

"I recognize your blade. Did you say *Rurik* Brimstone?"

"Rytlock," the charr snarled.

Logan shrugged. "I just figured since you stole Prince Rurik's sword, you probably also stole his name."

Rytlock lashed the air with the burning blade. "The sword's mine now."

"After this fight," Logan said, whirling his war hammer in a figure eight, "Sohothin will once again be in the hands of a human."

"*During* this fight," Rytlock spat, "Sohothin will once again be in the *guts* of a human." He looked back at the charr around him. "Turn those damned rifles around and chop them to pieces!"

Rytlock charged, ramming his sword toward Logan's stomach.

The man spun aside, his war hammer pounding the fiery blade. Sparks flew, and the sword clanged down to one side. Logan stepped in to kick his opponent's leg, and Rytlock staggered back in surprise and pain. The man meanwhile advanced, swinging his war hammer in a thundering arc overhead.

This time, Rytlock deflected the blow, leaned in, and planted a massive fist in the man's stomach. Logan flew back and crashed to the ground. He staggered up to one knee.

"You fight like a charr"—Rytlock laughed blackly—"though you fly like a grawl."

"Grawl don't fly."

"They do when you punch them!" Rytlock stomped toward the man and swung another massive blow.

Logan tried to dodge, but the flaming sword followed him. Growling, he jabbed his hammer out desperately. Sohothin engulfed the weapon, fire mantling the hammerhead.

Logan ripped his hammer free, but it sloughed a skin of red-hot metal.

The charr cackled. "Nice sword, eh?"

"Legendary."

"And you'll never wield it."

Again the roaring attack, again the argument of metal and fire, and again Logan stepped back, his hammer smoldering and his chest heaving.

Rytlock was a cat playing with prey. "At least you're doing better than your friends."

Logan glanced to one side where Wescott, Perkins, and Fielding fought back-to-back, surrounded by four charr. On the other side, Everlee, Dawson, Tippett, and Castor fought a similarly desperate battle against five charr.

"Is that how you fight?" Logan growled at the legionnaire. "Four on three? Five on four?"

Rytlock shrugged. "We fight to win. Foreign concept to you humans, I know."

Fury flooded through Logan, and he spun. His war hammer vaulted overhead and moaned down toward Rytlock's head. The charr rolled aside, the hammer cracking across his claws. He clambered to his feet and charged, Sohothin's fires roaring. The flaming blade struck a blue aura that Logan had painted in the air to cover his retreat.

Rytlock ripped his sword free of the barrier and said, "You're so *good* at retreating."

Despite his words, Logan took another step back, staring in horror—not at the sword, but at what it showed lurking behind the charr.

Two monstrous faces loomed out of the night. Their eyes were the size of fists; their mouths were gathered like sacks; their armored figures towered like cliff faces.

"Ogres," Logan stammered as he staggered back.

"What?" Rytlock roared, turning.

"Ogres!" Logan shouted.

A massive boot pounded the ground behind Rytlock, who whirled aside just before a spiked club crashed down beside him. The spikes impaled another charr and rooted him to the ground. The ogre flexed its sinewy arm, trying to yank the club free.

Recovering from shock, Logan charged the ogre, running up its huge club and arm and onto its shoulder. With a mighty swing, he buried his hammer in the brow of the beast. Moaning, the ogre dropped to its knees and rolled ponderously forward. Logan leaped to the ground.

"How about that?" Logan crowed.

"Turn around!" Rytlock snarled.

Logan spun to see a pair of hyenas soaring toward him out of the darkness.

His hammer rose and fell, and beside it, Sohothin danced, and the hyenas dropped before the man and the charr.

"Pets," hissed Rytlock. "Ogres always travel with them."

"I know all about ogres!" Logan snapped, clubbing another hyena.

But Rytlock wasn't listening, his sword slicing through an ogre's leg. Its club had been swinging toward Logan, but as the beast crumpled, the club flew free and crashed into the wall of the canyon. Rytlock leaped onto the breast of the fallen ogre and buried his blade in its heart.

"How about that?" Rytlock exulted.

Logan rose and hurled his hammer toward Rytlock. "What the—" Rytlock ducked, and the weapon spun by overhead and smashed into the face of another ogre. It staggered dizzily, shaking its head to clear it. Rytlock leaped up and struck the ogre's head from its shoulders.

Between them, Logan and Rytlock had felled three ogres and three hyenas, but five more of the beasts and ten more of their pets battled the other scouts and charr.

One ogre kicked its way through the crowd, hurling Tippett against the rock wall and stomping a charr warrior to mush. Another ogre tackled a charr, breaking its back. A third swung a club with Wescott impaled on it.

Logan ducked beneath the club, fetched his hammer, and smashed it into the beast's hip. A wet crack told of a broken pelvis, and the creature slumped to one side. Another blow from the hammer destroyed its spine.

Rytlock, meanwhile, dragged his burning blade across the hamstrings of another ogre. As it dropped, he plunged the sword into its skull and fried its brain.

Two charr chopped at a third ogre like woodsmen working a great bole. It was an agonizing end, but the ogre made its opponents pay for it. Its flailing hands clutched their heads and pulped them.

The last of the defenders, Logan and Rytlock retreated back-to-back within a circle of hyenas. The snarling creatures darted in, snapping at the legs of the warriors. They responded with hammer and sword. Bashed and burning, hyenas yelped and withdrew.

And now it was down to one human, one charr, and two ogres.

One of the ogres was young and broad; the other was

old and narrow. The young one demanded, "Why have you invaded my lands?"

Rytlock hitched a thumb at Logan. "*He* invaded. I just followed."

The old ogre growled, "You attacked Chiefling Ygor, son of Chief Kronon."

"I want no trouble," protested Logan. "My quarrel is with the charr."

"Your excuses mean nothing," the chiefling said. "The sentence is death."

"Chiefling Ygor has spoken!" pronounced the old ogre.

With that, the ogres charged, their massive morning stars descending like meteors.

Logan and Rytlock rolled away as the weapons impaled the ground.

"Get back here," the old ogre growled. He swung a wild shot after Logan.

Logan tried to leap over the blow, but it caught his boot and flipped him over. Desperate to bring him down, the old ogre lunged sideways and bashed Logan with his elbow. Logan barked with pain, staggering out of reach.

Meanwhile, Chiefling Ygor traded blow for blow with Rytlock. Sparks flew as the weapons met. Sohothin glanced off the morning star to graze Ygor's leg. The ogre roared in fury and reeled back out of range.

The old ogre charged up protectively before Ygor and rushed Rytlock. A roundhouse swing of the morning star caught the flaming sword and wrenched it out of Rytlock's hands. Sohothin flew through the air and crashed down to gutter at the base of the rock wall. The old ogre kicked Rytlock onto his back and towered over him, morning star poised to strike.

"The honor of the kill goes to the lord of the hunt."

Ygor stomped up on the other side of Rytlock and raised his morning star. "My pleasure." The weapon moaned in the air as it fell.

But it never reached Rytlock, because a war hammer shattered Ygor's hand. Shrieking, he reeled back, and the old ogre caught him.

Rytlock scrambled toward Sohothin, but Logan ran for the sword as well.

"Get away from my sword!" they both yelled.

Rytlock grasped Sohothin and rolled over.

Ygor lunged atop Rytlock, trapping him beneath his crushing weight.

Rytlock gasped, the air driven from him. He bashed the chiefling's shoulder, but only managed to get him to roll to one side.

Logan meanwhile brought his hammer down on Ygor's temple. The chiefling hissed, slumping to the ground beside the charr.

"Wow, do *you* owe *me*," Logan said.

A second later, a huge claw latched around him. The old ogre, eyes cracked with rage, hoisted Logan into the air.

Rytlock scrambled to his feet, grasped the ogre's belt, and launched himself up to bury Sohothin in the creature's heart. The blazing blade pierced the great muscle and boiled the ogre's blood. His eyes went black; his claws opened.

Logan tumbled to the ground.

Rytlock landed beside him. "Now *you* owe *me.*"

"We're even," Logan replied, steadying himself on the dead ogre. "I saved you, and you saved me."

"We aren't even," Rytlock snorted. "The life of a charr's worth more than the life of a human."

Logan laughed. "Then by that logic, *you* owe *me.*"

Rytlock spat a gobbet of blood, which spattered the ground. "Once I get my breath back, I'll *kill* you."

"Yeah, me, too." Logan spat a glob that sailed just past Rytlock's mark.

The charr glared at him.

Logan said flatly, "I have to check on my troops."

"I as well!" Rytlock grumbled. "But I'll still kill you afterward."

"Course."

They staggered out into the darkness of the canyon and checked for signs of life, but there were none.

"We need more light," Logan said.

Rytlock rumbled, "We need pyres."

"Which means we need wood."

"Which means *you* gather wood." Rytlock looked at the sword that flamed in his hand. "I'm the one who has the light."

Nodding wearily, Logan strode to the woods and gathered deadfall. He hoisted it and dumped it in a pile, his forehead dappled with sweat.

"One more pyre," Rytlock said. "Can't burn charr with humans."

"True," Logan replied. "That'd be disgusting."

"Hey!"

Logan returned to the forest, gathered another

armful of wood, and dumped it on the other side of the canyon. Rytlock stepped up to him, thrusting his sword into the pyre and igniting it. Then he went to the other pyre and did the same.

"All right, then," the charr said. "Let's get to work." He sheathed the blade.

The two foes turned their backs on each other and went to gather their dead. Logan knelt above each of his fallen friends, speaking a prayer to Grenth and kissing their foreheads. Rytlock meanwhile knelt above his comrades and sang an ancient war song of the Blood Legion. He cradled the head of each warrior just as the primus of their fahrar had first cradled them—"First breath to last . . ."

The man and the charr hoisted the fallen and carried them to the pyres and bedded them in flame.

Soon, twin fires sent twin columns of soot into the sky.

It was hard work—kneeling and whispering and lifting and hauling and burning—eleven humans and ten charr. And when the work was done, Logan and Rytlock staggered, bloodied and soot-blackened.

"I suppose we have to kill each other now," Logan said.

"Yeah," Rytlock replied dully.

"You're going to die like a dog."

"I'm more like a cat," Rytlock pointed out.

Logan shook his head. "You can't die like a cat. They have nine lives."

Rytlock spread clawed arms. "That's what it's going to take!"

A new voice—a woman's voice—broke in and said, "You two have the strangest conversations."

GOLEMANCY

Garm yelped—a strange sound from a dire wolf—and his claws skittered on the stone floor as he ducked back from the huge golem.

Eir also leaped back, her mallet before her.

"Oh, nothing to fear," Snaff assured. He patted the golem's metalwork ankle. The leg was articulated with arrays of aura pumps and servos. "She's harmless." Snaff frowned. "Well, not exactly harmless. She could kill us with one swat if she wanted to . . . but she doesn't *want* to."

"How do you know?" Eir asked.

"Because she doesn't want *anything*," Snaff explained. "Oh, let me show you!"

He scrambled up onto the stone table where the golem sat, clambered onto her leg, and climbed the metal piping that crisscrossed her barrel-shaped torso. Reaching the golem's face—Zojja's face at five times the height—he waved his hand in front of the stone eyes. "See? Nobody's home."

Garm trotted in a wide circle around the golem, watching it warily.

Eir had not lowered her mallet, and her other hand hovered near the chisels on her belt. "But why?"

"Why, what?" asked Snaff, lounging happily in the metal collar of the creature.

"Why make this thing?"

Snaff slid down the broad torso of the creature and landed on the thing's legs. "I just feel that every golem ought to have a good head on her shoulders—especially the eighteen-foot-tall ones. Not that the Arcane Council agrees. They're churning out golems with no heads at all—easy to build, sure, but they're as dumb as posts. What's the point of that?"

"He doesn't do anything the normal way," Zojja noted.

Snaff glanced fondly at his creation. "I think I'll call her Big Zojja."

Normal-size Zojja stomped her foot and stared daggers at him.

"And she'll have quite a ferocious look when she gets into combat."

"Into combat?" Eir asked.

Snaff nodded. "She's a war machine."

"War machine!"

"Why not? Wars shouldn't be fought with flesh and blood. Somebody might get hurt. I'm hoping to revolutionize war—make it the province of golems without people involved at all. Let them bash each other's brains out. The nation with the best golems wins." He gestured behind him to another stone table where a second metal warrior lay. "I'm what you call a philanthropist."

Eir laughed. "We pronounce it *profiteer*." She slung the mallet at her waist and wandered between the tables, surveying the golems.

"They're a special design of mine," Snaff said. "Ceph-alolithopathic."

Zojja broke in, "It means 'psychic blockheads.'"

Snaff smiled patiently. "You see, these golems are designed to be fitted with massive basalt heads, which provide resonance points that channel energy into these powerstones"—he lifted what looked like a golden laurel and pointed to the small powerstones embedded around it—"which infuse the signals through the cranium of the wearer, allowing remote experience of somatic sense and reciprocal control of motor functions."

"What?"

Zojja sighed. "You can control the golem with your mind."

"Precisely," Snaff said. "Very experimental. No one else is even close to doing this sort of thing. It's difficult not to wax poetic about one's own inventions." He carried the golden laurel to his apprentice. "Would you be so kind, my dear? After all, it *does* have your head."

"Fine," Zojja said, taking the golden laurel. She slid it down until the ends rested on her ears and the middle cradled her skull. The moment gold contacted skin, the powerstones began to glow.

"It's working!" Snaff said, clapping his hands as if he had expected it wouldn't. He turned and pointed toward the golem's forehead. "It's working! You see?"

The large powerstone in the golem's forehead glowed with crimson light. Ripples of energy spread out across the golem's face, somehow seeming to soften the stone. When the ripples rolled across the creature's eye, a black iris formed, and a pupil opened, shining red light.

"It can see!" Snaff cried.

The golem lurched up from the table, metal feet pounding stone, and took a booming step toward Eir.

"Look out!" she shouted, and dragged Snaff back from the gigantic foot.

Growling, Garm retreated as well.

But Zojja stood unmoving in the path of the golem. Well, not actually unmoving. She lifted her leg, and the golem took a thunderous step toward her. She lifted her other leg, and—

"Look out!" Eir shouted, snatching Zojja out of the path of the golem.

The golem's foot boomed brutally just behind Eir.

Zojja squirmed in Eir's grip, her feet kicking the air as if she were a child having a tantrum.

Behind Eir, the golem broke into a loose-limbed run.

Eir held Zojja out at arm's length. "What's she doing?"

Snaff's voice sounded distant and sad. "She's running away."

Eir turned to see the huge golem bounding up the staircase, heading for the skylight above. Every kick of Little Zojja's legs became a step for Big Zojja—who just then vaulted out of the ziggurat.

"Help me chase her down!" Snaff shouted, running for the stairs.

Eir glanced from him to Little Zojja, whose feet were still flailing. "What do I do with *her*?"

Snaff pointed to a small door. "Lock her in the closet until we get back!"

Carrying Little Zojja to the closet, Eir shoved her inside and slammed and locked the door. Moments later, small fists were pounding inside the closet, and big fists outside the ziggurat.

"Hurry! The golem's getting away!" shouted Snaff as he ambled up the stairs.

Eir dashed up behind him and hoisted Snaff to her shoulders and vaulted through the skylight. She emerged in hot, humid Rata Sum.

"There she is!" Eir exclaimed, pointing upward, toward the city center.

Big Zojja climbed the stairs with the loose-limbed excitement of a child who was running naked.

"Can we catch up?" Snaff asked dubiously.

"Of course," Eir replied.

Garm shot out past her and vaulted up the switch-back stairs. His black jowls hung loose as he tore past the stony slope where Master Klab had launched his puff-ball. Beyond it, Garm closed in on Big Zojja. He nipped at her heels, snarling.

The golem turned her uncanny stone head down toward him, eye beams scanning. Then she broke into a real run, leaving Garm behind.

The great wolf slowed to a stop and stood there, panting, waiting for his master to catch up. When Eir arrived, they ran on together.

"Some would call this an anomaly," Snaff murmured as he bounced on the norn's shoulders. "But to have an anomaly, you have to establish a baseline."

Eir glanced at the inventor. "*This* is your *baseline?*"

"I put it down to high spirits," Snaff said with mock cheer. "When you're used to having legs that are two feet long and suddenly have legs that are ten feet long, well, you want to take them out for a stretch, don't you? It's not an anomaly."

Just then, gongs sounded from nearby towers. The clangor spread outward until all of Rata Sum was ringing. Asura voices joined the cacophony, resolving to a single word: "A-no-ma-ly! A-no-ma-ly."

Snaff snarled, "Haven't they been *listening?*"

Emergency crews poured out of the sides of the cubes, looking around in shock to see what sort of mayhem had been unleashed *this* time.

Big Zojja bolted onward, cracking tiles and shattering stones on the bridges. She rushed across one of the giant stone cubes, then vanished around its edge.

"No!" Snaff shouted.

Eir ran up to the edge of the cube and skidded to a stop, with Garm beside her. They looked down at the jungle far below.

Snaff squeaked, "Where is she?"

Eir blinked. "If she fell, there should be a golem-shaped hole in the jungle."

"She's up there!" Snaff shouted, pointing.

They all looked up along the slanting edge of the giant cube. There, Big Zojja teetered, heading for the top.

"She'll fall to her death!" Snaff shouted. "We've got to get up there!"

Eir grabbed on to the side of the cube and began to climb. Garm scrambled up alongside her.

Snaff meanwhile wrung his hands. "I've murdered her. That's what I've done. I've quite simply discombobulated my apprentice. And she was a genius! Oh, wretched man that I am!"

"Shhh," said Eir.

"What?"

"Shhh! She's just ahead."

At the peak of the stony slope stood Big Zojja, with legs fully extended and arms lifted high and stony face raised.

Snaff wailed, "The posture of an idiot! I've reduced Zojja to an idiot!"

"Shhhh!" Eir reiterated.

Snaff fell silent.

In the hush, the asura, the norn, and the dire wolf watched breathlessly as a great white puffball drifted up over the edge of the pyramid. Wind-filled bags of silk surrounded the terrified figure of Master Klab. At the base of the puffball, a dozen or so skyhooks hung, testimony to the failure of rescue krewes.

Big Zojja stood on the block of stone, lifted her golemic arms, snagged a few of the skyhooks, and hauled down.

The moment that the puffball reached the top of the pyramid, Master Klab unbuckled his harness and fell at Big Zojja's feet. "Thank you! Thank you! Where is your master? Where is your creator?"

Snaff stepped up behind the bowing man and tapped him on the butt. "Ahem. That would be me."

Master Klab looked behind him and managed to sputter, "Oh, yes! My good friend Snaff."

"Good friend?" Snaff replied.

"Well, *friend* is not so much the word. More like *role model.* Even *idol.*" Klab wore a sick smile and seemed to throw up in his mouth.

"Really, Klab, I think you might be wise to give up larking about in the sky. A bit dangerous, don't you think?"

"A bit," Master Klab allowed as he mopped the cold sweat from his forehead. "Maybe I should go back to my study of frostometrics."

"Yes, excellent idea. Iceboxes *are* more your speed." Snaff turned toward Big Zojja. "Come along, now. Let's head back to the laboratory for a few more adjustments." The golem nodded and followed its master. Once they were out of earshot of Klab, Snaff began to mutter, "I've got to solve the problem of spacial dislocation experienced by the pilot—that and the business about flailing legs and arms and all the dangers they present. Can't just be locking pilots into closets... *unless* they were mobile..."

"What are you talking about?" Eir asked, regaining her breath.

"Mobile closets," Snaff muttered, grinning.

Eir blinked. "I don't know what that is."

"A cage—no, a cockpit. We'll put it in the abdomen—you know, with a harness and all so that the driver can kick her legs and punch her arms as much as she likes and ride along in safety!"

Eir nodded. "You think you could make these machines controllable?"

"Of course."

"Because, in wartime, a machine has to be completely in control."

"Yes, of course," Snaff replied, adding innocently, "What's this about?"

"You have these . . . hypercephalic—"

"Cephalolithopathic."

"Yes . . . these golems that people can control with their minds. And I need warriors who can fight the Dragonspawn—"

"Your point being?"

The norn sighed. "Here's what I propose: I'll carve your head, so you can have a golem just like your assistant, if you'll agree to march these golems against the Dragonspawn as your . . . um, what do you call it?"

"Beta test?"

"Right."

The asura inventor sighed contentedly. "It's just the sort of arrangement I had hoped for."

STRANGER DANGER

Who said that?" Logan asked, silencing Rytlock with an upraised hand. "Listen."

Only the crackling fires spoke in the dark canyon. Neither warrior could hear anything else, let alone see beyond the pyres.

"Wasn't me," Rytlock growled. "Sounded womanish."

"It *was* womanish," said the voice.

Rytlock and Logan drew their weapons.

Logan stepped away from the pyres, war hammer ready in his hand. "Who is it? Show yourself!"

"I *am* showing myself," the woman replied flatly. "I'm standing right here. The problem is you're fire-blinded. If you want to see me, step away from the light."

"Yeah, right," Rytlock snarled.

"Why don't *you* step *into* the light?" Logan asked.

"You want all three of us to be fire-blinded?"

"Yes."

There was a sigh. Then she emerged from the veiling

darkness—a petite woman with silvery hair and porcelain skin. She wore glossy travel leathers crossed with vine motifs, which clung tight to her young body. Her spike-heeled boots also looked like dark seedpods, lifting her three inches taller than she would have stood.

"A sylvari," groaned Rytlock. "Always trouble."

Logan stepped toward her. "What are you doing here?"

Her eyes shone like jade. "Talking to you."

Logan blinked. "No, I mean, *why* are you here?"

She sighed. "You asked me to step into the light."

"See what I mean?" growled Rytlock.

"Which is a bad idea since the smell of blood is drawing predators from miles around," she continued, "and those pyres are like beacons to bring the ogres."

Rytlock huffed. "*Bring* the ogres? We just *killed* the ogres."

"Yes," the silver-haired woman said. "You killed *some* of them."

"Do you live here?"

"No."

"Then how did you get here?"

"I followed you."

"Why?"

"Because you were moving. It's impossible to follow someone who is standing still. If I hadn't moved, I would have lost you. Thus, *follow*. You ask the strangest questions."

Logan flung his hands up in frustration.

Rytlock stepped forward, Sohothin before him. "You saw what this sword can do. Give us your name."

"I'm Caithe. But what does my name have to do with what your sword can do?"

Rytlock rolled his eyes. "It was a threat."

"I'm not the one in danger here," Caithe said.

"Is *that* a threat?" Rytlock asked, eyes growing wide.

"Not a threat. A warning."

The charr laughed harshly. "You? Warning me?"

"Yes."

"About what?"

"Being killed."

"You think you can kill me?"

"No."

Rytlock stared at her, waiting for elaboration. None came. Finally he asked, "So, who, then?"

"Chief Kronon."

"Who's that?"

"The chief of the local tribes."

"What does he want with us?" asked Rytlock.

"You killed his son, Chiefling Ygor."

"The one with the iron helm," Logan said, snapping his fingers.

Caithe continued placidly, "When Chief Kronon finds out, he and his hunters will track you down."

Rytlock stared at the dead ogres lying between the pyres. "We've got to get out of here."

The sylvari clenched her teeth. "That's exactly what I was telling you but was sidetracked by all those *hows* and *whys* and ridiculous commands to come into the light so that all three of us could stand here and be surrounded by devourers."

"Devourers!" Logan blurted, just before the first giant scorpion scuttled into view.

It was a devourer, all right, its armor as thick as plates

and its two tails curved in deadly arcs above its back. The
creature ambled up just behind Caithe.

"There's a swarm," she said in a lecturing voice, "which
means we'll all be fighting. Now, I've seen you two fight—
too much power, too little care—which means you'll win,
but not before the ogres get here, which means we all lose."

Claws clicked the ground behind Logan. He spun to
see another devourer creeping up on him.

"I've got one, too," Rytlock announced, raking his
sword out before him. The darkness beyond shivered with
scaly claws and venomous stingers. "Hate these things.
They're attracted by the smell of death. It's their food."

"But the pyres," Logan said. "We burned the dead!"

"So they want their food *cooked.*"

"Too many!" Logan hissed as a pair of devourers
scuttled up to him. He swung his hammer, and their
tails darted down to spurt venom into the air.

Rytlock's sword was even worse, drawing the great
scorpions like a candle flame.

"Put away your weapons," the sylvari said easily.
"Devourers have better weapons than you. You need to
dictate the battle. Draw the monster in. Get it to strike,
but when you want it to."

Whirling around, Caithe flung her arms toward the
sky and set her feet wide apart, becoming a living X
before the giant scorpion. It scudded forward, its scales
shivering with anticipation. The two poisonous tails
quivered, and drops of venom hung from their ends.
The devourer snapped its pincers and clicked its feet,
watching for an opening. Suddenly, both poisonous tails
lunged toward Caithe.

She flung her hands back from the stingers, which jetted poison. Then, with catlike reflexes, she grabbed the tops of the stingers.

"What are you doing?" Logan shouted.

The sylvari only smiled again as those muscular tails lifted her up over of the devourer's snapping claws and carapaced back. Caithe raised a spike-heeled boot and brought it down on the base of the scorpion's tails. Her heel punched through the thick armor and into the nerve core. The two great tails wilted, slumping to the ground.

"Every creature's got weak points," Caithe said as she drew a knife from her belt and stabbed the beast's brain. "Learn the weak points, and you can lockpick them. For these devourers, the weak point is where the two tails diverge."

A half dozen devourers swelled out of the darkness.

The man and the charr traded annoyed looks and launched into battle.

Logan brought his hammer down on the back of a devourer—except that the beast shied back, and the hammer rooted in the ground. Logan dropped it and pivoted to run, but the devourer surged up to trip him. Pincers grabbed his ankles and pitched him backward. Logan landed on the scorpion, back-to-back, his hands reaching up to catch the twin stingers before they could sink into his stomach. Gobs of venom slid down his arms as the muscular tails struggled to break his grip. The venom made his hands slick, and he was losing hold.

"Weak points," said a voice, and Logan looked up between the tails to see the smiling sylvari. She kicked her heel into the divergence of the spines. The tails slumped. Caithe leaned over Logan and jabbed between his legs to stab the scorpion's brain. Smiling grimly, she helped Logan to his feet. "Try it my way."

With his hammer mired beneath a dead devourer, he had little choice. As another giant scorpion approached, Logan lifted his arms and spread his legs as Caithe had done. When the tails struck, he reared his hands back, caught hold of the tails, and rode them up to the weak point. A solid stomp wilted the stingers, and another crushed the brain of the beast.

Caithe had already finished off half a dozen the same way—and Rytlock had burned two others to sooty husks. The last three devourers surrounded the charr, though.

"Let's give him a hand," Caithe said.

Logan dragged his hammer free and rushed to aid his onetime foe. He pounded the spine of one devourer, crushing it and wilting the deadly tails. Caithe meanwhile plunged her dagger into the back of another.

But the final scorpion bounded at the charr, grabbing his legs and knocking him to the ground.

Rytlock rammed his sword into a joint in the carapace. The scorpion's eyes grew fire-bright, then cloudy white, then cracked like hard-boiled eggs. Smoke oozed from the shell in a hundred places.

"Smells like thundershrimp," Logan said.

"Never had it," Rytlock snorted, crawling on his elbows out of the grip of the thing's dead pincers. Next moment, the creature burst into flame. Rising to his feet, Rytlock heaved a satisfied sigh. "Well, that's three for me. How many for you, Logan?"

Reluctantly the man said, "Two. But one was yours. You owe me."

"Stop it."

"I killed seven," Caithe said. She went among the devourer bodies, slicing off the tails. When she finished, she cut off the stingers and leaned the tails against the pyre to cook. Kneeling, she dug a hole and positioned a stinger in it, point up.

"What are you doing?" Logan asked.

"Burying their stingers."

"Why?"

"The ogres won't be able to run as well on stung feet." She nodded to the two warriors. "Well, lend a hand."

The man and the charr bent, digging as well. In a few minutes, the three had set their devourer-tail traps. Caithe smiled dazzlingly. "We need to go. I can hear them."

"Hear who?"

"The ogres." She cupped a hand to her ear. The man and the charr listened. Beyond the crackle of sizzling fat and the chorus of distant locusts came the thunder of boots on ground. Occasionally, a cackle or yip announced that hyenas ran with the party. Then a deep-bellied horn sounded. "That would be Chief Kronon and his hunters."

"How does he know about the chiefling?" Logan wondered.

"He doesn't—yet. Let's go." Caithe snatched up one of the roasted scorpion tails, peeled off the charred scales, and took a bite of the white flesh within. "They're delicious, but don't eat the venom glands." She set off at a light-footed run from the canyon.

The man and the charr watched as she disappeared into the darkness. Rytlock growled, "Why should we trust her?"

Logan shot him a disbelieving look. "Why should I trust you?" He snatched up his own scorpion tail and jogged after the sylvari.

"Good point." The charr grabbed two more tails and chased after his strange allies. "Thundershrimp, eh?"

Chief Kronon's feet pounded the ground, and his heart pounded his ribs. His scar-crossed chest pumped like an old bellows, and he ached—not with the running, but with every father's fear: that his son had stirred up terrible trouble.

"Ygor is rash," Chief Kronon growled.

Beside him, Warmarshal Rairon blew upon a great horn. The mournful cry pealed out across the mountains, but no answering cry came from Chiefling Ygor's horn.

Chief Kronon shook his head violently. His son was idealistic and rash and perhaps gone.

Kronon had lived 240 years, enough time to bury many sons. The chief had been born the very year that the Great Destroyer, champion of the ancient dragon Primordus, had awakened. His great-great-grandsire had been born in the year that magic had come into the world. The greatest of his grandsires had been born before there were any humans.

The ogre race was ancient, but Ygor was young. He cared only for "the hunts," slaughtering humans and charr that strayed into ogre lands. "He is foolish and reckless and rash."

Chief Kronon led his hunters up a wooded slope and thrashed past a stand of trees. He and his retinue emerged on a rill and staggered to a halt.

There, on the mountainside above, a canyon was lit by a pair of pyres. The ogres had smelled them from twenty miles away—burning human flesh and burning charr flesh. Only now, at the edge of dawn, did they see the light of them.

"We don't burn our dead," the chief said to no one.

"No, lord," Warmarshal Rairon replied.

"The winner of this battle is burning the dead."

"Yes, lord."

A groan escaped Chief Kronon's lips, but when the warmarshal glanced his way, the chief only ran forward.

He climbed a slope of scree and then a mossy hillside and a narrow trail through another thicket and at last reached the canyon.

There, between the pyres, lay ogre bodies.

Warmarshal Rairon charged into the clearing, past dismembered devourers and slain hyenas. When he approached the ogres, though, he shouted and fell to the ground. "Stay back! It's trapped."

Chief Kronon halted, holding out his arms to keep the rest of the group back.

The warmarshal reached to his foot, where the white stinger of a devourer was embedded. The venom gland still pumped. Rairon pried the stinger loose, then reached to his thigh and pulled out a second. "There are more stingers," he gasped, "in a circle around the pile."

Kronon nodded grimly.

Already, Rairon was stiffening. He looked up with cloudy eyes. "It has been an honor to serve you, my chief."

"You have served well."

The warmarshal went gray like a statue and toppled backward.

"Clear them away."

The hunters tentatively moved forward, digging in the sands to remove the scorpion stingers. At last, they announced, "It is safe, lord," and backed away. "Your son lies here."

Chief Kronon approached the spot, seeing Chiefling Ygor sprawled out, arms spread and hands open, never to close again.

Falling to his knees, the chief murmured, "My son. My son. You will be avenged."

He reached down to the chiefling's belt, which bore the horn he used in the hunt. Chief Kronon pulled the horn from its thong and set it to his lips and blew a long, mournful cry. Then he let his hands fall to his sides and roared into the sky, "You will be avenged!"

Four miles away, Caithe, Logan, and Rytlock were running across a hanging valley when they heard the lonely horn.

"I think he's found the body," Logan said.

Then came an anguished roar.

"He's definitely found the body," Rytlock added.

Caithe still led the way, faster and more lithe than the other two. "Ogres can outrun all of us, and their hyenas can outrun them."

Rytlock laughed derisively. "Where's the weak point on a hyena?"

Caithe replied, "Unfortunately, it's halfway down the throat."

"I'll reach in and see if I can find it," Rytlock replied.

"Better to just keep running," the sylvari said, her silver hair lashing her ears. Logan noticed now that it was not quite hair, but rather more like the fronds or leaves of a plant.

"You knew the ogres were hunting us," Rytlock said. "Why didn't you stay away?"

Even as she ran, leaping small cracks in the ground, Caithe shrugged. "You two were trying to kill each other. That's what charr and men do. But then, you were trying to save each other. That's not what they do. I was . . . intrigued."

Logan asked, "Are you still intrigued?"

"More like baffled." Just then, the voice of a hyena ripped the air, and more yipping followed. "They've seen us."

"Half a mile back," Rytlock huffed, glancing over his shoulder. "We've got—what?—a minute?"

"Just keep running."

The three did for the first forty seconds, rushing side by side across the grasslands while hyenas bounded after.

"I wouldn't be in this mess if it weren't for you," Rytlock snapped.

"You wouldn't be in this mess if you'd left Ascalon to us," Logan replied.

The hyenas were snapping at their heels.

Rytlock drew Sohothin and backhanded two of the beasts right behind him. They squealed and fell away.

Another peal from the ogre horn announced that the brutes had sighted their quarry. The ground shook with the footfalls of the ogres.

Logan hoisted his war hammer. "We have to turn and fight. The hyenas will drag us down."

"No! Just keep running!" Caithe shouted.

"What's the point?" cried Rytlock. "You got some secret fortress hidden in your pocket?"

"Yes!" Caithe said, suddenly dropping away into a narrow cleft in the ground.

Eyes wide, Logan ran up on the same cleft and skidded to a halt in front of it. The steep crevice plunged away into unseeable depths, and the sylvari had vanished into it.

"Look out!" Rytlock shouted, running a hyena through with his flaming sword.

"Thanks," Logan replied, pulping the head of another.

As they fought the snarling beasts, both warriors backed toward the deep crevice.

"You think she did that on purpose?" Logan asked, mowing down another hyena.

"Of course!" Rytlock growled through clenched teeth. "She's sylvari!"

More hyenas converged out of the grasses, their fangs snarling.

"I'll give her the benefit of the doubt," Logan said as he leaped into the gap, sliding away between walls of stone.

Rytlock rolled his eyes and killed another hyena. "I'm not going to be outdone by a human and a twig." He sheathed Sohothin and jumped down the crevice, too.

HEADS OF THE MILITARY

Eir stepped back from carving another huge basalt head. It showed Snaff's face—the quirky rumple of his brow mirrored below in a slight smirking lip, the wide and happy eyes, the long nose, and those ears like milkweed pods.

"How do I look?" Snaff asked, posing nearby.

Pacing across the stone chips that littered the floor of Snaff's laboratory, Eir said, "You look good."

"Good?" Snaff said dejectedly. "Not dashing?"

"I've never seen you dash. . . ."

"How about brave?"

"Sure," Eir said as she brushed rock dust from her hands. "Brave."

Snaff waddled up beside her and stared at his likeness. A smile crept onto his face, and he said, *"Brave."*

"Well, that does it for the second head," Eir said. "What about the body?"

"Oh! Zojja's been working hard on my design," Snaff

said enthusiastically. He grasped the norn's hand and led her over to a short drafting table covered with sketches. All showed a spherical cage with a leather harness suspended within. "The cage is for protection, of course, like your rib cage, because inside it is where the driver will be suspended. These straps will hold the person secure within the center of the cage, with side straps to stabilize in case the golem falls over."

"Ouch," Eir said.

Snaff nodded. "Yes, and you see that there's plenty of clearance for flailing arms and legs."

"Show me how far we are."

Snaff led Eir to the worktables that held the metal golems. From the belly of Big Zojja, a blinding light flashed, and acrid smoke whiffed into the air. The light ceased, and Zojja's head popped from the opening, her hair slightly singed. She set smoking hands on the golem fuselage.

"Have you been welding by hand again?" Snaff asked.

"It's fastest," Zojja said dismissively. "But I've got to make sure my eyes are shut."

"How are the cockpits coming?" Snaff went on.

"Nearly done. Both are welded to the frame. Then you can hang your rigs."

"Ingenious," Eir marveled.

Zojja huffed. "Only if you trust metal over magic."

"Eir," Snaff interrupted, "I don't think I've shown you the laurels. . . ."

"Wait," Eir said, staring at Zojja. "What did you say?"

"I said I don't know why the two of you are putting more trust in golems than in magic."

"They're *magic* golems," Snaff volunteered with a weak smile.

Eir waved him off. "No, wait. This isn't about magic or metal. This is about Zojja disagreeing with the plan."

Zojja nodded tightly. "Exactly."

Eir folded her arms over her chest. "So you don't think your master's designs are good enough?"

Zojja's eyes flared. "Of course they are!"

"So you don't think your *welds* are good enough?"

"My welds are rock solid!"

"So you don't think *my plans* are good enough."

Zojja pointed at her. "*There* you go."

Eir nodded. "Well, your reservations are noted, but the plan goes ahead."

"Then we're all going to get killed."

Eir laughed angrily, shaking her head. "No, we won't. I promise you, we will kill the Dragonspawn, and every one of us will walk out of there alive."

Zojja cocked her hips. "If I die, it'll be too late to say I told you so."

Eir towered above the asura. "Your master is a kind man. You could have much worse. In fact, every asura I have encountered would make a much worse master."

"Thank you very much," Snaff said. "And now, about the laurels—"

"But he has one fault," Eir continued, never looking away from Zojja. "He lets you pretend *you* are the master."

"That's because he recognizes that I am a genius," Zojja said archly.

Eir shook her head. "You *work* with a genius, and yet you disdain everything he does. He treats you with respect, and you act as if he is your enemy. One day, you will be without him, and then you will see who the true genius is."

Zojja rolled her eyes. "Nice speech."

Eir clenched her hands, gritted her teeth, and turned away.

Snaff smiled and blinked placidly. "Let me show you these wonderful laurels." He retrieved a pair of golden torcs from a nearby table and brought them over. Powerstones in red, yellow, purple, and green gleamed in settings of gold. "Beautiful, aren't they? The stones are selected to map to the activation zones of our minds."

The word *minds* cast a pall over Eir's face. "Yes. Minds. There's the flaw in my plan." She glanced over her shoulder, then looked back down at Snaff. "The Dragonspawn takes over minds. He corrupts them. His power infuses them, tempts them. He turns those who want to kill him into those who want to serve him. These machines are no good unless we can block his mind powers."

Snaff grinned like a boy who had studied well for a test. "He can't. That's why I've placed these here," he said, tapping a powerstone embedded in the shoulder piece of Big Zojja. "The gray stones repel mind auras. Out here on the shoulders, they'll create a field that will block the Dragonspawn's mind. He can't reach us, and he can't take over our golems."

Eir slapped Snaff on the back, a move that shuffled him a few steps forward. "You *are* a genius. But could you put some gray stones in a necklace for me and a collar for Garm?"

"Of course," Snaff replied offhandedly, but then said, "You know, *nobody* else has this technology. Everybody else is making golems *without heads!*"

Eir feigned shock. *"No!"*

Snaff nodded deeply. "Their golems fumble around, while mine combine the genius of an asura with the power of a titan! *Nobody* can do this stuff!"

"They all think he's cracked," Zojja explained flatly as she jumped down from the belly of her golem. "I agree. Sometimes."

Eir laughed ruefully. "So, is everything ready?"

"Everything except the head of my golem," Snaff said. "You can put that into place while I get your gray-stone necklace and collar made. Then we'll have a meal and a rest, and tomorrow—"

"We march on the Dragonspawn."

She headed back toward the worktables, lifted the huge head of Big Snaff, and slid it into position atop his metalwork body. When the stone base contacted the metal frame, loops of steel rose to engage the stone shoulders and clamp down tightly. Then Eir had only to set a powerstone in the head of the creature. It fused with the basalt, sinking in and rooting.

Big Snaff sat up.

Eir set the other powerstone, and Big Zojja rose, too.

Garm and Eir stood between those towering creatures. Snaff and Zojja wandered over to join them. They stared in wonder at what they had wrought.

"There is a certain sick calm before battle," Eir said. "The panic of the heart that something has been left undone, that we are not ready for this." She looked at the two asura, only rising waist high, and at her wolf, who rose only to her ribs. "We *are* ready."

Snaff clapped his hands once and then rubbed them eagerly. "Then let's feast."

A pig turned on a spit within the laboratory's ironwork forge, and among the coals below, potatoes nestled in chain-mail sleeves. Wild onions and butter-soaked leeks simmered in iron skillets. Cornflower cakes rose on the hearth, and little pitchers of honey and gravy warmed there, as well.

The four warriors lined up along the hearth and loaded pewter plates with this bounty. Then they gathered around the great stone table where Big Zojja had been built. Even Garm had a place. Though their plates were heaped with smoked pork and caramelized onions and leeks and cornflower cakes, they sat in silence, unsure what to say.

At last, Eir spoke. "Spirit of Wolf," she breathed, her voice husky in the hot jungle air. "Spirit of Bear and Snow Leopard and Raven, we eat this meal tonight in preparation for war tomorrow. We fight not just for the norn but for you, for all races. Be with us. Help us prevail against the Dragonspawn."

With those words, the spell of regret over them all was shattered. They ate and talked and laughed but did not speak of what the dawn might bring.

•   •   •

The first red glow of sunrise filtered through the skylight of Snaff's laboratory and shone across his two massive golems: a twenty-foot-tall Snaff and an eighteen-foot-tall Zojja. Both stood with their cockpit hatches open, ready for their drivers to climb in.

"Well, my dear," Snaff said, "let's take them for a spin."

Zojja gave a rare smile and clambered up the leg of her golem, into the cockpit.

Snaff climbed up as well, pulling the cockpit hatch closed behind him. He stepped into the spherical cage and strapped himself into the leather harness. Leaning toward a speaking tube, he shouted, "Can you hear me?" His voice rang through the metal.

A tinny reply came: "Yes."

"Make sure you fit the straps securely. We're going to get jostled. And make sure your laurel is tightly in place."

"Yes, Father," Zojja said sarcastically.

Snaff slid the laurel onto his head. The jewels on the gold band glowed to life, and the metal affixed to Snaff's skull. He blinked as his eyes lost focus in the cockpit. They regained focus above, staring through the red pupils of the golem. "I can see! Through the golem's eyes! Well—hello down there, my norn friend!"

Servos whined, and Big Snaff's giant hand waved beside his giant head.

Eir waved back a little sheepishly.

"It's spooky to be so big."

"Yeah, spooky," Zojja replied in a metallic voice.

"All right! Gang's all here," Eir said as Garm loped up beside her. "Let's get this attack going." She led the way, striding up the stone steps that led from the laboratory.

Garm followed at her heels, and behind him came the two Bigs.

Rata Sum had never seen such an odd procession. The norn warrior Eir Stegalkin marched down the side of the ziggurat, followed by her dire wolf, Garm, who was taller than two asura stacked. Behind came two asura who were taller than five—the wide-eyed Big Snaff and the intense, young Big Zojja.

They climbed toward the city center, the switchback stairs shaking with their footfalls.

That morning, even the geniuses who loved to sleep in rolled out of their beds to gape at the procession.

Master Klab, for one, staggered up from within his workshop and stood beside his ruined puffball, which was unceremoniously lashed to a stone curb. He blinked in annoyance at the mechanical parade, saving a particularly deep scowl for "Master" Snaff. "Bit of rubbish," Klab snarled, though he couldn't quite turn away from those strange stony heads, those carefully engineered trusses, those expertly aligned welds. Yes, Klab had recently been saved by that very golem, looking so much like Snaff's own apprentice, but no genius wants to be beholden. Zojja showed how beholden he really was—and how much of a genius Snaff really was.

"I hope you fall off the city!"

But the band navigated the bridges safely on their march to the center of town, heading for a particular asura gate.

Eir and Garm strode through, feeling the membrane of magic snap around them. The sultry air of Rata Sum gave way to the biting cold of Hoelbrak.

Of course, the asura gate had not been constructed with twenty-foot golems in mind, so Big Snaff had to crouch and nearly crawl to get through. The air rippled around him as he passed. "I hope the Dragonspawn has a bigger door."

"If he doesn't, you can make one," Zojja replied as she shuffled through behind him.

Then they were all in Hoelbrak, standing on a cobbled way between tents and rough-hewn lodges. The bodies of the Bigs pinged and crackled as the metal contracted from cold. Standing at their full height, the golems could peer over the thatched rooftops, past the defensive bridges that ringed the settlement, and out to snow-covered tundra and ice-choked mountains.

"Out there is where the Dragonspawn is," Zojja said grimly.

"Not much longer," Snaff assured.

As the group marched down the lane, walls shuddered, thatch shivered, and norn came running out in all states of undress, bellowing and bearing weapons.

"What's happening?"

"Earthquake?"

"Invasion?"

"For the love of Wolf—!"

"We're being attacked!"

"Stop!" shouted Eir, lifting her hands to the crowd. "You are not being attacked. These magnificent creatures are fashioned to battle the Dragonspawn."

A susurrus of shock moved through the crowd, and someone shouted, "Golems can't do the work of norn warriors!"

"*I* am a norn warrior," Eir said, "and I am doing this

work. But let me ask you this—what becomes of norn who go to battle the Dragonspawn?"

The crowd sighed in frustration, and a nearby woman said, "The men return . . . as frozen icebrood. The women return . . . not at all."

"Exactly. But we are warded by powerstone magic that will block his aura." She tapped the gray stones that shone from the epaulets of her armor. "And these warriors of steel and stone cannot be corrupted by the Dragonspawn's power. With these provisions, Garm and I and our metal allies will reach the inner sanctum of the Dragonspawn.

"And we will tear him apart."

8

DEEP PLACES

As Rytlock dived into the crevice, he thought, *Why am I following a pollen-brained sylvari?*

A hyena nipped his heel.

Oh, yeah, that's why.

Then there was no more time for thinking. Only plunging. And cursing.

Rytlock dropped through the narrow cleft and into a cavern. Below him, Logan and Caithe were tumbling into the darkness.

"Great idea!" Rytlock shouted. "Really flipping great!"

"I heard you the first time!" Caithe yelled.

Just then, there came a huge splash, and then a second, and then . . .

Ow! The water was hard. Rytlock smashed through the surface, and the flood closed over him. Bubbles chattered everywhere, but there wasn't a gulp to breathe! He lashed his claws through the water—kicked and flailed (wasn't this how humans swam?) but only sank.

Then the water above exploded again. Something else had just plunged into it, something that was now swimming toward the surface. Rytlock grabbed on to the thing and let it lift him. He reached the air and gasped.

The thing yipped and giggled. A hyena.

"A hyena," Rytlock snarled. "Who knew they floated?"

"Rytlock!" Logan shouted.

"Yeah?"

"There's hyenas in the water!" Logan warned. "Just killed one."

"Got one of my own."

"Snap its neck!"

"Do they float when they're dead?"

There was silence. "How would I know?"

"You just killed one. Did it float?"

"I didn't *hold on to it*!"

Just then, a thud and a splash told of another hyena's arrival. In moments, it, too, was gasping at the surface. When it heard the struggles of its packmate, it swam toward Rytlock.

"Ah, good," Rytlock said. "This one was getting tired. . . . Hello."

The scavenger lunged for Rytlock, but he bashed it back, grasped it around the midsection, and hauled it beside him. The hyenas paddled desperately while Rytlock leaned back. "I've got two hyenas now."

"Snap their necks!"

"Do they float?"

"You're ridiculous!"

"You're *both* ridiculous," interrupted the sylvari.

"You survived?" Rytlock yelled. "Damn."

"I just saved you from the ogres!" she shouted back indignantly.

"You just dropped us into a cesspool a hundred feet below the ground."

"It's not a cesspool. It's an underground river," Caithe responded. "Can't you feel the current?"

Rytlock squeezed the hyenas into submission. "Yeah."

"That's why I led us down here," Caithe said. "I can feel the ways of water and wind, the ways of nature. I'll get us out of here. Follow my voice."

"I'd have to *listen* to it."

Logan stroked toward her and shot back over his shoulder, "How're the hyenas holding out?"

The truth was, they seemed to be weakening. Rytlock whispered, "Follow the sylvari. She's young and tasty."

Whether or not the scavengers understood, they did paddle generally in Caithe's direction, carrying the charr with them. The chant of the river changed, echoes coming more quickly ahead, and then there was water-smoothed stone underfoot.

Rytlock strode up it, feeling the waters recede. "Finally," he said, dropping the hyenas into the water and kicking them sharply in the backsides. "Get off with you!" Yipping, they swam away.

"There's a cave mouth up here," Caithe called from ahead. "A slight breeze is pouring into the cave, so there must be an opening on the other side."

"I'm following," Logan said, feeling his way forward through the darkness. "Keep talking, Caithe."

"Yeah. Keep talking." Rytlock was in torment. Not the

Realm of Torment, with its fire and severity. That place would've been homey. No, this was a uniquely charr torment—with churning water and buoyant hyenas and a pesky human and a starry-eyed sylvari leading a parade of fools.

They stumbled through the passage that Caithe had found, trading the terrors of an underground river for the annoyance of stalactites hitting their faces and stalagmites jamming their toes. And the cave wasn't entirely dry. Something scuttled on the ground and squashed wetly underfoot with each step.

Ahead, Caithe staggered to a stop. "Oh. Well, *that's* something. . . ."

The man and the charr came up behind her. "Whoa."

They stood at the edge of a gigantic cavern, dimly lit by fading blue stones embedded along the walls. The light of the stones revealed a ruined underground city. Cobbled streets ran between rock-walled buildings, and a crumbling palace stood on a prominence on the far side. Many buildings were missing their roofs, and many windows were marked with soot where fires had burned. Cracked columns shored up the ceiling high above.

An eerie wind meandered past, like the brush of a ghost.

"What *is* this place?" Rytlock asked.

"It looks dwarven," Logan said. "Who else would have a whole city that nobody knew about?"

"But what happened to them?"

"Destroyers," Caithe broke in. "Creatures of living lava—the minions of the dragon Primordus. I've seen other villages destroyed this way."

"Well, when you live in a hole in the ground, you've got to expect to run into things like that," Rytlock said. "The question is whether they're still here." He stepped past the other two and marched down toward the city.

"We're following her, not you," Logan called.

"When I can see, I follow no one." Rytlock paused, looking down at his foot and seeing the remains of albino frogs crushed between his claws. "I'm finding my own way out of here."

As Rytlock marched away into the gloomy ruins, Logan shook his head. "Good riddance."

"We shouldn't split up," Caithe said.

"Not much choice." He turned to her. "Where to now?"

"It's strange. I sense a presence here. Something magical."

"Well, then, lead the way."

Caithe stepped out ahead of him and strode down the slope. Logan hoisted his war hammer and went along.

The city was indeed built on a dwarven scale: Logan had to duck his head to look through windows. Markings on the walls had the deep-etched angularity of dwarven runes, and along the main way was a metalwork shop every hundred paces.

"Definitely dwarves," Logan said. He peered into a burned-out building, with charred tables and chairs and a burst beer tun.

Caithe meanwhile stood at the corner of the building, peering down the cross-street. "Yes. Dwarves."

Logan came to her, rounding the corner to see the undeniable proof—a dwarven skeleton in chain and plate armor lying on a pile of rubble.

Caithe crouched down to look more closely at the rubble pile. The broken stones seemed almost to fit together. "Here's what killed him."

"What?" Logan asked. "These stones killed him?"

"These stones are the remains of a destroyer—a monster of elemental magma. A whole hive must have erupted into this chamber and burned every living thing in it."

"They conquered it only to vanish?"

Caithe nodded grimly. "Destroyers care only about killing. They are forged from the molten heart of their master—Primordus, first of the Elder Dragons to rise. The dwarves forestalled his coming, but at a terrible price. They are all but gone now, and Primordus is rising to destroy all races."

Logan took a deep breath. "All right. Let's try to keep things a little lighter, yeah? How about finding this presence of yours down here?"

Caithe lifted her head, listening, and closed her eyes. She breathed deeply and pointed. "This way."

She set off down the street—a wide, cobbled way that grew wider as they went. Soon, the avenue split around medians, where stone sculptures depicted dwarves—working, fighting, drinking. One tableau showed dwarves in battle against destroyers.

"Just ahead," Caithe said, hurrying forward.

Logan marched double time up the avenue, which bent around the massive wall of a dwarven palace. On the far side, the avenue entered a great arch against the stone wall. Logan scratched his head. "They must have been carving a new passage when the destroyers attacked."

"No." Caithe pointed toward the base of the arch, where a massive blue crystal hung loose from its facing. As a breeze wafted past, the stone swung toward the wall, which sparked slightly. "This is an asura gate. It's probably from when Primordus was first put back to sleep. Watch." She knelt beside the stone and pressed it into its housing.

Suddenly, the gate flashed with light.

Logan and Caithe shielded their faces. Only as their eyes adjusted could they see what strobed within the archway.

Visions. Beautiful visions . . . a grassy plain where wild horses ran . . . a deep lagoon encircled by leaning palms . . . a great glacier with snowcapped peaks in blue . . . a sere desert where crystalline statues stood . . .

"Ow!" Caithe said, letting go of the crystal. It was glowing red, and smoke rose from a chunk out of one side. "It's damaged. Someone smashed it to close the gate."

"Can we get it to work long enough to get out of here?" Logan asked, pushing the stone into place again.

. . . a deep rain forest . . . a hamlet in a hanging valley . . . a bustling harbor jammed with junks . . . a white city with gleaming spires . . .

"That was Divinity's Reach!" Logan said, stepping toward the gate. Already, though, the scene had changed to a city-size white tree within a steaming jungle . . .

"And that was the Grove!" Caithe said.

Logan hissed, releasing the crystal and shaking his hand. "That thing's overloading. We'll have just one last chance at this before it blows completely. And if we jump through at the wrong time, who knows where we'll end up."

"Maybe I can call to the Grove. Maybe the tree can prolong the contact."

She began to sing:

> *Oh, come to me, heart of the wyld.*
> *Oh, hear this lost sylvari child,*
> *Away from wood and glade and briar—*
> *Entombed within a world of fire.*

Rytlock was still hearing Caithe's vibrant voice echoing through his head. It was almost as if she were just around the corner.

"That's it," Rytlock growled, sliding Sohothin upward. A feeble blue flame flickered around the twisted metal blades and then flared to life, roaring and crackling. "Ah! Light!"

The fire shone across the ruined street where he stood, revealing burned buildings and shattered walls, dwarven skeletons and dead destroyers. But it also revealed something else. Something worse.

Live destroyers.

They hunkered in an alcove of the cavern wall, their lava figures barely flickering with fire. But the flaming sword seemed to awaken them. One destroyer shifted, its insectile head rotating toward him. Fire blazed from eye sockets and mandibles. The beast jolted up, joints liquefying to lava and arms rising.

Rytlock took a step back.

The other two destroyers shifted, too, standing.

Oh, come to me, heart of the wyld . . .

That wasn't a memory. That was Caithe's voice.

Two more destroyers rose. Now there were five of them.

Rytlock could take five destroyers. He'd be a little charred by the end of it, but—

Then about ten more stalked out of the alcove.

He turned and ran. These were destroyers, and there were too many of them, but he could even the odds if he found Logan and Caithe.

Entombed within a world of fire . . .

"Not yet, I'm not!"

Logan heard the bray of a drunken mule. "What was that?"

"Someone's coming," Caithe replied.

The air shook with massive footfalls.

"By the sound of it, a bunch of someones."

"Maybe destroyers," Logan said. He was using his shirt to hold the broken crystal in place. "Do you see the Grove?"

Caithe turned back to the archway as images flashed, one after another: a desolate tundra . . . a deep-hewn canyon . . . a storm-tossed sea. "No."

Logan looked behind them where a fiery light

glowed along the palace wall. "We're just going to have to jump for it."

"We don't want to end up in the sea."

"Watch for a good place."

. . . a smoldering battlefield . . . a calving glacier . . . a trackless swamp . . .

Logan looked back again and saw that the fiery light came from Sohothin, clutched in the pumping fist of Rytlock. The charr ran full out down the avenue with an army of destroyers right behind. "Just about anyplace!"

. . . a blazing desert . . . a venting caldera . . . a green glade—

Caithe grabbed Logan's arm and hauled. "Now!"

He barged after her through the flashing gate and tumbled down on a grassy meadow. A moment later, the magical membrane burst apart again, emitting Rytlock at a run. He stumbled and rolled beside them.

"Together again," Logan noted.

Rytlock had no time to reply, though, as the gate popped thrice more before closing.

Three destroyers had vaulted through the magical meniscus, and they landed in the meadow.

LAIR OF THE DRAGONSPAWN

Beneath a frigid blue sky, Eir led her wolf comrade and her metal allies. Steel feet crashed on glacial ice. Cogs ground and servos whined. Stone heads and silver skins reflected triangles of light across ice-choked peaks.

They marched up a valley with a glacier running through it. The center section was smooth like a frozen river, but the outer sections had cracked into countless parallel crevices. A thousand feet ahead, a wide cave slanted into the glacier. It didn't seem so much a cave as the mouth of a slain titan, giant icicles like fangs jutting all around it.

From Big Snaff, a metallic voice spoke. "Those look daunting."

"They're worse than you think," Eir replied. "Look *within* the cave."

Creatures paced there—five-hundred-pound wolves of ice. Hackles bristled across their shoulders, and claws cracked the ice beneath them. With eyes that glowed blue, they stared out at Eir and her comrades.

"They're corrupted wolves that once defended our homeland," Eir said. "Now they defend the despoiler."

Snaff's golem shuddered, taking a step back.

"What's wrong?" asked Zojja.

"There are more than wolves there."

Staring through the huge eyes of his golem, Snaff saw giant, white bats dropping from the ceiling of the cave. They spread icy wings and shrieked, echolocating their prey.

"Let's take them on!" Eir roared, charging.

Garm galloped beside her.

"Charge!" Snaff roared as the Bigs followed.

Eir and Garm reached the ice cave first and bounded within. Icy bats swarmed them, but her axes and his teeth ripped their wings away. Bats tumbled from the air, shattering on the ground.

The ice wolves came on—baying as they charged.

Eir turned toward the first and smashed her axe through its brow. Metal crashed on ice, broke into the creature's watery brain, and pulped it. The ice wolf fell at her feet.

"That felt good."

Another wolf leaped for Garm's throat. He dodged to one side, caught a foothold, and lunged back to fasten jaws on the icy neck. Garm bit down, and the whole head broke loose.

More ice wolves converged.

One clamped its jaws on Eir's forearm, ice skirling on her steel armor, and a second lunged for her foot.

She kicked, but the wolf held on, and she staggered unsteadily back.

Meanwhile, two other wolves circled Garm. One darted in to bite his throat, but Garm leaped atop it and smashed it to the floor of the cave, shattering its head. Even as it slumped, though, the other clambered atop it and bounded on Garm, shoving him to the floor.

But then steel pounded ice. Big Zojja struck the wolf's head, and cracks raced through it. The head calved and cascaded down in a glittering shower.

"Great job!" shouted Snaff from within his golem, which was marching through the cave, kicking ice wolves to pieces with his massive feet.

Eir also kicked hard, breaking loose the jaw of the wolf that held her foot. Pivoting, she swung her axe against the creature that clutched her right forearm. The beast cracked and fell. Eir rained more blows on it until it shivered apart.

In moments, only the ice bats were left, dying like mosquitoes with each sweep of the golems' hands.

When the bats were gone, Big Snaff strode jauntily up to his comrades and flexed his metal fingers in satisfaction. "Better than anything Klab could invent."

"Better than anything the Dragonspawn's seen," Eir said with a laugh, kicking at the remains of an ice wolf. She gazed deeper into the cavern, seeing a throat of ice that descended into the glacier. "Let's take this battle below!" Eir strode away at the head of the group. "I wonder what lies ahead."

A few giant strides later, they saw. The ice cave descended through a water-smoothed throat into a deep, dark belly. Meltwaters had formed ropy lines of ice, and on that rumpled ice stood warriors.

Norn or once-norn, they were tall, garbed in armor and furs, bearing staffs and spears and swords. They might have been defenders of Hoelbrak except for the dead blue light that shone in their eyes.

"They are recently turned norn," Eir said. "There will be no joy in killing them."

The rimed norn, now icebrood, raised a deep-throated war cry and ran at the heroes.

Eir strode toward them and spread a gauntlet tipped in chisels.

Roaring, the enemy rushed her.

She raked fingers through the first one, spilling him on the floor, and kicked the chest of the second to flatten him and ran across him to the third, who received her axe in his head. Garm, too, tore through these warriors.

Killing them was like killing her kin.

The golems were especially deadly. The icebrood gushed beneath their feet.

It was a sickening triumph to break bones and burst veins. But Eir and her friends did their grim work. Garm shook them like rats. Snaff and Zojja bashed them with metal fists. And Eir ended them on her chisels.

When it was done, Eir and Garm and the golemic asura stood side by side, mantled in gore.

Snaff said quietly, "We killed them here so that they would not kill in Hoelbrak."

Eir gazed around the dark cave. "We didn't kill them. We ended them. The Dragonspawn killed them." She peered deeper into the ever-descending cave. Another chute slid down into total darkness. "We're very close. Already, we've destroyed his defenders. Now we're poised to strike at the Dragonspawn's heart and be rid of him forever."

With that, she strode across the bloodstained ice and launched herself over the edge of the chute. Garm bounded close behind.

There was a moment's pause as Big Snaff and Big Zojja looked at each other. Then Snaff ran forward and leaped over the edge, and his apprentice followed.

At first, it was just sliding—velocity and vertigo. Armor and metal joints skirled on shoulders of ice. Eir and Garm slalomed down into darkness, and Big Snaff and Big Zojja followed, spinning like tops. Their minds were spinning as well, with a fear that Zojja voiced for them all. "How will we get back?"

Before anyone could answer, the chute dumped them out in a deep place, so deep that the glacial ice above no longer glowed with sunlight. They skidded across the floor of that cavern and spun to a stop, leaving chaotic score marks.

Eir rose, followed by Garm, Big Snaff, and Big Zojja.

"Well, here we are," Eir said.

It was preternaturally cold—bone-shattering. Spell conduits hardened and hydraulic humors thickened. Webs of frost formed on steel skins.

"Bigs, what do you see?" Eir asked.

"The ceiling is a mass of icicles, gigantic icicles," Zojja said. "Thirty feet long, some of them."

Eir asked, "What other threats?"

"The floor is clear," reported Snaff. "No defenders. No wolves. No icebrood. Nothing."

"Let's march," Eir said. As she and Garm led the charge, the Bigs marched behind.

Big Snaff stiffened. "There's something approaching, dead ahead."

"Halt," Eir said.

They did, staring into the murk.

Out of the depthless dark, something emerged.

Its body was fashioned of living ice. It had a long head like a cattle skull, and its eyes glowed with eerie blue flame. The rest of it seemed skeletal as well, with an arching spine draped in white robes. A blue-gray vapor circulated among its icy ribs, forming the body of the creature. Gaunt arms lifted clawed fingers, and gaunt legs spread talons on the ice. The creature reached to its sword belt and drew out a blade that was so cold it roiled with frost.

"The Dragonspawn," Eir said.

"He's not a man at all," Zojja murmured.

"A tibia of ice. A fibula of frost." Snaff spoke in a hushed voice. "Skull of a minotaur. Tail of a drake."

"Sounds like a spell," Zojja said.

"That's what he is," Snaff said. "He's just like the Bigs—a marionette moved by a hidden mind!"

"He's just like me . . . ," Zojja replied in a dreamy voice.

Eir looked at her. A faint blue glow pulsed in Big Zojja's eyes, matching the eyes of the Dragonspawn. "Look away!" Eir shouted, averting her gaze. "Don't look at it. Don't lock eyes with it. It's trying to freeze you."

With an effort of will, Big Zojja turned away from the

glowing visage. The blue pulse faded from her eyes, and she shook herself. "How can we fight something we can't look at?"

The Dragonspawn's elongated head turned toward his foes. Eyes glowed bright blue. The beams splashed across Eir, Garm, Snaff, and Zojja. They shielded their eyes, but the monster was seeping into their minds.

"Look away!" Eir called. She turned, seeing that Big Snaff and Big Zojja already stood motionless. "No!"

MAGMA MONSTERS

Three destroyers advanced across the meadow, searing plants with every step.

"I'm not afraid to play with fire," Rytlock snarled, hoisting Sohothin. He shot a glance at Caithe. "Careful, twig. You might get yourself singed."

Each destroyer strode steadily toward one of the comrades.

Rytlock lunged at the nearest destroyer, thrusting Sohothin. The blade burned through the creature's stony skin and plunged into its heart.

The destroyer halted, arms shuddering and head falling back as Sohothin transfixed it. The creature's molten joints flared, and its chest expanded with spinning energy. Fiery light intensified in its amorphous face.

"Damn," noted Rytlock.

The destroyer brought its pincers swinging together to crush Rytlock's head. Stone knuckles crashed—

But the charr rolled away beneath them. He scrambled up and stared accusingly at his sword. "What'd you do?"

"You're *feeding* it," Logan said while backing away from the destroyer that stalked him. "You might as well attack a Krytan with a baguette. Move back."

Rytlock growled, "Retreating is a good strategy. Very human. Use your hammer, for blood's sake! Break some stones!"

"All in good time," Logan said, leaping back over a patch of long grass. His hand painted a blue aura in the air, a slim band meant to trip up a destroyer.

His pursuer swung a stone claw that missed, then stepped in the long grass and tripped on the guardian aura. The destroyer overbalanced and crashed into the ditch.

A blue aura lit Logan's hands and spread to encompass his hammer. The glow seemed to hoist him into the air, and he brought the weapon down in a massive overhead stroke. The blow struck the destroyer's solar plexus and shattered it into five pieces.

"Let me get in on that!" Rytlock said, bounding over to land flat-footed on the creature's spine. Rocks snapped, and lava welled up between the broken parts.

"Nice footwork," Logan said, "but, of course, you've brought *yours* over here."

Rytlock's destroyer rushed the man, reaching for him, but Logan ducked beneath the grasping claw, spun on his heel, and hammered the beast's thigh. More rocks snapped. The destroyer roared, stumbling toward Rytlock.

"Get out of the way!"

Rytlock jumped off the fallen destroyer as the other one crashed down on its back. "Better yet!" the charr enthused. He scooped water from the spring and flung it on them. The droplets struck and sizzled, solidifying magma. "How do you like that?"

"Nice," Logan said, splashing both monsters.

"While you two mess around," Caithe said, "I've had to keep this one occupied by myself." She moved wraithlike, ducking beneath an arm, reeling back from another, and diving between its legs.

"Nice, as well," Logan said.

Behind him, the two destroyers climbed up from the ditch.

"None of us can take a single destroyer," Logan noted, "but maybe together, we can beat all three."

Puffing a sweaty lock out of her eyes, Caithe said, "What's the plan?"

"Well," Logan said as he ducked a hundred-pound fist, "I seem best at defense."

"Which means retreating," Rytlock said as he kicked a destroyer in the chest. The monster reeled back unsteadily.

"And Rytlock seems best at being offensive," Logan said.

"Hey!"

"Which leaves me," Caithe added as she high-stepped away from her destroyer. "What's my role?"

"You deliver the killing blow—like with the devourers."

Rytlock landed a haymaker on one destroyer's

jaw—then shook out his claw. "These aren't scorpions. They're magma monsters. You can't stab them in the tailbone."

"Not the tailbone," Caithe replied as a destroyer grabbed her and began to squeeze. "But magic has channels just like nerves. Weak points." She thrust a dagger into the lava joint at the creature's shoulder, twisted, and cracked the arm loose. It clattered to the ground as the destroyer staggered back and Caithe stepped away.

Meanwhile, the charr dodged behind a boulder, a lava creature in pursuit. "What's the plan?"

"We take out one foe at a time," Logan responded. "This one, for instance." He was slowly backing away from a destroyer. "I draw one in"—Logan hooked his war hammer on the lowest limb of a nearby birch and yanked himself up, scrambling onto the branch. The destroyer grasped the tree, setting it alight—"then Rytlock attacks."

The charr rushed up behind the destroyer and kicked its knee sideways, shattering it. The destroyer crashed to the ground.

Amid flaming branches, Logan shouted out, "And then Caithe delivers the kill."

The sylvari bounded over to sink her stiletto into the back of the destroyer's neck. She wrenched the blade in an arc, and the destroyer's stony head rolled away. She drew out her stiletto and said, "Their necks are weak: all magma. Cuts like butter."

The lava in the destroyer's joints turned gray, and the solid bits decayed into separate stones.

"Pretty good," Logan said.

"Damn good," Rytlock said.

Caithe grinned at the other two. "Let's do another."

They turned and strode side by side toward the other two destroyers.

One roared, flecks of lava flying from its mouth. It charged.

Logan broke from the other two, charging as well.

The destroyer reached with massive hands toward him.

Logan slid beneath them and rammed his war hammer into the monster's groin. He posted the butt of the haft in the ground, and the beast's momentum carried it over the hammer. The destroyer hung in the air for a split second, then crashed face-first to the ground.

Rytlock followed on, leaping onto the monster's back and marching double time. His claws shattered the stony skin, leaving the creature a pulpy mass. Lava oozed up, and Rytlock leaped free, patting out the flames on his dewclaws.

Caithe arrived, her white stiletto spearing the neck of the monster and twisting to rip loose the head. She kicked it away. "Too bad you can't put these on a pike."

"I was thinking rock garden," Logan responded, watching the head roll down the green slope.

Rytlock joined them above the kill, which crackled and dissipated to dust.

The team turned toward the final destroyer.

It stood at the edge of the meadow beneath the tree its comrade had set alight. It planted its massive feet and lifted its brutal arms and roared with the voice of a volcano.

"Here goes." Logan rushed it.

The destroyer's hands dropped down.

Logan sprang over them. He bounded off one rock wrist and onto the creature's shoulder.

It reached up to swat him.

Rytlock's shoulder crashed into the destroyer's stomach. Rytlock leaped free as the flaming minion toppled.

Caithe plunged her white stiletto into its neck and twisted, harvesting the monster's head.

She stepped back. The ropy ends of neck cooled. The beast shuddered and segmented and settled on the ground. In moments, it was a pile of rubble and ash like the other two in the clearing . . . like thousands in the ruined city of the dwarves.

"We're getting good at this," Logan said with a laugh.

"Yeah." Rytlock nodded breathlessly.

Caithe kicked the pile of smoldering stone. "Teamwork."

The man, the charr, and the sylvari grinned at each other, then turned awkwardly away.

Rytlock looked around. "So, where do you think we are?"

Logan scanned the green glens and hardwood glades, the gentle hillsides sloping down toward golden plains. "It's not Ascalon. Not since you lot moved in. I'd say Kryta. But we can't know until the stars come out."

"I'm hungry," Rytlock groused, sitting down on a fallen tree.

"Yeah," Logan agreed, plopping down as well. "Scorpion tail doesn't stay with you."

Caithe shook her head. "There may be some grubs for you two in that log. I'll see what else I can find." She drew her dagger and stalked off into the brush.

The charr and the man sat on the log, looking out at the green landscape. Long moments passed before either spoke.

Logan said, "This is crazy. We're supposed to be killing each other."

"I never do what I'm supposed to do."

Logan huffed, "Me neither."

Rytlock cocked an eyebrow. "What do you mean?"

Taking a deep breath, Logan said, "I've got this big brother in Divinity's Reach. He's in the Seraph, for gods' sake. Guarding the *queen,* even—"

"One of *those* brothers."

"Yeah," Logan said, pointing at him. "He wears armor that shines like a mirror . . . white everything . . . stands by the queen all day. I was supposed to follow him, but a white knight casts a long shadow."

"Heh. You're pretty far from that shadow."

"Huh?"

"Mercenary scout for a supply caravan in the Blazeridges?" Rytlock said. "That's about as far from your brother as you can get."

Logan looked at his hands. "Guess so." They sat awhile in silence before he asked, "You got any brothers?"

"About a dozen," Rytlock said with a rueful laugh, "and a dozen sisters."

"Big family."

Rytlock shook his head. "Charr don't have families. We have warbands. The bonds are even stronger."

Logan's eyes grew wide. "Was that them, back there? That funeral pyre?"

"Course not," Rytlock snapped. "Those were Iron Legion. I'm Blood Legion."

"You guys all look alike," Logan said with a shrug. "So, where's your warband?"

"Back east somewhere. I left them."

That comment hung in the air between them. "Why?"

"My reasons are my own."

Just then, Caithe returned, flopping a brace of dead rabbits down on a nearby rock. "All right, so, I hunted them. You cook them."

"Sure," Rytlock said, relieved to end the conversation. "I'm a good cook."

Logan blasted a laugh. "Yeah, right! Charr cooking?"

"What's wrong with charr cooking?"

"It's right in the name!"

"Shut it," Rytlock advised, "and don't open it again until there's roasted rabbit."

Caithe brushed off her hands and sat beside Logan. They watched as the charr cracked burning branches from the birch and piled them into a campfire. He sharpened three other sticks into spits. Sticking a claw into each rabbit's pelt, he ripped it away to reveal the meat. Then he slid the spits through the gutted rabbits and propped the skewers in the flames.

"So, you come from a grove?" Logan asked Caithe.

"*The* Grove," Caithe corrected.

"A whole lot of trees."

"The Pale Tree. I was born out of it. Out of a seedpod. I am one of the Firstborn."

"Coming out of a tree—" Logan whistled. "Must be weird."

Caithe's brows canted. "And your method isn't?"

They sat for a while, the scent of cooked rabbit coming to them on the air.

At last Logan ventured, "How come you left the Grove?"

"I knew everything there. I left to learn more."

"Admirable."

"What do you mean?"

Logan shrugged. "Lots of people stay right where they were born. They don't want to know anything else. Maybe that's what's wrong with the world."

Caithe shrugged. "I think Elder Dragons are a bigger problem."

Logan laughed. "Yeah, I guess they are."

Caithe looked deadly serious. "They *are*. We just fought the minions of one of them—Primordus. He was the first one to rise, and he's still spreading his power through the deep places, like that dwarf city. But there are others. The Ice Dragon Jormag is taking over the northern mountains, and there's another dragon in the black heart of Orr. Who knows how many more are rising."

Logan nodded politely. "Not one for small talk, are you?"

Caithe's eyes were wide and guileless. "Why talk small when there are such big things happening?"

"Perfectly done!" Rytlock announced as he lifted three smoking rabbits from the fire. "Black outside and pink within."

Logan nodded as he dutifully received his meal, and Caithe did likewise.

Holding his own charred rabbit, Rytlock sat down on the log and began to eat. The charr's eating habits—gnawing teeth and flying meat and grunts of satisfaction—at first put the other two off. But soon all three were feasting. The rabbit was delicious—a creature alive half an hour ago, slain unknowing, and roasted moments later.

As he bit into a haunch, Logan said, "I'd never guess you could cook."

Rytlock wiped grease from his chin. "You'd be amazed what I can do."

The comrades ate in silence as the sky deepened to dusk.

"Kryta," Logan said at last, staring upward.

Rytlock glanced at him over the picked skeletons. "What?"

"That's where we are. That constellation overhead puts us two days' march west of Lion's Arch."

The charr's face darkened. "Long way from Ascalon."

Logan smiled. "Come on. You'll *like* Lion's Arch. Everybody there's from somewhere else."

"Whatever," Rytlock said. "Surely they'll have a gate back to the Black Citadel."

Nodding, Logan glanced at the stone scabbard hanging from Rytlock's belt. "You can go through such a gate, but you're not taking Rurik's sword."

Rytlock barked a laugh. "I'd like to see you stop me."

IN THE COLD

Eir ran up to Big Snaff and Big Zojja and pounded their metal hides. Whether because of the blows or the aura of her gray powerstones, the two golems jolted, and the otherworldly light left their eyes.

"Where are we?" came Snaff's tinny voice.

"You're in battle with the Dragonspawn," spat Eir. "Wake up!"

Big Zojja shivered. "Point me at him. I'll get him."

They were back, in control. Their eyes no longer glowed with the blue-white aura of the Dragonspawn. Eir turned toward their foe.

The Dragonspawn stood with hands outflung, eyes gushing wrath on Garm.

"No!"

The dire wolf stood enveloped in blue-white energy. Power sluiced past his gaping jaws and coursed over his hackles. It sought entry. It probed for a chink that would let its icy talons reach into his heart, into his mind. But there was no such chink.

Garm had only one alpha, now and forever.

"This is our chance!" Eir shouted to the Bigs. "Let's go!"

Eir stepped out from behind her dire wolf into the full brunt of the boreal blast. More frost etched across her armor, but she strode toward the Dragonspawn and broke into a run.

Garm did, too, alongside her.

Big Snaff and Big Zojja joined the charge.

"Ten more paces," Eir cried, "and the Dragonspawn will be a pile of ice!"

But in five more paces, he was gone. The air folded around his frozen figure and closed on him.

Eir took three more strides before stumping to a halt.

Garm, Big Snaff, and Big Zojja pulled up alongside her.

"Where did he go?"

A sharp crack came from above. The comrades looked up to see an icicle the size of a fir tree break from the ceiling and plunge toward them. It didn't seem to move, only to grow larger.

"Back!" Eir commanded.

The golems leaped back, skidding on the icy floor.

The icicle struck, its tip hurling out hailstones. The shaft rammed downward, disintegrating until it reached its center, which struck the floor like a hammer. The cavern shook.

Big Snaff brushed ice off his steel hide. "Lucky for us, we got out of the way."

"We're not out of the way," replied Eir, looking up at the thousands of similar icicles hanging overhead.

Crack, crack, crack, crack!

"He's trying to drive us out," Eir cried. "Deeper! Run deeper!"

She ran forward, followed by golems that fissured the ice as they went. The four comrades ran headlong into the darkness.

Behind them, icicles fell. *Boom! Boom! Boom!* They hissed and burst like rockets. Frozen shrapnel rang across the golems' metal skins. *Boom! Boom! Boom!*

One icicle grazed Eir's elbow, dragging her sideways—away from another icicle that staved the floor before her. She spun past its disintegrating bulk over a field of slippery shards.

"Keep going!"

Garm leaped aside as an ice shaft struck before him, going off like a bomb.

Big Snaff and Big Zojja danced past two more columns while a third toppled before them like a felled tree.

"Jump!" Snaff cried.

The golems grasped hands and leaped as the icicle hit. Big Zojja and Big Snaff sailed side by side over the shattering ice. The two golems fell into a wave of crushed ice that picked up Eir and Garm and dumped them into another chute.

"Down we go!" Eir called.

For a time, there was only metal scraping ice and golems spinning and the wave breaking. Then the floor flattened out again in deep darkness. Eir, Garm, and the golems ground to a halt, and the last skittering shards of ice tumbled to silence.

"Now where are we?" Zojja wondered through her speaking tube.

Snaff replied philosophically, "Somewhere else."

"Somewhere he was trying to keep us from," Eir said as she rose. "This is probably his inner sanctum."

Something moved in the darkness.

The golems turned to see.

Ahead, the black air unfolded, and the Dragonspawn took shape. His figure glowed ice blue, and his soul whirled in a cyclone about him.

"It all comes down to this," Eir said, "the courage of four heroes—"

"And the golemancy of two geniuses," Zojja added.

"Against the Dragonspawn." Eir paused. "Spirit of Wolf, guide my work." So saying, Eir transformed from a towering norn into the aspect of her totem animal. She became a dire wolf like Garm, only standing on hind legs, with eyes like fire and a coat as red as blood.

Side by side, the red wolf and the black wolf charged through the inner sanctum, bearing down on the ice champion. Big Snaff and Big Zojja followed.

"Kal-throk-tok!" the Dragonspawn cried in a voice like thunder. He raised his sword of eternal ice. Dark magic roiled around it. He plunged the sword into the glacier beneath him, cracking through the frozen floor. The crack spread like black lightning, splitting one side of the glacier from the other.

Eir and Garm leaped to one side and Big Snaff and Big Zojja to the other.

Still, the crack raced along, up the far wall of the ice cave and onto the ceiling. The split grew wider, and above, light poured through the glacier.

A mile of ice had ruptured, and the crevice gushed sunlight.

Eir and Garm struggled to stay upright as the ice cave shook, and Big Snaff and Big Zojja scrabbled to keep from falling into the chasm.

"Kal-throk-tok! Borea-kal-lu-ki Joor-maag."

Suddenly, something else was in that ice cavern. A presence. It was as old as the world, as uncaring of mortal creatures. It was colder than a blizzard: not just the power to freeze but the *will* to, to see living things shiver to stillness and crack open. This was the power behind the Dragonspawn. He wielded only a portion of it—the portion that could pour through eye sockets and skeletal fingertips. Now, Eir, Garm, and the Bigs were in the presence of the power itself.

We are in its inner sanctum, and it is going to get rid of us, Eir thought. She shouted, "Get away from the crevice!"

Big Snaff and Big Zojja clawed their way toward the wall of the chamber.

Out of the fissure behind them, a blast of cold and snow erupted. It was like an inverted avalanche. Hunks of slush smashed into the golems and coated them and froze them. The storm hauled them off the floor.

"Get out! Jump!" Eir shouted.

The hatches of the golems opened, and first Snaff and then Zojja tumbled out. They crashed to the icy floor of the cave as their golems were hauled up on the erupting storm. The golems jolted up the chasm, occasionally smashing against the ice cliffs. Moments later, the golems flew past the surface of the glacier and were flung through the air on a storm of hail.

"We have to escape," Eir told Garm as she clambered toward the entrance to the hollow. Already it was filling in. If they stayed even minutes, they would be buried in the glacier's heart. "Climb out!"

On the other side of the rent, Snaff and Zojja also scrambled toward the chute that had brought them down. They would have to find handholds, some way out.

Even as Eir climbed, arms stiffening beneath the onslaught of snow, she knew what this was: failure. She had not been corrupted by the Dragonspawn, but she had not slain it, either. And if she knew the Dragonspawn, her people would pay for her hubris.

The ice cave had probably saved their lives. When at last the companions had crawled from it, they found a world buried in snow. It was more than ten feet deep and still falling. The sky was black overhead, disgorging the fury of the Dragonspawn. Snow, hail, sleet, and ice pummeled the ground and piled atop glaciers. Boreal winds whipped the white stuff into gigantic drifts and tormented pillars. Winter lightning mantled the mountaintops.

Anything that had once lived on the steppes was now battered to death or buried alive.

And this storm would be pummeling Hoelbrak as well.

A week later, when Eir, Garm, Snaff, and Zojja straggled into Hoelbrak, they found a city buried in snow. Many roofs had collapsed, and most lanes were impassable. And in the main lane, opened by the work of hundreds of hands and shovels, stood an imposing figure.

The snow-mantled man strode toward Eir and her friends. Light washed across him, showing an old, battle-scarred face wreathed in silver hair. The norn's blue eyes, though, shone with the fire of a young man.

"Knut Whitebear!" Eir gasped, dropping to her knee.

"Rise, daughter of snow."

Eir did, a chill running down her back. No one had called her daughter since her own father had died. It was as if he stood before her once again, disappointed.

Knut Whitebear brushed snow from his pelts. His eyes were grave and kindly. "You are so strong, so determined," he said, lifting his hand to straighten the tangled hair that fell to her shoulder, "it is hard to remember that you are just a child."

"I am not a child!" Eir replied.

"Oh? You march a pair of windup toys through my town. You tell everyone that they will kill the Dragonspawn, only to bring upon us a millennial storm that buries us alive?"

"We almost did it," Eir said. "We were so close. We were in the inner sanctum."

Knut's face stiffened. "This storm was worse than the icebrood. It has killed more—"

"What are you telling me?" Eir asked.

"The doors of my lodge are closed to you," he said simply.

"What?"

"You and your wolf and your companions."

Tears rolled down her face. "How long?"

"Until you can return with real warriors, not clockwork toys."

"We got further—"

"You failed," Knut said plainly, "and we have paid the price."

"But I will succeed. I will stop him! I'll bring better warriors."

Knut did not answer, but only turned to leave.

Snaff looked down at his feet. "Where are we supposed to find warriors?"

"We'll go where they gather," Eir said with a bleak smile. "We'll go to Lion's Arch."

PART II

SLAYING
MONSTERS

LION'S ARCH

Names?" growled the Lion's Arch gate guard—a norn holding a quill the size of an arrow.

"Logan Thackeray of Kryta, and this is Rytlock Brimstone of the Blood Legion, and Caithe, one of the Firstborn of the sylvari."

If the guard was impressed, he showed no sign, scrawling the names in a gigantic book on a stand. "What's your reason for visiting Lion's Arch?"

Rytlock muttered, "Just looking for an asura gate."

"Where to?"

"The Black Citadel."

The norn snorted, then wrote, *En route to the Black Citadel.*

"Not us," Logan said, pointing between himself and Caithe.

The guard looked at them. "What are you here for?"

"I'm a scout," Logan said.

"What kind? Seraph?"

"Um, no. My brother's in the Seraph, but I'm, well . . . freelance. Work for merchant caravans."

"I see," the norn said, arching an eyebrow and writing, *Unemployed.* "And what about the sylvari?"

"I joined them," Caithe said.

"Would you just let us in?" Rytlock pressed.

The norn glared at him. "What about the sylvari? Why does she want to enter Lion's Arch?"

Caithe's eyebrows rose thoughtfully. "Is it interesting?"

"What?"

"The city. Is it interesting?"

The guard scowled. "Of course."

"Then put that down," Caithe replied.

The norn wrote, *Not applicable,* snatched up a wooden stamp, and pounded it down on the entry. "In you go! Just don't break anything."

Logan, Rytlock, and Caithe shuffled into the vaulted city gate, passing beneath an iron portcullis that dripped rusty water down their backs.

"Why did he think I was 'not applicable'?" Caithe wondered.

"Ha!" Rytlock barked, but then frowned and shook his head. "I don't know."

The vault above them echoed with the clatter and tumult of the city ahead. As the three stepped out of the entryway, they caught their first real glimpse of Lion's Arch.

"Wow," said Rytlock.

The city was huge and a hodgepodge. To the left gleamed a wide bay full of great galleons. Their masts and rigging made a patchwork of the sky. A water gate guarded the entrance to this sheltered harbor, and pennants flew all down the docks. The docks teemed with longshoremen hauling skids from ships to warehouses. These warehouses themselves were former galleons, overturned on land. Many of the city's other buildings were also fashioned of ships washed ashore by the great flood. More than a few vessels had even been upturned to become strange towers, jutting skyward.

"A market!" Caithe noted eagerly.

Logan and Rytlock turned to see a manifold market spread beneath billowing blue sails. Stalls and tents crowded against each other, forming narrow lanes that thronged with people.

"They say everything's for sale in Lion's Arch," Logan noted.

Rytlock laughed. "Everything and everyone."

"Let's see," said Caithe, striding into the marketplace.

"Wait," Rytlock called, "we're looking for an asura gate!" But already the sylvari was approaching one of the outer stalls.

Within it, an ancient-looking asura sat surrounded by buckets into which he flung bits of a machine he was dismantling. Each bucket was marked with a coin amount—1g, 2g, 3g. Without looking up, the asura said, "What sort of mechanism are you building?"

Caithe's brow furrowed. "I'm not building a mechanism."

"Then you're blocking my light."

"What sort of mechanism are you *un*building?"

He looked up, eyes annoyed under linty brows.

"Something that had no right getting built in the first place."

"What was it?"

"A washing machine."

"Sounds helpful."

"Would've been if I had dirty friends like yours," the asura noted as Rytlock and Logan strode up. "Not that they would've used it. Nobody did."

"Why not?"

The asura sighed. "You wore it over your body, like a yoke. It washed the clothes while you walked in them—sprayed them, sudsed them, wrenched them, rinsed them." He pantomimed the machine squirting and snatching at his clothes. "People didn't like it. Got them wet."

"You should've called it a shower washer. People like getting wet in the shower."

The asura's hands stopped on the device. His face went pale, and he glanced regretfully at the buckets all around him.

Rytlock butted in. "Where's the nearest asura gate?"

"It was a problem with marketing, not design," the asura said despondently. "A *shower* washer!"

"Excuse me—the *nearest gate?*"

The asura scowled. "Did Master Drup put you up to this? Is he taunting me again?"

"Come on," Logan said to Caithe, taking her arm and leading her away.

The three companions strolled onward through the wonderland of strange goods—silken scarves, pewter chalices, clockwork toys, rundlets and hogsheads of ale, sheaves of spice, parchment, linens, fish, nails. Every needful thing and needless thing piled on tabletops beneath the luffing blue canvas. Here was a cart selling sausages and there a booth filled with blades. A stall selling ice cream stood beside a stall selling torture implements. And these varied wares were hawked by a varied group of merchants—humans and sylvari, charr and norn, asura and ogre.

"Why aren't they *killing* each other?" Rytlock wondered sourly.

"That's Lion's Arch for you. Live and let live," replied Logan. "Just don't mention the E-word."

"What E-word?"

"The place I was leading a caravan to. The place you wish didn't exist."

Rytlock hawked and spit. "*That* E-word."

"I don't feel well," Caithe murmured, leaning against Logan.

He caught her. "You look white."

"That's her color."

"All except your neck. There are little black lines—"

"I'm fine," Caithe interrupted, straightening. "Just a little out of breath."

Logan guided her to a half-wall out of the traffic of the main road and helped her sit. "Here. Just take a moment."

Caithe nodded, staring emptily ahead.

"What is it?" Rytlock rumbled.

Caithe shook her head weakly. "All these lives—all intersecting."

"Just ignore them," Logan advised. "You can be alone in a big city. Loneliest place in the world."

"That young man there." Caithe pointed to a teenage boy leaning sullenly beside a set of wooden stairs.

"Yeah? What *about* him?" Rytlock asked.

"He's trying to get up the courage to go upstairs and knock on the door and see if the girl is home."

The man and the charr looked at the nondescript kid, long hair veiling his eyes. Rytlock said, "How could you possibly know that?"

Caithe stared at them, amazed. "Don't you see the rose behind him?"

As she pointed it out, the flower seemed obvious.

"Good luck to him," Logan said.

"He needs more than luck. Look in the window." Caithe pointed to the head of the stairs, where a curtain waved in the breeze.

Rytlock stared. "So what? A curtain."

"See the hand on the sill beneath the curtain? The young man's hand?"

"What about it?"

"Why would a curtain be drawn at this time of day? And why would a young man be sitting beside it, watching another young man in the street?"

Rytlock's jaw dropped. "Seriously? Is this what you do? You watch, put things together, figure them out?"

"That man in the marketplace," Caithe said, nodding toward a swaggering fellow in a red greatcoat and black boots, "he's pretending to be a pirate for fear that he will be robbed, and the man beside him in the sackcloth shirt is pretending not to be a pirate so that he can pick his pocket."

"How could you possibly—," Rytlock began, but broke

off as the man in sackcloth slid his hand, branded with the pirate's *P*, into the other man's waistcoat. "Impressive."

"This could be good," Logan said. "This could be very good."

"This could be bad," Caithe echoed. "Very bad."

"What?" her comrades chorused, but Caithe was gone.

"Where did she—?" Rytlock began.

Logan pointed. "Up there!" She was about a block ahead of them, her lithe figure slipping easily through the jostling throng. Logan strode out after her, dodging through the steady flow of traffic. "Excuse me. Pardon me. Look out!"

Rytlock followed, his scowl clearing the way—that is, until another charr approached. The two locked eyes and traded fuming expressions as they marched into each other. They crashed like a pair of bulls, horns clacking and shoulders shoving.

"Out of my way," Rytlock thundered, hurling the other charr aside.

The other staggered a moment, dug his claws in, and drew a sword. "Says who?"

Sohothin leaped up, and Rytlock smiled. "Says he."

The fool eyed the epic blade, clamped his teeth together, and swung his own sword.

Sohothin cracked through the fool's weapon, cutting it in half and dropping the tip in the dirt.

The attacker stared down at his suddenly short sword, turned, and ran.

Rytlock humphed. He now had an open lane, especially since Sohothin still flamed in his grip. He strode down the vacated street between buildings fashioned of boats, heading toward a large circular theater in timber and plaster. Judging from the roar of the crowd, a show was going on within—a show that had drawn Caithe and Logan. Striding up to them, Rytlock sheathed his sword and said, "What is it?"

Caithe turned to him, eyes wide. "An atrocity."

"Bearbaiting," Logan said ruefully.

"Bear what?" Rytlock craned to peer through the archway into the triple-decked theater within.

A circling throng surrounded a patch of sand where a grizzly bear stood on its hind legs. A spiked collar was cinched around its neck, and a chain bound it to a stout post. Within its black coat ran rivulets of blood.

The same blood painted a spiked mace in the hand of a muscular brute. The man wore a grimacing grin and breathed excitedly as he circled just outside the reach of the bear's claws. "Want this? Want this?" the man asked, swiping the mace at the creature.

The bear roared and batted the weapon away. The crowd, their enthusiasm strengthened by the rows of bottles along the walls, roared back.

The man spun about, swinging the mace in a full arc and bringing it back to smash the bear's face. Spikes pierced the muzzle and cracked fangs. The bear reeled back, blood spraying from its jowls. A mad cheer rang from the crowd as the beast staggered against the post and almost fell.

But it didn't fall. Someone was holding it up with slender arms.

"I will stand with you, brother," Caithe said.

The crowd's bloodthirsty cheer faltered.

At the back of the crowd, Rytlock wondered, "How'd she get up there?"

"She's going to get herself killed," Logan said, pressing forward.

The bear could have bitten her throat or torn out her stomach, but it didn't. It seemed to know by touch that she was a friend.

The man with the mace thought otherwise. "Get away! I paid for five licks, and I'll get them."

"Yes, you will," Caithe replied, drawing her white stiletto and spinning it before her.

The man eyed the dagger and then his gory mace. He cocked a grin. "Seems you got a problem with reach, girl." He swung the mace at her head.

Caithe ducked, the spiked ball scraping along her shoulder. Lunging, she rammed her dagger into the man's hand and split his middle finger from his ring finger. Blood gushed, and the mace tumbled to the sand.

The man staggered back, cradling his bleeding hand. "She stabbed me! Get her!"

Six of the man's mates leaped over the half-wall that kept back the crowd. Swords rose from scabbards and cudgels from belts. The men grinned, and the crowd cheered.

Until Logan and Rytlock stepped up beside their friend.

Caithe smiled. "You love bears?"

Rytlock scowled. "I hate bullies."

"I thought you hated sylvari."

"I hate bullies more."

Logan muttered, "There's six of them and three of us."

"Hardly fair," Rytlock agreed, "for them."

One of the thugs snapped a whip, which lashed around Rytlock's neck. He reared back, yanked the man off his feet and into the air, and head-butted him. The man crumpled in a heap at the charr's feet.

"Now there's five."

A thug swung his sword at Logan. He bashed the blade down, stepped on the end, and smashed his hammer into the man's shoulder. The thug staggered sideways into one of his comrades. Both men spilled to the ground.

Meanwhile, Caithe deftly danced away from a morning star. The man who wielded it shrieked in frustration and swung at her face. Caithe dodged back and jabbed her dagger into the morning star's chains, fouling them. She wrenched the weapon from the man's hand and grabbed his throat. "You'll be getting sleepy," she warned as he went limp in her grip. She dropped him to the ground.

Beside the man fell two smoldering clubs, shorn off by Sohothin. The men who had held them moments before turned to run, but Rytlock kicked one into the other, and they crashed together to the ground.

"Anyone else?" the charr roared. "We got licks for all of you!"

The crowd stared back in terrified silence.

"Well, then, how about this?" Rytlock rammed Sohothin into the chain that bound the bear to the pole. Twisting, the charr shattered the chain, and the tormented grizzly was loose.

The onetime bravado of the crowd melted to terror. Screaming, they climbed over each other to get out the gate. The bear charged along the back of the crowd, snapping at them.

"We have to make sure he gets out of the city alive," Caithe said.

Rytlock's jaw dropped. "You've got to be kidding."

"What's a grizzly going to do in a city?"

Rytlock watched the bear swipe at screaming spectators. "He knows exactly what to do."

"He's our responsibility, now," Caithe said.

The charr's claws slashed that idea from the air. "I'm not responsible for anybody but myself. I'm going to find a gate to the Black Citadel."

Logan blocked his path. "About that gate—"

"What!" Rytlock roared.

"You can go through it, but you can't take Rurik's sword with you."

"Here we go," Rytlock said. Sohothin ripped through the air before Logan. "Just try to stop me."

Logan flung out his hands, and a blue ball of energy deflected the blade. Wreathed in flame, the legendary blade swung back behind Rytlock. Logan smiled tightly. "We'll see who stops whom."

Caithe shook her head, stepping back.

Rytlock spread his arms and let Sohothin blaze above him. "We fight to the death after all!"

Logan stood his ground. "I don't want to kill you. I don't even want to hurt you. But, you can't take that sword with you."

"It's my sword!"

"It's *Rurik's* sword! A *human* sword! You stole it from us just like you stole *Ascalon*."

"You're deluded."

Blue aura erupted from Logan's hands and swarmed across his hammer. He hauled it overhead to smash into the sand. A profound boom shook the bearbaiting den, flinging Rytlock backward against the half-wall. He smashed it to the ground.

"What are you doing?" Caithe shouted at Logan.

Rytlock roared as he climbed to his feet. "What he's doing is picking out his burial plot." He charged, and Sohothin fell like lightning.

Logan rolled away, flinging sand from his heels. Some of the grains flared like tiny meteors in Sohothin's mantle. The sword chopped through another half-wall, igniting years' worth of spilled spirits. Flames raced around the pit and leaped to the stands.

Scrambling along the base of the wall, Logan climbed to his feet and spun about, panting. "You're as slow as an ettin."

"You're as thick as one." Rytlock charged again.

Logan's hand painted an arc of blue energy in the air before him. He staggered back as Rytlock thudded into the magical shield.

Arcane energy sparked across the charr's front, but Sohothin cleaved through. It swept down at Logan.

Logan lunged to one side as the sword sliced past him. He whirled around and smashed his hammer into Rytlock's wrist.

"Ah!" the charr shouted.

The blow sent Sohothin flying through the air. It

spun just over Caithe's head and embedded in one of the support beams for the upper boxes. Flames clambered up the wood.

As Logan's mystic shield dissipated, Rytlock charged through it, gripping his broken wrist. "You'll pay for that!"

Logan struggled to get his hammer between him and the charr, but Rytlock backhanded the weapon. It flew through the air, crashing through the back wall of the theater. Rytlock then grabbed Logan and hoisted him in the air, ramming his back against the bearbaiting post.

"You have some nerve!" Rytlock roared.

Logan grabbed the chains hanging from the post and hurled them at Rytlock's face. The charr winced back, and Logan wormed from his grip. Dropping to the ground, Logan scuttled free and ran for the burning pillar where Sohothin was embedded.

Rytlock followed, roaring.

The gathered crowd roared, too, delighted to see the man and the charr battle in the burning theater. It truly was burning: walls of flame sent smoke and sparks high into the air.

Logan reached the pillar and started to shimmy up.

"No, you don't," Rytlock growled. His good hand pried Logan off the beam, hurled him into nearby seats, and reached up to snag the sword.

"No, *you* don't," said another voice—a deep voice accompanied by a cutlass grip ramming into Rytlock's throat.

He looked to see his attacker—a norn with a tanned, dreadlocked, piratical face. "Who're you?"

"Magnus, one of the Captains of the Ship's Council of Lion's Arch, head of the Lionguard," the man said grandiloquently.

"That's a lot to remember," Rytlock replied.

"Then just remember my nickname—the Bloody Handed." Magnus nodded at the brute squad around him. "You, my destructive friend, are under arrest."

Rytlock's shoulders tensed, bracing for another fight.

"You have no weapon," Magnus pointed out with a steely voice, "your wrist looks broken, and you're more than surrounded."

Rytlock shot a look over his shoulder, where more of the brute squad were dragging Logan from the wreck of seats. Two other Lionguard flanked Caithe.

"It's off to jail for the three of you."

IN SEARCH OF WARRIORS

Eir stepped from the frigid solitude of Hoelbrak into the bustling heat of Lion's Arch. At her heels, Garm trotted through the asura gate, and Snaff and Zojja brought up the rear. The four who had nearly destroyed the Dragonspawn now stood as strangers in a new city.

"Ah, Lion's Arch," Snaff said, clapping his hands together. He drew a deep draft of the salt-sea air and pounded his chest. "The Pirate Paradise. The Shore of the World. The Well of Races. The Freest City in Tyria—"

"The Place Where We Are," Zojja said dispiritedly.

Snaff looked out at the folk that streamed down the avenue—every intelligent race in Kryta, all going peacefully about their business, coursing through a rankling maze of streets. Here sprawled a marketplace under blue canvas, there towered a keep fashioned of an upended ship. "Being in a city like this is like being alive."

"You *are* alive," Zojja pointed out.

"Then I feel doubly alive."

A group of human warriors marched past, their eyes raking suspiciously across the dire wolf.

Eir set her hand on Garm's muzzle and drew him to sit beside her. "Exhilarating, yes, but we have a mission. We're here to find warriors. And I know where we can start: Captain Magnus the Bloody Handed."

"Norn, I assume?" Snaff asked. "Can't imagine an asura named Bloody Handed."

"Unless he was bad with a hammer," Zojja remarked.

"Norn, yes, and a sea captain. If anyone here could help us fight the Dragonspawn, it'd be Magnus. If he *will* fight." Eir pointed to the harbor, where tall ships were moored. "Let's get to the docks."

Garm trotted down the lane toward the forest of masts, black against the flashing waves. Snaff and Zojja had to jog to keep pace.

"Tell us about this Magnus the Bloody Handed," Snaff said.

Eir shrugged. "He is a norn who once adventured and gained great fame for himself. Now he is leader of the Lionguard, the peacekeepers of this city."

"Impressive," Snaff said.

"He's also a privateer—"

"A pirate?"

Eir shot Snaff a dark look. "Forget that you know that word. A privateer is sanctioned by the state to attack enemy ships."

"A legal pirate."

"Magnus is called the Bloody Handed because of what he does to those who insult him," Eir said significantly.

"But most often, those he fights are those who fight Lion's Arch. He's ruthless, but not for himself. For this city."

They strode out of a warren of maritime buildings onto the landings where ships unloaded. Lines of long-shoremen carried crates to great skids, where they piled them high. All around the dock, taverns and flophouses crowded, eager to trade easy virtues for hard cash.

"That's real work," Snaff said, nodding at the gangs. "Backbreaking, soul-crushing, hand-blistering work. They need more golems."

"Your solution to everything," Zojja said.

Snaff shrugged. "Magic could set these good souls free."

"Free to starve," Eir replied. "I don't think these good souls would thank you to hand their jobs to constructs."

Passing among the laborers, the band approached a great black ship—*Cormorant.* It was moored at the dock and built on a norn scale. The beam was twice as wide as that of a human ship, the masts twice as tall, the decks twice as thick. It was a monster of the sea, with massive black ratlines and thousands of feet of sail.

Of course, the sailors on that ship were massive, too. Norn they were, but their skins were burned brown by a ceaseless sun and a flashing sea. Their clothes were not meant for holding in heat but for shedding it. Instead of bear fur and caribou pelt, these sailors wore tan home-spun shirts and brown trousers tied off with old line. The higher-up seamen were garbed in leather vests over their homespun, and officers boasted greatcoats over linen.

Grandest of all, though, was Captain Magnus himself.

Intense eyes stared out beneath the silken band that wrapped his head. The captain's neck was circled with a collar of walrus tusks, over which streamed his overlong brown hair and overlong mustache. His bare chest was crossed by a pair of leather bandoliers that sported wide-muzzled pistols. At his waist, the bandoliers became a belt, which held up a woolen kilt that draped to his knees. Leather boots were strapped from knee to toe.

The captain's eyes fixed on Eir.

As she approached the *Cormorant*, Captain Magnus strode to the rail and propped one foot on a cask and propped one elbow on a knee and stared with undisguised interest. "In all the days since I left my homeland, I have not stared upon so beautiful a woman as you, or one with skin so fair. Fair to the point of whiteness. Blinding. Where is your tan, woman?"

Eir planted her feet on the dock and looked fearlessly into his eyes. "I fight ice monsters in black caves, and this fool of a norn asks me where my tan is."

Magnus scowled, his blue irises ringed in white.

Garm's lip drew back in a snarl.

Snaff and Zojja clutched each other.

Then Magnus laughed—a deep, threatening laugh. "And where do you think I've been, winning this brown skin of mine?"

"Lazing," Eir replied without hesitation. "Perhaps in a hammock, after a night of rum."

The scowl returned. "You think I won this ship, gathered this crew, by—*lazing*?"

Eir shrugged. "A typical man would not be able to. A typical man would have to work three lifetimes to gain a ship and crew like these. An extraordinary man could gain them with no particular effort. Hence, I assumed you were lazing."

Magnus's brow beetled as he turned her words over in his mind. "Why, sure! It was easy. A moment's thought." He leaned over the rail, allowing his magnificent pectorals to strain against the bandolier he wore. "When you have charisma, you don't have to work very hard."

"You'll have to work harder than that," Eir said.

"Who are you, porcelain girl, and why do you trade riddles with me?"

"I'm no porcelain girl. I'm Eir Stegalkin, who confronted and nearly destroyed the Dragonspawn, the greatest champion of Jormag."

"You confronted the Dragonspawn?"

"Confronted and nearly destroyed. We reached his inner sanctum—"

"If this is true, you *are* brave!"

"We seek warriors to join us to finish him."

Magnus's eyebrow cocked. "You want *me* to join *you*?"

"The Dragonspawn is the champion of Jormag. He has declared war on the norn nation."

"Jormag is a great threat," Magnus responded, nodding deeply. "But he is only one of three dragons who have arisen beneath our feet. The dragons are rising everywhere."

"Jormag is the dragon who afflicts your people."

"My people are in Lion's Arch, and the Orrian dragon afflicts us. I fight his champion—Morgus Lethe. He rules the sea. He sends dead things up from the bottom to sink ships and to feast on the living. I destroy his monsters. I save this city!"

"What about Hoelbrak?"

A slow grin began on Magnus's face, extending into his eyes. "The people of Lion's Arch are *my* people. I have chosen my battles." Magnus shook his head and laughed ruefully. "The world is changing, Eir Stegalkin. You must change with it. Perhaps I should ask *you* to join *me.* Get some sun on that lily skin."

Eir sighed. "When the Dragonspawn is dead, perhaps I will take you up on that offer. Just now, though, I need my own fighters."

Magnus's eyebrows lifted. "If it's fighters you need, it just so happens that I have a side business that specializes in them."

"What kind of business?"

"It's an arena where criminals can earn out of their jail sentences while providing the people of Lion's Arch with entertainment."

"Brutal."

Magnus let out a broad-beamed laugh. "They'd much rather fight in my arena than languish in a cell. I buy their billets, and the Lionguard makes sure they don't run off, and they fight until they've paid me back. It's in everyone's best interest." He grinned. "My booming enterprise might just be the place for you to find the fighters you need."

Eir shook her head. "I come asking after a norn legend and get sent to jailbirds."

Magnus laughed. "I saw a pair yesterday, a man and a charr. They fought like devils and destroyed a bearbaiting pit"—he paused to spit—"which I personally was glad of. But as head of the Lionguard, well, I had to lock them up. They're stewing just now in the dockside row house, but I'm about to send my agent to buy their billet."

"How much is their billet?"

"About five hundred gold."

Eir whistled. "Thanks all the same. If you change your mind about the mission—"

"I won't," Magnus said, smiling.

Eir turned away. "Come along, Garm."

"Nice wolf," Magnus called after her. "He'd be magnificent for boardings."

As Eir and Garm strode from the docks, she leaned toward her wolf and said, "You really would be."

He pricked up his ears.

Snaff and Zojja ran to catch up to them.

"What now?" Zojja asked.

Eir looked at the sky, deepening to dusk. "Now, we figure out another plan."

Caithe sat on a wooden bunk propped against a wall of thick-stacked stone. It was the only bunk in the cell, and she shared it with Logan and Rytlock. "We'll have to sleep in shifts."

"Logan better not sleep at all," Rytlock snarled as he leaned against the wall of the cell, "trying to steal my sword."

"*You* stole it first!" Logan growled, pacing along the bars at the front. "And now neither one of us has it. They confiscated it—*and* my hammer."

"Worthless hunk of metal! I can't believe you would compare my sword to your hammer!"

Logan whirled. "I *don't*. That's the whole *point*! I'm not carrying a fabled, sacred *charr* weapon."

"And neither am I, thanks to you!" Rytlock spat back.

"Enough!" shouted Caithe, suddenly standing between them, her slim hands held out to either side. "You're stuck together in a cell, and you're fighting over an empire? Over a sword that neither one of you has?"

The man and the charr snarled one last time before turning away from each other.

Just then, a dark-complected man strode up the cell corridor. He had a stern face beneath long black hair, and he wore embroidered silk robes. Behind the man came an entourage of muscular warriors.

Logan glanced nervously at them. "Those guys aren't Lionguard."

The man stopped, planted his feet, and crossed his arms over his chest. "You fight well."

Rytlock nodded. "If you're talking about the bearbaiting den back there, yeah, we sure do."

"I am Sangjo, an agent of Magnus, head of the Lionguard and member of the Captains—"

"The Bloody Headed," Rytlock interrupted.

"The Bloody *Handed*," Sangjo corrected with a wan smile. "He would like to purchase your billet."

"What are you talking about?" Rytlock snarled.

"Your debt to society—specifically, repairing the portion of the city you burned down," the man said sedately.

"Which is?"

"Five hundred gold."

Rytlock's eyes flew wide. "How are we supposed to get that kind of money?"

"Agree to Magnus's offer," Sangjo said placidly.

"Which is?"

"My boss is prepared to pay for your billet—if you agree to fight in his arena."

"What?"

"Master Magnus has an arena where you could fight for your freedom, earning money to pay him back. Or you could sit here and rot. It's your choice."

Caithe asked, "If we fought, how long would it take to pay him back?"

"Not long," Sangjo said, "perhaps a dozen matches— if you win."

"We can't fight," Rytlock said. "We have no weapons."

"Your weapons will be returned to you before each match and taken from you afterward."

Rytlock huffed, "Well, we can't fight for at least a week, since grawl-boy here broke my wrist."

Sangjo's enigmatic smile only widened. "Then let grawl-boy fix it."

Rytlock glared at Logan. "*You* could heal me?"

"Not all at once. A little bit now, and then an hour later, a little more."

"Why didn't you *try?*" raged Rytlock.

"You'd've taken my head off!" Logan shouted back.

"There's that," Rytlock growled. He sighed. "All right, I won't. Promise. Now, *get to it.*"

ARENA

Next morning, Logan, Rytlock, and Caithe walked among stern-looking warriors who led them from the jail to the arena. Rytlock's wrist was fully healed, but the rift between the man and the charr was only partially so. Last night, both fighters had fidgeted and fussed as Logan healed Rytlock. This morning, neither had spoken to the other.

They walked through a narrow set of winding lanes, with half-timber houses leaning over them. At last, they reached a much-trammeled plot of land with the overturned hull of a huge ship in its center. Many people milled outside the wooden hull, and money changed hands. A few of the people there stared with lurid admiration at Logan, Rytlock, and Caithe.

"Fresh meat," one man said darkly.

Rytlock reached for Sohothin but, of course, his sword and scabbard were gone.

The guards marched them toward a wide rectangular

entrance cut into one side of the overturned hull. The passage was preternaturally dark, shielded by a curtain of magic, but sounds came from within.

Feet pounded. Voices shouted. Swords clanged. Someone screamed.

"Are we making a mistake?" Logan asked.

"Quite possibly," Caithe responded.

Rytlock scowled. "You two got any money?"

"No," they chorused.

Rytlock swept his claws forward. "Then let's go."

The three strode among their guards through the mystic curtain. They emerged into a gigantic space—a huge arena carved into the ground. Rows of stone benches descended toward a broad, sandy arena. Warriors practiced there. To the right, a man and a centaur faced off. To the left, an ogre battled a charr. In one spot, a team of gorilla-like grawl assaulted a pair of scaly skritt.

"This must be the place," Logan said.

"This *is* the place," responded a new voice. Sangjo emerged from one of the nearby archways and glided placidly toward the trio. "Welcome to the arena."

"We're here for one reason," Rytlock grumbled, "to get back my sword."

Logan added, "And also to get back our freedom."

"So," Caithe said, "we're here for *two* reasons."

Sangjo's face was a cryptic mask. "The only reason to fight in the arena is to win."

"Right," Rytlock said.

"Let me show you around," Sangjo said coolly. He stepped away, leading them along a concourse among benches. "Below, of course, is the arena proper."

"Ah, the blood-soaked sands," Rytlock said. "How many die here per day?"

"None."

"None?"

"Battles are not lethal. Combat is to exhaustion."

Rytlock snorted. "Nothing to lose?"

"Actually, there's plenty to lose. Those who lose don't get paid. Those who win receive a cut of the total gate receipts."

"Which means . . . ?" Logan prompted.

Sangjo shrugged, descending a ramp that led beneath the stands. "If you're unknowns, as you are, a victory could bring fifty silver. If you're headliners, if you pack the place, well—a hundred times that."

Rytlock's eyes flashed like coins. "When do we get to it?"

Sangjo lifted his index finger. "First, the tour."

He led them down a ramp into a dark, curving corridor. Its ceiling was formed from the underside of the stone seats, and its walls were lined with cells fronted by thick iron bars. The floor of the corridor pitched inward to drain the waste of the things that lived in the cells.

"What've you got in here?" Rytlock asked.

"Everything—krait, dredge, skritt, hylek, human . . ."

"Human?" Logan gasped.

"Murderers, all of them. Convicted and sentenced. Like you, they had the choice of prison or the arena, and they chose the arena. Naturally, you'll have better lodgings, elsewhere. Unless you try to run."

The group walked past a cell where a pair of the giant, frog-headed hylek crouched and glared. One shot its mucous-mantled tongue out between the bars to wrap around Logan's leg. He kicked his foot loose and stomped on the tongue, which withdrew limply. The next cell held three krait—creatures with reptilian heads and human torsos and serpent abdomens. At sight of the group, the krait raised their neck frills and hissed angrily.

"What've you got in the way of grawl?" rumbled Rytlock.

"All in good time," Sangjo replied, "but first—" He gestured into the next cell, in which twenty or thirty rotting bodies shambled around in the darkness. Their rusted cutlasses grated on the ground. "We just got this load of Orrian undead."

"Undead?"

"Real crowd-pleasers. We let them get torn limb from limb since they're already dead. Of course, down here, they're a nuisance. They don't keep. They stink up the place."

"Not much of a challenge, fighting undead," Rytlock put in.

"You'd be surprised. They fight with weapons and with fury, and even after you dismember them, the limbs fight on." Sangjo slid a key from his pocket and fit it into the door of the cell.

Caithe's eyes grew wide. "What are you doing?"

Sangjo smiled. "Giving you a test." With that, he produced their weapons from his robes, handing Caithe her stilettos, Logan his hammer, and Rytlock—

"That's mine!" he growled, snatching Sohothin in its scabbard and knocking Logan's hand away.

Just then, the tide of undead hurled back the door of their cell and flooded out.

One monster charged Rytlock, ramming its blade at

him. He backhanded the rusted metal and kicked the creature in the groin, crushing its pelvis. The monster's legs went limp, and it slumped to the ground. Even so, its sword kept swinging. Rytlock stomped on its arm, cracking it in two.

Logan meanwhile ducked beneath another monster's cutlass, grabbed the beast's rotting hand, wrenched the blade out of tumbling finger bones, and impaled the monster on it. He let the creature fall on its own sword while he hoisted his hammer. "You might've given us a chance to prepare."

Sangjo stood beyond the fray, a warding wall glimmering before him. "Gladiators must be ready at a moment's notice."

Rytlock punched another undead creature in the head, breaking its neck, though the body still fumbled toward him. "Enough!" he growled, unsheathing Sohothin and ramming it into the creature's guts. Fire burst between ribs, and the whiff of roasted meat wafted upward. Rytlock kicked the cooked creature off his sword and turned to spit two more. "It's a sad thing when a group of friends can be torn apart by something as simple as undead."

Logan's hammer imploded the chest of another beast, which fell on a pile of two more. "That's three for me."

"Three?" Rytlock roared as he strode over his victims to impale another. "I've got three stuck between my toes, two more smoldering in the corner, and a new one on my blade." He shoved off his latest kill, which fell to the ground like a turkey from a platter. "Where's that damned sylvari?"

"Standing on seven." A monster toppled forward to reveal Caithe drawing her white stiletto out of its brain. The creature lay beside six others like fish on ice. "Pithing is what they call it. Stick in the blade, swish it around, and the brain's no good—even for an undead." She demonstrated on an eighth. "Also works on frogs."

"You mean hylek?" asked Logan. His hammer pounded the creatures around him, leaving broken, heaving forms on the floor. Whenever a figure moved, he whacked it. "That should be about twenty."

"You don't get to count the pieces," Rytlock said.

Still, there wasn't much counting left. Caithe pithed three undead while Logan felled two more, and Rytlock burned the last. In moments, the dark corridor was silent again, hunks of jittering flesh lying all around.

"Wow, they stink," Rytlock said.

Sangjo clapped, smiling serenely as his warding wall fizzled and vanished. "Well done. Ten apiece."

"The count was twelve, nine, and nine," Rytlock said.

"He's right," Caithe said. "I had twelve."

"*You?*" Logan and Rytlock said together.

"All of you passed," Sangjo told them happily. "Now, please stand to one side." He held his arms out, herding them back against the bars of the undead cell.

At the dark end of the corridor, a couple of enormous thuds resounded, followed by the noise of heavy metal scraping against stone.

"What's next?" Logan groaned.

Sangjo said, "An ettin."

"Bring it on!" Rytlock replied, waving Sohothin before him.

"Not a fighter," Sangjo clarified, "a janitor."

Just then, an ettin shoved a heavy sledge into view. The sledge had a scoop on its front end, gathering the pieces that lay on the floor and tumbling them toward some distant dump.

As the ettin rumbled past, Rytlock rumbled, "If he's not our next test, what is?"

Sangjo rubbed his hands together. "A battle on the arena sands. Your owner, Captain Magnus the Bloody Handed, has even given the three of you a name—Edge of Steel."

"How much are tickets?" Eir asked an old man who sat at the ticket booth.

"A silver for each of you."

Nodding, Eir reached into a pouch at her belt. "One. Two. Three."

The old man took the coins and slid them into a drawer. "What about the wolf?"

"He doesn't take a seat," Eir pointed out.

The old man squinted. "I won't get anyone to sit within ten feet, which means he empties about twenty seats. He's a bargain at one silver."

Eir drew one more coin from her purse and slid it into his hand.

He smiled, handing her torn tickets.

Eir led her group into the arena.

Beside her, Snaff offered, "It really is reasonable."

"We're going to have to find a way to earn some money," Eir replied.

They picked their way through the growing crowd, looking for seats that could accommodate them all. Most sections were designed on a human scale, though some shorter seats filled rapidly with asura and some taller ones with norn and charr. A few sections were merely stalls where quadrupeds could stand. Finally, Eir found a spot with mixed seating, where each of them could recline in comfort.

"Do you really think that this man and charr could be the warriors we're looking for?" Snaff asked.

"I don't know," Eir replied softly. "Magnus the Bloody Handed seemed to think so."

Trumpets played from the pinnacles of the arena, and the crowd rose to their feet and cheered. At the center of the arena, a man in multicolored robes climbed a set of stairs to a raised platform and addressed the crowd. Magic bore his voice outward to them all.

"Welcome, people of Lion's Arch. Welcome to the arena. It is a day for combat!" A glad roar met the words. "And we have some new blood challenging for a place in the gladiatorial games. Stand and cheer for Logan Thackeray, Rytlock Brimstone, and Caithe of the sylvari. They are the gladiatorial team called Edge of Steel!"

From one of the dark entrances, the three gladiators trotted out on the sands.

Eir, Snaff, and Zojja applauded, but few others did—and some even booed.

Edge of Steel looked small and tattered in their battle-scarred armor and clothes. The charr raised a halfhearted greeting to the people, but the man and the sylvari had the demeanor of people caught in a cold drizzle.

"And now, for this match, join with me in welcoming our opposing team. Our undefeated team—the Killers!"

The stands erupted.

"First, we have the centaur Mjordhein!"

The arena welled with cheers as a centaur strode from one of the arena gates. The massive figure had shaggy hooves and a body like a plow horse. His upper torso was muscular and topped with a horned head like a ram's.

"And second, we have the grawl Moropik!"

A gray-skinned gorilla-man bounded out of the dark corridor, lifted its furred face toward the crowd, and roared between widespread fangs.

"And last but not least, welcome the ettin Krog-Gork."

The spectators roared loudest of all for this lumbering brute, with its two heads and witless cries.

Eir, Snaff, and Garm sat back down.

"All right," Eir said soberly, "maybe there are no warriors here."

"You *think?*" Zojja shot back.

"Let the battle begin!" cried the announcer. His hands moved in elaborate gestures, drawing the amplification spell from his own throat and sending it down upon the gladiators.

Mjordhein plodded forward and bellowed, "For Ulgoth the Mighty! We will reap you like grain!"

"Yeah," the charr grumbled under his breath, though the amplification spell shared his response with everyone. A wave of amusement swept through the crowd. Rytlock looked up and bellowed, "And we'll eat you like meat!"

The stands erupted.

The centaur drew forth a quarterstaff fitted with a scythe, the grawl lifted a mace encrusted with obsidian shards, and the ettin raised a club the size of a horse's leg.

Edge of Steel stood ready with flaming sword and war hammer and stilettos.

The centaur broke into a gallop, leading the monsters across the arena sands. "Come along, two-legs! The centaurs are taking back what is ours!"

Logan also charged, shouting, "All that is yours is death!"

The man and the centaur came together. Mjordhein swung his bladed quarterstaff to cut Logan's legs out from under him, but Logan leaped. The scythe cut through air instead of flesh. Logan planted his foot on the centaur's steely hand and kicked his other foot into the creature's jaw. The centaur reeled as Logan flipped over and landed in the sand.

Mjordhein's eyes went red, and he dropped his massive horns and charged.

This time, Logan didn't dodge, instead bringing his war hammer down between the horns and atop the centaur's skull.

Mjordhein posted his legs, wobbled slowly on them, pitched backward, and crashed to the ground.

The crowd roared. Chirurgeons rushed out to aid the fallen centaur.

Meanwhile, the grawl turned toward Rytlock and charged: "For the Great One!" It swung its obsidian-bladed club at him.

The charr bounded in, flaming sword sliding along

one edge of the club and shearing away the stones there. When the grawl swung a counterstrike, Rytlock raked away the other side of the club.

The grawl staggered back, staring in amazement at his toothless weapon. He should have been staring in amazement at Rytlock, however, who swiped his fiery sword beneath the gorilla-man's face, setting his beard on fire. Hooting and wailing, the grawl bounded away.

Rytlock grinned at the stands. "Fricasseed—charr style."

The crowd ate it up.

Chirurgeons rushed out to aid the grawl, and one shouted, "Unnecessary brutality!"

"Unnecessary brutality?" Rytlock roared, wheeling about. "I like the sound of that!"

Laughter welled through the arena.

Of the Killers, only the ettin remained. It trained one head on Rytlock and the other on Logan.

"Where's Caithe?" whispered Rytlock, though everyone in the arena heard.

"I don't know," Logan whispered back. "Statistically, this one should be hers."

"Well, let's do this."

The charr and the man charged side by side toward the great monster. Logan swung his hammer at the beast's left leg, but its arm smashed him back. Rytlock met a similar fate on the right side, hurled back twenty paces. Both charr and man tumbled in the dust as the ettin rushed to finish them off. Horned feet pounded up to crush their heads—

But then the ettin staggered to a stop. Its knees buckled, and it plunged forward.

"Look out!" Logan shouted, rolling away.

Rytlock tumbled in the other direction.

As the ettin struck ground, its hunched back revealed a slender sylvari in black leather. She jumped free.

More chirurgeons arrived at a run, looking overwhelmed by this new team.

But the crowd went wild.

Eir and Snaff cheered as loudly as anyone.

"There you have it," called the announcer from his stand, "the fall of an empire. The undefeated Killers have now been defeated by Edge of Steel."

That name brought the fans to their feet and they cheered, "*EDGE OF STEEL! EDGE OF STEEL! EDGE OF STEEL! EDGE OF STEEL! . . .*"

The man, the charr, and the sylvari stood dumbfounded in the midst of it all.

Snaff turned to Eir. "They're the ones—the warriors we need."

"You'll never be able to afford them," Zojja put in.

"That's why I've got a different plan," Eir responded.

Zojja huffed, "Oh, here we go again."

Eir turned toward Snaff. "We can't buy them. But I bet I can make a deal with Magnus the Bloody Handed."

"What kind of deal?" asked Snaff.

"If he lends these warriors to us, then after we defeat the Dragonspawn, we'll lend some warriors to him."

"Who?" Snaff asked.

"Us."

EDGE OF STEEL

I could get used to this," Rytlock said as a platter of thundershrimp was set in the center of the table. The tails were huge, and the red shells had been cracked down the middle to reveal steaming white meat.

Edge of Steel had earned five hundred fifty silver for their victory in the arena. They'd paid three hundred of it toward their billet, but the rest was for rooms and a feast.

Caithe speared some of the thundershrimp meat, twisted, and ripped it loose. She popped the morsel in her mouth. "Tastes a bit like devourer."

"Less poisonous, though," Logan said, dunking his own piece in drawn butter. "And it wasn't trying to kill us."

Too hungry to worry with silverware, Rytlock clamped down on a section of meat and tore it free. He tossed it into his mouth and leaned back, staring at the smoky rafters above—once the bilge of a ship. "Ahhh."

"Are you Rytlock Brimstone?" asked a voice nearby, unmistakably charr, unmistakably young.

Rytlock turned to see a cub fresh out of his fahrar, brown eyes gleaming with hero worship. "Why, yes, I am."

"I saw you fight today," the young charr said. "Would you sign my sword?" He slid a wooden blade onto the table.

"Of course." Rytlock winked at him. Lacking a writing implement, Rytlock used his claw. He carved his signature boldly across the flat of the blade and handed it back. "There you go."

The young charr stared with white-ringed eyes at his practice sword and bobbed away.

Watching the cub go, Rytlock sighed, "Yeah, I could get used to this!"

Just then, the server brought three tall tankards of charr ale, setting them in the middle of the table.

"Old Regret!" Rytlock enthused. "I didn't think you could get this stuff outside the Black Citadel." He hoisted his tankard. "Here's to Edge of Steel."

"To Edge of Steel," chimed in the other two, lifting their ales and clanking the tankards.

Rytlock drained his in a single, long pull. Logan tried to match him but had to stop halfway, tears coming to his eyes.

Caithe took two gulps and set the tankard down, eyes wide. "Water from a peat marsh?"

"No," Rytlock said, tugging on the waistcoat of the server and handing his empty tankard over for a refill.

Caithe sniffed the drink again. "It's not sweat, is it?"

"No!" Logan laughed, winking at her above his ale. "Drink some more. It tastes better the more you have." As if to prove his point, he drained his tankard—while Rytlock drained a second.

Shrugging, Caithe took a few more gulps. She lowered the drink to see two faces leering at her.

"Well, what do you think?" Rytlock asked.

Caithe stared blankly back. "You two are not as ugly as I first thought."

Logan guffawed.

"You're not as insufferable, either," Rytlock said. "Neither one of you."

"I'm not sure why I said that," Caithe blurted.

Rytlock grinned. "It's in the name, girl. Old Regret. Makes you say things—true things, of course—that you'll regret later."

Caithe scowled and took another gulp, coming away with a foam mustache. "Things like what?"

"Things like . . . well, like . . ." Rytlock huffed, making a decision. "All right, here goes: being with the two of you is like being with the striplings."

"What?"

"That's what they called us," Rytlock reflected. "In my fahrar—that's the pack they put you in when you're born—in my fahrar they called the smallest of us the striplings."

"*You* were small?" Logan asked incredulously.

"I was the youngest. The smallest. They called me Runtlock."

"Runtlock!" Logan snorted.

"I made them stop," Rytlock growled ominously. "I

did, and the other striplings did. We banded together, and I was the leader. We taught the bullies a few lessons. Still can't stand bullies."

"But you *can* stand us," Logan said.

"Yeah—barely."

Logan took another pull from his tankard. "Well, it may be the Old Regret talking, but, you know—I always thought charr were bloodthirsty brutes—"

"We *are*," Rytlock interrupted, receiving another ale.

"But not *just* that," Logan went on. "You're also loud, foul, and pigheaded."

"What's your point?"

Logan clapped a hand on Rytlock's shoulder. "I'd rather hang out with you than with my brother."

Rytlock laughed. "Oh, yeah. The Seraph."

"Yeah. The white knight, you know—the perfect one. He's guarding Queen Jennah, and I'm guarding a caravan of salt pork. He's a Seraph, and I'm a grunt. He's always judging me—"

"*I'm* always judging you," Rytlock said.

"But I don't care what you think, 'cause you're a jack-ass like me. There. I said it: you're the jackass brother I never had."

"I'll drink to that," Rytlock proclaimed, crashing his tankard with Logan's.

Logan took another sip and then turned to Caithe. "What about you? Why do *you* put up with us?"

Caithe blinked. "You're interesting."

The man and the charr traded looks.

"She's got a point," Rytlock said.

Caithe continued, her foam mustache disintegrating

with tiny, fizzy pops, "Sylvari are one thing. We are born out of the Pale Tree, and no matter how far away the winds bear us, we still carry the life of the tree in us. Humans and charr, you don't belong to anything, not even your mothers or brothers. Not even yourselves. You spend your whole lives trying to find something to belong to—something worth it. And it seems like most of you never do." Another hiccup. "That's interesting."

"Yeah," Logan echoed hollowly. "Interesting."

Rytlock sighed. "Well, I'm sure not gonna belong to a tree."

Caithe stared hard at him for a moment before she laughed. She *never* laughed. The sound was strange, like bells ringing—rare and pure—and it left her comrades gaping. She glanced from one to the other, stopped laughing, and fell over.

"Here they are, the up-and-coming team of Rytlock Brimstone, Caithe of the sylvari, and Logan Thackeray. You know them as Edge of Steel!"

Rytlock, Caithe, and Logan jogged out to a smattering of applause. That was plenty, though: everything seemed *loud* this morning.

"So, what do you think Sangjo's got in store for us today?" Rytlock wondered.

"Get ready," Caithe broke in. "Here they come."

"And today, Edge of Steel faces a fan favorite," called the announcer, "the Northern Fury!"

Three norn warriors loped from the open gate,

massive in their animal hides and gleaming armor. The crowd greeted them with shouts and applause, and the Northern Fury lifted huge hands toward them.

"The Northern Fury?" Caithe said wonderingly.

"They're huge," Logan said.

"*I'm* huge," Rytlock reminded.

"We can defeat them easily," Caithe said. "They all have the same strengths—brute force and fury—and all the same weaknesses."

Across the arena, the three norn drew morning stars from their belts and broke into a trot, heading toward Edge of Steel.

"What are their weaknesses?" Logan asked as he pulled loose his war hammer.

The three norn were charging now, bellowing as they came.

"We'll see," Caithe said, her dagger in hand.

The first of the three norn ran directly at Rytlock, who raised Sohothin for the charge. The norn warrior arrived with skins flying and armor gleaming. Rytlock swung the flaming sword at his foe's morning star, severing the chain. The norn did not slow, ramming Rytlock backward. He rolled once and lunged to his feet, Sohothin forming a fiery figure eight before him. He shouted, "I know their weakness! They don't smell so good!"

"*You* don't either," Logan shouted back as he jumped out of the way of a morning star.

Its spikes impaled the ground, and the norn who wielded it yanked it back for another blow. The weapon fell again, and Logan barely scooted out of the way.

He spun and slammed his hammer into the norn's

hip guard. The thick metal plate rang, and the hammer jangled in Logan's grip.

Worse—the morning star swung at him again. He ducked, but the spikes snagged his leather armor, tearing it loose and dragging long lines down Logan's back.

"Arrhhh!" he growled. "That's it!" He charged the norn and buried his hammer in the warrior's groin.

A high-pitched whine came from the towering warrior, who bent over at the waist and fell like a tree. Logan scrambled out from beneath him as the norn smashed to the sand.

"One down," Logan said as he glanced over to Caithe.

She was scrambling across the back of the third norn like a squirrel running around a tree. He danced, trying to shake her loose. Caithe kept on, every once in a while jabbing her white stiletto into a weak point. The norn twisted and roared, gulped and giggled, bedeviled by the omnipresent sylvari and her ticklish blade.

As he convulsed, a wave of laughter rolled through the crowd. They began shouting, "Caithe! Caithe! Caithe!"

Now the norn was running and swatting, like a man beset by bees. His escape lasted only a moment before Caithe wrapped her arms around his neck and squeezed. "You're going to get sleepy," she announced as the norn went limp and tumbled to the sand.

The crowd went wild.

Caithe rolled free and stood up to survey the battlefield. She shouted to Logan, "Let's give Rytlock a hand!"

Logan turned and saw that Rytlock was in a desperate scrum.

Sohothin lay out of reach, twenty yards away, and a scorched norn held Rytlock in a headlock. Growling, the norn drove his weight onto the charr, hurling them both to the sands.

The two other members of Edge of Steel jogged up to where the charr and the norn wrestled.

"How you doing?" Logan asked.

Spraying sand from his mouth, Rytlock said, "How do you think? Stick a blade in him."

Caithe leaped onto the norn's back and jabbed her dagger into a buttock.

"Yow!" the norn yelped as he climbed off Rytlock.

Caithe leaped free, rolled on the sands, and came up with her stiletto ready.

The remaining norn stared, panting, at his foes, then looked beyond them to the two figures lying in the sands. The norn's expression went from anger to amazement. "You laid out my brothers?"

Caithe smiled, cocking her hips. "Want to see how?"

"There's an easy way and a hard way, my friend," Logan said, his comrades coming to stand beside him. "We're the hard way."

The norn nodded. "Then let it be." He charged.

"Let it be," Rytlock replied. He ran head-on into the towering warrior, knocking him to the ground.

The norn struggled to rise.

Caithe leaped on him, wrapped her arms around his neck, and squeezed.

The norn thrashed, trying to throw her off, but she clung on. In moments, he teetered and then toppled and flopped down, unconscious.

Edge of Steel emerged from a cloud of dust, their latest victim lying in the midst of it.

The stadium roared.

Rytlock grabbed the hands of his comrades and lifted them high. The cheer redoubled. "It'll be a thousand silver this time."

"Enough to buy some new armor?" Logan said faintly, his slick hand dragging from Rytlock's grip. He fell forward, and his friends saw four red stripes down his back.

"We need a chirurgeon!"

Logan got his chirurgeon—and a new plate-mail breastplate, an upgrade from his leather. Rytlock got his glory and his thundershrimp. Caithe got her name spoken on ten thousand lips: the woman who fought with the frenzy of a whirlwind.

They paid four hundred more silver toward their billet. "How much does that leave?" Rytlock asked Sangjo.

"Four hundred ninety-three gold," the man said with a serene smile.

Rytlock cocked his head. "Looks like we'll be fighting a lot."

"Looks like it."

The next day, they fought a band of charr. Rytlock was reluctant at first, until one of the charr walloped him in the head with a mallet. A quick healing touch from Logan revived him, and Rytlock was all business from then on. Logan acquitted himself well against them also, and Caithe discovered that charr could be monstrously strong but have numerous "weak points."

As Edge of Steel stood together atop the fallen charr, Caithe said to Rytlock, "No one has ever reported that charr are ticklish."

Rytlock nodded. "Ticklers do not live to report it."

The next day, they fought a band of six humans. It was Logan's turn to feel chagrined, triumphant over his own people. But it was as Caithe had said—they all had the same strengths and weaknesses. Only groups of mixed races and abilities had any hope of succeeding in the arena.

For two weeks, Edge of Steel went undefeated. Their wealth grew, and their fame with it. They moved further and further into the lineup, clearing away opponents before them. Humans, sylvari, asura, charr, and even mixed groups of all these. None could stand before Edge of Steel.

After two weeks came a second exhibition match, which Sangjo described as "an epic battle against a secret foe for the delight of a special personage."

"What do you think we're going to fight?" Logan asked Rytlock as they trotted out onto the sands, to the cheers of the crowd.

Rytlock humphed. "Who knows? Maybe a pack of skritt. Maybe a herd of centaurs. Could even be an oak-heart for all I know."

"At least an oakheart is flammable," put in Caithe.

The announcer called from his tower, "And before we announce the foe this afternoon, all rise in honor of our special guest—all the way from our ally Kryta, the most noble, most high, Queen Jennah!"

The stands erupted with cheers, and trumpeters along the upper courses played a fanfare that echoed beneath the wooden dome.

"Queen Jennah!" Logan whispered, looking up into the stands.

At the top, a pair of double doors opened, and white-garbed Seraph marched through. They descended the stairs with precision, unrolling a red carpet and tucking it securely onto each step.

Then the queen herself appeared, and mesmer magic projected her image out to hang above the center of the arena.

Logan turned toward that image.

Queen Jennah was young, powerful, regal—garbed in a white gown and wearing the mantle of Divinity's Reach across her shoulders. She had dark hair, tan skin, and riveting brown eyes.

"She's beautiful," Logan murmured.

The huge image that hovered above the sands spoke to everyone gathered there: "Thank you, good people of Lion's Arch. Thank you for this welcome to your beautiful city! Once you were a part of our homeland, and always you will be part of our hearts."

Cheers answered her speech.

"Today, before Commodore Marriner and the Ship's Council, I have confirmed Kryta's commitment to work with Lion's Arch for the good of Tyria's free races. Together, our people and yours declare an alliance. We will help you fight the Orrian undead, who threaten your shipping lanes, and you will help us fight the centaurs that raid our villages."

Applause filled the arena, and the image of Jennah smiled beautifully.

"She's wonderful," Logan sighed.

"I asked your excellent Ship's Council what great entertainment I must not miss in my brief stay, and they all turned as one to Captain Magnus the Bloody Handed, proprietor of this great establishment"—gleeful cheers interrupted her—"and he brought me here! And so, to all who do battle here today, I wish success and health and wealth!"

"All who do battle?" Logan stepped back breathlessly. "That's me!"

As Queen Jennah's mesmeric presence faded from the center of the arena, the stadium applauded her one last time. Waving to the crowd, she slowly descended the stairs, flanked by her bodyguards. Seraph bowed to her, one by one, as she passed.

Logan drifted toward her across the sands.

"Where are you going?" Rytlock barked.

"My queen," Logan muttered, his steps growing more sure.

Queen Jennah entered a private platform, with guards ranked in white all around her. She had other attendants, too—blue-robed men and women in courtly attire, their eyes sharp and scanning the crowd.

As Logan approached the stands, a number of the Seraph watched him in anticipation. Their swords raked free of silvery scabbards. One shouted for Logan to stay back, but he kept on walking.

Then another Seraph waved the others back and descended to the rail. "So, it's true—my kid brother's in Lion's Arch."

Logan blinked, only then seeing who it was. "Dylan!"

Dylan didn't return the greeting, and there was anger beneath his black brows. "What are you doing here? I thought you were guarding merchant caravans or something."

Logan averted his eyes—it had always been difficult looking into his big brother's relentless gaze. "My group was slaughtered . . . down to me."

"By what?" Dylan asked.

"By ogres." Logan glanced behind him, where Rytlock was taking practice swings with Sohothin. "The charr back there saved my life."

"Really," Dylan said coldly.

"Really," Logan responded, finally looking him in the eye.

Dylan nodded coolly. "So, now you fight beside a charr, in the arena?"

Logan shrugged. "Yeah."

"I shouldn't have expected more," Dylan sighed. "I hope the queen likes the exhibition match today."

"She hopes she does, as well," came a woman's voice behind Dylan.

He looked over his shoulder, surprised, then dropped to one knee. "My queen!"

Queen Jennah of Kryta stepped forward.

Logan's mouth fell open, and he staggered back.

The queen was stunning, her dark features set off by robes as white as lightning. Her eyes were sharp, and they pierced him, baring his inner thoughts.

Logan stood pinioned on those eyes. He wanted to turn away but couldn't. It was as if every other woman he had ever seen was just a statue, but Jennah was flesh and blood.

The queen smiled. "Rise, Captain Dylan, and tell me who this man is to approach my presence armed."

"Regrettably, my queen," Dylan said, "this gulping codfish is my brother, Logan."

Logan tried to speak, but there was no air in his lungs.

"Bow before your queen!" Dylan snapped.

Logan fell to his knees and bowed his head.

"Logan is your name?"

Logan nodded.

Jennah leaned forward on the rail, looking down at him. "Can he speak?"

Before Dylan could respond, Logan gasped out, "Normally, yes, my queen, I can speak. It's only in your presence that I . . . that I can't seem to find . . . you know, words."

Dylan looked from his brother to the queen. "Your Majesty, is he under a charm of some sort?"

Jennah shook her head.

"A charm?" Logan asked.

"Our queen is a mesmer of extraordinary power," Dylan said to Logan. "It's how she spoke to the whole stadium just now. I thought perhaps she had cast some strange glamour upon you to make you gabble so stupidly. Apparently, though, you come by it naturally."

"Stand, Logan Thackeray," Queen Jennah said.

"Yes, Your Majesty." Logan rose and brushed the dust from his knees. "Thank you, Your Majesty."

"Do not fear, Logan. If you're half the warrior that your brother is, you will do well today."

"I'd say he's *almost* half," Dylan put in.

"My queen," Logan replied earnestly, "I am not sure how good a warrior I am, but if I could fight this match for you, I would be ten times the warrior. Grant me a token—"

Dylan sternly shook his head at his brother.

But Queen Jennah leaned forward, drew a blue scarf from her robe, and handed it down to Logan. "Yes, Logan. Be my champion today. When you fight, fight for me."

Numbly, Logan stepped up and took the scarf as if it were a tender flower. The royal seal of Kryta was embroidered on one corner. "Thank you, milady. I *will* fight for you."

Dylan sighed, "Pity."

"Pity my foes!" Logan proclaimed.

"Give me reason," the queen said, smiling. She turned away and ascended the stairs.

Dylan looked down at his little brother and shook his head. "Hopeless." Then he followed his queen.

"She's going to watch," Logan realized, pivoting slowly and heading away. He stared at the scarf in his hand, marked with the emblem of the royal house, then lifted it to tie to his left shoulder plate.

As Logan approached his comrades, Rytlock wore a wry grin. "A little lovesick, are we?"

"She's my queen."

Caithe interrupted, "Let's forget about the queen and focus on whatever's behind that gate." She pointed across the arena, where men dragged a set of bars away from an entrance.

In the darkness, flames flared. They showed a massive form with red-glowing joints.

"Did you see what I saw?" Logan asked.

"Yep," Rytlock replied.

"Some kind of giant destroyer," Caithe said.

The announcer broke in on their conversation. "And now for the exhibition match this afternoon—the one you've been waiting for. In honor of our special guest, Queen Jennah of Kryta, and in honor of our new alliance with Kryta to battle the dragon menaces, we match up today the crowd favorites, Edge of Steel"—cheers flooded the arena, and the white-faced warriors dutifully waved— "against a minion of the dread dragon Primordus. Feast your eyes upon the destroyer harpy Racogorrix!"

The crowd roared.

Out lumbered the creature of living lava. It was shaped like a woman, but with the wings and talons of an eagle. It bounded forward across the sands, dragging a team of ten men, who held its enchanted shackles. Despite a metal muzzle fastened across the harpy's mouth, it screamed, and flame roared out.

"More magma magic." Rytlock hoisted Sohothin. "Probably impervious to this thing."

Caithe looked down at the skintight strapping she wore. "I'm wearing a wick."

"I'll take this one," Logan said, thumping his new steel breastplate.

"You kidding? That thing'll melt on the second barrage," Rytlock said.

"Then there can't *be* a second barrage," Logan replied. "Caithe, advance about a hundred paces ahead of us and draw it in. When it starts to dive, run back to us. Pass us before it reaches you. We'll take care of the rest."

Caithe looked warily at her comrades. "I'm trusting you with my life, as usual." She turned and stalked away, counting the paces.

Beyond her, handlers slid iron keys into the shackles that bound the harpy. The moment the restraints fell away, Racogorrix vaulted into the air. Its huge wings spread and beat. The shock wave sent a pulse through the arena. A second stroke, and a third, and the harpy circled slowly higher. Its shadow swarmed, horrible and huge, across the sands.

Caithe strode into the circling shadow. "Ninety-eight . . . ninety-nine . . . one hundred!" She stopped and glanced back.

Rytlock pointed into the sky behind her. "Start running!"

Caithe looked up to see that Racogorrix had reached the top of its spiral and had now turned to swoop down on her. She began to run.

Rytlock muttered, "So, what's the brilliant plan?"

"Put your sword away."

Sohothin slid it into its stone sheath. "And . . . ?"

"Cup your claws and lean forward."

The charr grinned, fangs splaying. "You want me to throw you?"

"Precisely."

As Rytlock bent down, cupping his claws, Caithe ran full speed toward him across the sand. The black shadow of the harpy fell over her, growing larger with each step. The harpy screamed, and a gout of red flame billowed down toward Caithe.

The crowd leaped to its feet.

The harpy was nearly on her.

She ran full out past her comrades.

Rytlock hurled his shoulders back, flung his arms up, and launched Logan into the path of the beast.

The crowd screamed.

Fire burst over Logan, enveloping him.

Agony.

He couldn't see a thing but swung his hammer where the head should be. The cloud of flame rolled past, and the hammer crashed down across the harpy's stony shoulder.

"Damn."

The beast slammed into Logan. He folded across its shoulder, hammer wedged beneath its wing. Screaming fire, the creature carried him away.

Logan caught a foothold on one of the harpy's talons and flung himself up onto the monster's back.

Racogorrix banked above the roaring crowd, jigging right and left to shake Logan loose. It snarled fire back along its neck, but he ducked, only singed.

The harpy circled, spotting Rytlock and Caithe below, and dived toward them.

"Oh, no, you don't," Logan muttered. He lifted his hammer overhead and, with one massive stroke, bashed the harpy's brow.

Stones broke, and magma gushed out, but still the harpy flew.

A blue aura gushed from Logan's fingertips and wrapped around his hammer. He hoisted the weapon overhead and roared.

The enspelled weapon crashed into the head of the

harpy and broke it free from the body. The magma joints grew gray and seized up.

Suddenly, the harpy was not flying but falling.

Dead weight.

Rytlock ran away in one direction and Caithe in the other.

The ground rose up to meet the harpy. It crashed down and flipped over, breaking into hundreds of pieces. Logan was flung a few dozen paces through the air. He tumbled end over end in a welter of sand.

Then there was a blow to the head and blood in his nose and nothing else.

When he awoke, the first thing Logan saw was Rytlock's face, his whiskers curled at the ends. "He's back!" Rytlock said.

Caithe moved into view and smiled her rare smile. Beside her, Dylan appeared, his white face flushing red. And then, even Queen Jennah was there.

Logan couldn't breathe. And suddenly . . .

Jennah stood above him, smiling. Her hand gently touched the royal scarf tied to his armor. "You *are* a champion, in the mold of your brother."

"I fight for you . . . forever."

"Ssh, now . . . rest."

Logan opened his mouth to reply but once again lost consciousness.

16

AGREEMENTS

The summer sun beat down on Rata Sum, but within Snaff's ziggurat, everything was cool.

He and Zojja and Eir worked away contentedly in the shade. Eir pounded her chisel, breaking loose a few more chunks of sandstone. She glanced at Snaff. "Keep flexing."

Snaff snorted, tensing his chest muscles. "I've never flexed so long."

"You're the one who wanted a 'buff golem,'" Eir reminded. "Besides, it can't be harder to flex muscles than to actually *use* them." A few more blows knocked the last of the large pieces from the sandstone block, which now had the rough shape of Snaff—only five times larger. Eir switched to a smaller chisel. "I've never carved sandstone before. Very soft. It doesn't hold up."

"All the better," Snaff said enigmatically. "So, you're confident in this plan of yours?"

Eir nodded. "I know we can defeat them. They don't plan. They just react. They wait until their opponents attack, and then they exploit the weaknesses they see. If we don't attack, they'll have to, and we'll be a mystery." Eir carved a long, swooping curve that would be the lid beneath Snaff's left eye. "Let me turn the question on you, Snaff: Are you sure about this sandstone golem? Zojja says no asura has ever created anything like it."

"No other asura could—well, maybe Oola, or one of her students, but nobody else."

"But *you* can?"

"We'll see," Snaff said with a grin.

"You'll have *control?*"

"Yes, but not with a single powerstone. With millions."

She shifted to the lower lid of his right eye. "A pretty expensive golem."

"No. I've designated one powerstone for each body part, and then ground them into fine powder. Each grain is a minipowerstone. We're going to spread them over the whole statue once it's finished. I'll have power over every inch."

"Ingenious."

"Thank you." Then Snaff coughed into his hand. "By the way, once you're finished carving this statue, we'll have to deconstruct it."

"What?" Eir stepped back and stared at him. "How do you deconstruct a statue?"

His smile grew devilish, and he pantomimed giving it a push.

"You're cracked."

"Thank you."

"Flex!"

The day after downing a destroyer harpy, Logan was back on his feet and fighting like never before. He credited the scarf of Queen Jennah for healing him, but of course the chirurgeons didn't hurt.

Sangjo was anxious that his newfound team keep fighting—especially since they still had such a large billet to pay off—but Edge of Steel seemed in no particular hurry to pay up. Logan had used his cut to complete his plate mail, Rytlock had moved on from thundershrimp to skale omelets, and Caithe had rented a private room in a tower near the arena, where she could "keep an eye on everyone."

The delirious winning streak continued. Even two months in, Edge of Steel was undefeated. They headlined the arena and bashed all comers: warriors and elementalists, devourers and drakes, humans and charr and whatever—no team could defeat them, and Lion's Arch hailed them.

Then Queen Jennah herself hailed them—or at least Logan.

The message came on a scroll of fine parchment, sealed with wax that was imprinted with the royal signet. Logan's eyes lingered on that emblem, the same sewn into the scarf on his shoulder. Then he broke the seal and unrolled the scroll and read:

From Her Royal Majesty, Jennah,
Queen of Kryta,
Regent of Ascalon
To Logan Thackeray,
Gladiator of the Arena in Lion's Arch

Greetings:

Your presence is required. Report to the royal palace in Divinity's Reach, Kryta. We will receive you at our convenience.

"She's calling me," Logan gasped, eyes darting again across the scroll. "She's summoning me." It was still morning. He had time to don his best clothes and go through the asura gate to Divinity's Reach and see his queen—all before the night's match. He looked again at the letter in his hand. "She's calling *me*."

An hour later, Logan was stepping through an asura gate, leaving behind the hurly-burly streets of Lion's Arch and stepping into the white splendor of Divinity's Reach. Sultry winds gave way to cool stillness, the loud menagerie of species to the sedate capital of a single, ancient people.

Humanity.

Divinity's Reach was the last bastion of human glory. White limestone walls, great statues, shrines to gods—Divinity's Reach was the world as it had once been, as it would be again.

It was laid out like a great wheel, with the high outer walls as its rim and six inner walls radiating like spokes from the hub at its center.

Logan stood in that hub—a broad, beautiful parkland with green lawns stretching to white pavements, beyond which rose great shining buildings. The buildings were grand, with columned porticoes and hanging galleries and friezes carved in their tympana. The carvings showed scenes of glory from Kryta's past, scenes of beauty from Ascalon before the fall.

This was the heart of the greatest human city on Tyria.

That building was the Chamber of Ministers.

Those white-walled barracks housed the Seraph.

Beyond them lay one of six elevated high roads, each dedicated to a god that the rest of the world had forgotten.

Logan turned to his right, seeing at last the glorious palace of the queen. It was a magnificent structure of spiraling columns and recessed arches, rounded roofs and overhanging stone gazebos and spires reaching to the sky. Before the royal palace sat an amazing domed garden. The dome consisted of a wrought-iron framework covered in a skin of glass. Circular limestone walls rose to a lattice of iron, holding up vast panels of glass. The sun beamed through them onto suspended orreries and solar clocks. Mature oaks and elms and beeches towered among winding paths and trim green lawns.

Logan strode toward the palace gate.

A Seraph emerged from a guardhouse, his armor gleaming mirror-bright but his brows glowering cave-dark. "Who approaches?" he barked while Logan was still half a block away.

"I am Logan Thackeray."

The storm clouds around the guard's face suddenly parted. "Logan Thackeray? *The* Logan Thackeray?"

Stepping up, Logan nodded. "Yes."

"You look a lot smaller up close."

"You've seen me in the arena?"

"Are you kidding? I was there when you killed that destroyer harpy. I've seen you a couple times since then. You're terrific!"

"Thanks."

The guard suddenly straightened. "Erm, what is your business here today?"

"I'm here to see Queen Jennah," Logan replied simply.

"No one sees the queen except by special appointment."

"How's this?" Logan lifted the scroll and unrolled it. "A summons from the queen herself."

The guard squinted at it, reading. Then he stepped back, set a horn to his lips, and blew three times. "One of her attendants will come gather you and take you to her."

Beyond the guard, a Seraph strode from the arched doorway of the castle. It was Logan's brother, Dylan. He smiled ruefully as he approached. "You're blowing the horn for my kid brother?"

The guard blurted, "The queen has summoned him."

"*Him?*"

Logan lifted the scroll.

Dylan scowled as he read it. "What would she want with *you?*"

Logan refused to be daunted. "I don't know. She no doubt has heard of my acclaim."

"Acclaim?" Dylan huffed.

"Yeah. You may not know this, but I'm one of the greatest warriors alive. The arena doesn't lie."

Dylan sniffed. "Follow me." He led Logan into a side garden ringed with tall windows and balconies.

"Wait here, Brother, until we are summoned into her presence."

Logan glimpsed a pair of wooden swords leaning on a nearby bench. "What are those for?"

"Practice matches," Dylan said offhandedly, then a smile cracked his face. "You say you're the greatest warrior alive?"

"I don't," Logan corrected. "Everyone else does."

"Then, how about you show me." Dylan gestured toward the practice swords in the side garden.

"All right." Logan entered the garden—benches circled around an elaborate white fountain, with sculpted shrubs standing sentry over beds of flowers. "Nice spot for sparring."

Dylan lifted one of the wooden swords and used the blade to hoist the other, flinging it to Logan.

Logan caught the sword and took some practice swings. "I'm used to a war hammer."

"You *would* be." Dylan bowed regally. "Pounding things. All power, no finesse."

Logan bowed likewise.

Dylan lunged, his sword striking Logan's breastplate.

Logan staggered. "I wasn't ready."

"You bowed." Dylan followed the first stroke with an overhand blow.

Logan dodged, letting the sword swing past, then elbowed his brother out of the way. Spinning, Logan retreated. "In the arena, we don't bow."

Dylan pivoted. "Yes. I've seen what you do in the arena. You fight like a charr."

"Thank you."

"That wasn't a compliment. And that last shot of yours didn't count. We're fighting with swords, not with elbows." Dylan charged again, sword jabbing.

Parrying the blow, Logan stepped behind one of the benches.

"Out of bounds," Dylan called. "That's a second point for me."

Glowering, Logan whacked Dylan's blade out of the way and stepped back into the garden. "Is that how it's played here? Battling for points?"

"That's the civilized way."

Logan was about to respond when he spotted a figure on a balcony high above the garden. It was she, the queen—Jennah.

His heart pounded.

Dylan lunged, his sword ramming Logan's breastplate. "That's another touch. Three points."

"That wasn't fair! I was looking at the queen."

"She *is* mesmerizing you," Dylan said, grinning. "I'm beating you three points to zero."

Logan huffed. "Of course you can beat me if this is a parlor game. But I thought it was a duel."

"It *is* a duel."

"Then let's forget about touches and out of bounds. The one who wins is the one who stands over the other."

"Fine with me."

Smiling, Logan flipped the practice sword over in his

hand, catching the narrow end and swinging the cross-piece as if it were a hammerhead. Dylan ducked back and glared. Logan laughed. "That's more like it."

With a snarl, Dylan rushed forward, sword stabbing.

Logan's hammer cracked the blade to one side, and he bulled through to ram Dylan backward, causing him to sit down on a garden bench.

Distant laughter drifted down from the balcony.

Logan stepped back, giving his brother room.

"That counts for nothing," Dylan said. "I didn't go out of bounds, and you used your shoulder."

"It counts for me knocking you on your ass."

Dylan roared murderously, swinging his sword to brain his brother.

Logan sidestepped.

Dylan's blade struck a stone bench and rattled stingingly. "Why, you—"

Laughing, Logan scurried away.

Dylan followed with sword swinging.

Logan bounded onto a bench and leaped to the next and the next while Dylan's sword swiped impotently at his heels.

"Stand and face me!"

"This is how we do it in the arena."

"What, run away? Stand and face me!"

Logan planted his feet on the grass and raised his hammer. "Here's my face."

"Almost as ugly as the other side," Dylan noted as his sword jabbed.

Logan's hammer bashed the blade, entangled it, and yanked it free, flinging it behind him.

Shrieking in frustration, Dylan head-butted his brother.

Crack!

Both men staggered back. Logan shook his head, trying to get the multiple images of Dylan to coalesce. His brother meanwhile shambled backward, eyes crossed and hands flailing for balance. Logan's vision cleared just in time to see his brother stumble back into the fountain and sprawl into the water. He thrashed ridiculously for a moment, but then sat back against the central figure. It was a mermaid spitting water, which rolled down his face. "I hate you."

Logan bowed. "I love you, too, Brother." He rubbed his forehead, wondering if his skull was cracked. When he dropped his hand, though, he saw the queen on her balcony, beckoning to him. "I must go. Our sovereign calls."

Straightening his clothes, Logan strode from the garden toward the royal residence. He held his summons up before him, and the first Seraph he encountered led him up a broad stairway. At the top, they reached a high chamber with columns on either side and a thick red carpet down the center. Courtiers in samite and silk lined the carpet, turning to see this rough-and-tumble gladiator in their midst. They watched him, eyes narrowing and mouths curling in smiles of disdain.

Logan didn't care what they thought. The queen had summoned him, and he had come.

She awaited him, sitting at the end of the red carpet, on a throne of gold.

Logan strode toward the queen of Kryta.

Pallid-faced guards dressed in blue and gold—the Shining Blade—stepped up protectively around her throne.

Logan flashed them a smile and then went to his knee, bowing. "Greetings, Your Majesty."

"Rise," she commanded.

Logan got to his feet and stared wonderingly at her. She was more beautiful than before—her brown hair pulled back from her neck, her dark eyes locking with his, her lips a red to match the rich robes that mantled her. He almost forgot the words he'd been practicing: "Your Majesty, I came the moment I received your summons."

She smiled dazzlingly. "You *must* have. I sent it just this morning."

"I am at your command."

"Then I command you to stand with me." The queen rose from her throne. Logan stood there numbly as his queen stepped up next to him. She grasped his hand—her fingers soft but strong—and turned him outward to face the roomful of courtiers. She lifted their hands together. "Friends, senators, courtiers—" She looked pointedly at a proud bald man with a long goatee, and said in an almost growl, "Minister Caudecus—I want to introduce this young man to you. He is a warrior of a new stripe—a gladiator who slew a minion of Primordus in my honor. This is Logan Thackeray."

The courtiers nodded politely, donning smiles and clapping gloved hands in a muffled ovation.

"He fights for me," the queen went on, "as certainly as his brother fights for me. Yes, I have champions beyond the Seraph and the Shining Blade. I have champions such as this warrior. I said he was of a new stripe, but in fact, he is of a very old stripe. He is a hero, like Rurik of old."

Again came the muted applause, the supercilious smiles.

Logan blushed as the queen lowered his hand and squeezed his fingers. She leaned toward him and murmured into his ear, "Thank you for answering my summons."

He squeezed her hand in return. "I will always answer your summons."

"*Will* you?" she replied in a voice of sudden steel. Turning toward him, she pinioned him on her gaze. "Then you will be bonded to me." She lifted her hand as if in blessing, but then reached out to lay her palm on his forehead and lace her fingers into his hair.

Power poured through her touch.

It roared into Logan.

The queen's mind entered his own mind like a thief through a window. But he welcomed this thief. He took her hand and led her deep within and showed her vistas of memory.

They walked together at the height of the Blazeridge Gap as stones buried the charr.

They swam together through the depths of the underground river.

They fought side by side in the meadow against the destroyers.

They stood hand in hand on the arena sands before the Killers.

Logan showed her every moment: when he was a boy

clapping his hands red as his brother was inducted into the Seraph; when he was a young man leading his first scouting party to escape a wildfire; when he was first blooded, slaying a centaur raider and taking the creature's war hammer; when he was most proud, using that hammer to destroy a minion of Primordus in the name of his queen. . . .

Jennah's hand broke from his forehead, and she stepped back, catching a slight breath. Once again, the two of them were standing in the throne room, staring wide-eyed at each other.

Jennah whispered, "The things you have done."

Logan smiled. "The things I will yet do—in your name."

The senators and courtiers of Divinity's Reach listened in silence.

Jennah glanced toward them and drew a deep breath, becoming the queen once again. "You are bonded to me, now, Logan Thackeray," she pronounced, speaking to everyone. "If ever I am in mortal peril, I will call to you, and you must come to me."

"Yes, my queen," Logan said, dropping again to one knee.

Jennah's eyes moved among the courtiers, fixing on certain ones. "Let those who plot against the throne beware."

"Where've you been?" Rytlock asked.

Logan wandered dumbstruck onto the arena sands. "I'm not exactly sure."

"Sangjo wants to talk with us," the charr growled. "All of us."

Caithe walked up to join her teammates. "Something about a big matchup."

The three walked side by side through the main trainer's gate into the foul-smelling underbelly of the arena. They passed among rows of caged gladiators, who hollered excitedly to see Edge of Steel among them, and reached an infirmary, whose operating tables just now were empty. Beyond the tables, Sangjo stood in conference with a female norn, her dire wolf, and a pair of asura.

Wending among the empty tables, Edge of Steel approached. They stopped a few strides away, planted their feet, and folded their arms over their chests.

Logan spoke for them. "You wanted to see us?"

Sangjo dipped his head. "I've just arranged a special match for you."

"With whom?" Logan asked.

"With this group—Eir, Snaff, Zojja, and Garm." As Sangjo named them, he pointed to each one.

Rytlock blinked. "Are they suicidal?"

"No," replied the norn named Eir.

"You've seen us fight, yes?"

The little asura named Snaff waddled forward and nodded happily. "Oh, yes, many times. We've studied—"

"We've seen you fight," broke in the norn. "We're ready."

Rytlock strode along before the group. "How many matches have you fought?"

"We fought the Dragonspawn," Eir responded.

"Did you win?" Rytlock asked.

"No."

The charr lumbered over to Sangjo. "What is this? Is it some kind of trick?"

"It's no trick," Eir responded. "It's a bet."

Rytlock turned toward her. "A bet with whom?"

"With your owner—Captain Magnus the Bloody Handed."

Rytlock scowled. "What kind of bet?"

"If we beat you in the arena," Eir explained, "he will lend you to us on our quest to slay the Dragonspawn."

"What?" Rytlock snarled, backing away among his teammates. "He can't lend us out to fight a dragon champion."

"He's afraid," Snaff said in a stage whisper.

"Afraid of what?" barked Rytlock.

Snaff shrugged. "Of us, of course."

The charr made a hawking sound. "Of you?"

"You're afraid we'll defeat you. That's the only way you'd have to face the Dragonspawn—which, by the way, we've already faced and will again." Snaff turned to his comrades. "Maybe they aren't as tough as they look from the stands."

Rytlock roared with wounded pride and blurted, "We'll beat you. We'll *destroy you!*" He looked toward his comrades, who nodded shallowly. "Sangjo, you better promote this match. I want this place packed the day we shred these four."

Sangjo said simply, "It shall be done."

The evening sun cast long shadows as Eir, Snaff, Zojja, and Garm headed toward the Lion's Arch asura gate.

"That cost us," Zojja groused.

"Money well spent," said Eir. "*My* money well spent. We couldn't afford their billet, so a bet with Magnus was the only way to win them. And even if we win their *billet*, we also have to win their *respect*. And the only way to do that is to beat them."

"How?" Zojja wondered.

"Oh, we'll beat them," Eir replied, "and with Edge of Steel, we'll bring down the Dragonspawn, too."

Zojja sniffed, "You make it all sound predestined."

"It is, Zojja. We're the Dragonspawn's destiny."

CONTEST

For the first time in two months, Edge of Steel canceled their scheduled match.

The fans were outraged.

"They will not fight tonight or tomorrow," proclaimed Sangjo, standing in the announcer's tower. "Or the next night or the next."

Boos answered his pronouncement, welling up around the arena.

"What's the matter?" Sangjo asked. "There are plenty of other gladiatorial teams."

A chant of *"Edge of Steel! Edge of Steel!"* began in one sector of the arena and propagated through the whole. It shook the stands and washed across the other gladiatorial teams waiting below. In the announcer's tower, Sangjo smiled secretly and waited for the chants to die down. After five minutes, they did.

"Friends. Friends—they *will* fight again. In five days, you will see them face their greatest rivals ever."

A wild cheer went up. The cry evolved into a single chanted question—"*Who? Who? Who?*"

"In five days, you will see."

Throughout those five days, Sangjo furiously promoted the match. He sent out a small army of stable hands to stand in the streets and shout teasers. The one bit of information they did not divulge, though, was whom Edge of Steel would fight.

Edge of Steel themselves spread the news through the taverns of Lion's Arch. They promised "a strange challenge," "a brutal whupping," and "a bloody massacre," depending upon which group member was giving the report. Soon, the taverns rang with speculation about the mystery challengers.

But even Edge of Steel knew little about their opponents. Just after laying down their challenge, the foes had vanished through an asura gate. They were a complete mystery.

As Edge of Steel worried about their unknown foes, Lion's Arch boiled into a frenzy over them.

Then the night of the match came.

Crowds clogged the streets all around the arena, shutting down traffic as they jostled to get inside the huge overturned ship. The stands filled with hundreds and then thousands. Banners announced the crowd's favorite—Edge of Steel—but no one knew the name of the challengers.

Then the time for battle came, and Sangjo ascended the announcer's tower to call out, "Welcome, everyone, to tonight's epic spectacle. The famous versus the obscure, the known versus the unknown. The heroes versus the villains. Many have asked who these challengers may be. Now is the moment you will see for yourselves. Here they are, Dragonspawn's Destiny!"

The crowd leaped to its feet, applauding and cheering—craning to see what great menace would emerge from the gladiators' hold.

The barred gate rolled back, and from the darkness waddled two tiny asura onto the newly sanded arena floor.

A rumble of uncertainty answered, followed by a roar of derisive laughter. These two? They looked like aphids. Shouts of outrage began to pierce the laughter.

"What is this?"

"No!"

"A joke!"

Then, a towering norn warrior stepped from the darkness, dragging a huge bow from her shoulder. She drew from her quiver three heavy-headed arrows, each bolt the height of a man. When a great black wolf loped out beside the woman, the furor of the crowd died down, and a few people began to chant, *"Wolves! Wolves! Wolves!"*

But then the men rolled the gates closed. No more wolves emerged—no more creatures at all.

Heckling shouts filled the stands.

"And now, the team you have come to cheer for, the champions of the arena, the undefeated. They are Caithe, Rytlock, and Logan, but you know them better as Edge of Steel!"

The air turned solid with cheers.

From a gate on the opposite side of the arena trotted the sylvari, charr, and human, and the shouts redoubled.

The gladiators lifted their hands in greeting, and the fans responded with a growing chant.

"Edge of Steel! Edge of Steel! Edge of Steel!"

"And now, let the match begin!"

Rytlock ripped Sohothin from its stone scabbard and stabbed it skyward. The blade added its hungry roar to the roar of the crowd. Logan meanwhile lifted his war hammer from his belt and swung it in a series of deadly figure eights. Caithe pulled the daggers from her bandoliers and twirled them before her. The three stared across the arena sands at the norn, her wolf, and the two asura.

The storm of cheers quieted, and a watchful hush fell over the crowd.

Edge of Steel stood, waiting.

So did Dragonspawn's Destiny. They didn't move a muscle.

"What's taking them so long?" Rytlock asked.

Logan said, "Probably terrified."

The members of Dragonspawn's Destiny still stayed put.

"Probably *planning* something," Caithe said.

An ugly rumble began in the crowd and rose like a wave.

"Don't they care that they look like idiots, just standing there?" Logan asked.

Rytlock snarled. "Don't we?"

With that, he strode forward and broke into a run. Sand flew up in a dust cloud behind him.

"Let's go," Logan said with a sigh, bolting after his comrade.

Caithe lit out as well, catching up to Logan, who caught up to Rytlock. Side by side, the gladiatorial champions charged across the sands toward their mysterious foes.

Dragonspawn's Destiny had still not moved. They seemed frozen in fear.

Rytlock roared a war cry, and his comrades took it up.

At last, the norn warrior moved. She nocked three arrows, hoisted her huge bow, and let fly. The arrows arced up above the sands and then came whistling down toward Edge of Steel.

"Dodge!" Logan called out, swerving to one side as Caithe and Rytlock swerved to the other.

The arrows swerved as well, falling upon them.

"Knock them away!" Logan cried, swinging. His war hammer cracked the shaft that angled toward him, but the head of the arrow sprung open, releasing a metal net. It spread over him and draped to his feet. He tripped and sprawled to the ground, seeing that Rytlock and Caithe were down as well. "Damn it!"

Logan struggled to get free, but the metal mesh clung to his armor. He fought against it, managing to drag the clinging stuff from his left arm. His right was still fouled.

The norn warrior rushed across the sands toward him, pulling a heavy mallet from her belt.

Desperate, Logan stood up, though the mesh still clung to his war hammer.

The norn was there, and her mallet fell like thunder.

Logan tried to leap aside, but the maul smashed his breastplate and sent him tumbling across the sand. He rolled to a stop and staggered up, finally yanking his war hammer free. The norn warrior was stalking toward him, her red hair gathered in braids.

This was not going to be an easy fight.

Rytlock, too, was in trouble. He had scrambled up from the metal net but had left Sohothin within it, hopelessly tangled and sending up metallic smoke.

Worse, the dire wolf was upon him. It leaped for his throat, its jaws gaping.

Rytlock crouched, curling into a ball.

The wolf's massive teeth closed over the neck piece of his armor. The fangs skirled on the metal as the wolf flew past, carried by its momentum. It pounded to the ground just beyond Rytlock and turned, snarling.

He rose and snarled back, his claws out.

The dire wolf eyed him and began to circle, looking for a chance at the charr's throat.

Rytlock laughed. "You look flammable to me. If I had my sword, there'd be wolf on the menu."

The dire wolf lunged, fangs bared. It bashed into Rytlock and knocked him to his back. Its teeth snapped just short of his throat. Roaring, the charr raked his claws down the wolf's neck, drawing blood. The beast reared back and brought its massive forepaws down to pound Rytlock's chest. Breath blasted from his lungs, and once again the wolf lunged for his throat. Rytlock rolled aside, and the wolf got a snoutful of sand. It sneezed massively and bounded off the charr.

Rytlock scrambled to his feet and struggled to regain his breath. The air around was thick with shouts. The crowd chanted, *"Edge of Steel!"* but also, *"Des-ti-ny!"*

They didn't care which team won. They only wanted a spectacle, and they were getting it.

On one side of the arena, Logan and the norn warrior traded hammer blows. On the other, Rytlock and the dire wolf circled each other, snarling. That left one other member of Edge of Steel, the one who always struck the killing blow. . . .

Caithe, too, had escaped her net, and she stalked toward the two asura. They lingered near the arena wall as if petrified. She had a dagger for each one, and she could easily plant them from thirty paces. She was nearly in range. Flipping a blade in her hand, Caithe caught the keen tip of it and raised it to throw at the male asura.

But he threw something first—a handful of red sand. It flew out and whiffed down in front of Caithe.

Did he want to blind her? He would have to throw better than that.

Caithe took two more steps. In range. She threw her dagger—

Except that the ground shifted underfoot, and the blade spun off-target, only nicking the asura's ear.

He didn't even flinch, focused instead on the sand beneath her feet. It was mounding up. The asura spread his fingers toward the ground, and it rose in response.

Caithe's feet sank to midcalf in the clinging sand. She tried to pull them free but plunged to her knees. Clawing the stuff only trapped her hands as well.

Quicksand! But it wasn't watery. It was firm—like muscle.

A huge sand creature was emerging beneath her. Its back arched from the arena floor and revealed a head with pointed ears. Caithe's feet were mired in its shoulder. Sand sifted away to reveal broad but stumpy arms and stocky legs. The golem stood to full height—a gigantic asura in the likeness of the older asura.

The golem moved as the asura moved. He lifted a hand to his shoulder and pressed firmly down, and the golem's hand lifted the same way, driving Caithe to midthigh in the sandy golem. She stabbed the thing with her daggers, but the blades only sank away, lost in the all-consuming sand.

Caithe shouted for help, but her teammates couldn't possibly hear over the roar of the crowd.

Why are they laughing? Logan wondered, but he had no time to look.

The norn's mallet thrummed the air. Logan leaped aside as the maul cratered the ground. He hurled his own maul around in a sudden, desperate stroke. The head missed the norn but struck the handle of her mallet, breaking it. The blow also jarred the norn's hands. She staggered back.

It was Logan's first opening, and he took it.

Spinning, he whirled the war hammer in a moaning circle.

The norn tried to leap away, but the hammer struck a glancing blow to her ribs. *Crack!* Breath blasted from her. She staggered back, fell to the ground, and gasped.

A cheer resonated from the crowd.

Logan turned and saw that Caithe was half-buried in the shoulder of a—what was that thing? A sand golem?

He ran toward the golem, raised his hammer, and brought it down against the golem's leg. Steel struck sand and flung away a divot of it. The remaining sand, though, grabbed hold of his weapon. Logan pulled it free and struck again, blasting more sand away. The leg was thinning, the golem tottering. Logan chopped like a lumberjack.

The golem reached its massive hand down to grab him, but Logan dodged away. He smashed one of the sandy fingers, obliterating it. Still the hand reformed and took another swipe at him.

As Logan spun out of reach, he glimpsed the little asura making the same motions as the big one: a puppeteer.

Ducking another attack, Logan rushed up to the asura, hoisted him off his feet, turned him over, and shook him. A golden laurel fell from his head.

Twenty feet behind him, the golem toppled onto its back and shuddered. Sand sifted away from Caithe's legs, and she clawed her way out of the dissolving monster.

A great cheer erupted.

"Let him go!" came a shout.

Logan turned to see the other asura, the apprentice, staring him down. He laughed. "Let him go or what?"

"Or this!" she responded, flinging her hands out.

A bolt of lightning erupted from her grip, smashing into Logan and hurling him across the sands. His nerveless hand lost hold of the asura, who toppled separately. Logan also dropped his hammer. It tumbled to the ground as he did. Logan staggered up, jangled by the blast, and grabbed his hammer in numb fingers.

Meanwhile, the asura apprentice flung the powerstone laurel to her master. He donned it somewhat dizzily.

From the sands, the huge golem mounded up, taking shape again and hulking to its feet. As the asura puppet master marched in place, the sand golem lumbered toward Caithe.

"No!" Logan roared, and ran toward the golemancer.

The sand golem meanwhile snatched up Caithe in one fat fist.

Logan was ten feet from the golemancer when another bolt of blue blasted into him and hurled him back.

He crashed over the sands only to have sands crash over him: the sandy fist. That damned golem clutched him in one hand and clutched Caithe in the other and ran toward Rytlock.

Rytlock turned to escape, but the wolf lunged against his back and knocked him down.

Next moment, the lumbering golem arrived and slumped down, burying Rytlock to his chest.

There was a moment of stunned silence in the arena as the norn warrior strode back to join her battle-scarred wolf and the two asura geniuses.

Then all eyes shifted to Edge of Steel, buried in sand.

The crowd erupted. Every voice shouted, every hand clapped, and the roar of it all evolved into the cry *"Des-ti-ny! Des-ti-ny! Des-ti-ny!"*

In the infirmary beneath the arena, the two gladiatorial teams met once again. Chirurgeons tended Garm's many claw wounds and Rytlock's many bite marks; they set Eir's broken ribs and Snaff's dislocated shoulder. But most of all, they kept Edge of Steel from murdering Dragonspawn's Destiny.

Rytlock roared, "You hid a *golem* in the arena!"

"We're *golemancers,*" Snaff replied. "What did you think we were going to do? Stand there and get slaughtered?"

"Actually, yes."

Eir gasped as the chirurgeon set plaster to her bruised side. "Then you failed to plan."

"Of course we didn't plan," Rytlock snarled. "We're fighters, not engineers."

"Which is why you need us," Zojja put in.

"We don't need anybody," Rytlock spat.

"We defeated you," Eir said. "You're not invincible. But together, we *can* be."

"Why would we ever join you?"

"Because we own you now," Eir said. "We made a bet with Captain Magnus the Bloody Handed, and we won your billet."

Rytlock convulsed, his claws raking out and narrowly missing his chirurgeons. "Damn it!"

"You have no choice," Eir said coolly. "You will go with us to fight the Dragonspawn."

Rytlock was trembling with fury, unable to speak.

Logan set a hand on his shoulder. "She's right. Trick or no trick, we've got to go."

Snaff winced as a chirurgeon set a hot towel on his shoulder. "The fact is, you three aren't gladiators."

"Aren't we?" barked Rytlock.

Snaff shook his head. "Of course not. You're heroes. You don't need to fight trumped-up battles against prearranged foes." He looked around at the stone ceiling. "You should be out beneath the sky, fighting *real* monsters."

Rytlock, Logan, and Caithe looked at each other, unsure what to say.

Snaff sighed. "We went after you because you were the heroes we needed. We set this whole thing up, crossed continents, designed golems, bet with our own lives to win your billet and to win you to our side. Yes, we can force you to join us, but we don't want henchmen. We want heroes."

Again, the members of Edge of Steel traded glances.

At last, Logan spoke for them all. "Tell us about the lair of the Dragonspawn."

From Her Royal Majesty, Jennah,
Queen of Kryta,
Regent of Ascalon
To Logan Thackeray

Greetings:

I have received word that you and your comrades are leaving the arena to go on a quest. Congratulations. I always felt that your courage was wasted on gladiators: you were meant for greater things.

But I fear that this quest is beyond even a hero such as yourself. Dragon champions are not to be trifled with. They are of themselves tremendously powerful, but they also tap into the inexhaustible power of their lords, the Elder Dragons. This Dragonspawn is the greatest champion of ancient and wicked Jormag and has destroyed countless heroes—whole companies of norn.

As your queen, I could forbid you to do this thing, but I have seen you defeat a legion of charr. I have seen you slay devourers and destroyers, centaurs and ettins and worse. If anyone could defeat the Dragonspawn, it would be you.

So, I will not forbid it. I will trade fear for hope and look forward to congratulating you on this latest and greatest of your victories.

Your queen,

Jennah

THE CALM BEFORE

Two weeks later, an amazing group passed through the Hoelbrak asura gate. First came Eir Stegalkin, her head breaking through the magical membrane beside the head of Rytlock Brimstone. The woman and the charr marched side by side, pulling a wagon behind them. The wagon was fully loaded, with a tarp strapped across its contents. On the tarp sat Snaff, looking quite satisfied, and Zojja, looking somewhat sour. On one side of the wagon walked Logan Thackeray in his much-scarred armor, and on the other side strolled Caithe of the Firstborn. Behind the conveyance loped the dire wolf Garm.

As this group emerged from the gate, the norn guards spread out in a semicircle around them. Two guards stepped before the wagon, planted spear butts in the road, and leaned the points toward Eir and Rytlock.

"Halt, there, Eir Stegalkin, by order of Knut Whitebear!" demanded a tall guard with blond braids.

Eir halted.

"Chilly welcome," Rytlock noted, looking impressed.

"Tell Knut Whitebear that I have returned with a band of warriors to slay the Dragonspawn," Eir ordered.

The guard nodded and turned to go but caught himself. "*I* give the orders here."

"Go tell him."

The guard's eyes locked with hers in a staring contest that he quickly lost. "That's *exactly* what I'm going to do." He handed his spear to the guard beside him and stormed off. "We'll see about this."

The other guard, his hair dirty white like glacial runoff, hitched his chin at the wagon. "What've you got in there?"

"Provisions," Eir said simply.

"Like what?"

"Like meat. Charr eat meat."

The charr flashed a smile.

The guard stared at Rytlock. "You look familiar. Are you a gladiator?"

Rytlock's smile only deepened. "One-third of Edge of Steel."

"Edge of Steel!" the guard said, smacking himself in the head. "Of course! You're famous. Everybody was talking about you, coming and going through the gate—so I went and saw you. Incredible! When you killed that destroyer harpy—"

"Racogorrix, yeah," Rytlock supplied, hitching a claw over his shoulder. "That was Logan—"

"I thought the crowd was going to tear the place down!" the guard enthused. His eyebrows suddenly knitted. "Hey, did I hear something about you guys losing a match?"

It was Eir's turn to smile. "*We* beat them."

"*You*? You three? You and these two?"

"We're geniuses," Snaff explained.

Eir nodded. "We three and the dire wolf. We're called Dragonspawn's Destiny."

"Yeah. Whoa! You beat Edge of Steel, and they *joined up* with you? That would make you, like, Edge of Dragonspawn's Steely Destiny . . . uh, what do you call yourselves?"

"Destiny's Edge," Eir supplied.

Just then, the first guard returned, followed by a broad norn warrior with much scarred skin. Knut Whitebear's eyes were black pits beneath his glowering brows.

Before he could speak, the second guard blurted, "Do you *know* who this *is*?"

"Eir Stegalkin," Knut said, addressing her.

"Not just her, but these are Destiny's Edge—the best gladiators ever with the band that beat them!"

Knut ignored the guard. "*This* is your band?"

Eir met his gaze. "Rytlock is a Blood Legion soldier, and Logan has fought for Queen Jennah. They, with Caithe, one of the firstborn sylvari, slew an ogre chiefling, his warband, and his hyenas. They killed devourers and destroyers and went undefeated in the arena in Lion's Arch—"

"But the rest of these are the same hapless creatures you took before—"

"The rest of these defeated this undefeated team in combat not two weeks ago," Eir said flatly.

Knut nodded, impressed, but doubt still lingered in his eyes. "What of those blasted clockwork creatures?"

"Do you see any?" Eir asked. "This is a force like no other. We go north to destroy the Dragonspawn."

Knut gritted his teeth. "You'd better not fail again, or his wrath will fall on us all."

"It won't happen again. We'll destroy him this time."

"Outlaw, huh?" Rytlock muttered as he and Eir drew the heavy wagon through Hoelbrak.

"Outcast, more like," Eir corrected, "temporarily."

The charr nodded. "An outlaw steals a pig. An outcast pretty much destroys a whole city."

"That's right."

Rytlock mulled the response for a while before asking, "What did you do?"

"Brought on a blizzard—twenty feet of snow. Ice sharp as daggers. Roofs caved. People died. The Dragonspawn did not like being nearly killed."

The charr whistled through his teeth. "Never leave an enemy alive. That was your mistake."

"It's the Dragonspawn's mistake, too."

Well north of Hoelbrak, the charr and the norn staggered to a stop and parked the wagon on the tundra. Just beside the wagon lay the wreckage of Big Snaff.

"There's one of them," Eir said.

The damage was severe. The golem's stone head had split in half, with Big Snaff's left eye and nose and mouth lying close by but the rest of his face some fifty feet away. His golem body lay in three pieces nearby—two mangled legs and a battered torso with broken arms.

Snaff and Zojja jumped down from the wagon to investigate. After a few minutes of stooping and peering, Snaff called back, "Worse than I thought."

"What happened to it?" Rytlock asked.

Eir pantomimed a pair of talons hoisting the golem into the air and letting it go.

"You mean, you marched that thing in against the Dragonspawn, and it hurled it back out?" Rytlock asked.

"Many miles back out," Eir replied.

"The stanchions are shattered," Zojja reported. "The servos are split. We could salvage some thylid crystals—maybe—use some of the gear work elsewhere—maybe—but there's no way this golem's going to fight again."

Garm let out a howl, his nose pointed north.

The team looked to the horizon, where the other broken figure lay.

"Take them there," Eir commanded.

The dire wolf trotted to Snaff, bit down on his shirt, and hurled him up across his back. The wolf then did the same for Zojja. Once the two were seated, he galloped out across the mossy ground, heading for the next wreck site.

"Let's go," Eir said, hauling on the wagon.

Amazed and unnerved, Rytlock staggered forward, pulling as well.

That night, the group gathered around a campfire. Eir and Rytlock reclined on the wagon they had hauled all day while Caithe, Logan, and the two asura perched on pieces of scavenged golem. Actually, the asura didn't perch. They worked. With wrenches and screwdrivers, mallets and awls, they struggled to resurrect the wreckage.

"This Snaff matrix won't fit inside the Zojja fuselage," Zojja complained.

"Do your best," Snaff replied, not for the first time. "It just has to *work*. It doesn't have to be pretty." He was currently replacing the shattered ankle joint of the golem.

"Can we march by morning?" Eir asked.

"Yes. Yes," Snaff responded absently, "by morning."

Logan took a deep breath of the frosty night air and looked to Eir. "Tell us about the Dragonspawn."

Eir nodded pensively. "The Dragonspawn isn't so much a man but a creature of ice and cold. He leads an army of the icebrood and Sons of Svanir."

"I've heard the name," Logan said. "What are they, anyway?"

"Two hundred fifty years ago, a hunter named Svanir and his sister Jora led a band of norn to slay the wolves that ruled Drakkar Lake. They were crossing the frozen waters when a strange presence grasped Svanir's mind. It whispered seductions to him, promised power and prey. It was a voice of infinite hunger and hate, and Svanir listened to it.

"Jora heard the voice, too, but it terrified her. She refused its dark gifts and tried to drag her brother away, but he struck her and told her she was weak, told her he had discovered the well of power. She fled.

"Svanir remained to commune with his newfound lord. In time, the voice began to change him. It taught him to hate all living things. It stripped him of his human form and made him a champion—half bear, half norn, encrusted with ice. Svanir wandered the wastes in madness, attacking any who came near. He became a monster that his own sister had to destroy.

"Over the next hundred fifty years, the voice seduced more norn, and they joined the cult, becoming the Sons of Svanir. They believed they were drawing upon the ancient voice, but in fact it was drawing upon them, gaining the power to rise.

"And it did rise. One of the Elder Dragons. Jormag was its name.

"We fought Jormag—gladly we fought it, for norn are made for battle. But never had we fought a beast like this. It was a living blizzard. It and its minions froze us where we fought and buried our lands in snow and ice and tore apart Gunnar's Hold with a massive glacier. It took our lands. It drove us south.

"And despite the destruction, there are still foolish norn who hear the call of Svanir and seek the power of Jormag. In the end they are reduced to icebrood themselves, flesh wrapped in ice, fed by malevolence and hatred."

As Eir's tale fell to silence, her comrades stared into the fire and listened to it crackle.

At last, Rytlock said, "You want us to destroy a living blizzard that defeated the entire norn nation?"

Eir's eyes were fierce. "I want us to destroy the dragon's champion, his right arm. When the Dragonspawn is dead, Jormag will be maimed. Then we can strike the dragon's heart."

Rytlock took first watch while Eir, Caithe, Logan, and Garm took their rest. Wrapped in blankets, they nestled down on the mossy tundra, seeking warmth. Only the two asura worked on. By the middle of Rytlock's watch, Zojja had became cruel and cranky, like a tired child. Her verbal barbs grew sharper by the minute, and at last Snaff sent her off to sleep.

Rytlock walked the perimeter. Overhead, a sickle moon tore through rags of cloud. On the icy desolation all around, moon shadows flitted like ghosts. Rytlock shivered. "We should let the dragon keep this place."

At the darkest corner of night, Rytlock returned to the camp to wake up Logan.

"You're quite a pair," came a nearby voice, accompanied by the rasp of a socket wrench.

"Hm?" Rytlock turned to see Snaff straddling the leg of the golem and working by the faint blue glow of a powerstone.

"You and Logan," Snaff replied, flashing a smile. He turned back to the conduits he was repairing. "After all this time, a charr and a human make peace."

"Ha!" Rytlock blurted, but then glanced toward the sleepers. He went on more quietly, "It's not peace. More like mutually assured destruction."

Snaff laughed. "Ah, it's more than that. He idolizes you."

"He covets my sword. It's not the same."

"Oh, it *is* the same. What little brother doesn't want what his big brother has?"

"And what big brother doesn't hate his little brother for wanting it?"

Snaff nodded. "Yes. I suppose that's part of the dynamic. Love and hate hand in hand. Apprentices feel the same way toward masters—love them for all the knowledge they have, and hate them for the same reason."

Rytlock glanced over at Zojja. "Nah. You're her whole world. She just doesn't know it yet."

"Funny how that works," Snaff said philosophically. "People become part of you, and you don't realize until they're gone."

"Right. Listen, uh, my watch is over and Logan's up next."

"Good, good. He'll be good company."

By the next morning, Rytlock, Logan, and Eir had each taken a watch while Snaff worked on. Soldering and shaping, rewiring and refitting—by the time he was done, Big Zojja had been resurrected. She stood at the edge of the camp, dented and dinged but ready for action.

Eir gazed soberly at the result. "You've worked a miracle."

"That's what I do," Snaff said with a smile.

Zojja rubbed sleep from her eyes. "Too bad the other one couldn't be salvaged."

Snaff's smile never wavered. "That's all right. We brought a spare."

"A spare?"

Snaff donned a powerstone laurel, and with a boom and a hiss, the tarp on the wagon bulged up and rose. The canvas dragged away to reveal the sand golem, towering there and grinning like his master.

"*That's* why the wagon was so heavy," Rytlock groaned. "Least we won't have to drag it any farther."

"Exactly."

Eir looked around at her crew—Big Zojja and Sandy, Little Zojja and Snaff, Garm, Caithe, Rytlock, and Logan. "All right, everyone, we have a long hike today, and a tough battle ahead. We have water and food for two more days. Beyond that, we'll have to live off the land."

"Oh, there's one more thing we need," Snaff broke in, fishing in his pocket. Behind him, Sandy seemed to do the same. Snorting, Snaff pulled off the powerstone laurel, letting the golem slump in a heap in the wagon. Snaff then pulled from his pocket a vial of gray dye. "We need tattoos."

"Tattoos?" Eir asked.

"As you know, the Dragonspawn has a mesmerizing aura that takes hold of minds. Last time, we combated it with gray powerstones on our armor—but if the stone gets struck from the armor, the result could be fatal."

Eir nodded, trying to follow the thread. "Yes, but— tattoos?"

"Powerstones in our skin!" Snaff enthused, holding up the vial. Tiny stone chips shimmered within the dye. "They'll block the mind of the Dragonspawn." He pulled back his tunic, showing a beautifully inscribed emblem that read DE. "That for us, Destiny's Edge, you know? Zojja has one, too. Show them."

Zojja huffed and pulled back her collar, revealing the same DE pattern in a slightly less deft hand.

"I did hers, and she did mine. Give us half an hour, and we'll have the rest of you done."

Reluctantly, the others agreed. Snaff inscribed the emblem onto Logan, then shaved a clear patch on Rytlock and Garm and did the same. Zojja took a bit more time and care to work on the shoulders of Eir and Caithe. In the promised half hour, though, the deed was done.

"Here," Snaff said, slipping the vial of gray dye into Eir's hand. "I'm always breaking things."

Eir took a long look at the vial, and an uncommon smile spread across her face. "I know just what to do with this." She slid the vial into her pocket. "Let's move out."

Claws, boots, bolts, and sandy pseudopods set out across the tundra, heading for the icy peaks in the north. They walked in a loose group, Caithe scouting ahead and Garm loping behind. Zojja rode within her golem, and Snaff rode atop Sandy's head.

The party moved at speed, and the land rolled back around them.

In time, Rytlock and Logan happened to be walking side by side. Neither wanted to fall back, and neither could casually stride ahead. As the awkward silence stretched, Logan at last ventured, "Listen. I know things haven't been right, not since I tried to take Sohothin."

The charr's hand settled on the hilt of his sword. "You'd better not try again."

"No. That's the whole thing. I never should have tried to take it. Sohothin is your sword. I see that now."

Rytlock looked Logan in the eye for the first time in weeks. "Really?"

"Really."

"You don't mind seeing a charr carry a 'man's sword'?"

"It's not a man's sword. It's a hero's sword. It's yours."

They walked a while longer in silence. Rytlock caught sight of Snaff, who just smiled back at him.

"It's going to be bad, you know," Rytlock said.

"Yeah," Logan said. "Worse than any gladiatorial team. Worse than destroyers or devourers or ogres."

Rytlock nodded. "Well, I've gone into a lot of battles with a lot of good warriors. You're as good as any of them."

"Thanks."

"The one thing they had that you don't—"

"Oh, here it comes."

"—is a Blood Legion pendant." Rytlock drew a chain from around his neck. On it hung the maroon and silver crest of the Blood Legion. "Here. Put it on."

Logan took the pendant and looked Rytlock in the eye. "I don't know what to say."

Rytlock gritted his teeth. "Damned human. You don't have to say anything. Just put it on."

"Thanks," Logan replied feebly, slipping the pendant around his neck.

"It's an honor wearing that thing, you know," Rytlock said, "an honor I don't think any other human has ever been given. It means we're brothers."

Logan flashed him a smile. "Oh, you're much better than *my* brother."

"I know," Rytlock replied with a laugh. "I've *seen* your brother."

Logan nodded, tucking the pendant between his breastplate and his chest. "Thanks. I want you to have something, too."

"What is it?"

Logan untied the silken scarf that Queen Jennah had given him. "You saw the day I got this."

"Yeah," Rytlock said heavily. "You killed Racogorrix that day."

"I fought for the queen that day." Logan handed the scarf to Rytlock. "You know how much she means to me, but I want you to have this."

The charr lifted his claws away. "I can't take that."

"Damned charr! Don't you know how to receive a gift?"

Reluctantly, Rytlock took the emblem from his friend's hand. He looked for a place to tie it—armor? hackle? horn? At last, he tied it to his sword belt. "Thank you." He looked around, seeing the rest of the group stare at him. Clapping his claws together, he said, "All right now. How much longer to this lair? I'm ready to kill a Dragonspawn."

INTO THE LAIR

Eir and her companions stood atop a frozen ridge and gazed down at the lair of the Dragonspawn. The wide cave mouth was fronted by rows of jagged ice, standing like fangs or horns in terrible clusters.

"You never told us about that," Rytlock pointed out. He patted the hilt of Sohothin. "Lucky for us, I brought an ice cutter."

Eir shook her head. "We can't go through it. It'll be filled with icebrood. We'll have to go *over* it."

Rytlock turned to her quizzically.

She smiled and said, "Avalanche."

Logan frowned. "Conditions have to be just right."

"He should know," Rytlock snarled in remembrance. "Guy specializes in rockslides." Under his breath, he added, "Jerk."

"I think we have *exactly* the right conditions," Eir said cryptically.

Just then, Big Zojja pounded up behind the others, her

footfalls cracking the ice they stood on. From the cockpit within, Little Zojja piped up, "Right conditions for what?"

The ground trembled again as Sandy thundered to the top of the ridge.

"What'd I miss?" asked Snaff, who stomped to a halt between Sandy's ears. "Sorry I lagged a bit. Set off a little avalanche back there."

Eir's smile broadened. "I brought along a pair of avalanche machines."

Caithe gestured along the rim of the valley, where a thick snowpack clung. "That ridge ahead should do the trick."

"Perfect," Eir said.

"Perfect for what?" Snaff and Zojja chorused.

Eir reached up to Sandy's head and lowered Snaff to the ground. "Can Zojja drive that thing from a distance?"

"Sure," Snaff said, "as long as she has the laurel."

"Come on out, Zojja," Eir commanded.

The windscreen on the cockpit cranked open, and after buckles clanged loose, Zojja emerged and climbed down the golem's leg. "What do you want?"

Eir said, "I want you and Snaff to march your golems on ahead to trigger an avalanche—one that'll sweep down over those defense works and bury them."

Snaff's eyes lit. "That'll be fun!" He began pumping his arms and stomping his feet, and Sandy marched excitedly away across the ridge.

Zojja glowered like a teenager watching her father dance. "You're enjoying this too much." Reluctantly she began marching as well, and Big Zojja pounded out after Sandy.

The two golems had crossed about a quarter mile of icy ridge before anything happened—but it happened all at once.

A thunderous *boom*! shook the ice, and a crack shot like black lightning along the ridge. The whole face of the ridge broke free. It slid down as one thick ice sheet, grating over the cliff face. A network of cracks raced through the ice, and it shattered into huge boulders. They stampeded down the side of the mountain and swarmed over the labyrinth. House-size ice chunks flattened the defensive works. Walls smashed and spikes shattered. Whatever icebrood might have lurked in those defenses were crushed. Hundreds of thousands of tons of ice wiped the barriers from the world.

"Perfect!" Rytlock said.

"Not quite," Eir replied, pointing toward the ridge.

Sandy had had one foot on either side of the crack when it gave way, and now the sand golem was struggling not to tumble down the slope. Already, its legs had stretched to twice their usual length. Big Zojja grasped Sandy's hand and tried to pull it back up.

"It's no good!" Snaff yelled. "Let go!"

"Too late," Zojja replied.

In the distance, Sandy toppled, dragging Big Zojja after it. They rolled together down the ice-ravaged rock face.

Little Zojja shook with each impact, eyes glazing.

Snaff grasped her. "Separate your mind!"

Down below, Sandy's head crashed into an outcrop of stone.

Snaff staggered, "Wow! That smarts."

Out across the ice field rolled Sandy and Big Zojja, clinging together like a giant, dirty snowball. They held each other a moment more before limbs of sand broke away from limbs of steel. A battered and gritty Big Zojja staggered back and toppled to the ground while Sandy shuddered as it reformed itself.

Meanwhile, on the ridge, Snaff released Zojja. "Are you all right?"

"Feel like I got run through a gearbox," Zojja said.

"Do you need to rest?" Eir asked them.

"Not me," Zojja replied huffily, "but I'd say the Big me is out of service."

They all stared down at the tableau, where Big Zojja lay twisted with smoke rising from her joints.

"That's not good," Eir said.

"Sandy's fine," Snaff put in hopefully, seeming to check his pockets.

The sand golem was meanwhile reshaping itself. It gave a massive wave.

Eir reached down and hoisted Zojja to her shoulders. "Phase One is complete, but we're down to a single golem. Someone grab Snaff. Let's move!"

Rytlock picked up Snaff, slung him onto his shoulders, and growled, "Don't touch the horns."

The asura sheepishly released them. "Sorry. They look like handlebars."

"I don't need to be steered," Rytlock said.

"Can't steer a steer," Snaff quipped.

"Shut up."

"Right."

Rytlock ran after Eir, with Logan and Caithe following.

Garm brought up the rear, his black head turning from side to side to make sure they weren't followed.

Moments later, the group reached Big Zojja. She was, indeed, beyond repair. One leg was shattered outright, and the conduits had been ripped from the knee of the other.

Zojja leaped down from Eir's shoulder. "That's a wasted night." She turned to Snaff. "I told you you put too much trust in metal."

Snaff was too grieved to reply.

Eir scowled at Zojja. "You seem almost gleeful that the golem is wrecked."

Zojja grinned. "I almost am."

Eir huffed. "Good luck fighting without it."

"I've been expanding my portfolio of spells for this," Zojja said with a grin. "*Fire* spells. You'll see how magic can trump machine."

"I hope," Eir said, watching Zojja march jauntily away.

Snaff stepped up beside Eir. "You must forgive her. She's a genius in the rough."

"She won't follow orders, she won't listen to others," Eir muttered.

"You're both strong-willed," Caithe broke in. "You're not followers."

Eir and Snaff gaped at her.

Caithe was wide-eyed. "Well, look, she's leading the charge."

They turned to see that Zojja had broken into a run.

"Let's go," Eir said ruefully, turning and charging after her. All the others followed. It took only a few moments for them to catch up to Zojja and pass her.

The group ran to the ice cave. It yawned darkly before them, a thousand icicles hanging overhead.

"Wouldn't like to get one of those down the back," Rytlock said.

"Rytlock and Logan, you'll take the fore," Eir said. "Garm and I will back you up. Sandy will back us up and give cover for Snaff and Zojja. Caithe, you're the rear guard. Weapons, everyone."

The group shifted into position. Sohothin roared from its scabbard, and Logan's war hammer spun in circles around him. Zojja cracked her knuckles and sent flames leaping into the air, while Sandy remolded one stretched-out leg. Behind them, Caithe scanned the rubble field, her daggers whirling.

Eir nocked three arrows. Their heads sparked with arcane energies prepared by Zojja.

Rytlock eyed the arrows. "More nets?"

"You'll see." Eir drew the bow until the string pinged with tension and then let fly. The three shafts whistled away into the cave, diverging from each other. Simultaneously, the arrowheads burst into three red fireballs. As they flew, the flames intensified to orange and yellow and white and blue.

They lit up a ceiling crowded with giant icicles. Among them lurked dragon minions in the form of ice bats.

"Whoa!" Rytlock said.

Another explosion came from each arrow. Shock waves cracked the icicles loose, and blue flames melted the wings of the bats. Giant icicles and watery bats plunged, crashing side by side on the icy floor of the cavern.

"Awesome," Logan said.

"Phase Two complete," Eir noted, then shouted, "Charge!"

Logan and Rytlock broke into a run, leading the rest into the ice cave. Ahead lay shattered icicles and bats flailing in their death throes. The flaming sword and the war hammer ended their torments.

As they ran on, Rytlock called over his shoulder, "What's ahead?"

Eir replied. "More dragon minions. They might be transformed norn, or more ice bats. I expect something much bigger, though. Stay sharp."

The team passed beyond the killing fields, rushing down a smooth throat of ice into a deeper, darker chamber. Eir fitted another shaft to her bow and let fly. The flaming comet soared through a deep, broad ice cavern with a smooth ceiling. There were no icicles, no lurking bats—only a colonnade of frozen pillars lining either wall.

"It doesn't feel right," Logan said.

Rytlock barked a laugh. "Course not. It's a monster's lair."

Together, they ran down the center of the chamber, between the pillars of ice.

A groan echoed up the cavern, as if the glacier itself moaned in pain. The floor shook beneath their feet.

A splintering sound came from a pillar to one side of Rytlock. He swung his flaming sword toward it, seeing the shaft pull free from the wall.

It wasn't ice, but an icy giant.

It lunged toward Rytlock, hurling a mace at him. He

ducked, but the icy spikes bashed one shoulder. "Damn!"
he growled. "It would have been nice to know about
these!"

Eir nocked another shaft and loosed it, point-blank.

The arrow cracked into the ice giant's chest and
exploded in its transparent heart. Red flame evolved to
orange and yellow, melting ribs. The fire turned white
and beamed from the giant's astonished eyes. Then the
wretched figure toppled.

Eir scrambled back as the massive warrior struck
ground. It burst open, its melted heart gushing across
the ice.

"Help!" shouted Logan from across the chamber.

Eir and Rytlock looked, seeing that he had been
snatched up by another frozen giant. The thing had lost
an arm, which lay in shattered ruins on the floor, but its
other arm hoisted Logan toward a mouth that bristled
with fangs.

Zojja rushed up to the creature and set her hands on
its leg. An orange curtain of flame blazed from her fingertips and ripped through the leg. The flame split the
icy limb and sent steam blasting from it. Falling back,
Zojja slapped hands on the other leg and blasted it, too.
The thighs of the giant slid outward over the calves and
cracked, dropping the torso. It struck ground and shattered. Cracks raced up it, and blocks of ice dropped loose.
The fangs that were just then biting down on Logan dis-
integrated, and the thing came apart around him.

Buried to his chest in chunks, Logan said, "Nice job,
little one."

"Little one!" Zojja seethed.

"You'd rather be big? Like Eir?"

"No," Zojja grumped. "Little is fine."

They turned to see that their teammates had the other giants well in hand. Sandy was pummeling the next two, and Caithe had scrambled up the back of a third. As it thrashed, she plunged her dagger into the seam at its neck and twisted. The neck cracked. The head slid off its massive shoulders and plunged face-first to crash on the floor. Bits of giant skull skittered out all around.

Eir, meanwhile, loosed shaft after shaft at the remaining giants.

Boom! Boom! Boom! They fell.

Suddenly, there was only silence in that deep, dark place.

"Onward!" Eir called.

Leaping over melted monsters, the companions formed up again and charged deeper.

"Ahead is the inner sanctum," Eir called out to them. "The Dragonspawn will be there."

They ran onward a thousand more paces before they reached the end of the chamber.

And it ended abruptly.

The team stopped atop a cliff that overlooked a deep, dark chamber. They couldn't see the bottom, but the space was far from empty.

A guttural roar erupted from it—a mob incensed at the sight of invaders.

"The inner sanctum," Eir said. She raised her bow and shot an arrow into the chamber. It flared, showing a mob of norn warriors—or once-norn.

None retained a fleshly body. All now were made of

ice and stone. Some had great spiked clubs for hands. Others had frozen plates jutting from their backs. Still more had monstrous faces stretched by forests of icy fangs. The arrow flew past them, showing perhaps five hundred before it struck the far wall and exploded.

"What in the Foefire are those things?" Rytlock wondered.

"Icebrood. Hundreds of years old, corrupted by the Dragonspawn. We'll take this battle to them."

"Phase Three?" Rytlock guessed.

"Phase Three," Eir said. "Snaff, stay up here and control Sandy. Caithe, stay here as well and guard him."

"Yes," the sylvari agreed.

"What are *we* doing?" Rytlock asked.

"You, Logan, Zojja, Garm, and Sandy are going down with me to fight them, to draw out the Dragonspawn." Turning, Eir nocked three shafts and sent them down into the cavern. Three more arrows followed, and three more before the first volley struck the floor. The arrowheads exploded, blasting apart their foes and clearing a patch at the cliff's base.

Eir slung her arm over Sandy and said to Logan and Zojja, "Climb on."

They did.

"Sandy, give our charr friend a ride," Eir commanded.

The sand golem grasped Rytlock and slung him up to piggyback.

"Take us down," Eir ordered.

The golem bounded from the cliff's edge and plunged. On the way down, Eir loosed six more shafts, tearing holes in the enemy army.

Sandy landed at the base of the cliff, legs flexing to take the impact. Eir, Logan, Rytlock, and Zojja rolled free and scrambled to their feet. Garm landed heavily beside them.

"Charge!" Eir shouted, sending arrows ahead of them. Explosions cleared the way.

Behind her came Sandy, marching over the icebrood. Giant feet crushed the ice minions, and giant hands smashed them. The few icebrood that evaded Sandy ran headlong into the charr, the man, the asura, and the dire wolf.

"At last, real combat!" Rytlock roared.

He reared back as a frozen sword glanced off his armor. Lunging, he rammed Sohothin through the body of an ice monster. The creature split, shards sliding past each other to splash on the ground. Rytlock spun around and seared the head off another warrior.

Logan meanwhile traded blows with one of the icebrood. Its ice axe rang against his breastplate, but his war hammer cracked against its knee. The warrior toppled to its back. Logan leaped on it and emptied its head with his maul.

He jumped back and flung his hand out. His fingers smeared blue aura in the air, solidifying it in a shield before Zojja. The icebrood pounded up to the shield but couldn't reach the asura apprentice.

Zojja sent gouts of flame bursting from her hands and melted the monsters all around.

Garm bulled through ranks, smashing them down to break on the icy ground.

Shattered shards, broken bodies, steaming pools—the comrades flattened the icebrood.

But then a blue-white light erupted in the center of the chamber. It emerged from the icy floor and pierced the ceiling and cast all in its horrid glow. Out of that shaft, a figure took shape. Its crystalline back was hunched and spiky, and spiraling energies infused its frigid frame.

"The Dragonspawn!" Eir cried, halting her team.

Even the icebrood fell back from that horrid presence.

The Dragonspawn's eye sockets beamed a wicked blue light across them all, and its icicle fingers weaved strange magics in the air. It spoke in a voice like ice grating on stone. *So, you have killed a hundred of my warriors?*

It was hard to reply, hard to scrape words together. The shaman's mind was filling the chamber, infusing every mind with its aura. Only the tattoos kept the companions' minds from being taken over entirely.

At last, Rytlock managed a few words: "We've killed . . . half your army."

A deep moan came, a sound of infinite misery that evolved into a drone of delight. *Not half. Not one-tenth!* The Dragonspawn flung out its algid arms, and purple light jagged from its fingertips.

The walls of the cavern shattered, tumbling to the floor to reveal more of the icebrood. Rank on rank, the dragon minions stretched into the unseeable distance.

Your sandman and your tiny band cannot kill them all. Nor will you kill me. Instead, I will make you my own.

Eir closed her eyes, fighting against the Dragonspawn's aura. She mustered the words "You have no power over us."

So many have said that, the shaman replied, *and have been wrong.* It beckoned to its troops. *Come to me!*

Thousands of icy feet pounded the ground. The icebrood converged on Eir and her companions.

"We must escape," Logan muttered, fear creeping up his spine.

"Sandy can get us out," Rytlock added.

Eir shook her head. "That's the Dragonspawn talking."

Rytlock said, "Your plan has failed."

"Not yet." Eir pulled another exploding arrow from her quiver.

"What are you going to do?" Rytlock raged.

Eir drew the gray vial from her pocket. "Adapt the plan." She rammed the vial into the explosive head and said, "Phase Four." Eir aimed at the Dragonspawn and launched the shaft.

The arrow whined through the air and crashed into the shaman's icy chest. It exploded. A fireball engulfed the Dragonspawn, embedding tiny gray powerstones all across its figure. The shaman's mesmeric mind, which once filled the cavern and drowned out all other minds, suddenly imploded.

The mental onslaught ceased.

Eir and the others could think again.

The Dragonspawn was cut off from every mind in the chamber—cut off even from the mind of its master.

The marching armies faltered. A thousand ice warriors halted. They had obeyed the Dragonspawn because it was the champion of their lord. Now, it was only a terrible, foreign power in their midst. They turned from Eir and her comrades and turned on the Dragonspawn.

They were no longer marching but running, converging on the spectral creature. The icebrood tore into the Dragonspawn. They ripped off its icy arms and cracked open its body and shattered its head. Each time a shard came away, though, the storm of energies around the Dragonspawn whipped wider. It became a whirling cyclone. Its circling arms bashed into its attackers.

"Is *this* what you planned?" Rytlock yelled.

"In the end." Eir nodded. "The lust for power turns on itself."

The swirling storm of blue magic around the Dragonspawn picked up the icebrood and smashed them together. They broke into flying shards of ice and stone, which spiraled around the dragon champion. It was taking a new shape, not as a single entity but as an ice storm. The souls and bodies of its minions were becoming part of the champion. Already, the cyclone of ice and stone whirled fifty feet high and twenty feet wide, and it roared as it consumed even more of the icebrood.

"The Dragonspawn seems to be winning," Rytlock noted. "What's Phase Five?"

"Escape," Eir said grimly. She turned and ran, with Rytlock, Logan, Zojja, and Garm close behind. Eir shouted back to Sandy, "Get us out of here!"

THE NEW CHAMPIONS

The Dragonspawn whirled, a wintry cyclone ripping apart the icebrood. Their ravaged bodies—shards of ice and stone—only added to his spinning form. The vortex shuddered as it grew. Already, the storm reached the ceiling of the ice cavern.

Eir meanwhile reached the ice cliff, with Garm beside her and Logan and Rytlock arriving next. Eir shouted back to Sandy, "Hurry up! We've got to ride you to the top!"

Sandy stretched its legs, pounding up to the cliff. It turned toward Eir, laced gritty fingers together, and held its hands out to her.

She hitched her foot into the golem's hands and launched herself up, intending to reach its shoulders.

Sandy had other ideas, hurling her straight up the cliff face to where Snaff waited.

Rytlock goggled. "It just killed her."

Eir soared upward, reached the top of the cliff, and clawed her way to safety.

"Actually, it just saved her," Logan noted in awe.

Sandy snatched Logan up in one hand and hurled him like a spear. Shouting, Logan spiraled up toward the cliff top. He tried to see where he was going, but everything was a concentric blur. Just when he was losing momentum, topping the arc, Eir snagged him out of the air and dragged him onto the cliff.

Below, Rytlock looked dubiously at the golem. "That's not going to work for me. I weigh more than—"

Sandy grabbed his wrists and ankles and swept him off his feet, so that he hung like a hammock between the golem's hands. Rytlock roared in humiliation as the golem spun around, building up momentum. At last, it flung the charr. Rytlock whirled like a horseshoe, wailing all the while, toward the top of the cliff. When he reached it, though, he was turned the wrong way, his back striking the icy edge.

"Damn."

Down he slipped, plunging toward his death—

Except that Eir grabbed his arm and hauled, and Logan latched onto his armor and pulled as well. They scraped him up the ice edge and dumped him safely atop it.

"Thanks."

"Look out!"

Rytlock rolled away just as a black dire wolf materialized out of the darkness, bounding onto the ice sheet where the charr had lain. On the wolf's back rode a red-faced asuran apprentice.

Eir made a quick visual check. "We're all here except Sandy." She turned to Snaff. "Climb Sandy out!"

But the asura master didn't seem to hear. He was running in place, his eyes gazing into the darkness.

Eir knelt before him and said quietly, "We're all safe. You can climb him out now."

Snaff's head shook briefly, and he kept running.

"We lost," Eir admitted. "That thing'll rip Sandy apart."

Still, the asura ran.

"It'll take his body and use it. It'll take *your mind!*"

Snaff stopped running.

Rytlock held out his flaming sword and craned over the cliff's end. The fiery light faintly sketched out the figure of Sandy far below, plunging into the huge cyclone of ice. Boulders and hailstones pounded him. At first, they only dented the golem, but then a huge chunk of ice smashed into Sandy's arm, ripping it off.

"Get him out!" Eir implored.

It was too late. The cyclone ripped away more of the golem. Powerstone-laden sands eroded into the vortex. Sandy stood only a heartbeat more before the final crystals were torn away.

Gone.

Snaff went rigid, his eyes wide, gazing into horrors. Then he began to spin as if he held a dance partner. He picked up speed, turning faster and faster.

"It's got him for sure," Rytlock said.

"No," Zojja broke in, watching with wide eyes. "No. *He's* got *it.*"

And then they saw: The cyclone flexed like a giant arm and shoved up against the ceiling of the cave. The ice moaned. The storm whirled tighter. The ceiling cracked.

The cavern shook.

"He's trying to bring the place down."

Snaff crouched down for a moment, then thrust his arms up again.

The vortex gathered itself like a spring and then launched upward. It smashed into the ice, and a thousand cracks radiated out.

The ceiling slumped.

"We better get out of here," Logan said.

"Not until he's done," Eir replied.

Snaff crouched down and launched himself upward again, and the cyclone did likewise.

It bashed through the ceiling.

Gigantic icebergs hailed down. They smashed through the cyclone, dispersing it, and shattered the icebrood and continued to cascade, filling the chamber..

"He's done," Rytlock said, scooping up Snaff.

"Let's go," Eir agreed, hoisting Zojja.

The companions turned and ran, blown forward by a gale as the cavern collapsed. Hunks of ice pummeled their backs.

Then sparking blue energies swept out around them.

"Ball lightning!" Eir shouted, ducking one sphere.

"Don't let it touch you!" Zojja yelled. "It's the leftover essence discharging!"

More spheres shot out through the chamber and rebounded off the icy walls. Lightning arced from sphere to sphere. The companions ducked and weaved as they ran amid the glowing globes. Stray tracers lashed them or jolted into them, each stinging with the frigid mind of the monster . . . but his power was fading.

At a run, the invaders launched themselves up the next throat of stone and ran on through the hall where the ice giants had died. The ceiling was cracking apart, spilling sunlight across the broken figures below. The cracks spread down the walls, and great hunks of ice caved inward. Massive blocks pounded down all around them.

Speed was the thing, and Rytlock, Eir, and Logan poured it on. Caithe struggled to keep up, but Garm snatched her up and hurled her onto his back.

A house-size hunk of ice plunged from above them.

The dire wolf's claws skittered on the icy floor as he struggled to outrun the block.

Boom! The slab staved the floor right behind Garm. A black line snaked after him, splitting the ice at his paws.

With a yelp, he dodged away from the opening rift, following Rytlock, Eir, and Logan through the chamber of the ice bats. A few more bounds brought them out of the collapsing cavern and into the spanking sunlight of the glacier. Still, they ran, rushing beyond the avalanche zone until they could stand on scoured bedrock. Only then did they turn to look at what they'd wrought.

Behind them, the lair of the Dragonspawn imploded. The ceiling fell in, and millions of tons of ice buried the horrors that lay below. The roar of it—the earth-shattering roar of it—was like a deafening ovation.

The Dragonspawn was gone.

The Dragonspawn and a thousand of the icebrood were destroyed.

Logan whooped, "How's that for a job well done?"

"It's not done yet," Zojja said, nodding toward Rytlock, who set down Snaff.

"Snaff," Rytlock said, staring into the golemancer's eyes. "Snaff. Snap out of it!"

Snaff reached numbly to the golden laurel that encircled his head and drew it off. The red powerstones in it flashed and then faded to darkness. He blinked at Rytlock. "That *hurt*."

"Guess it was kind of a rough ride."

"Not that," Snaff said in a weary voice. "Getting crushed by a glacier."

Eir laughed. "You did it, though, you know? You destroyed the Dragonspawn."

"No." Snaff shook his head, looking around at them all and smiling weakly. "*We* did it."

"They did it!" shouted the crier in the marketplace of Hoelbrak. "Destiny's Edge destroyed the Dragonspawn! They slew a thousand of the icebrood!"

As Eir and her friends marched proudly into Hoelbrak, norn warriors gathered along the central way to stand at attention. Bakers and brewers and weavers brought loaves of bread and barrels of ale and robes of wool. Towering hunters and rangers stood shoulder to shoulder and cheered as the band passed through their midst. Norn children—as tall as Logan but wide-eyed and young—pushed through the crowd to gawk in awe as the famous warriors passed, then darted through back alleys to take up new positions and stand in awe again. After squeezing in a third time, the children ran off to empty fields where they made believe they were the slayers of the Dragonspawn. The girls argued over which was Eir and Caithe (and Zojja), and the boys fought over who was Rytlock and Logan and Snaff (and Garm).

But the one who seemed most appreciative of all was Knut Whitebear. He waited for the honorees outside the hunting hall, flanked on both sides by the Wolfborn. A smile lurked within Knut's braided beard, and his eyes sparkled like flecks from a glacier. As Eir and her friends approached, Knut lifted arms mantled in white bear-skin and said, "Welcome home, daughter of Hoelbrak, daughter of the norn." He stepped forward, unfolding an ermine cloak.

Eir knelt so that he could set the cloak on her shoulders.

"You who once were outcast have returned to us victorious, as a norn should. Well done. You and your friends"—he paused to look at each of them—"are welcome now and forever in Hoelbrak."

The crowd cheered, and Knut Whitebear clasped Eir's hand and raised it overhead.

She shot him a fierce look. "You should not have doubted me."

He grinned, not looking at her. "I did not doubt you. I doubted that anyone could do what you set out to do."

"I have greater things I will do."

"I hoped you would say that." Still holding her hand, Knut Whitebear led Eir and the others into the great hall of Hoelbrak, to the fang of Jormag, embedded in the ground. The fang was a sacred relic from the dragon, harder than diamond. Thousands of norn had tried their blades against it, but none could even dent the fang. Walking beside it, Knut leaned his head toward Eir. "So, when will you challenge the dragon's tooth?"

Her smile faded slightly, but she turned to the revelers all around and cried out, "Let the feast begin!"

A great cheer rocked the rafters of Hoelbrak.

And what a feast it was! The fires of Hoelbrak had been stoked, and six caribou turned on spits above them. There were kettles of stew and mounds of bread and barrels of beer. The whole hall filled, with revelers arriving throughout the day and evening. Every warrior in the area converged to gaze on this ragtag band, came to lift a mighty flagon to their health and hear them tell their tales of valor.

As the ale and mead flowed, the crowd thickened around Snaff and Zojja, the best storytellers in the group. Snaff's account was florid and fantastic, and Zojja's interruptions were comically earnest. When they pantomimed Sandy's fight against the whirling cyclone, the hunting hall filled with laughter and cheers.

Caithe endured the festivities as long as she could. The crowd was unsettling to her—so many people crossing paths, so many false words spoken. Snaff was perhaps the worst. Everything he said was an exaggeration, which meant a *lie*, but still the norn roared with approval.

"Why should the Dragonspawn's defeat be commemorated with lies?" Caithe wondered to herself as she stepped from the hunting hall.

"You never could enjoy a party," came a voice like scarlet silk.

Caithe gasped, turning to see Faolain. "What are you doing here?"

"I've been following you," Faolain said, standing in her black-orchid dress, leaning in so that her warm breath wafted across Caithe's ear. "I've watched you risk your life to kill a dragon champion. Foolish girl."

Caithe stared quizzically at her. "You act as if it is nothing."

"It *is* nothing. Your life is too precious for this."

Caithe pushed Faolain back. "I don't belong to you."

"Don't you?" Faolain's black fingernails flashed to pull back the collar of Caithe's shirt. There, above her heart, a black handprint marked her skin. "Your heart belongs to me."

"No!" Caithe said, prying Faolain's hand loose and turning away. "I reject the Nightmare."

"But you love me." Faolain nodded toward Eir and Rytlock within the hunting hall. "Do they love you, as I do?"

Caithe scowled. "I don't know what they feel. They are a mystery to me."

"But I am not. There are no mysteries between us." Faolain's black eyes grew suddenly intense. "Join me! The Dream is only a dream. The Nightmare is the reality."

"Leave me."

The dark sylvari took an unsteady step toward Caithe. "My love is poisoning you. You cannot be without me."

"Go!"

Snaff was in the middle of another retelling when Caithe staggered into the hunting hall as if drunk—except that she had tears running down her cheeks.

Snaff broke away from the group he had been entertaining and approached Caithe. "Tears?"

Caithe dashed them away. "They're nothing."

"Nothing? They're everything. They're what you *feel*. Why are you crying?"

"It's nothing," Caithe averred, rubbing her hand on her cheek.

Snaff said levelly, "You wouldn't cry unless the world itself was in danger."

Her eyes glistened. "It is!"

"What danger?" Snaff asked.

"The dragons. No one is fighting the dragons, but we must. We stopped a dragon champion, but what about the power behind him?"

"You're right," Snaff said gently, "but that's not why you're crying."

Caithe stared at him, her eyes wide but searching, trying to decide if she could trust him. "It's that someone I care about has chosen the wrong path."

Snaff bowed his head and pursed his lips. "Anyone I know?"

"No." Caithe shook her head. "Another sylvari. She has gone to Nightmare."

Snaff nodded. "I'm sorry. Every creature must choose her own path."

"But what can I do? I have to save her."

Snaff smiled sadly. "You can't save anyone but yourself. I can't save my own apprentice, though she means more to me than the world. I can only be good to her and hope she notices, hope she learns from me." His expression clouded. "She will outlive me, as she should. She will face horrors that I will not. And in those moments, I hope she remembers my strength, not my weakness."

Caithe stared at him for a searching moment. "She will. She will remember."

"And this one that you care about—she will remember, too."

The east was gloaming with approaching dawn when at last Eir and her comrades bid farewell to the other revelers. They staggered to the rooms prepared for them—the finest in Hoelbrak, which meant huge beds and simple linens and great basins for washing. It was more than any of them could have hoped for, and each was asleep the moment his or her head hit the pillow.

They slept all through the day and into the next night, awakening to hear the sounds of more merrymaking— *norn* merrymaking, which sounded like a continual bar fight punctuated with ferocious laughter. Norn were streaming into Hoelbrak from dozens of miles away—the wild wanderers and the loner nomads who had only just heard of the Dragonspawn's destruction and of the team that did him in. Every one of these new arrivals had suffered beneath the terrible reign of the dragon champion. Every one had battled the icebrood. They now gathered to give thanks and gawk, to have a drink or five and celebrate heroes whose deeds would be retold for generations.

Eir retired from the second night of celebration a little earlier than the others, and Garm went with her. He watched her with interest. She had that look—the look of planning something.

First, she went to the statue of her father. "I did it, Father. I killed the icebrood, and the Dragonspawn, too."

She paused as if expecting some response from the stony figure. The old man only returned her gaze, his eyes seeming to look beyond her.

Eir looked down at her feet. "I know. There's still the dragon. He's crippled now, without his greatest champion, and maybe we can strike."

Still, the statue watched her impassively.

Eir went to her drafting desk, drew out a scrap of paper, and began drawing. At first, the figure was the Dragonspawn, and then, the Dragonspawn devolving into a cyclone, and then Sandy being pulled into the monster. She sat back and blinked.

Garm nuzzled her.

"Perhaps it is time to make a try at the old wyrm."

The wolf looked levelly at her.

She smiled, ruffling the fur between his ears. "I'll start by chipping its tooth."

Next afternoon, before the celebrations began in earnest, Eir strode down the lanes of Hoelbrak. Her carving belt jangled, her axes and mallets hung in hand, and her dire wolf jogged beside her.

"She's going to take on the fang!" shouted one of the norn revelers.

Many followed this living legend as she made her way toward the hunting hall. The crowd seemed to swell with each step Eir took. They had heard the magnificent tales of the Dragonspawn's defeat, and whatever this woman planned next must be even more spectacular.

Among the crowd were Eir's companions, following with excitement and a mixture of other emotions. When Rytlock and Logan had heard what Eir planned, they had wanted to lend their weapons to the attempt. Snaff had even wanted to bring Sandy to bear. Eir refused them all, saying she was their leader, and that if she was not strong enough to break the tooth, they would not face the dragon.

Caithe and Zojja were not starry-eyed about the prospects, either. Caithe knew all too well the power of the dragons, and she feared that Eir was only setting herself up for failure. Zojja, on the other hand, thought it absurd that physical attacks could do anything against a magical creature.

Dragging along a crowd of believers and skeptics, friends and foes, Eir reached the hunting hall of Hoelbrak and hurled the doors open. She strode in, and the crowd around her flooded in as well. Eir headed straight toward the central feature of the hall—the Fang of the Serpent. This relic of the dragon had been brought back by the great hero Asgeir and rooted in the floor of the hall—a challenge to all norn champions. If they could not chip or dent or scratch the fang, they had no hope of facing and defeating Jormag himself.

Eir strode up before the fang, which was eight feet tall, broad, curved, and icy white. The crowd murmured excitedly as they settled in around it. Eir's eyes traced across them all, and she bound her red hair back from her shoulders.

"You have heard great tales of us, of the ones who slew Jormag's champion. But we did this thing only to weaken the dragon himself. I've come here tonight to see if he is weak enough that we can face him."

The crowd applauded, watching avidly as she drew two great axes from her belt. When she began to swing the axes in wide arcs, though, the spectators fell back.

"Spirit of Wolf, guide my work."

The two blades crossed in midair, and then Eir lunged forward, and the heads came down on either side of the tooth. They crashed into it, their keen edges biting into the hard whiteness—but no. *It* was biting into *them.* The axes skirled down the fang in a shower of sparks, their faces worn away in curves.

Eir looked at the blades, burrs rising from their ruined edges. She tossed the axes aside. "Axes are for trees," she said, and the crowd laughed. Eir drew from her belt a large, keen chisel and a great mallet. "Imagine these on your own tooth."

As the crowd cringed, Eir positioned the chisel in a line that ran the length of the fang. She raised the mallet and brought it down with a *crack.* The fang showed no damage. She reared back with the mallet and pounded the chisel again. *Crack!* Still no fault shown on the fang. Then she took a deep breath and struck it an almighty *CRACK!*

The fang was unharmed, but the chisel's end had curled over.

Eir dropped the chisel and mallet beside her. She also let fall the whole belt of tools. Closing her eyes, she raised her face toward the dark rafters high above and said, "Spirit of Bear, guide my work."

She swung her arm at the fang, but before she could strike it, fingers had become claws. The foreleg of a great grizzly lashed at that tooth. Claws rasped across it but left no mark. From the other side, more claws ripped at it. These were claws that could tear down a young tree, could scratch stone, but the fang stood, inviolate. Now fully a bear, Eir lunged in to set her own massive teeth against the dragon's great tooth. Enamel skirled, but no harm came to the Fang of the Dragon.

Eir reeled back, her figure transforming again into that of a norn warrior—shaking, sweating, enervated, and defeated. She looked out numbly at the crowd.

Rytlock stepped up, pulling Sohothin free. "Let me have a shot at that thing."

Logan arrived with hammer in hand. "Me, too."

"No!" Eir snapped. "We're done here. Let me through! Let me go!"

Her friends pushed back the crowd and moved in to hold her up as she went.

"It's fine," Snaff said softly as they moved along. "So, we're not ready yet. But we *will* be. We'll defeat the dragons. Together, we can defeat anything."

That night, there were more gifts and feasts and stories and ale. But Eir was quiet through it all, and all the comrades felt the weight of what had happened. Even more norn had flooded into town. From hundreds of miles, they had come, and the merrymakers from the last two nights had not dispersed. The sound of the ongoing party was like a logging camp next to a stockyard beside a slaughterhouse.

"With an army like this, they could have done it without us," Eir muttered.

She gathered her companions and led them to her workshop. "I've had about as much of this as I can take," she confessed.

Rytlock laughed out loud, but then looked around at the others, saw that they agreed with Eir, and sullenly stared at his claws.

"Norn ale is stiffer than most," Logan said, rubbing his forehead. "And norn pints are gallons."

"That's what I *like*," Rytlock said.

"And here they are!" came a new voice at the workshop door—a deep voice that was somehow both jovial and ferocious. Eir and her companions turned to see Captain Magnus the Bloody Handed. He towered in the doorway, his pistol-strewn bandoliers gleaming in the lantern light. A smile lurked beneath his long mustache. "I came all the way from Lion's Arch to toast Destiny's Edge, the slayers of the Dragonspawn—and yet, no one knew where you were."

"Here we are," Eir replied.

Magnus sighed, his breath ghosting from his nostrils. He stepped into the workshop. "Well, anyway, congratulations!"

"Something like that."

Magnus set his boot on a nearby chair and leaned toward them all. "Now I need a favor."

Logan said, "What kind of favor?"

"Help me hunt down and destroy another dragon champion."

Rytlock arched an eyebrow. "*Who* is this dragon champion?"

"His name is Morgus Lethe," Magnus responded. "He rules the black seaways beyond Lion's Arch—he and swarms of undead. They attack ships and tear through their hulls and drop them to the bottom. They kill hundreds of sailors a week and turn them into more undead."

"Can't you handle a few undead?" Rytlock asked. "After all, they *are* prekilled."

"One by one, they are nothing, but where there's one, there's a thousand."

Logan put in, "If you haven't noticed, there are only seven of us."

"Yes, but you defeated a thousand before," Magnus replied. "And I have a personal score to settle with this devil Morgus Lethe. In life, he was a norn like me, captain of the *Cormorant* before me. Since he fell among the undead, they have known our every move, our every route, our tactics, our vulnerabilities. I need—"

"You need strangers," Eir interrupted.

Magnus nodded thoughtfully. "You've destroyed one dragon champion. Help me destroy another."

"We must," Caithe said. "If we are not yet powerful enough to face down a dragon, we must face down their champions. We must fight them."

Logan shrugged. "Sounds less dangerous than another night of celebration in Hoelbrak."

Rytlock growled. "I'm not leaving until *tomorrow.*"

Caithe, Logan, and Rytlock exchanged looks, and Caithe spoke, "We'll go."

"Of course we'll go," Eir said, "all of us. We go not just because you asked, but to destroy another dragon champion—"

"Wonderful!" Magnus proclaimed. "Morgus Lethe, prepare to meet Destiny's Edge!"

From Her Royal Majesty, Jennah,
Queen of Kryta and so forth . . .
To Logan Thackeray

Greetings:

The news spreads through Kryta of your conquest of the Dragonspawn. Congratulations, my dear Champion. I knew that my trust in you was well placed. Your brother was relieved to hear the news as well, though he hid it with annoyance. Comparing your battles against icebrood to his long days guarding castle walls, I can see why he might be jealous. I hope that, someday, you both find common ground and brotherhood.

I had hoped you would return to Divinity's Reach, but I hear that is not to be. With the news of your victory also came a report of your next mission: to face Morgus Lethe, champion of the dragon Zhaitan.

It seems you are most alive in the heart of danger.

My heart tells me to forbid you to go. I should. An entire army would have difficulty facing Lethe. You are my champion, not one of Captain Magnus

the Bloody Handed's sailors. But I know you will
not turn away from danger. Not when doing so
could aid Kryta. And in that, I support you.

But if you lose to Morgus Lethe, it would be
worse than losing an army.

So, your Queen must allow you to go. Yet still,
I think of you often. I imagine you marching across
blasted tundra, battling monsters in caves of ice,
standing stalwart against our enemies. Perhaps I
am just imagining the battles you fight, but I choose
to believe we have a deeper bond. When you are
finished killing Lethe—which I know you will do—I
hope that you will come to Divinity's Reach. I would
see you once more, and greet you as a true hero of
our grateful nation.

Your grateful queen,

Jennah

MORGUS LETHE

Two weeks later, Captain Magnus the Bloody Handed led a pair of tiny geniuses on a tour of his gigantic galleon—the *Cormorant*. "Through here, we have the captain's quarters," Magnus said as he pushed back a pair of twelve-foot-tall doors. "A little cramped."

"Spacious! Tremendous!" Snaff said.

Zojja started to march off the dimensions of the room.

Snaff went on, "We could fit two golems in here if we put the table, bunk, ale cask, and so forth into storage."

The captain colored slightly but managed a laugh. "No. This is the *captain's* quarters, not the golems' quarters."

"Fifty feet wide by forty feet deep," Zojja announced with satisfaction.

"Fifty by forty?" Magnus said. "It's hardly twenty-five by twenty!"

"I'm using asuran feet. More accurate," Zojja said. She glanced at his boots. "I'd never measure in norn feet!"

Huffing in annoyance, Magnus reached down to cup the asura's backs and shuffle them out of his quarters. "How about we look in the hold? Plenty of room in the hold for golems."

"The hold!" Snaff gazed admiringly at the captain. "Where you *hold* things. You maritime types are quite literal, aren't you?"

Captain Magnus shepherded them across the deck, ignoring the sniggers of his mates. He jabbed fingers into a wooden grate and yanked it upward. "There it is— the hold of the *Cormorant,* big enough for a thousand large crates."

Snaff and Zojja waddled up to the hatch and stared down into the huge, dark hold, loaded with crates and casks. The asura began muttering back and forth.

"A thousand large crates? I'd say ten thousand large crates."

"He's talking norn-large, not asura-large."

"Ahem," Captain Magnus interrupted. "How does it look to you?"

"Most suitable!" Snaff pronounced with a grin. "Of course, we'll have to off-load all this cargo, and you won't be able to man the cannons you have down there, and we'll need to cut six new hatches, three along each rail, with trapdoors—"

"Cut new hatches? With trapdoors? The crew will fall through!"

Sighing, Snaff climbed up on a nearby barrel so he could look the captain in the eye.

"What is it?" Magnus asked.

"Eir said we needed to turn your ship into an undead

destroyer," Snaff explained patiently. "This is how we'll do so."

Captain Magnus stroked his black mustache. "I suggest a change of plan. You'll not be turning *Cormorant* into an undead destroyer. You'll be doing it to *that* ship." He pointed to a vessel moored nearby. "A barque."

Snaff dubiously scanned the ship. "*Bark* like a dog?"

"No, *barque* like a ship. You should know barques. They're asuran. Just your size."

It was not just small. It was decrepit.

"Hmm," Snaff mused. "Looks burned."

"Part of it is. But, look, it's seaworthy. It's got a solid hull. That's all you really want, right?"

Snaff sniffed. "It's too small."

"Take two, then," Captain Magnus said, gesturing to a second barque docked in the shadow of the first. It was somehow even shabbier.

"Where'd you get them?"

"Saved them—but only just—from Morgus Lethe," said the captain. "Both crews—asuran crews—were lost."

"Sadly, asuran krewes are often lost," Snaff said reflectively. After a few more moments of thought, Snaff jabbed his hand out toward the captain. "We'll take them. Very soon, those barques will be barking at Morgus Lethe!"

Smiling ruefully, the captain took the asura's tiny hand and shook it.

The preparations for war took two months.

While Snaff and Zojja labored away to retrofit the

pair of barques, Eir, Logan, Rytlock, Caithe, and Garm learned the ways of the sea. Captain Magnus took them out in the *Cormorant* for training expeditions.

They learned how to keep their feet on rolling decks, how to climb ratlines in a gale, how to furl and unfurl sail, how to hurl grapnels and board ships and fire blunderbusses. More than once, a companion ended up in the drink, and sadly for Rytlock, no hyenas were near at hand. After his first plunge, sinking like a stone, Rytlock was required to wear a safety line tied around his waist. Of course, when they used it to to haul him out of the sea, he rose backside first. Rytlock quickly learned to swim, if only to shuck that embarrassing line.

He also learned to keep down his lunch, though he would often be a little green beneath his dark fur.

Meanwhile, Eir learned the charts, the currents, and the hazards of the local seaways, as well as the lairs of their enemy. Captain Magnus made sure they never approached the unholy sanctum of Morgus Lethe, for to do so would be to draw him out, but he showed Eir on the charts where it lay. It was a maelstrom above a great graveyard of ships. To go into those waters would be certain death—unless they were prepared.

At last, they were.

The galleon *Cormorant* breasted through gray waves beneath a gray sky. Her sails snapped white overhead, straining with the elemental wind that Zojja had called up to carry them across the sea. The deck of the ship groaned beneath four hundred boots—crew at battle stations. Gunners loaded cannons, fighters drew blunderbusses, and necromancers readied vials of enchanted acid. Grim-jawed, they braced for war.

Captain Magnus the Bloody Handed manned the helm. His eyes glowed with the thrill of the hunt, and his hands held the wheel in a steady beat against north winds. Beside him stood Eir Stegalkin, slayer of the Dragonspawn. Logan, too, was there, assigned to guard Snaff and Zojja. The two asura stood nearby, wearing golden laurels and swaying slowly. Rytlock and Garm were stationed along the starboard rail, tasked with deck-to-deck fighting, and Caithe had taken up her position in the crow's nest.

Eir had planned out the whole battle, giving assignments to each of her friends. She had even asked Zojja to enchant every weapon aboard to strike hard and true against undead. Everything was in place.

Now, they just waited for Morgus Lethe.

"Do you think we've scared him off?" Eir asked, scanning the choppy waters ahead.

Captain Magnus shook his head. "Lethe doesn't scare off. The *Cormorant* gives him pause, aye, but only until we're fully above his lair." The captain nodded to the fore. "We're approaching it now."

Eir perched a hand over her eyes and saw it—a hundred yards beyond the bow, a black maelstrom. A wide, roaring pit opened in the choppy seas, and water rushed down into some black abyss. "The lair of Morgus Lethe, champion of Zhaitan."

"Aye. That maelstrom swirls above a deepwater drop-off, where the sea falls away to a bottomless rift. It's a

maelstrom that drags ships down. Beneath that vortex
lie a thousand wrecks, home of Morgus Lethe's undead
navy." Captain Magnus lifted his ear, listening to the slap
of waves before the *Cormorant.* "They'll hear our bow
wave, see the shadow of our hull. It'll bring them up.

Captain Magnus spun the wheel, and the bow shifted
to point south of the whirlpool. Sails bellied full as they
tacked into a run. "Split up the barques," the captain
commanded, "one north and one south."

"Aye, Captain," Snaff and Zojja chorused. They closed
their eyes, and red powerstones gleamed in their golden
laurels.

In the boiling wake of the *Cormorant,* a pair of asuran
barques rode low in the water. They seemed to be heavily laden cargo vessels, ripe for the picking. In fact, they
held a surprise—one linked to the golden laurels on
the asura's heads. As they sent impulses from the powerstones, one barque veered north and the other south.

Caithe called down from the crow's nest, "There's
something shifting in the maelstrom!"

Eir went to the starboard rail and stared down at the
green-gray waters. They sloped away into a deep vortex.
The heart of the whirlpool was black, but in the swirling waters, Eir glimpsed shadowy figures. An emaciated
arm, for just a moment, and then what seemed a knobby
spine, and then a skull draped in ratty hair or seaweed or
something. These shapes were distinct only a moment,
pressing against the spinning membrane before vanishing again.

Captain Magnus shouted, "Fighters to the rail!"

Seamen stepped forward, cutlasses and cudgels

raised. Rytlock dragged Sohothin from its stone sheath, and Garm shouldered up beside him.

Eir meanwhile brought her bow into position and nocked three arrows. She trained them on the waters that sucked away just to starboard.

There were more glimpses—here, a half-rotten leg, there, a battered rib cage, and then across the inner curve of the whirlpool, a long line of skulls pressing up through the film of water and rising. Vacant eye sockets gushed brown water.

Eir released the bowstring. Three shafts whistled away to crack through three decaying faces. Still, the creatures rose, fletchings jutting from nasal cavities and cheekbones. The monsters emerged from the whirlpool as if the water had no grip on them. They rushed the gunwales of the *Cormorant,* and their skeletal finger-nails clawed its boards. With daggers in their rictus grins, they climbed.

Eir released three more arrows, which snagged in three more skulls without destroying the monsters. Eir slung her bow on her shoulder and pulled a great mallet from her belt. "Here we go."

With a gurgling roar, the first line of rotting crea-tures reached the rail.

The crew of the *Cormorant* replied with a roar of their own. They attacked, blunderbusses blasting and cutlasses swinging.

Heads rolled from shoulders, but bodies climbed on. Sailors hacked hands from wrists, and arms from shoul-ders. The bodies merely fell into the whirling soup as more Orrian undead emerged.

Rytlock rammed Sohothin into one, lighting it like a lantern. Fire sizzled in its eyes, and it plunged away into the water. Sohothin punched through the rotting chest of another undead, roasting its heart, then slashed down the midline of a third.

Beside him, Garm bit the head from a skeleton and spat the skull into its body. The decapitated creature plopped down into the whirlpool. With a sick growl, Garm chomped the rib cage of another creature and shook his head, ripping the bones apart.

The *Cormorant* was pulling clear of the maelstrom, but the sea beyond boiled with even more undead.

They lunged up en masse, clawing toward the rail.

Three swift strokes of Eir's mallet reduced three of the foes to greenish paste on the side of the ship. Then she stepped back. "Keep them pinned down," she called to Rytlock and Garm. "I've got to help Logan guard the asura!"

The charr and the wolf tore through many more.

Eir retreated to join Logan beside Snaff and Zojja. "How're they holding up?"

"See for yourself," Logan said.

Snaff and Zojja swayed hypnotically. Their eyes hung wide, and the red powerstones in their laurels flashed.

Eir glanced aft toward the two barques that her friends controlled. Both had sailed past the whirlpool, but both were now swarmed by rotting corpses. They clambered up the gunwales and vaulted over the rails and shambled across the decks—only to drop into a clever set of trap-doors. The spring-loaded hatches dumped the undead belowdecks and slammed closed again, ready for more.

Meanwhile, beneath the planks, gears spun and bones splintered and meat ground into a gray paste, which oozed out the portholes. The two barques were golems of a sort, steered from afar. Instead of cargo, their holds contained powerful meat grinders.

Snaff and Zojja destroyed undead by the hundreds. Even Morgus Lethe could not hope to raise the chum that poured from the barques.

A nearby roar brought Eir's attention back to the aft deck of the *Cormorant*, which now swarmed with undead.

Eir smashed one to the deck and spun to kick another in half and turned to fling a third over the rail. It was heavy work, like shoveling sand from a pit that kept filling.

Logan meanwhile painted blue aura in the air around the asura, making a shield that would guard them. He spun around and pounded skeletons like tent pegs. His hammer crashed into their heads and drove their spines down to scatter across the deck.

But wherever two fell, three more rose.

Worse, yet, before the bow of the *Cormorant*, another ship lurched up from the depths. It was a ship of the undead, huge and hoary, with black masts like burned-out pines and a riddled hull and sails hanging in tattered ribbons. It disgorged the sea from its decks and hull and rose up, tacking toward the *Cormorant*.

Captain Magnus saw the ship and the monster at its helm: Morgus Lethe. "They're coming alongside! Load cannons. Hoist grapnels. Prepare to board!"

As the undead ship hove up alongside the *Cormorant*, gunnery teams lit fuses and stood back. Cannons blew. They shot crystal orbs filled with acid, which broke upon the ship and sprayed out over it and ate at it. Still, the vessel bore on. Boarders hurled grapnels, the metal weights thudding to the decks and rattling as they dragged back to lodge in the ship's rail. Heaving mightily, the men hauled the ships together.

"Board her!"

The men cleated off the lines and leaped for the deck of the undead ship, careful to avoid the spots eaten by acid.

Rytlock and Garm went with them, bounding side by side onto the enemy vessel. Their feet left solid wood and landed on rot and slime.

"Squishy," Rytlock said.

Garm's hackles rose, sensing enemies, though the deck was clear.

"Where are they?" Rytlock snarled, holding up Sohothin to light the darkness. "Show yourselves!"

The hatches flew back, and undead sailors stomped up in greatcoats emblazoned with ancient heraldry.

"Pistols!" shouted a nearby seaman.

The sailors lifted blunderbusses and discharged them. The shots ripped through the undead to pepper the waves beyond. Tossing aside their guns, they slashed with cutlasses. Though blades cleaved flesh and bone, the undead came on.

Fingers of death, cold as the grave, pierced the sailors' flesh and ripped it warm from their bones. They screamed as they came apart. At the moment when each died, though, the screaming stopped, and what was left of their flesh turned gray.

The shivering cadavers then spun about to join the ranks of the undead.

"Not good!" shouted Rytlock, swinging Sohothin like a torch to keep the undead at bay. Garm circled behind him, snarling at the wall of monsters.

Behind the phalanx of undead, a figure strode down from the aft deck and crossed over amidships. The man was large and amorphous beneath a tattered cape—a norn warrior. He lurched forward on leech-covered legs and strode toward the fore of the ship.

"That's him," Rytlock said. "That's Morgus Lethe."

But to reach Lethe, they would have to fight through a wall of undead.

While the battle raged on both decks below, Caithe began her invasion from above.

She leaped from the crow's nest of the *Cormorant* and slid down the ratlines, knocking off numerous undead on her way. Then she swung out onto the lowest spar and balanced lithely across it. The yardarm extended beyond the ship's sides, nearly touching the boom of the undead ship. It was a simple thing, therefore, to walk out on a beam of solid wood and walk in on a beam of rot.

Caithe reached the mainmast of the enemy ship and wondered at it, soft and slimy to the touch. "Weak points." She drew an enchanted dagger from her hip and plunged it into the mainmast. It gave no more resistance than wet clay. She twisted the blade, wondering if it would—"Amazing!"

The mast severed and tilted outward and plunged.

With a great whoosh, the upper half of the ship's mast dropped to the deck, smashing a dozen undead below. Staying in the tops, Caithe could cut down the mizzenmast and the fore and the aft—

Except that undead were climbing the ratlines toward her.

She winged a dagger at one of them, but the blade buried itself in the thing's chest, and it just came on. That didn't work. Caithe ran along the spar, slicing loose the lines that held the sail and gathering the cloth. She flung it around the ratlines, pinning the undead to it. She tied off her trap with a double-shank knot.

On the other side of the mast, though, undead had topped the spar and were treading toward her. Caithe approached, cutting more lines. The first creature grasped her shoulder, icy fingers piercing her skin. Screaming, Caithe wrapped one of the severed lines around its neck, cinched it, and kicked the dead man from the spar. It jolted out, hanged in midair.

This was fun. Why were the others so frightened?

Hauling on another line, Caithe swung away from the undead that reached toward her. She landed on the mizzenmast and cut it down as she had the main. Then she grabbed a line and swung out and around, back toward the bow of the boat, landing on the foremast. In moments, it, too, went tumbling. Now, only the aft mast stood, but no lines remained to swing to it.

Caithe leaped down from the spar, striking the deck and rolling. She came up, ready to run toward the aft, but a huge, fetid figure rose before her: Morgus Lethe.

He turned empty eye sockets toward her, and water streamed through his rotten cheeks. "Where do you think you're going?"

"To the aft deck. I want to cut down the last of your masts."

"Don't you know who I am?"

Caithe lifted an eyebrow and said, "Captain Lethe?"

"The same." He reached beneath his tattered greatcoat and drew forth a cutlass that dripped with black ichor. "I have a blade that sucks the life out of any living thing."

Caithe nodded politely. "Only if you hit me with it." She lifted her white stiletto. "I'm pretty good at killing things, too."

Captain Lethe's vacant eyes turned toward the blade. "I'm sure you are. But you can't kill me. I'm dead already." He lunged for her, his cutlass spattering black ooze.

Caithe cartwheeled away, careful not to let the ichor touch her. She leaped up on a nearby barrel and bounded out past a pile of rotten line. The black stuff spattered the deck just short of her and burned through.

The captain stalked forward, swinging his cutlass. "I'm your destiny, you know. I'm the destiny of all living things." He lunged for her.

On the *Cormorant*, the battle had become brutal. Undead swarmed the ratlines and sails. The fight in the tops sent a steady hail of bodies down to pound the decks below.

Those decks were awash in monsters. Logan and Eir stood back-to-back, smeared with gray flesh and black blood. Logan still painted aura in the air around them, but the undead clawed their way through it. His hammer smashed them back, and Eir used axes to tear them limb from limb.

Between these two grisly defenders, Snaff and Zojja huddled, clinging to each other. Their minds spun as their meat-grinding golems ate up the things that swarmed their ships.

But perhaps Captain Magnus had it worst. The undead formed a thicket around him. His axe cut through arms like branches. All the while that he defended the *Cormorant,* he stared at the enemy ship, at the creature that marshaled these undead.

All would be lost if Morgus Lethe did not fall.

With a roar, Captain Magnus the Bloody Handed plowed through undead and leaped rail to rail and landed on the deck of the undead ship.

On the enemy ship, Rytlock and Garm fought a rotting host. The undead raked them with bony fingers and bit them with horrid teeth.

But the charr and the wolf gave as good as they got. Sohothin rammed into them and ignited their tattered flesh. Garm meanwhile clamped fangs on the monsters and ripped out their bones. Rancid meat spattered him. It clung and stung. No matter how many undead they slew, more marched up from the hold, barring their way to Lethe.

Garm suddenly howled, and Rytlock turned to see why. There, on the aft deck of the undead ship, Captain Morgus Lethe towered over Caithe, his black cutlass raised to strike.

FIGHTS AND FEASTS

Morgus Lethe roared, lunging at Caithe.

She spun aside, letting the black-oozing cutlass jab beneath her arm. Meanwhile, she rammed her own stiletto between two of Lethe's ribs.

Lethe only laughed, a hacking sound. "I have no heart to pierce."

Caithe buried a second stiletto in his chest. It, too, brought only mockery.

"You cannot kill me!" A blast of grave air broke over her as Morgus lunged with his cutlass.

Caithe twisted aside, but the undead captain fell atop her. His blade struck the deck beside Caithe, and Morgus roared, writhing.

In his back stood the axe of Magnus the Bloody Handed.

"Whose blade!" hissed Morgus, clawing at his back.

"Mine," Magnus said, stepping on the haft and driving the blade deeper through his spine.

Morgus jolted on the planks. "You can't kill me! *I am death!*"

"Now you're *dead*!" Caithe said, ramming both stilettos into his skull. She twisted, and the cranium severed and fell in two halves. Where the brains should have been was instead a nest of maggots. The voracious vermin erupted from the skull and spread out all across the whole horrid figure, eating as they went.

Caithe scrabbled back.

In moments, Morgus Lethe was stripped to bone. Then the bones, too, were eaten away. At that point, the worms fell to the planks, twitching.

"It's ending," Magnus said, reaching out to take Caithe's hand. "Zhaitan's champion is destroyed. . . ."

Caithe reached down to pluck her blades from the writhing ruins of Lethe. "What now?"

"Now, we must fight our way back to our ship," Magnus said.

Side by side, Caithe and Magnus battled the hosts of Lethe. Caithe's stilettos split more heads, emptying them on the deck, while Magnus's axe harvested them whole.

They headed toward the rail, but it was too late. The ship was sinking.

"Down we go," Magnus said.

The ship plunged into the water, dumping Caithe and Magnus throat-deep in sloshing waves.

Worse, the undead hordes that had been crawling up the sides of the *Cormorant* now fell into the water around them. Caithe and Magnus swam and fought, slicing their foes apart, a job made easier because the undead had lost much of their will.

The hosts of Zhaitan sought the abyss as living things seek the air.

At last, Caithe and Magnus reached the *Cormorant*. Caithe grasped a line that hung in the water and pulled herself out of the soup. Magnus followed.

The deck of the *Cormorant* was ravaged. Rotting corpses lay interspersed with the freshly dead.

"What a mess," Caithe said as she stepped over the rail.

"Caithe! You're alive," called Eir from the aft deck. She was ruddy-faced, red hair torn wildly from its braids, but she smiled with triumph.

Caithe climbed the aft stairs. "Not just alive. Victorious!"

"Yes," added Logan, "though some of us feel less than victorious." He glanced at Rytlock, who was vomiting over the aft rail.

Only then did Caithe notice Snaff and Zojja, who stood in swooning concentration beside Eir. They were bringing up the two barques. Both were smeared with undead and scratched from stem to stern.

Magnus the Bloody Handed stepped up and bowed to them all. "You have done it. You have slain another dragon champion."

"Yes," Caithe said. "Him *and* his followers. Do you see?" She gestured beyond the aft rail of the *Cormorant*, where the whirlpool closed. The once tormented sea settled into its regular rhythm, the waves rising and falling like breath.

Magnus nodded, his face lined with deep gratitude. "Now Destiny's Edge has purchased its own billet. All of you are free."

The Ship's Council of Lion's Arch announced a feast for Destiny's Edge, slayers of Morgus Lethe. Every captain wanted to host the banquet, and every dignitary wanted to attend—with supporters and family and friends. As a result, no ship was big enough, and measures had to be taken to keep out undesirables.

In the end, the feast took place in the middle of the Grand Harbor aboard not one but seven ships, connected via gangplanks and swinging lines. Each ship sought to outdo the others. Every deck was holystoned, every bit of brass polished, every rail festooned. Lanterns blazed upon the spars, sending a warm and manifold light down over the elegantly garbed partygoers.

Even Eir and her companions wore new clothes—greatcoats in dazzling white. They were gifts from Magnus the Bloody Handed, tailored from the first shipment of fine wool to pass the erstwhile lair of Morgus Lethe. Each coat designated its wearer an honorary member of the Ship's Council.

"I think we look dashing," Logan said, "as white as Seraph."

"I think we look like waiters," Rytlock griped. His brawny shoulders bristled beneath the yards of white cloth, and his horns continuously snagged the coat. "I can't move!"

"Luckily, all you have to do is shake hands."

It was true. From the beginning of the party until

well into the evening, Destiny's Edge stood as a long line of dignitaries filed past and shook their hands.

The companions coped with varying degrees of success. Eir and Logan were the most gracious, nodding and thanking people. Snaff and Zojja didn't understand how to keep the line moving, though. Whenever someone would say, "I don't know how you did it," Snaff would leap in with, "Well, let me tell you! It all began with the design of the hold golems . . ." Then he would spin a long, elaborate tale, all the while shaking the person's hand so that he or she could not get away, with Zojja breaking in every fifth word with a correction.

The companions were, of course, stationed on the finest of the seven ships—the *Pride*—a great war galley that belonged to Commodore Lawson Marriner of the Ship's Council. He was a man of contrasts. The finery of his greatcoat contrasted with the leathery skin of his seafarer's face, and his quick movements aboard ship and his even quicker mind belied his age. When finally the receiving line ran out, the commodore showed the members of Destiny's Edge around his ship.

"It's a warship, yes," the commodore said as he guided Rytlock and Logan into the stateroom beneath the aft deck, "but it's also one of the meeting places of the Ship's Council." The room was lavish, with silver leaf and red velvet drapes. In the center stood a great, round table in oak, where the commodore and the captains of Lion's Arch routinely met to do the city's business. Just now, though, the table was loaded with thundershrimp and clams and swordfish and squid. "Avail yourselves."

Rytlock grinned and grabbed a plate. "Ah, seafood."

"I'm surprised a charr would like seafood," Commodore Marriner remarked.

"I like any food I can spear with my claws," Rytlock replied.

There was plenty to feast on, of course—ales and wines and cheeses and breads and every other bounty of this bountiful city. Loaded down, Logan and Rytlock staggered out the cabin door and seated themselves on the capstan. There, they ate, listening to a nearby conversation.

"It's the size advantage, for one," said a young asura, her skin smooth despite sea and sunshine. She was speaking to Snaff, Zojja, and Caithe, and judging by her short greatcoat, she was a person of importance. "I mean, a norn in the hold—it's a comical thing. And on deck they're constantly getting whapped by the boom. 'Bring a ship about and there's a norn in the drink' is the old saying. And have you ever seen one climb the ratlines? Looks like a mantis in a spiderweb."

Rytlock laughed, a shrimp flying from his mouth.

"I can imagine," Snaff said encouragingly. "Go on, Captain Shud."

"Captain?" Rytlock wondered.

"Shhh," replied Logan. "I want to hear this."

The captain went on, "An asuran ship, though, there's a thing to behold. We fit everywhere—the tops, the decks, the holds. And we can run more sail than any norn ship. We can set the boom four foot off the deck, not twelve. No, the seas were meant for us—"

"Not to mention the innovations," broke in another asura, who was shorter than the first. The tail of his greatcoat pooled on the deck.

"What innovations, Captain Tokk?"

"Well, things like retractable keels so you can sail in three feet of water, and retractable masts so you can sail beneath bridges."

"Fascinating," Snaff said. "I'd like to learn more."

"Well, *I* would like to learn more about you and your goals."

"Ehh?" asked Snaff, his mouth hitching.

Captain Tokk smiled, his face beaming red. "Well, you've done so much for the norn in defeating Jormag's champion, and then for Lion's Arch by defeating the Orrian dragon's champion, but what have you done for our own people?"

Snaff blinked. "Well, I invented completely new forms of golems, ones that allow the controller to move them while moving their own bodies. I call it double sight."

"What else?" Tokk pressed, smiling in a self-important way.

"Well, I've innovated sand golems—actual golems that rely more upon the powerstone dust that controls them than on the substances that make up their physical forms."

"Exactly," Tokk said as if he hadn't heard a word. "Nothing. It's time for you to pay back your homeland by defeating another dragon champion."

Snaff blinked away his frustration. "Another dragon champion?"

"It's rising near the city, in the jungle beyond the swamp."

"Yuck," Snaff said.

"I *know!* Mud, mosquitoes, those bushes that stick seedpods to your pants—"

"Sticker bushes—"

"Thanks," Tokk replied. "Yes, in such a horrid place is where a champion of Primordus is rising."

"Just name him!" Snaff said, scowling now. "Imagine the cheek, rising near Rata Sum!"

"He is called the Destroyer of Life," Tokk said, his eyebrows lifting as if his own words amazed him. "His master, Primordus, was the first of the Elder Dragons to rise, and he wreaked havoc on the dwarves. They slew his first champion, the Great Destroyer, and we allied with the dwarves to fight back the tide of minions that boiled up from the deep places. For centuries, we had them driven back. But the old wyrm found a new champion. The Destroyer of Life is forged of stone and magma. He is raising more armies of destroyers."

Snaff now was shaking one small fist. "We'll get you, Destroyer of Life! And why shouldn't we? We're the killers of dragon champions!"

Tokk grinned. "So you think you and your comrades could destroy the Destroyer of Life and his army?"

"Of course," Snaff said resolutely.

The party lasted all night and stretched straight through till morning. As guests boarded boats and rowed back to the docks, the comrades found themselves lingering together around the council table and the ragged remains of the feast.

"You know," Rytlock said as he hoisted a barrel and poured the dregs of the ale into a stein, "that's *two* we've done for the norn."

Eir glanced at him in annoyance. "What?"

"You know—the Dragonspawn was for Nut White-Face—"

"Knut Whitebear."

"And we did this one for Morgan Bloodfist."

"Magnus the Bloody Handed. How much ale have you had?" Eir asked.

Rytlock pointed a claw at her and sighted somewhat unsteadily down it. "Not enough to not be able to recognize that it—I mean, to *not* notice it's been all norn favors so far."

"Fine," Eir said. "Noted."

"All I mean is, maybe next time we do something for the charr," Rytlock ventured, downing the stein in one gulp.

"Yeah," Logan said with a laugh. "Let's destroy Ebonhawke. But afterward, we have to help the humans by destroying the Black Citadel."

Rytlock looked at his friend with surprised admiration, and then with shocked disgust, and then with a mixture of the two, which looked very much like a hangover.

Logan went on, "Instead of rushing into another fight, why don't we do some—I don't know—*diplomatic* missions. For instance, Queen Jennah has requested our presence in Divinity's Reach—"

"That's it!" Rytlock crowed. "We'll conquer Divinity's Reach!"

Everyone but Logan laughed at that.

Snaff shook his head. "It's no good doing things for humans or charr, but there *is* an ancient threat rising beneath Rata Sum."

"What threat?" Eir asked.

"Another dragon champion: the Destroyer of Life.

He's raising an army of destroyers to erupt from the ground and swarm the jungles and destroy Rata Sum."

Eir arched an eyebrow. "How much have *you* been drinking?"

"It's true. Captain Tokk told me," Snaff said. "Rata Sum doesn't have effective defenses. Sure they have the peacemaker golems, but they're used mostly to prevent krewes from stealing each other's secrets. I've tried to sell them true battle golems, but no one on the council listens to me. This is just the sort of threat I was imagining: there's a volcano under the jungle, and its spewing out destroyers. Perfect!"

"You want us to fight a *volcano*?" Rytlock asked.

Snaff bubbled excitedly, "We could come up with a caldera plug or maybe caldera crème—or even a giant spear like people use to lance a boil."

Eir smiled. "Excellent ideas, all. But first, we'll find out what really is happening beneath Rata Sum. Then we'll make our plans and our golems. If the Destroyer of Life *is* rising beneath the jungle, he's just made seven deadly enemies."

From Logan Thackeray
To Her Royal Majesty, Jennah,
Queen of Kryta,
Regent of Ascalon
Friend of all Humankind

Greetings,
    As you have no doubt heard, Captain Magnus

the Bloody Handed, his troops, my comrades, and I have destroyed Morgus Lethe. This brave coalition of norn, human, asura, sylvari, and charr fought for many reasons; but as always, I fought only for you.

Perhaps you have also heard that we were in the midst of celebrating this victory when the threat of another dragon champion came to our ears: the Destroyer of Life. It is a new champion of the Elder Dragon Primordus, and it rises near Rata Sum, homeland of two of my dear friends.

I made a case for traveling to Divinity's Reach first, but my comrades are too eager to fight again, too fearful of what would happen if we let the situation in Rata Sum simmer. Eir keeps us busy with preparation.

Just say the word, though, and I will leave them and come to you. I desire more than anything to see you again, face-to-face. It is my sole consolation that you are before me every time I close my eyes.

Let me know what you wish, and I will obey.

Your humble champion,

Logan

From Her Royal Majesty, Jennah
To the Magnificent Logan Thackeray

Greetings:

I knew you would kill Morgus Lethe. The

champion of a dragon cannot stand before the champion of a queen. Your works bring honor and glory to yourself and to me.

Yes, of course I had expected you and your comrades to appear before me, but this next mission does take precedence. I have been in long-term negotiations with the Arcane Council of Rata Sum for a restored asura gate into Ebonhawke. The new gate will bind our farthest outpost to our greatest city. Long the asura have stalled, fearing a backlash from the charr. But when I received your letter, I at last had the bargaining chip I needed.

I will allow my champion to fight this fight, and in return, I will get my superior gate.

This is your greatest service yet to me, Logan, but I recognize the price we both are paying. I fear to lose you, and I want more than anything to see you again. But you cannot fight for me by standing around the halls of Divinity's Reach. The last thing I need is another polished advisor. They are just statues compared to a flesh-and-blood champion.

So, fight for me. Defeat the Destroyer of Life. And in our long separation, I will content myself with letters and with visions of your heroism.

Your queen,

Jennah

BATTLE ON THE LAKE OF FIRE

D amned inconvenient," Zojja said a month later as she tromped behind Caithe and Snaff through deep jungle. "Why'd the Destroyer of Life have to rise so far from civilization?"

"Just be glad he did," Snaff said.

"But the mud," Zojja said, not for the first time. "And the bugs." She slapped her neck, and her hand came away red. The burst body of a gigantic mosquito was pasted to her palm. She shook the insect from her hand, then saw another giant mosquito land on Snaff's face. "You got one!"

Snaff went cross-eyed, staring at the gangly critter. "Look at that proboscis!" he said in genuine wonder. Just then, the bloodsucker rammed its snout right through Snaff's left nostril. He sneezed, a blast of air that shot through the proboscis, inflated the mosquito, and popped it. Snaff gazed cross-eyed at the limp thing, then dragged it from his face. "A design flaw, I'd call that."

From up ahead came a whistle.

Snaff's face brightened. "That would be Caithe. I wonder if she has found something."

The two asura pushed past ferns and fronds and entered a clearing. Caithe stood at its edge, looking down at a black rift in the ground. Sulfuric smoke rose in a long curtain from it.

"That looks like a way in," Snaff blurted.

Caithe held up a hand to signal that the two asura should stay still. Then she stalked soundlessly up to the rift, dropped to hands and knees, and stared within. After a few moments, she motioned her two comrades over.

The asura waddled toward her as quietly as possible, though their stubby legs stirred up the undergrowth and cracked sticks. Soon, they reached the brimstone-reeking rent, knelt beside it, and gazed within.

The jagged cleft descended into a dark cavern beneath the ground, south of Wildflame Caverns. As the asura stared, their eyes grew accustomed to the murk, and they could make out a red glow at the base of the cavern.

"What *is* that?" Snaff murmured.

In moments, it was obvious: A thousand feet down lay a huge lake of fire. At its center hulked a tormented volcano of ropy black stone. The caldera at its peak was filled with white-hot lava, and red stone poured down the sides. Gases hissed in gray jets from the slopes of the island, and the lake of fire boiled. The whole chamber rumbled like the belly of a titan.

"We're going to need a way to get down there," Caithe said.

Snaff nodded, writing on a pad of paper. He made a

second bullet on his pad. "We'll also need some way to freeze the caldera. That's the source of all this lava."

"Isn't Master Klab working on a magic icebox?" Zojja asked.

Snaff sighed. "Klab. Yes. Magic icebox. He hasn't a romantic bone in his body. Here *we* are, trying to save Rata Sum from destroyers, and there *he* is, trying to keep food cold!"

"Still, we could use some of his arcane crystals," Zojja said.

Snaff scowled.

"Write it down. *K-L-A-B.*"

Snaff dutifully scribbled. "Now, as to the enemy, there's neither hide nor hair."

"What do you mean? The chamber is full of enemies. Look!"

Snaff and Zojja peered back down into the rift and saw what Caithe meant: The lake of fire was boiling, yes, but not with gas bubbles. It was boiling with destroyers. They were being birthed from the lava—an army of them crawling onto the tortured sides of the island.

"I thought that's why you wanted to freeze the caldera," Caithe said.

"It was," Snaff assured. "Of course it was." He touched the tip of his stylus to his tongue and wrote down, *Destroyers everywhere.* He smiled up at the sylvari. "And I suspect those keen eyes of yours have clapped onto the Destroyer of Life itself?"

"Yes," Caithe said simply.

"Really?" Snaff blurted. He ahemed and regained his composure. "Show me."

"Right there." She pointed toward the caldera far below. "There, on the right edge. It's calling those creatures up out of the lake."

Snaff goggled for a moment into the darkness, then nodded sagely. "Very good, Caithe. Eir will be quite pleased with the reconnaissance we've gathered." He reached to smack his backside and fling away a bloody mosquito. "Now, let's get out of here."

Eir and Rytlock hoisted a massive metal chassis from the scrap heap and dragged it across the floor of Snaff's workshop. Steel skirled on stone.

Eir winced. "Dragging these things is like fingernails on slate."

"Or horns on the ceiling," Rytlock said.

The chassis shrieked all the way to the granite workbench where they laid it down.

"That should give him enough scrap for building," Rytlock said.

Eir swung her arms and cracked her back. "What do you think Snaff's design is worth? Fifty destroyers? A hundred?"

"You're fighting the battle already, aren't you?"

Eir smiled, brushing red hair back from her eyes. "Every day, I fight it over and over until one day I find that I've won. That day, I know the strategy I'll use."

"And this fight, coming up," Rytlock said, "on a lake of fire beneath the ground against an army of magma creatures—against the dragon champion of Primordus?"

"What about it?"

"You think we can win?"

"Ask me tomorrow."

A month of tomorrows had passed, and summer blazed over the Tarnished Coast. Caithe emerged from a thick forest of bamboo. She turned silvery eyes up toward a break in the forest canopy. A thin curtain of smoke rose there. She whistled and rushed ahead toward the nearby rift.

Behind her, a huge figure shoved through the bamboo and stepped out—Big Snaff, rebuilt and better than ever. He had a water cannon mounted above his left hand and rock drills inserted into his right. His chest was an armored cockpit in which Snaff hung on a harness, sending signals through a powerstone laurel. Big Snaff stepped forward, letting the bamboo snap back.

Luckily, little Zojja was too short to be hit in the face by it. Though Snaff had begun work on a new Big Zojja, she was far from complete. Instead, Zojja was controlling a group of golems that Snaff affectionately called the Wheels of Doom.

Fronds parted to allow seven great wheels of silver to roll placidly after Zojja, across the jungle floor.

"A good fire would clear this place," Rytlock snarled, stepping through the trammeled gap.

"Your solution for everything," Logan said as he followed.

Rytlock raised an eyebrow. "Haven't burned *you* down yet."

Behind the bickering pair came Eir, her face red from the sweltering march. "We'll be there shortly," she said as she flung sweat away from her brow.

Garm appeared at her side, looking equally withered by the heat. He was fitted out like a warhorse in fireproof metal bardings.

Eir fondly set her hand on his helmet. "I wish it'd be cooler below ground, but that's where the magma is."

Garm panted miserably.

Ahead, Caithe whistled.

"Sounds like she's found it," Eir said to Garm. "Let's catch up."

In a clearing ahead, Caithe gestured toward a black rift that rankled across the jungle floor. Big Snaff stepped aside as Zojja brought the Wheels of Doom through. The seven silvery wheels rolled one by one through the group and headed for the rift. The first of the great disks dropped into the crack, wedging half-buried. A second and third wheel rolled onto the rift and fell in behind the first. Soon, all seven of the special golems were bedded in a line down the crevice. Their metal frames began to hum, energy building within.

"You'll want to get back, Caithe!" Zojja shouted, her eyes half-lidded and fluttering.

Caithe looked up, blinked in realization, then bolted away from the disks.

A moment later, the wheels ignited with white blasts and red flames and a sound that drove the air from their lungs. The explosions tore the rift open. The ground came to pieces in blossoming fire and billowing ash. It slumped down. The floor of the jungle poured into the gap and became a great ramp of debris that descended into the cavern.

"Nice!" Rytlock said.

"If my calculations are correct, this ramp should lead

to the volcanic island," Snaff said. "It also should have crushed about a hundred destroyers."

Eir smiled. "Time to crush more."

"Charge!" Snaff proclaimed, and his golem bolted into the roiling dust cloud.

The others followed close behind, running into that infernal realm.

They rushed down the ramp, leaving the green of the jungle floor and passing into the gray cloud. A thousand strides on, the dust cleared, and the crimson heat of the magma chamber flooded over them.

Now they could see: The ramp led across a bloodred sea of lava and ended on a volcanic island at its center. The ropy black stone was teeming with destroyers—their insectoid figures steaming as they cooled. Every moment, more of the monsters clambered up out of the magma pool.

"Be careful where you step," Logan advised as the group ran toward the island.

"And if you drop something," Rytlock added, "just let it go."

Eir laughed grimly. "The problem is, the lava isn't just in the flows. Some of it's walking around."

Ahead, destroyers were pouring onto the ramp. Black-backed creatures climbed up from the boiling sea, and red-backed creatures scuttled down from the volcano.

Eir shouted to Snaff. "Clear the way to the caldera! Let's see what steel and muscle can do against slag and stone!"

Big Snaff bounded down the ramp, unfolding the fingers of its left hand, which now were wide nozzles.

Powerful jets of water erupted from them and struck the magma monsters, exploding into steam. The spray also hardened the beasts in midstep. They tumbled over, cracking, as more destroyers climbed over their backs. They, too, fell. Three rows, four rows, five—the destroyers formed a steaming henge before Big Snaff.

He arrived at a gallop, his metal feet coming down on destroyer backs and crushing them to the ground. He pounded the creatures flat and ran onward. His water cannons paved the way in destroyers, and his feet tamped down the road for the rest of the warriors.

Ahead, the ramp ended, and the slope of the volcano began. It swarmed with black-shelled destroyers.

Even as his left arm poured water on his foes, his right arm whirred with diamond-tipped drills. Big Snaff swung his grinding fist through a phalanx of magma monsters. It shattered their rocky hides and hurled apart their glowing guts. He rammed the drill down on lava heads, sending the bodies slumping.

Snaff gazed around at the carnage. His golem was delivering on his promise and more—perhaps a hundred destroyers were down, and the corridor to the island was open.

He was doing his job. Now it was up to the others to do theirs.

With twin axes, Eir smashed back destroyers. Blue power-stones embedded in the axe heads froze the monsters with one blow. A follow-up stroke shattered them like ice.

Garm meanwhile crashed into more of the magma

monsters. The powerstones on his battle armor flashed blue as well, and he toppled the creatures like statues.

Rytlock wore powerstone gauntlets that ripped through the beasts, and Logan's hammer and Caithe's stiletto had likewise been enchanted.

Zojja, who had cast all these spells, brought up the rear, water spraying from her fingertips to hiss across any destroyers that rose behind them.

At the front, Rytlock roared, "Are we in range? Do you see it yet?"

"There!" shouted Caithe, pointing to the rim of the volcano high above.

The others looked to see a massive figure climb from the caldera and stand silhouetted against the vault of stone. The huge destroyer, covered in rocklike hide and steaming from magma joints, was amorphous and horrible, its body only just solidified from the lava sea where it lived. It seemed a gigantic mantis of stone.

Eir glanced at the molten lake all around them, at the shapeless figures swimming through it, heading for shore.

This was their general. This was a dragon champion, right arm to ancient Primordus.

And it was watching them.

"I'm going after the Destroyer of Life," Eir announced. "Guard me!"

Rytlock and Logan surged up before her, smashing destroyers.

Eir stepped back and slung her axes at her waist and lifted her bow. She pulled from her quiver an arrow with a blue powerstone head. Cold light gleamed from it, and frost drifted down in a glittering cascade. Eir nocked the shaft, aimed for the massive figure, and released.

The arrow soared like a comet, trailing ice crystals. It arced across the ceiling of the magma chamber and plunged to strike the Destroyer of Life in the chest.

The powerstone exploded, hurling a storm of ice off the massive figure. It did not fall, though, did not even flinch. In moments, the flurry ceased, and the blue stone went dark.

The Destroyer of Life batted the shaft away.

Gritting her teeth, Eir nocked three more blue-headed arrows and shot them into the superheated sky. They shrieked as they went and smashed side by side into the huge figure. More explosions, more spewing ice, but the Destroyer of Life yet again knocked the shafts away.

"Now what?" Rytlock roared, head-butting a destroyer.

Eir stepped back, gazing in dread at the dragon champion. Despite the searing heat, her face went white. "I don't know."

THE DESTROYER OF LIFE

At the edge of the caldera towered the Destroyer of Life—a massive primordial mantis of stone. Fire blazed from its eyes and joints and roared through its thorax. At its feet lay four burned-out arrows, and at its back boiled a white-hot caldera—the source of its power. The Destroyer of Life gazed down at the lake of fire, where more of its minions emerged, oozing rock. They were infinite, his destroyers. No puny band could stand against the tide of them.

The Destroyer of Life pulled a magma bow from its back and fitted a white-hot shaft to it. The arrow burned with primordial fire. Once woken, it could never be quenched. The champion of Primordus drew back on the metal string, sited the red-haired woman below, and released.

Eir and her comrades watched as the white-hot shaft curved downward, smoking through the air, and came straight for them. They leaped aside. The arrow drilled into the volcanic rock nearby, and flame awoke within the hole.

"He's going to be a challenge," Caithe noted.

Above, the Destroyer of Life lifted his arms and roared. His minions answered, the shout sounding like a volcanic eruption.

"Hold them back!" Eir commanded. She fitted and loosed three more shafts.

They struck the Destroyer of Life and spewed frost but did nothing more.

"They don't work!" Rytlock growled, climbing up a smoldering mound of destroyer parts. "Try something else!"

"Buy me time!"

Logan's powerstone-enhanced war hammer pounded the head of a destroyer. The creature's outer skin solidified. Another blow ripped the skin loose. The magma monster stood there shivering as if it had been flayed. A new shell of rock began hardening on its amorphous form. "Oh, no, you don't." Logan struck again. The shell cracked, and magma gushed out across the ground.

Rytlock meanwhile plunged steel gauntlets into the chest of another rock creature and tore the thing in half. "I love these gloves!" he exulted. Just then, a second destroyer bashed into him, flinging him to the ground. It rushed him, but Rytlock lifted his foot, planted it on the steaming torso of the thing, and flipped it overhead to break on the lava field. Rytlock struggled to his feet as a third destroyer charged him. It would have tackled him and set him on fire except that Caithe plunged a powerstone-stiletto into its neck. It froze up like a statue and broke into a thousand pieces.

"Thanks," Rytlock said.

A destroyer charged Eir, grabbing her arm and burning it brutally. She cried out, kicking the monster back. As it staggered, she dropped her bow and grabbed an axe and buried it in the destroyer's lava-gushing head.

Still, she swooned back, her arm blackened where it had touched her.

More destroyers surged up, but a great deluge poured down upon them all—a sudden rain that healed Eir's burns and Rytlock's bruises and every wound they had suffered so far. The rain also solidified the rock monsters around them, letting axes and hammers do their work.

When the work was done, the comrades turned within a circle of smoldering stones to see Zojja, drenched but grinning. "A healing rain, don't you think?"

"Thanks," Eir said, turning with an axe in each hand. She brought them down in a brutal rhythm, slaying destroyers two at a time. But the tide of magma monsters was unending, and the Destroyer of Life still commanded the caldera, still sent red-hot shafts down into the battle.

One iron arrow struck Big Snaff's left hip, melting the joint. The golem teetered sideways and crashed to the ground.

"Damn it!" shouted Eir.

Rock monsters hurled themselves onto him. They would have torn him apart if Zojja hadn't laved the fallen golem with conjured water.

The Destroyer of Life next turned its bow back on Eir, loosing a shaft that moaned as it fell.

She heard it just before it struck and ducked down, seeing the iron arrow impale Big Snaff's foot. Somehow, the metal caught fire.

"Primordial flame!" Eir realized. "The core of the Destroyer's power." She turned toward Rytlock. "Give me a gauntlet!"

Rytlock ripped the powerstone-enhanced weapon from the chest of a destroyer, shucked the glove from his hand, and flung it to Eir.

She grasped it and shoved her hand within. Then she reached down and snatched the white-hot arrow from Big Snaff's foot. The primordial arrow screamed in the clutch of that frigid gauntlet.

Eir spun about, nocking the blazing-hot arrow on her bow and drawing back. The bow burst into flame. She sighted on the Destroyer of Life and released.

The scarlet shaft soared up beneath the vault of the magma chamber.

Crying out, Eir dropped her bow, which flamed for a moment before it was wholly consumed. It fell to ash.

The primordial arrow was falling now toward the dragon champion.

"Come on!" Eir said through gritted teeth. "A *little* luck..."

The shaft descended to smash into the Destroyer of Life's face. Primordial fire pierced through to primordial fire. A holocaust erupted from every joint of the beast. The flames roared, going red-hot and white-hot and blue. Then came a deafening *crack*. The rocky figure of the Destroyer of Life blasted apart. Hunks of basalt cascaded all around, trailing fire. The conflagration chased the pieces down from the air, plunging them into the red-hot lake below.

"Ha ha!" Logan shouted.

Rytlock roared, "The Destroyer of Life is destroyed!"

But there was no time to celebrate. Destroyers were pounding Big Snaff, denting his chassis and tearing away the armor around the cockpit.

"Help Snaff!" Eir ordered as her mallets bashed a pair of destroyers away.

A moment later, Logan and Caithe and Rytlock arrived. Logan's hammer knocked the head from one destroyer, sending the pulpy thing flying. Rytlock's gauntlet ripped out the chest of another. Caithe's stiletto severed the neck joint of a third.

They were falling more easily now. The Destroyer of Life had been their conduit to the power of the dragon. With him fallen, the destroyers staggered, stunned.

Still, there were dozens to slay.

Eir and her comrades demolished the rock beasts that swarmed Big Snaff, but the golem was burning.

"Get him out!" Eir called, ripping back the heat shield over the cockpit. A great cloud of steam rose from it, but once it cleared, Eir could see Snaff lounging in his harness and grinning in triumph. "We did it!"

"Yes," Eir said, helping Snaff climb from the golem's chest. "I'm glad."

Snaff rubbed his hands together. "Time to deploy the caldera plug." He reached to one corner of the cockpit and hoisted a bluish cluster of arcane crystals, dangling from a single cord.

Rytlock rolled his eyes. "You think that thing's going to work?"

"Probably not," Snaff replied with a shrug. "After all, Master Klab made it. Still, we need to give it a try."

"Let's go, then," Eir said, returning the gauntlet to Rytlock.

He slid it on, grinning, and flexed the metal gloves. "On to the caldera!"

With powerstone mallets in hand, Eir led the group in a march up the subterranean volcano. Logan followed to her right and Rytlock to her left. The two asura trundled along behind this advancing wedge, trailed by a watchful Caithe and a growling Garm. Here and there, a destroyer would rise from the smoldering wreckage of the army and charge the group, only to be frozen and bludgeoned and shattered.

Minutes later, the companions reached the crater where the Destroyer of Life had exploded. The blast had carved out a fifty-foot hole in the basalt, and chunks of the champion lay all around. A hundred feet farther on, the team reached the caldera itself, a vast pool of white-hot lava. Within it swam the figures of half-formed destroyers.

Snaff hoisted the caldera plug and stared dubiously at it. "Let's hope Klab knows what he's doing."

"We have to get the stones to the center," Eir said, "but my bow is destroyed."

Snaff took a long look up Rytlock's arm. "Looks like we've got a natural catapult."

"Heh heh. Hand me that thing." Rytlock took the crystalline bundle, sniffed it once, and said, "Stand back." Rytlock pivoted, letting the bundle swing in the air around him. He whirled around and around, gathering speed, and the bundle whistled with wind. At last, grunting, Rytlock released it.

The crystalline bundle flew through the air. It arced upward, growing small, and soared to the center of the caldera. The plug plunged like a meteor, struck the lava, and sank, leaving a black hole. A blue light erupted from the hole, and the edges cooled and hardened.

"Well, that was pretty much a bust," Snaff said.

But the caldera plug wasn't finished. The white-hot magma cooled to red-hot, and then to brown. In a wave out from the central hole, the molten rock solidified, first a mere skin, then a thick plate with cracks running through it. Steam shot up through cracks, and the plate darkened as it thickened.

"It's working," Snaff said incredulously.

Rytlock shook his head. "The crystals did nothing against the Destroyer of Life."

"It was made of elemental fire," Eir said. "Now that the Destroyer of Life is gone, the power of the dragon is cut off. This caldera has once again become natural lava."

The solidifying plate turned black as the heat below it went out. Rivulets stopped flowing from the caldera. Soon, the sea of fire would become a smooth expanse of black basalt.

"It worked!' Rytlock exulted.

"Yeah," Snaff replied emptily. "I just wish I didn't have to tell Klab."

Rytlock arched an eyebrow. "What do you mean? He'll be pleased."

"Exactly."

Whether Klab was pleased or not, the rest of Rata Sum was. It was a heroes' welcome. The walkways of the city were lined with shouting and laughing asura, and children rushed out to drape them with necklaces fashioned from discarded ether crystals.

The Arcane Council stood on one side of Snaff's ziggurat and cheered more loudly than even the children.

Walking in the midst of his friends, Snaff said dourly, "Oh, no."

Zojja turned to him. "What do you mean, 'Oh, no'?"

"Those are the councilors, my dear."

"Of course they are."

"What do the councilors do?"

"They run the city."

"Yes, but the other thing they do is try to rope other people into being councilors so they can go back to inventing."

Zojja laughed. "You think they'll appoint you to a position?"

"I *know* they will! Just the sort of spiteful creatures they are!"

Zojja tried to look serious. "Too bad we don't have Big Snaff. You could attack."

"Too bad," he echoed darkly.

The companions came to a stop before the Arcane Council.

Councilor Thud waddled forward and lifted his hands, calling for silence. "On behalf of the Arcane Council and empowered as I am by the Arcane Council, I, Councilor Thud—"

"They're going to stick me with pest control," Snaff hissed to Zojja. "I just know it. Thud's been looking for a patsy for months."

"—do hereby welcome the genius Snaff and his apprentice, Zojja—"

"I built those cockpits!" she whispered peevishly.

"—and their allies from lands far removed—"

"He can't find the end of this sentence," Snaff noted.

"—to Rata Sum and confer upon such genius the highest honor—"

"Wait just a moment!" shouted Master Klab, inventor of the flying puffball and, most recently, the caldera plug. "What did Snaff do to deserve this honor?"

Councilor Thud's eyebrows fluttered like moths. "He . . . well, he designed a golem and marched it out to defeat the Destroyer of Life before his destroyers could attack Rata Sum."

"Yes, yes, all that. But in a matter of weeks, perhaps days, another army would have spilled from that hole in the ground. Whose invention stopped that? Whose invention ensured peace for years to come?" When Councilor Thud mistook this for a rhetorical question, Master Klab exasperatedly said, "*Mine!* That's whose!"

"I thought you were working on a magic icebox," Snaff offered innocently.

Master Klab whirled on him. "*Not* the icebox, but the cold-stone crystals that drive it—the bundle of cold-stone crystals that I gave you to solidify the volcano—the *caldera plug!*"

"Oh, *that*," Snaff averred. He turned to a nonplussed Councilor Thud and said, "He's quite right. His volcano stopper—"

"Caldera plug!"

"Yes, that thing—it really did save the day. Whatever honor you were about to bestow on me should instead go to genius Klab."

Master Klab shot a look of astonished suspicion at Snaff.

A moment later, the suspicion was vindicated when Councilor Thud reached up to the mantle that draped his shoulders, lifted it, and said, "On behalf of the Arcane Council, I hereby appoint Master Klab to the role of director of pest control."

"And iceboxes," added Snaff.

"No. That would just be silly." Thud said as he lowered the mantle around Master Klab's neck.

Klab's red face went green, and he suddenly realized he'd been had—a fact made obvious when Thud and Snaff heartily shook hands, congratulating each other.

The new director of pest control swayed unsteadily.

But the one who actually swooned was Caithe. She grabbed her heart and fell to the ground.

Logan knelt down, seeing that her face looked as white as paper. A cold sweat dappled her skin. "Heat exhaustion! We need water!"

As asura scrambled to get water, Caithe blinked at Logan and shook her head. "No. It's not the heat. It's Faolain. She's poisoned me."

"What?"

"She serves the Nightmare Court, and her touch has poisoned me." She reached to her collar and pulled down, showing that a hand-shaped tumor had formed above her heart. Tendrils of rot reached out from it across her skin. "As I fight the Nightmare, the poison spreads. I must join her, or die." And with that, she collapsed in Logan's arms.

DRAWING THE POISON

hile the rest of Rata Sum celebrated across the bridges and walkways of the city, Eir and her companions gathered down below in the quiet darkness of Snaff's workshop.

Caithe was not doing well. She lay on one of the smaller workbenches, a pillow cradling her now feverish head and woolen blankets piled on her shivering form.

Eir was cleaning the infection, using work rags and a bottle of spirits she had hijacked from Councilor Klab's victory table. "She kept this illness secret from us for so long. I only hope it's not too late." Eir tossed an infection-laced rag in a nearby brazier, where it flashed and burned away.

"Don't give up hope," Zojja offered. "They're sending for the chirurgeon—Madame Dort."

Snaff shook his head miserably.

Just then, a clatter at the head of the stairs announced

the arrival of Madame Dort, genius of malaises and melancholia. She trundled down the steps, her metal toolbox rattling against each one as she came. "Never fear! Madame Dort is here."

The companions looked at each other, eyes tinged with dread.

Madame Dort waddled over to the workbench, clanked her toolbox down beside it, flipped the heavy metal latches, and flung the thing open. The box held an assortment of bone saws and cranial drills, and what must have been an artificial hip. Madame Dort stared avidly at Caithe. "What can I amputate?"

"Get out!" Snaff growled.

Madame Dort stared at him in shock. "But I'm a genius of malaises and melancholia—"

"And misery."

"Well, now—"

"Get out!" Snaff raged, his face turning red. "You'll not lay a finger—let alone a saw—on our friend."

Madame Dort huffed, slamming the lid of her toolbox. "Pray that *you* never need my services."

"Excellent advice, madame," Snaff said, eyes blazing. He hoisted the toolbox and nodded toward the stairs. "Most excellent."

Madame Dort took her toolbox and stomped away.

As the woman ascended the stairs, Eir stared down at Caithe's feverish form. "What do we do now?"

"It's all right," Caithe murmured. "She's coming."

"You're awake!" Eir said, kneeling beside her. "Who's coming?"

"The one who did this to me. The one who can undo it."

"Who?" Eir said as she brushed silver hair back from Caithe's face.

"The Grand Duchess Faolain of the Nightmare Court."

It was midnight before Faolain came, and she was so silent that she stood among them before any of them realized it.

Garm was the first, leaping up from his blanket and standing with fangs bared and a low growl in his throat. At the sound of it, Eir startled awake and grabbed her mallet. Next moment, Rytlock and Logan were at the ready, too, weapons surrounding the stranger.

Despite the heat, Faolain wore a thick, black hood and cloak that covered all but her long, thin face. Her eyes were black, reflecting the fires of Sohothin, and her voice was unnerving. "One dear to my heart is here." Attenuated fingers emerged from the cuffs of the woman's cloak and reached up to pull her hood back. A shock of black hair spilled out. "I am the Grand Duchess Faolain."

"Of the Nightmare Court," Eir supplied.

Rytlock snarled, "*You* did this to her."

"Her love did this," Faolain said, staring at the black infection spreading above Caithe's heart. "She wants to be with me."

"You have to *un*do it!" Rytlock hissed.

"*She* must decide that. I have laid my hand upon her heart, and her heart has received me. Her love for me is poisoning her to you. Her presence with you is poisoning her to me."

"Faolain!" gasped Caithe, her head turning on the workbench where she lay.

Faolain's eyes grew wide, and she swooped past the companions to sit on the workbench where Caithe lay. "Yes, Caithe! I am here."

Caithe riled on the workbench, half-awake and half in dream. "You have gone to darkness."

"And you are coming with me."

"*She* decides!" Eir said.

"Yes," Faolain went on. "You decide. Will you reject me or reject these so-called friends?"

"If you take her from us," Rytlock growled, "you will not leave this place alive."

Faolain's black eyes blinked placidly. "If I take her from you, Rytlock Brimstone, none of you will survive this day." She drew off her cloak, dropping it to the workshop floor and revealing a suit of black leather over a leanly muscular frame. Faolain brushed silver hair back from Caithe's pale face. She was sweating again. "You cannot oppose me, Eir Stegalkin, onetime sculptor; Logan Thackeray, onetime mercenary, and Snaff and Zojja, formerly of Rata Sum—"

"*Formerly?*" Snaff objected.

"Rootless, all of you are. You do not belong in the lands that gave you birth. Now you belong to no one and everyone," the sylvari said with a smile. "You are killers of the Dragonspawn—slayers of dragon champions."

"And she's one of us," Eir said. "Take away this infection!"

"*If* she chooses," Faolain said, leaning in to gaze at Caithe. "What do you wish, dear heart?"

Tears were streaming down Caithe's face, and her head whipped back and forth. "I don't know! I don't know!"

"Let me *show* you!" Faolain's black fingernails sank into the festering wound over Caithe's heart.

Caithe jolted, her back arching up from the workbench.

Sohothin moaned above the sylvari's shoulder, but Rytlock stayed his hand.

Faolain spoke words that slashed the air.

She was there when the man and the charr killed the ogre chiefling.

Faolain was there. *They certainly know how to kill things. They could aid the Wyld Hunt.*

You hate the Wyld Hunt. You hate the Ventari Tablet and all who follow the Dream.

No, Faolain said, clinging to her like a shadow. *The tablet twists the Dream. The tablet is corruption. Would that we could draw it from the sylvari, and the Tree herself . . .*

She was there when Caithe sat on her bunk in the jail of Lion's Arch.

Faolain was there when Sangjo arrived to buy their freedom. *You see, now, how they work. They buy each other and sell each other. You are a commodity.*

At least we fight the dragons.

You must do what you must do. . . .

She was there when the Dragonspawn was a cyclone of ice crystals and stone in the heart of the glacier.

Faolain was there when it engulfed Sandy and enclosed the mind of Snaff and then brought down the roof. *Jormag will not like this. Not one little bit.*

That's the whole idea.

Yes, it is.

She was there when Eir sent the iron shaft of the Destroyer of Life back to him, elemental fire to elemental fire, to blast the champion from the world.

Faolain was there as the companions obliterated an army of destroyers. *And now, you slay a champion of Primordus himself.*

We do.

How you flail at the branches of evil while the roots grow fat.

She was there, clutching Caithe's head and heart as the sylvari's companions hovered behind them, their weapons ready.

Faolain was there to spread the blackness through Caithe. *It is a fool's errand you are on. You have killed dragon champions but have not faced a true dragon. And, even now, another is coming into the world. It will destroy you unless you join me!*

Caithe lurched, hurling Faolain's hands back from her heart. She looked wildly around, then locked eyes with Faolain. *How can you know this? How can any mortal?*

Faolain blinked. *The same way you know. We watch.*

We see the new dragon's champion preparing for it. A champion by the name of Glint.

A new champion?

An old one, her loyalties long concealed.

Then take the poison from me, so that I can fight it.

Faolain's mouth dropped open. *The poison is your love for me.*

"Take it! Turn it to hate!" Caithe said. "I will fight the one who rises!"

Faolain stared long, drawing a deep breath. "I will take it," she said aloud, but then added, "It is not over between you and me."

Faolain's black eyes grew wide, and her mouth twisted. She lunged forward, once again gripping Caithe's heart. Nails sank into Caithe's flesh and drew out beads of blood. The black infection drifted beneath Caithe's skin, coalescing around Faolain's fingertips. Then, like needles, her nails drew the blackness into them. Tendrils of corruption reached up through Faolain's fingers and across the back of her hand and into her wrist and up her arm.

Faolain yanked her hand free. Black rot riddled her fingers, ascending through her arm. She flexed the limb, hissing with exquisite pain. "Oh, love turned to hate, to poison. It deadens me." She staggered back from the workbench, nearly running into Rytlock.

The charr waved Sohothin behind her. "Remember this?"

"Let me go! I have released her!"

"Yes," said Caithe, sitting up. "Let her go!"

"She's a monster."

"Let her go!"

Faolain stooped to lift her black cloak from the floor. She slid her rot-riddled hand into it and stepped past Rytlock. "This, too, will heal. My arm will be mine again." She glanced at Caithe. "And so will you."

"Get out!" Rytlock roared.

Faolain was visibly shivering as she walked up the stairs, out the blasted top of the ziggurat, and into the night of Rata Sum.

Logan lingered on the stairs, watching, but the rest of the companions gathered around Caithe.

"Are you well?" Eir asked. "Truly?"

"Yes. And I know what we must do."

"What?" asked Rytlock.

"A great evil is rising. An ancient evil. We haven't fought the true evil yet, but only the mortal champions. Now we must fight a true dragon. He is rising. His champion is bringing him out."

"Faolain showed you this?" Rytlock asked. "Surely she was lying."

"There is only one hope to stop this new threat: we must slay the dragon's champion."

Rytlock shrugged. "Well, we've killed the others. Why not this one?"

"What is this champion called?" asked Eir.

"She's another dragon—a lesser dragon," Caithe said, "though ancient in her own right. Humans call her Glint."

"Glint!" Logan said. "*The* Glint? Keeper of the Flame-seeker Prophecies?"

"The same," Caithe said.

"Are you kidding me? She helped stop the Lich Lord. She helped stop the titans," Logan went on. "Why would she turn against us?"

Caithe looked levelly at him. "Glint is the champion of the one who rises."

"Glint is a friend of humanity," Logan argued.

"Very few of us are human," said Zojja.

Logan said nothing, but after a moment he nodded.

"Glint is in the Crystal Desert," Rytlock grumbled. "That's a long walk."

"There's no time to walk," Caithe said. "We must arrive in a matter of days."

Snaff snapped his fingers and trundled off across his workshop.

"Where's he going?" Rytlock wondered.

Over his shoulder, Snaff called back, "I've got a device that could get us halfway there!" He disappeared into a closet, and there came the sound of clattering metal. Something heavy crashed to the floor; then Snaff emerged, seeming to carry nothing except a smile. "It's one of the cleverest things I've come up with."

"What?" Rytlock asked.

Snaff reached in his pocket and pulled out what looked like a metal coin. "I call it a 'hole in my pocket.' But it's actually a mini, portable asura gate, of my own fabulous design." He flicked the coin, and as it tumbled in midair, it expanded. Metal filaments slid over each other and reoriented, broadening into a hoop, then a wide ring. The metal circle came down to strike the floor, wobbling itself flat. The moment that the entire circumference of the circle touched the floor, the flagstones within it vanished, showing a patch of wind-blown sand.

"Whoa," Logan said. "Where is that?"

"I can tune them only to known places, and this one's tuned to just south of Ebonhawke."

"How far south?" Rytlock said in alarm.

"Out of arrow range," Snaff assured flatly.

Logan frowned. "What if the charr are sieging?"

"Out of range for them, too. In the desert! Where do you think I got all that sandstone for Sandy?" Snaff clapped his hands together and rubbed them. "Now, let's gather up supplies and golems and go see this Glint!"

From Her Royal Majesty, Jennah,
Queen of Kryta
To the Most Magnificent Logan Thackeray

Logan:

Another dragon champion lies slain at your feet—the Destroyer of Life and his thousand min-ions. Well done! You have saved Rata Sum, and you have won for us an upgraded asura gate into Ebon-hawke. To think—a year ago you were guarding a caravan to Ebonhawke. Now you have made such caravans unnecessary. Thank you!

Still, I must say that I was greatly troubled to read your account of the incident with Faolain of the Nightmare Court. None of her ilk can be trusted. They cling to a demented view of the world. When I read your account, I almost called you to me, but that would only have been selfish.

If Glint is helping her master rise, you must face her down and slay her. But Glint has been an ally to humankind. I am torn. If I had to choose, I would trust her more than the Nightmare Court.

This mission is yet another danger for you to face in my name, in the name of all Tyria. So, go, my champion. Go slay a lesser dragon to stop an Elder Dragon.

Yours always,

Jennah

From Logan Thackeray
To Her Royal Majesty, Jennah,
Queen of Kryta

My Queen,

This may well be my darkest hour. I, too, remember what Glint has done for humanity, and to go to slay her seems inconceivable. But if this act can stop the holocaust of an Elder Dragon's rising, I must do it.

Your letters pierce me like arrows. How I long to see Divinity's Reach, our home. But more, I long to see you. Every moment of every day, I hope to feel your call, so that I can throw aside everything that doesn't matter and run to you. I would throw aside the whole world if I had to. But I know that the only way you will call to me is if you are in mortal danger. I never want that to be the case.

So I will remain your champion. I will fight on for you, these thousand miles away. I will even kill Glint if I must. But all the while, I will have your face before me—your eyes that pierce to my soul.

Your champion,

Logan

PART III

BATTLING
DRAGONS

26

SEEKING THE SANCTUM

The Crystal Desert sun beat down on a strange company. At the head walked warriors in white burnooses—Eir Stegalkin, Logan Thackeray, and Caithe of the Firstborn. Behind them came Rytlock Brimstone and Garm the wolf, their backs bared to the blazing sun. Next were a pair of newly designed Bigs, with Snaff and Zojja suspended within.

This army was marching into battle against another dragon champion: Glint.

Eir perched a hand over her eyes and squinted toward a ridge that ran across their path. "Either Glint's sanctum is very close, or we'll have to climb that ridge."

Caithe shook her head, eyes closing to consult the map in her mind. "The sanctum is beyond the ridge, but we will not have to climb. There's a defile that cuts through, just ahead."

Rytlock stomped up beside them. "A defile? Oh,

perfect!" He shot a look at Logan. "Any jackass could send a rockslide down on top of us."

"It's the only way," Caithe insisted.

Rytlock stared at the ridge. "I don't like it."

"You don't have to," Eir said.

The companions marched onward toward the defile, but an hour later, it looked no closer. The ridge only grew taller, the walls of the crevice only steeper. Four hours later, they stood at the entrance to the narrow canyon.

Eir stared at the cleft ahead, then flashed a sharp look at her comrades. "Well, here we go."

She marched up the loose scree at the ridge's base and headed into the defile, followed by the rest of the companions. Somehow, the heat of the plains was all the more intense within. The sun baked one wall of stone, which turned the cleft into an oven.

"Wow, it's hot," Eir said, her voice echoing from the walls. *Those two asura are like chestnuts in an oven.*

"Very compassionate," Snaff replied tersely.

"Did I say that out loud?"

"Must have. I heard it out loud," Snaff said. *Your brain's so close to the sun, it's probably getting baked.*

"It's hot enough, we don't need to be sniping at each other," Eir replied. *And don't even start making tall jokes. You don't know how many short jokes I've suppressed.*

Short jokes! Oh, yes, you're above us all, aren't you, Miss Titan?

Leave her alone, Zojja put in. *You can't stand having someone else in charge of you.*

"Would all of you just shut it!" Rytlock snarled.

"That's just the thing," Eir said. "We haven't been talking."

"Oh, you haven't?" the charr roared. "News to me." *You never stop talking. All these soft races, all they do is talk talk talk—talk you to death.*

"Soft races?" Logan spat. *What about short races— Runtlock and the striplings?*

I'm twice your height now.

Yeah, and four times my weight, Gruntlock.

Gruntlock!

"Don't you see what's happening here?" Eir asked.

Oh, I'm sure you're about to tell us.

She knows everything.

Yes, quiet everyone! Let's listen to the mighty norn.

"We're hearing each other's thoughts," Eir said.

Brilliant!

Thanks for explaining the obvious.

"The things we would never say to each other are coming right out."

"Well, maybe they *should* come out," Rytlock growled. "I gave this guy a Blood Legion pendant, and he's calling me *Gruntlock.*"

Logan replied, "It was a private thought. And I wouldn't even have thought it if you hadn't called us soft."

"I was talking about how you people won't shut up!" Rytlock roared.

"It's not a matter of shutting up. You're reading our thoughts!"

"Well, then, stop thinking!"

Easy for a charr.

"What kind of a place is this?" Caithe wondered.

It's the kind of place we have to get through, Eir responded, *which will be much easier if we all take Rytlock's advice and stop thinking.*

How do you stop thinking? wondered Snaff and Zojja simultaneously.

You haven't heard a thought from me in a long while, Rytlock put in. *Do what I do.*

Grunting keeps you from thinking? Logan thought. When Rytlock turned on him, he said, "Sorry. It was there in my brain before I could stop it."

You think of me as an animal, Rytlock raged.

Garm shot him an angry look.

"Not an animal," Logan said. *More like a monster.* Rytlock's eyes grew wide. *I mean, a good one—a good monster that'll fight on our side.*

So, you think I'm a traitor to my race?

You're fighting beside a human being. You're supposed to be killing me—

I may change my mind.

Eir broke in, *You have to shut down your thinking. Or if you can't do that, think nice thoughts.*

In other words, don't think about Klab, Snaff told himself.

Zojja hurled her hands up. *You're obsessed with him.*

He makes iceboxes!

You don't respect anyone but yourself.

I respect you.

Yeah, right—genius in training.

Haven't I promoted you?

No.

Well, now you're an almost-genius.

Thanks a lot!

You just jumped a whole level!

An imaginary level! I just helped defeat three dragon champions, and everyone still sees me as nothing more than your assistant!

Is that all you can think of? What I call you? The whole while that we're working together, you've been thinking you're *the real genius!*

Now we both know it! And what's all this "working together" crap? You order me around like I'm no better than Garm!

The wolf turned angry eyes toward Big Zojja.

So, I should worry about this cockpit weld, should I? Snaff wondered. *Put some kill feature in it, did you? Something to get rid of the master so you can take his place?*

Is that what you think? You think I would compromise a design like that? That I would try to kill you?

It's the secret desire of every apprentice, Snaff thought, adding, *but not so secret now.*

Eir yelled, "Why can't you two *stop thinking?*"

Snaff and Zojja both thought, *We're asura.*

"We're being tested," Caithe said softly.

That brought silence, with only the sounds of feet marching through the defile.

"We can hear each other's thoughts because Glint is listening to our thoughts. She's trying to understand why we're approaching her sanctum. She's trying to drive us away."

She may succeed, Eir thought.

Don't act like we're the only problems here, Rytlock thought.

"We need to stop," Caithe said. "She knows what we are thinking, that we are divided. She'll use it against us. Think thoughts that *unify* us!"

There came a flash from Logan's mind—Caithe stabbing her stiletto into the tail of a devourer, then her smile later as she pulled the roasted meat from the shell.

And from Rytlock's mind—the image of Logan launching up to drag down Racogorrix in midair.

Then from Snaff—Zojja bent over a golem, removing the ankle joint he had designed and replacing it with her new version, much stronger and simpler.

From Zojja—Snaff describing the defeat of the Dragonspawn, his eyes aglow and his hands gesturing to a ring of norn admirers.

From Snaff—Eir with hair drawn back and arms speckled with sweat and rock dust flying as she carved a perfect likeness of him.

From Logan—Caithe single-handedly bringing down the mast of a rotten ship and swinging away from undead.

From Rytlock—Logan mowing down undead.

From Zojja—Rytlock lifting a tankard.

From Caithe—Eir laughing at a joke.

From Garm—guarding them all.

And suddenly, they were through.

The sun-baked defile was behind them, and the companions stood on the edge of a great sand sea.

"We made it through," Caithe said. "She couldn't drive us away."

Eir shook her head. "You're right, Caithe. She couldn't drive us away, but she *could* drive wedges between us. We'll never defeat her unless we fight as one." Eir looked around at her companions. "I know you heard some unsavory things from me, but you must understand that I've hand-selected each of you. I trust each of you—*all* of you—with my life."

Her companions nodded, looking down at the sands.

"Damn it!" Rytlock spat. He turned and clapped Logan on the back. "Sorry about some of those things I thought."

"It's fine," Logan assured him. "And sorry about that whole thing about being a monster."

Rytlock laughed. "I kind of liked that."

As the two Bigs ground along, side by side, Snaff spoke through the tube, "You really are a genius, you know."

"Yes," Zojja replied. "I know."

"You'll be your own master any day now."

"Don't say that."

"Okay, I won't," Snaff replied in a tinny voice. "But I *will* think it. You're ready for it. I'm just selfish. Where am I going to find another apprentice like you?"

Eir meanwhile turned to Caithe and said, "You didn't share a single unkind thought toward any of us."

"I don't have a single unkind thought toward you. If I did, I'd say it."

"I suppose you would," Eir said with a laugh. She looked out on the rolling sand dunes that stretched forever into the distance. "Now, where is this dragon sanctum?"

"It's hidden in a crystal of sand," Logan said. "But how do we find it?"

"Yeah," Eir said. "I'm glad you can't hear what I'm thinking."

Big Zojja strode up and clanked to a stop, and a metallic voice came from within. "I can find it."

The others looked at the golem in amazement, and Eir said, "How?"

"Scan for magic." Zojja said. "Glint is incredibly powerful. She could not completely hide her magical signature. I can use the cockpit cage as an antenna of sorts. Tune it to magical frequencies." Big Zojja began walking out into the vast desert.

Eir looked askance at Big Snaff. "Really?"

The golem seemed to shrug, then waddled out after Big Zojja.

Eir nodded, took a swig of water from her canteen, and followed, as did the rest of the companions.

The companions wandered beneath the staring eye of the sun, following Big Zojja, as Little Zojja used her cockpit cage to pick up a telltale tendril of magic. She always proclaimed that the sanctum was before them, but twice they crossed their own trail. Never did they find that one grain of sand that held the sanctum of Glint.

Big Zojja trudged up a hill. Her ankle joints made an agonized hiss, ball sockets crisscrossed with score marks from the sand. The golem planted its feet wide and settled into position. Steam jetted from a pair of air locks on its shoulders, and the blast shield on the torso cockpit creaked open. "Ah! Cool air!" came the voice from within. Straps were unsnapped and buckles unbuckled, and Little Zojja jumped down amid the others. "It's hot in there."

Exhausted and sunburned, Eir trudged to the top of a dune, dropped to her knees, and lay on the still-warm sands. "This is as good a place as any."

Zojja quietly approached. "It's *close by.*"

"You've said that all day," Rytlock noted as he, too, collapsed to the sands.

Logan trudged up, yanked off one boot, and poured a mound of sand to the ground.

"No *wonder* we couldn't find it!" shouted Rytlock. "The sanctuary's been in Logan's boot!"

"Har, har," Logan replied.

Zojja clamped her teeth together. "You're such a charr."

"Where *is* the damned place?" Logan asked.

Zojja closed her eyes and spread her hands. "It feels like . . . it feels like it's every direction."

"No wonder we've been going in circles," Rytlock murmured. He took two gulps from his canteen. "Nearly gone."

Eir handed out hardtack and jerky. "We'll have to begin again tomorrow. We need rest."

Big Snaff arrived in much the same way as Big Zojja. The asura genius climbed from his cockpit and lay down with the others.

"It's going to get cold tonight," Caithe said.

"Cold?" Rytlock asked.

"The desert gets cold at night. I wish we had something to burn."

"I'm burning," the charr said. "Sit next to me, and you'll be plenty warm."

The group didn't say much more as the stars came out above them—millions of them. Their blue light seemed to drag the heat out of the sand. As night wore on, the companions shifted closer and closer together, sharing warmth.

At the darkest corner of night, Rytlock drew Sohothin and laid it on the sand between them to keep them all warm.

One by one, they dropped off to sleep.

They were awakened by the first, knifelike rays of the sun as it pierced the eastern sky. All awoke then except Zojja, who was already standing, eyes closed and hands reaching out to sense the sanctum. "It's right before us. Somewhere right here. In a grain of sand, but which?"

Logan dug his hand into the grit. Sand drained through his fingers, falling in little piles. "A thousand thousand crystals, and one of them holds a sanctuary."

Snaff soberly watched the grains tumble. "Reminds me of poor old Sandy." He suddenly struck his head. "Sandy! Of course!"

"What?" asked Logan.

"Sandy was made of billions of grains of sand—not one," Snaff explained feverishly. "We could hide him in the arena because everyone could see him without even knowing it. It's the same with the inner sanctum. It's not in a single grain. It's in *all* of them! Zojja was right—we're in the middle of it! Just open your eyes!"

As they all stared around them, the cloaking magic eroded.

The sand moved—grains fusing to become crystals and crystals fusing to become gems and gems to become rods and columns and walls and colonnades. Diamond pillars rose all around them, and great archways formed to join them. The arches, too, expanded into a dome the color of the sapphire sky. Walls solidified between archways, and beneath them, the sand became a floor as smooth as glass.

In moments, where there had been only trackless desert, there was now a gigantic sanctuary.

"Weapons out, everyone!" Eir commanded as she nocked three shafts to her bow.

Out came the other weapons—the fiery sword and the spinning hammer and the white-bladed stilettos. Snaff and Zojja scrambled up the legs of their golems and hastily buckled themselves in, powering up the massive machines.

"We're here," Zojja whispered incredulously. She peered down one of the golden colonnades that led away from the central dome. "We're in the sanctum of a dragon."

"And *she's* here as well," Eir warned, "somewhere."

The companions turned back-to-back, gazing out at the beautiful palace.

On one side of the main dome was a crystalline tree. Its leaves were formed of emeralds that glowed with their own light. On the other side hung a huge spear of quartz, suspended above a pedestal. Its blade, too, seemed to glow from within. Each of the three great archways from the main dome led to a golden colonnade. Two of the colonnades extended to distant entrances, beyond which stretched the desert.

But the third colonnade was dark.

From it, an ancient voice emerged as dry as sand: "*At your peril do you wake a dragon.*"

"Form up! On me!" Eir shouted as she drew back her bow and pointed the arrows toward the darkness.

Garm posted himself before her, black hackles jutting and eyes blazing. Rytlock sidled up on Eir's right and Logan on her left. Caithe took her place just behind Eir, ready with her daggers, and Big Snaff and Big Zojja lumbered up to either side of the group.

The companions stood, ready to attack, but they couldn't see the dragon—only claws the size of the asura and enormous eyes floating in the darkness.

The beast spoke again, her ancient voice rattling through them. "*I know why you have come.*"

"We've come to stop your master from rising," Eir responded.

A laugh answered, quiet but shaking the sanctuary: "*You cannot stop it.*"

"But we *can* kill you!" Rytlock roared, charging with Sohothin raised.

Suddenly, out of the darkness, crystalline scales and fangs and claws burst from the colonnade and smashed into Rytlock and his companions, hurling them down. Eir hadn't even time to loose her arrows before the beast's rocklike head struck her and Garm and threw them across the floor. Logan swung his hammer against the massive shoulder of the beast in the moment before it flung him to the floor. The dragon bashed against Big Zojja and Big Snaff, who toppled and crashed to their backs. Only Caithe escaped the dragon's assault, flattening herself as the wyrm rushed by overhead.

Destiny's Edge skidded like toys across the floor.

Gigantic wings grasped the air. Glint wheeled within her sanctuary and landed on the other side. Before her, the companions lay stunned and gasping. Glint towered over them. Her head was mantled in crystalline spikes, sharper than swords, and her body was a mass of muscle and scale. Each leg was as wide as a millennial oak, and each foot was tipped in razor claws. Most horrible of all were her wings—stretching from one side of the sanctum to the other.

"Form up!" Eir shouted as she staggered to her feet.

Her friends struggled to gather.

Glint reared on her hind legs and roared. The sound solidified the air.

The companions fell again.

Only Eir remained standing, gripping her ears to block out the roar. As soon as the dragon's shriek ended, Eir snagged three new arrows from her quiver and nocked them and drew back her bow. These were explosive charges, designed to pierce dragon armor. "You will not raise your master!"

Glint's eyes flashed fury, and her front legs pounded the floor. She stalked forward, claws scoring the marble at her feet. "I have no wish to raise him."

Eir's hand didn't waver, but neither did she shoot. "You can't deceive me, serpent!"

"*I* can't—but a wretch from the Nightmare Court *can*?" asked Glint.

Eir's bow trembled as the dragon stalked toward her. "*We kill dragon champions!*"

The dragon halted, gazing at the explosive arrows aimed at her eye. "Soon, you will get a chance to kill a true dragon." With a sudden lash of her tail, she batted the bow and arrows away. They skidded out of reach.

Eir's hands trembled, numb, but she remained standing.

"How little you remember," growled Glint. "How little you know."

"We know who *you* are!"

"Do you?" roared the dragon, rearing up and spreading her wings through the vault. "I am Glint, Keeper of the Flameseeker Prophecies, Protector of the Forgotten, Foe of the Lich Lord, and Downfall of the Titans! Three thousand years ago, I was set here as a guardian of the world. Three hundred years ago, I welcomed heroes such as yourselves, hailing them as the Chosen who would destroy the titans and save the world. But did they remember? Did not the very heroes that I sent return to battle me again? And now *you* come to slay *me*?"

"Do you know who *we* are?" Eir shouted back. "We are Destiny's Edge, Slayers of the Dragonspawn, Ruination of Morgus Lethe, Damnation of the Destroyer of Life. We have crippled Jormag and Zhaitan and Primordus in their very lairs, and we will not stand aside while you raise yet another Elder Dragon to ravage the world!"

"I know who you are, Eir Stegalkin." Glint dropped her foreclaws to the floor again and stared into Eir's eyes.

"I know the fight you have fought and the damage you have done to dragonkind. More, I know the fight that is ahead of you, and your vanishing hope of success."

"We *will* succeed!"

"*If* you stand together, you will," Glint said, watching as the other members of Destiny's Edge straggled to gather around Eir. "All seven of you, if you stand together—you can win."

Eir stared unblinking into the eye of the dragon while her comrades formed up around her. "Why would you tell us this?"

"Because your battle is not against me. As before, I am your ally."

"*You* would help us stop the dragonrise?"

"No one can stop it. But I will fight beside you against my master."

"Tell us his name!"

The dragon's massive eyes slowly slid closed, then opened again to focus on Eir. "His name is Kralkatorrik."

The name crackled through the air, as if it were crystallizing.

"Why would you fight against your very master?"

Glint nodded in thought and turned away. Her voice sounded ancient and hollow. "Long ago, I lived in a dragon-dominated world. I saw how they feasted on all flesh, on all minds, on all life. I saw how they ate until there was nothing left to eat, and then fell, sated. The darkness of those days slowly gave way to a new dawn— a bright world that did not remember the rapacious beasts. From that time to this, I have feared one of those sleeping dragons. My master, Kralkatorrik.

"But three hundred years ago, the dragons' bellies were empty, and their minds were awakening. Three hundred years ago, the sons of men fought me before they understood that I was their ally."

Eir's brow furrowed. "Why would you ally with humans against your own kind?"

The dragon's great eyes went gray. "I can hear the thoughts of creatures. I am an oracle. I heard their plots against my master, stopped them before they reached him, killed them in their tracks. But I also felt their agony, their loss. It grieved me.

"At first, for centuries, I defended my master. But I could hear his thoughts, too, and I knew that if he rose again, all good things would come to an end." Glint blinked, staring at Eir. "Now is that time. Even now, Kralkatorrik is rising."

Eir gritted her teeth. "Then we *will* ally with you. Your master will rise to face Destiny's Edge *and* a dragon such as himself!"

Glint shook her head. "If you call me a dragon, you must call him a mountain. If you call me a monster, you must call him a god. Even as I fight beside you—and I will—we will be battling a hurricane."

"How can we battle a hurricane?" Eir echoed.

Glint bared her fangs. "I will show you."

DRAGONRISE

Tyria should have known. The signs of the dragonrise were everywhere:

The earthquake that shook Rata Sum.

The tidal wave that carried ships into the streets of Lion's Arch.

The geysers that erupted in the tundra beyond Hoelbrak.

The pall that hung over the Black Citadel.

Tyria had been wracked by such terrible birth pangs before.

The people should have guessed that a dragon was rising.

Ferroc Torchtail's hackles rose. He didn't like the look of that mountain—how it hulked there—spiky, scaly, massive . . . unnatural. He certainly didn't like that his warband was marching *toward* it. He had a feeling of doom.

The last time he'd felt this way, a landslide had buried his centurion.

It had been a year earlier, when Centurion Korrak Blacksnout was marching his legion through a narrow defile in the Blazeridge Mountains. Ferroc was posted in the rear, the position of ignominy—far from the initial charge and the first kill and (as it turned out) the landslide that crushed the leaders. Blacksnout's decapitated body was found on the other side of the landslide.

In shame, Ferroc and the rest of his legion had returned to the Black Citadel. For months, they'd gotten the worst assignments.

This one was no different: go investigate a strange mountain.

Locals said the mountain was moving. They said it grew every night. It shook, it rumbled, it sent down landslides.

Oh, good—*landslides.*

Land was sliding even now. Boulders rolled end over end down the slope and leaped as their edges caught the mountainside. They trailed dust behind them.

Ferroc's warband was marching to fight *what*—boulders?

"Why are we still heading *toward* it?" Ferroc wondered aloud.

Legionnaire Kulbrok Torchfist sneered over his shoulder, "To find out!"

"Find out what?" Ferroc asked. "How it feels to be crushed by a twelve-ton boulder?"

"To find out why the mountain is rumbling."

"Why do mountains rumble?" Ferroc mused, ticking

off possibilities on his claws. "Maybe they're *volcanoes.* Maybe they're *fault lines.* These are reasons to march *away.*"

Kulbrok cast a piercing look at him. "We're charr. We march *toward* such things."

Ferroc nodded. "Yessir." But he let his pace slow ever so slightly, allowing Kulbrok to stride out ahead and the other charr to sift past. He was going to end up in the rear of the column again. The place of ignominy.

The place of survival.

"Aha! *There's* something to fight!" shouted Kulbrok, a good fifty yards ahead by now. He lifted a great sword and pointed toward a crack in the side of the mountain.

The crack was bleeding—not blood, but creatures. A big, fat Gila monster waddled from the crack, only to get bigger as it emerged. Now the size of a crocodile, now the size of a marmox, now the size of an elephant— why was it getting bigger? And beside the giant Gila monster scuttled a horned lizard. It, too, was growing. Its scabrous skin swelled outward, and its eerie face grew larger and stranger, and its blood-spitting eyes became *crystal-shooting* eyes.

They were no longer creatures of skin and scale. They now were crystalline monsters. Jagged spikes jutted out all around their heads and all down their backs and sprouted from their gigantic tails.

"Does anybody else see those things?" Ferroc asked.

"Charge!" Kulbrok replied.

The centurion bolted ahead, followed by his lead warband. Swords darted up and down in their pumping fists.

Ahead, the horned lizard reared up. Crystals shot from its eyes and hailed across Kulbrok and his warband. Many fell, but others ran on. Kulbrok crashed against the raised muzzle of the beast and fell beneath it. Throat spikes gored him. A few warriors rammed swords into the horned lizard, but the blades clanged off its stony flesh. The lizard whipped its spiked head from side to side, impaling the charr.

"Didn't anyone else see that thing?" Ferroc repeated emptily.

Other charr attacked the giant Gila monster—with a worse outcome. It waited for them to strike, ducked back, then lunged to snap them up like so many beetles. Poisonous teeth clamped down on bodies and bones, armor and weapons. With horrid gulps, the giant Gila monster swallowed warrior after warrior.

"Charge!" shouted Legionnaire Longtooth, leading another warband toward the monsters.

But they no longer faced just a horned lizard and a Gila monster. Now vast snakes emerged from the cleft— king rattlers wider than a charr and longer than a warband. They, too, had rocklike bodies and bad tempers.

They ate Longtooth and his soldiers.

Ferroc had slowed to a halt, marching in place. At least he wasn't backing up—a fact that changed when he realized that giant horned lizards and Gila monsters and rattlesnakes were nowhere near as terrifying as *whatever would create giant horned lizards and Gila monsters and rattlesnakes.*

Who cared what came out of the cleft? What was *coming out of the mountain?*

The witnesses had been right. The mountain was moving, shifting, growing.

One of the foothills shuddered. Gravel and sand sifted down its side, revealing rows of horns. Beneath one curve—a curve that looked suspiciously like a giant eyebrow—opened something that looked suspiciously like a giant eye. More rocks shifted, and another eye appeared, surrounded by horns.

"Do you *see* what that thing *is*?" Ferroc shouted.

"Attack!" commanded another charr, charging up the hill. A dozen warriors followed.

Before they reached the thing, an enormous snout shuddered up out of the mountainside and bared great fangs. Fire bloomed out of the mouth, engulfing the charr.

As the horrible breath poured over them, they solidified like statues.

By all rights, the charr warriors should have died, but they were still moving—twisting, becoming something different. Fur became scales, hackles became spines, and everything seemed made of crystal. They no longer looked like charr, but like . . . giant stone monsters. And they turned around and stalked toward the remaining warbands.

Ferroc was unabashedly backing away now. Whatever was happening on this strange mountain, it was beyond him.

Then the titanic head broke free of the mountainside and rose on a muscular neck. The neck looked as if it would stretch from one end of the Black Citadel to the other. It was rooted in powerful shoulders of stone, and wing nubs, and actual wings. With an earthquake, the gigantic wings cracked free of the encasing ground and rose ponderously into the air. Those wings stretched to the unseeable distance on either side of the mountain.

They blocked out the sun.

Across the ridge, spikes of stone flexed slowly.

Rocks sloughed from scaly ribs.

Talons cracked out of bedrock.

The dragon rose from the mountain.

It was the biggest living thing Ferroc had ever seen. It *was* the mountain—a thousand feet high with a wing-span that shadowed the world.

The dragon inhaled its first breath in millennia and then released it in a titanic shriek.

The sound crossed all registers, pounding Ferroc's chest and hurling him back. He hit the ground, his ears bleeding. He tried to scream, but no air was left in him.

The sky had no room for another scream.

Then it all went silent.

Ferroc staggered to his feet and looked up.

The dragon was spreading its crystalline wings. They became the sky. Sinews flexed, and bones folded, and miles of wing gathered the air. A sandstorm roared out. It struck Ferroc and hurled him across the wastelands. He crashed to the ground—how strange not to hear the sound of it!—and felt his bones break.

He was going to die.

An Elder Dragon—a creature of legend that Ferroc had never thought to see with his own eyes—was rising above him.

Another gale.

The thing must have lifted into the air. A thousand tons of dragon was hurling down a million tons of air.

Ferroc Torchtail crawled across the ground. His broken limbs ached, but he struggled to find cover.

Then the dragon's breath flooded over him.

He was transfixed.

Transformed.

Hackles melted to spines, hair to scales.

Legs crystallized.

Ferroc was becoming something new. The dragon's kiln-hot breath was hardening fear into fury and turning him into a giant.

Then the golden gale moved on, pouring on new ground and baking it and transforming it. The dragon scudded away like a thunderhead.

Ferroc stood in the burned and branded wake of the beast, and with his last conscious thought, he hungered to serve Kralkatorrik.

Chief Kronon and his ogre warriors and their hyenas had penetrated deep into southwest Ascalon, only half a day's march from Ebonhawke. They had destroyed three human scouting parties already and planned to kill plenty more before storming the fortress. Charr had already laid siege there, but Kronon and his tribal allies would charge across their backs and take the walls of Ebonhawke.

The life of Chiefling Ygor was worth a hundred charr and a thousand humans.

What was this, though? A black cloud rolled across

the sky, spitting lightning. What kind of storm was this, with eyes that glowed like coals?

A golden thunderstroke broke across Chief Kronon and his warriors.

It bathed them. It broiled them. It turned their muscles to crystals and their bones to stone.

He felt that he was dying.

He felt that he was solidifying—a pupa becoming a wasp.

He grew twice his height before his hide hardened. Then his bones warped to basalt. His hair elongated into stony spikes.

When the thunderstroke ceased, it left Chief Kronon and his army rocklike and massive, more powerful than ever. It left their hyenas like lions carved of stone, except that they moved.

The beam passed on, but the dragon's mind remained. It suffused Chief Kronon's thoughts—gritty like sand. Itchy. It made him forget vengeance for the dead chiefling. It made him only want to follow.

Chief Kronon watched the beam go. It was heading south, toward Ebonhawke.

That was where the master was going.

Chief Kronon flexed crackling arms. "Follow!" he shouted. Even his voice rang like crystal. "Follow!"

"Kralkatorrik is coming," Glint announced in her sanctum. "Fighting him will not be like fighting me. Your golems and weapons cannot harm him. There is only one thing that can."

With a grace that belied her size, Glint slid past the companions and reached the other side of the sanctum. She snatched up the crystal spear that hung there and swung it twice before her. It moaned hollowly as it cut the air.

"This spear was carved from one of Kralkatorrik's own spines," Glint explained. "It can pierce his hide, can find his heart." She thrust it out to Rytlock. "Take it!"

Rytlock stared for a moment at the spear, then clamped his claws around it.

"You must strike the killing blow, right here." Glint motioned to her side, tapping a groove between her ribs. "You must be running when you deliver the stroke, with all your weight behind the lance. Can you do that?"

"Yes."

"I will battle him in the air. I will drive him down toward you. He may be on the ground for only a moment. That is when you must strike."

Snaff piped, "I can help you keep Kralkatorrik on the ground."

"How, little one? Fighting Kralkatorrik is like fighting a sandstorm."

Snaff grinned. "Yes. I have some experience with sand. One of my best friends was made of the stuff."

"This is no time to brag," Zojja said.

"I'm not bragging," Snaff tutted. To the dragon, he said, "I'm an expert in creating powerstone portals into minds. They are portals, except that you don't walk through them with your body, but with your mind. No one else has even attempted this kind of work."

"And how will you survive in the mind of an Elder

Dragon?" Glint asked. "It has no reason. It has only hunger. Rage. Greed."

Snaff nodded. "I play to the hunger, rage, and greed. I become the itch that must be scratched."

"How?" Glint asked bluntly.

Snaff strode over beneath the emerald tree. "What are these green gemstones hanging here?"

"They are petrified drops of blood from Kralkatorrik—blood from his last battle. For thousands of years, I have gathered them from the sands of the desert and hung them on that tree, keeping them from mortal hands. They are magically potent."

"They're like *power*stones," Snaff said avidly, "but tied to the life force of Kralkatorrik." He plucked an emerald leaf from the tree. "Do you know what I can do with these?"

Glint seemed almost to smile. "What?"

"That one golem I mentioned—Sandy—was made out of billions of grains of sand and thousands of powerstone chips. I controlled Sandy with a powerstone laurel, which sent thoughts from my brain into tiny gemstones within him."

"But you don't have time to build a golem," Logan objected.

"I don't need to build one. With these crystallized drops of blood—thousands of them—I could take hold of your former master."

Glint's eyes grew wide.

"We'll pack these blood droplets into exploding arrowheads, and each one that pierces his hide will fill him with thousands of powerstone fragments. They'll be salted through him by the time I need to take over his mind."

Glint shook her head. "You cannot match the will of an Elder Dragon."

Zojja set her hands on her hips. "He stared down Jormag. He can stare down this one, too."

"He can do it," Eir assured Glint, "but we're going to need more than powerstone arrows. We need to get more of these emeralds attached to the dragon sooner." She snapped her fingers. "Those laurels you make, Snaff—could you make something like that for the dragon?"

Snaff's eyes lit. "Yes. Yes, I could! It'll take a rib out of the cockpit of my Big, but I could fashion a powerstone piece—maybe a yoke or torc—that could clamp onto the dragon."

"And Glint," Eir said, "could you fasten the yoke about Kralkatorrik?"

"He would not submit to that."

Eir strode toward her. "Then battle him. For millennia, you have wanted to stop your master. Now, you can do it. Battle him in the skies and place on him a powerstone laurel—a yoke that will give us access to his mind."

Glint's eyes narrowed as if she saw the fight in the sky. "It will take time. You will be overrun by his minions before I can place the laurel."

"Trench works!" Eir said. "U-shaped fortifications in the sand. There are three colonnades—three entrances to this sanctuary. We'll dig a deep trench before each one—"

"And fill them with enspelled dragon-blood stones," Zojja said.

All eyes turned on her.

"I can make them stick to minions," she said. "I can make them embed themselves, and then Snaff can take over their minds. He can use the minions against each other—keep back the tide until you have placed the dragon laurel."

"Perfect idea," Eir said, giving Zojja a rare nod. "And when Snaff must shift his mind from the minions to the master, we all will guard the three doors, keeping him safe until Rytlock can deliver the killing blow."

"How can you keep back thousands of giant monsters?" Glint asked.

"Garm and I can hold one gate, Caithe and Logan can hold another, and Big Zojja can hold the third."

SIEGE AND STORM

Though a besieging army of charr camped on the plains to the north of Ebonhawke, the fortress itself was decked for celebration. The royal banners of Kryta hung beside the emblems of Ebonhawke, and trumpeters lined the curtain walls. In the courtyard below, the Ebon Vanguard stood at attention in their dress uniforms, every inch of black armor polished. Their dark figures were outshone by the 144 white-garbed Seraph who stood at attention around their queen.

Queen Jennah had traveled to Ebonhawke not via the treacherous Shiverpeaks but via the restored asura gate. For years, the gate between Ebonhawke and Kryta had been unreliable, not maintained by the xenophobic human outpost or the last human monarch that could aid it. Years of neglect, though, had been undone by recent treaties. With the defeat of the Destroyer of Life, the asura had sent their best minds to repair and improve the ancient asura gate between Ebonhawke and Divinity's Reach.

Today, Queen Jennah was officially declaring the renewed asura gate open. She stood before the assembled might of Ebonhawke and gestured to the glimmering gate behind them.

Her majestic figure was projected by a mesmeric aura above the crowd, and she spoke to them all. "With this gate, you are no longer alone in the wilderness. With this gate, Ebonhawke is connected to the heart of Divinity's Reach. The asura will maintain it, and it will not fall into disrepair again. Through this gate, supplies will come to you—food and weapons and armor and medicines. Through this gate, reinforcements will come—new recruits and seasoned veterans and even, in time of great need, these white-garbed warriors."

That brought applause from some, but murmurs of uncertainty from others: "We don't need Seraph."

"They're better for parades than battlements."

"She sends them, she'll send orders."

The queen went on, "Through this gate, you will go on leave, out of a land of constant war and into a city of eternal peace, out of the rigors of battle and into the splendors of the greatest city on Tyria. Through this gate, your wounded will go to Vanguard Hospital in the heart of Divinity's Reach, to be cared for as all heroes should."

The warriors cheered that thought, but their celebration was interrupted by the distant rumble of thunder. A few of the trumpeters on the wall turned to gaze north, where a black cloud was boiling up.

"From this day forward, except at time of imminent danger, this gate will remain open—a road between humanity's bravest outpost and its brightest city."

The Seraph applauded these closing words, and the Vanguard joined in. But another peal of thunder—louder and nearer—interrupted the ovation. The trumpeters turned again to see a black cloud eating up the sky.

The queen signaled for the Krytan Fanfare.

Only a few horns began it, but others joined in, swelling the refrain.

A voice spoke in Queen Jennah's ear: "We must get you to safety." It was Countess Anise, a Shining Blade exemplar who was always beside the queen. Anise grasped the queen's arm and impelled her down from the platform.

Dylan Thackeray met the queen on the steps. "My queen, a storm threatens."

Jennah glanced between her bodyguards. "Since when have I feared rain?"

"It's more than rain." Dylan fell in step beside the queen and Anise. "Something stirs the sky, my queen."

The Krytan Fanfare faltered.

Dylan halted, drawing his sword and looking to the wall.

Trumpeters quit midsong and turned toward the stairs. They rushed down while warriors rushed up.

The black cloud was spreading with preternatural speed. In heartbeats, it engulfed the sky. Waves of dark magic riled through the belly of the cloud, and red lightning flickered horribly. In the far west, a strange golden beam tore down from the cloud to rake the horizon.

"I'm going up to see," Dylan told the queen. "Countess Anise, get the queen to the keep, to an inner chamber, and let no one and nothing through to her."

The countess scowled. "Do not tell me my duty, Captain Thackeray. She will be safe."

Anise and two other guardians led Queen Jennah toward the keep of Ebonhawke.

Dylan watched them go. Those Shining Blade always surrounded Queen Jennah, pretending to be greater protectors than he. Let them prove it now. The best way for Dylan to guard the queen was to learn what this storm was.

He rushed up the stairs along the curtain wall. The walkway at the top had long since been vacated by trumpeters, but the Ebon Vanguard remained, staring out.

The sky was black, and the storm overhead convulsed like a living thing. All around the ravenous cloud, dust devils ripped up the ground. Sandstorms boiled, and siroccos screamed.

"The charr'll have a hard time of it," Dylan muttered with satisfaction.

He looked down on the brutes' encampment on the northern plain. Their tents were ranked in even rows surrounded by great iron siege engines. The charr had closed off the eastern and western roads, and their sappers had dug zigzag trenches approaching the walls. Though the charr had besieged Ebonhawke for years, they seemed serious about bringing down the fortress this time—serious about shutting down the asura gate. By the look of the earthworks and war wagons, they were only a month from bringing their siege to storm.

But another storm was overtaking them.

Charr stood in the lanes between their tents, horned heads cast back, eyes fixed on the boiling skies. The storm would be hard on them, indeed.

Movement drew Dylan's gaze. He looked beyond the charr encampment to the dry fields in the far north. Something was advancing there. It looked like a sandstorm—a long line bounding forward across the wastes. But the storm clung to the ground, and it seemed too solid to be sand.

"What *is* that?" asked a young watchman nearby. He peered intently at the line, his head forward, his hands braced on the battlements.

He looked so like Logan that Dylan had to glance back at the young man to make sure it was not he. But no. Why would Logan ever enlist to fight for humanity?

"That's another army," the young watchman said, straightening up.

"Impossible," Dylan replied. "It's moving too fast."

The watchman shook his head. "An army of giants."

Next moment, Dylan himself could see them— huge ogres running across the plains with jagged hyenas in their midst. Dylan had never seen such massive ogres, and light glinted from them as if their skins were crystal.

"To arms!" shouted a nearby lieutenant. The call was echoed along the wall and throughout the bailey below. Watchers loaded crossbows and lifted longbows, ballista crews readied great bolts, catapulters rolled huge stones into their mechanisms.

A crack of lightning split the sky.

The thunder shook the heavens and didn't stop.

Dylan gaped in awe at the voracious bolt.

It struck a charr siege tower, setting the wood ablaze, then jagged like a knife through their camp. It didn't cease, its crackling column ripping open the ground, setting the camp on fire, frying every charr in a hundred feet. The rolling thunder of the bolt solidified the air. Lightning lashed with a will through the charr camp before vaulting to the wall of the fortress itself.

"Look out!" Dylan shouted, but his voice was lost to the thunder.

The lightning smashed the wall, incinerating a catapult crew. It blasted stones apart and hurled ten-ton rocks into the courtyard. One great boulder rolled to crash into the asura gate, toppling it.

The lightning leaped onward to Ebonhawke Keep itself. It exploded the guard station atop it and tumbled the burning warriors to the courtyard below.

The strike then vaulted to the back wall of Ebonhawke and ripped it open as well.

Capering and cackling, it tore on southward, across the Crystal Desert.

Only as the blinding glare eased and the thunder retreated was there room to think.

Stunned, Dylan stared at the lightning's path—the fires that burned the charr camp, the great breach in the northern wall, the toppled ruins of the asura gate, the shattered height of the keep, the blasted rift in the southern gate . . .

It was as if the god Balthazar had run his finger through camp and fort—a boy mixing black ants with red—so that human and charr would annihilate each other.

But it wasn't just humans and charr.

There were ogres, too.

Already, the ogres were charging into the northern part of the charr camp. Rifle blasts ripped out from the charr, but not a single ogre fell. They roared in, their clubs bashing charr, their hyenas tearing through tents. More gunfire. More clubbing. The ogres bounded through the charr as if they were not there. In moments, they would break through the encampment and surge across no-man's-land.

"Prepare to fire!" shouted an Ebon Vanguard lieutenant.

All along the wall, bows drew taut and ballistae creaked and catapults strained.

"Fire!"

A hail of bolts and shafts and boulders vaulted down onto the ogres and hyenas. The arrows only glanced off them. One ballista impaled an ogre, bringing him down, and two of the catapult stones smashed others, but the rest came on.

Armed for hand-to-hand combat, Dylan would be no help on the wall. He turned and descended the stairs into a courtyard in turmoil. Warriors rushed to their posts or struggled to close the breaches in the walls. Dylan strode among them, heading toward the keep.

He would defend it with his life. With his life, he would defend his queen.

Queen Jennah and her three Shining Blade bodyguards had just entered the armory on the fifth floor of the keep when lightning struck. *Boom!* It was like being inside a drum. The walls shuddered, the floor shook, and stones and bodies plunged past the windows.

Hands gripped the queen, steadying her. It was Countess Anise—pale, thin, beautiful, and angry.

"What was that?" the queen wondered aloud. "There was *mind* in that stroke."

Countess Anise said, "Yes. I felt it, too."

The queen stepped up to the window, drawing Anise with her. She stared out into the tormented sky and said, "We are mesmers. We know minds—how to touch them, how to turn them. Let us meditate on the mind in this storm."

Anise channeled thoughts into her.

Queen Jennah of Kryta, staring from a window high in Ebonhawke Keep, peered into the mind of darkness.

It was unlike any she had wrestled before.

A sandstorm. A chaos. Bottomless hunger. Endless outrage.

She glimpsed it for just a moment, but that was enough. In that moment, *it* had glimpsed *her.*

Crying out, Queen Jennah reeled back from the window. Countess Anise caught her, staring in dread at her queen.

"That's what they look like," Jennah said, panting. Her eyes were like mirrors. "That's what it's like to look into the mind of a dragon."

This was Dylan's finest moment. In Divinity's Reach, he had stood vigil beside Jennah through a hundred silken parties and a thousand confetti parades. Now, in the fortress of Ebonhawke, he had his one chance to truly defend her.

Dylan stepped out before the keep, his sword bared. "What comes?"

Something was fighting through the breach in the curtain wall—something huge. Dylan saw golden eyes and snapping jaws and spiked hackles. Vanguard troops clustered before the breach, shoving polearms into it, but the creature still came. Suddenly, a crystalline hyena burst through the rift, breaking it wider. The beast landed on a line of warriors, stone paws crushing them and stone teeth ripping them apart. Behind it, a dozen more of the monsters came.

"Giant hyenas!" shouted one of the guards.

More warriors rushed in to bring down the gibbering creatures, but their blades bashed uselessly off the rocky hides. The hyenas bounded atop the defenders and ate through them. Dozens fell, and the creatures loped forward into the courtyard.

One hyena stalked straight toward the keep.

Dylan lifted his sword, staring at the spiky creature. "What *are* you?"

It came on snarling, its legs gathering speed. It leaped.

Dylan stepped aside, letting it crash into the side of the keep, then rammed his sword into its neck. The hyena wailed, scabrous claws skittering on broken flagstones. Dylan drove his blade deeper, and the hyena shuddered to stillness.

"*That* is for the *queen!*" Dylan cried, dragging his

sword from the wound. He grinned as another of the beasts stalked toward him.

Its eyes were wide, circling in mad hunger, and its nostrils flared with the scent of fresh blood.

Dylan waved his sword. "Is this what you want?"

The hyena bounded toward the blade.

Dylan drove the sword into its mouth. Steel cracked through the creature's palate and rammed into its brain. Wheezing and gushing, it fell atop the other hyena.

Another beast gibbered as it bounded toward him.

Dylan spun, his sword barely lifted before the hyena pounded into him. It hurled him back, smashing him against the keep. He rattled down the wall. The hyena lunged a second time. Stunned and breathless, Dylan wedged his sword between himself and the creature. The blade clacked through the thing's teeth.

The hyena reared back, yanking the sword out of Dylan's hand and flinging it away. The creature yipped and turned its bloody grin on its prey.

Dylan drove himself back against the banded iron door and scrambled to his feet. Weaponless, he lifted his fists. "Come on now."

The giant hyena cocked its head, blinked glassy eyes, and lunged in to bite. Despite the punches to its muzzle, the hyena's fangs bit through the man's right thigh and spilled him to the ground.

Groaning and mantled in blood, Dylan pulled himself back up the door. "Get back!"

It grinned at him and darted its head in again.

It tore him apart.

THE DESPERATE HOUR

As Eir explained her plan, Logan stepped back from the others.

A sudden voice spoke in his head: *Come to me, Logan Thackeray. I am in Ebonhawke. I have need of you.*

"She's calling to me," Logan muttered. "Queen Jennah is calling to me. . . ." His knees buckled, and he dropped to the floor. "No!"

"Are you all right?" Rytlock asked, striding up beside him.

Logan gaped at his friend.

"Come on! Spit it out. We've got an Elder Dragon on the way."

"Queen Jennah," Logan muttered. "She's in trouble."

Rytlock grasped Logan's shoulder and hoisted him to his feet. "What are you talking about?"

Logan said. "She's calling to me! I have to go!"

"What?"

"She needs me!"

"*We* need you!"

"I swore an oath—"

"Yeah, to us."

"No, to *her*."

Rytlock's eyes blazed "You're part of my warband. You are my brother. You can't abandon us!"

Logan turned away, striding toward Snaff. "Give me the hole in your pocket."

The asura genius turned from the dragon-blood stones he had been working and lifted his eyebrows. "Huh?"

"Let me see that hole-in-your-pocket thing."

"This?" Snaff asked, dragging forth the coin-size portal.

"Don't let him—," Rytlock began, lunging, but Logan batted the portal from Snaff's hand.

It flew, tumbling through the air, and expanded into a wide circle with a slender metal edge. The ring tottered flat upon the floor, opening up the portal back to the land south of Ebonhawke.

Logan stepped toward it, but Rytlock grappled him. "You're not going!"

"Let go of me! I have to go. I'll come back."

"What if you can't come back?"

"I *can* come back. I *will!*"

"What's going on?" asked Eir, approaching.

"He's leaving," Rytlock said.

"Leaving?" she said, gaping at the hole in the floor.

"I have to defend Queen Jennah."

Eir looked levelly at him, and her voice was stern. "You have to do what is *right*."

"*Thank you,*" Logan said fiercely, ripping his arms free of Rytlock and leaping through the portal. He seemed to hang for a moment above the sands, but then vanished, and the portal vanished with him.

"What just happened?" shouted Rytlock, his claws swiping the air. "Why did you *say* that?"

Eir said numbly, "I wanted him to stay. . . ."

"Well, he *didn't*. He's gone."

"He's gone," Eir repeated stonily.

The others were gathering now, stunned.

Eir straightened. "We can't change that now. We have our plan."

"Logan was crucial to the plan! It's all about keeping Snaff safe long enough that I can strike the blow. I can't guard Snaff while I'm running with the spear."

"We'll have to guard Snaff without him."

"There are three entrances to the sanctum. We *need* Logan!" Rytlock shot back. "He's our best defender. He's always beside me!"

"He's not beside you now," Eir snapped. "Snaff, get that powerstone yoke ready—now. Rytlock, Caithe, and Garm—prepare your positions. Kralkatorrik will find this place and find all of us. Get ready to defend!"

Logan dropped through the portable portal device, seeing Rytlock and Eir disappear above him. Once he had plunged through the floor of Glint's sanctuary, the portal closed up, becoming as small as a spinning coin.

Logan grunted as he hit ground. He tucked and rolled across the sand dune.

The pocket portal dropped in the sand beside him.

Logan gripped it, hot as it was with the energies it had expended, and slid it into his pocket.

Only then did he look up to see the horror before him.

Ebonhawke rose from the sandy wastes to the north, her curtain wall shattered, her keep battered, and her courtyards roaring with the sounds of battle.

The queen was in there.

If I call, you must come to me.

Logan ran, heart pounding. The sand yanked at his legs, but he tore up the dune, heading for that break in the wall, three feet wide from top to bottom.

But the breach was not unguarded. As Logan ran forward, Vanguard archers stepped from it, their bows raised and arrows drawn. "Halt! Who goes?"

Logan staggered to a stop, panting, and lifted his hands. "I am Logan Thackeray, brother of Dylan Thackeray—"

"*The* Logan Thackeray?" one of the guards said, squinting. "Slayer of dragon champions?"

"Yes."

Both archers now lowered their weapons. "Are *we* in need of *you*! There are giant ogres and hyenas within. They gutted the charr army to reach us and are fighting inside our walls."

"The queen summoned me. I must go to her!"

"Come along!" they shouted, gesturing him forward. "She's in the keep."

Logan ran to the cleft and pushed past the archers, who slapped him on the back as he went. More Vanguard within greeted him, their blood-spattered faces tinged with hope. Logan rushed past them and into the courtyard.

It was in chaos. Stone-skinned hyenas ran rampant through it, tearing apart the Ebon Vanguard. Crystalline ogres climbed the walls. Warriors poured arrows down on their heads, and some jabbed between crystals, but most bounded away. An ogre with hairlike stone spikes topped the wall, swung his arm, and knocked five archers over, into the bailey.

These crystalline horrors were the minions of Kralkatorrik.

Hoisting his war hammer, Logan ran on toward the keep.

A contingent of Seraph stood around the base of it, battling hyenas.

Logan heaved his hammer overhead and brought it down on the skull of one beast. It crashed to the ground.

"Thanks," said a breathless Seraph.

"Let me pass," Logan ordered, pushing through the ranks to reach the banded-iron door beyond.

The sight that greeted him there was horrifying.

Dylan lay beside the door, mantled in blood, his eyes wide, his mouth hanging open.

"No!" Logan shouted. He dropped to his knees beside his brother. "Dylan, no!"

Those wide eyes turned. What was left of that bloodied chest shuddered with a bubbling breath. "Logan . . ."

"You're alive."

"Not much longer . . ."

Blue aura erupted from Logan's fingers, and he touched the wounds in his brother's chest. They glowed, flesh beginning to knit, but the holes were too wide.

"Don't prolong it . . ."

"I have to save you."

"You can't."

"The queen—she summoned me. I have to go to her."

"It's pointless. We haven't enough warriors. They're eating through us. The defenders are all dead."

"It's never pointless—"

Dylan hacked a laugh, looking up into his kid brother's eyes. "Funny to hear that from you."

With that, Dylan Thackeray shuddered to stillness.

Logan leaned forward and kissed his big brother's forehead. "I won't let you down. The defenders are not all dead."

Logan stood and pounded the door. "In the name of Queen Jennah of Kryta, let me in! I am Logan Thackeray, her champion!"

A wooden beam grated, and the door creaked open. Logan forced his way through the gap, only to find a sword at his throat. "What business have you opening— wait, you're Logan Thackeray!"

"Where's the queen?"

The guard hitched a thumb up the stairs. "Five floors up, surrounded by Shining Blade. Nothing gets past them."

"Safe," Logan said, "but only if we win the battle in the courtyard. Which way to the dungeon?"

"Down those stairs, but watch yourself. Hundreds of charr down there—nastiest brutes you ever want to meet."

"Yeah," Logan said, "just the guys we need."

He rushed down the spiral stairs and came to a deep chamber of barred cells with a corridor between them.

A set of keys hung on a hook by the wall, and Logan snatched them up. He marched down the corridor between the cells.

When the inmates caught sight of him, they growled and hooted.

"Silence!" Logan shouted.

"Who are you to command us?" barked a grizzled warrior missing an eye.

"I am Logan Thackeray!"

"Logan Thackeray? Friend of the famous Rytlock Brimstone?"

"The same."

"Slayer of the Dragonspawn and Morgus Lethe and the Destroyer of Life?"

"Yes, yes—all of that," Logan said.

"Who cares?" the one-eyed charr bellowed, and his fellows barked with laughter.

"*You* care!" Logan shouted angrily. "Or, you should, because right now, the minions of a new dragon have slain your armies and are assaulting this keep!"

A shout of glee went up from the cells, and the one-eyed warrior snarled, "Good luck to them."

"May I remind you that you are *in* the keep? You'll be crushed in your cells—or worse."

"*You're* the one who trapped us, human!"

Logan held up the keys. "And I can release you—if you will fight beside me."

Laughter roared from the cells, a deafening sound.

"You are a stupid young man!" the one-eyed warrior growled.

"How's that?" Logan asked.

"Because we'll swear anything to get out, and the moment we're out, we'll kill you."

"No, you won't." Logan lifted the Blood Legion amulet from his neck. "Because I am your brother."

"Bring that emblem here!" said the one-eyed charr. "Let me see that!"

Logan stepped up before the charr, whose single eye scrutinized the amulet.

"He stole it! He took it off Rytlock's corpse."

"No! He gave it to me willingly," Logan said. "We have a common foe. These crystalline ogres are not just attacking the humans in Ebonhawke. They are attacking your people on the plains outside."

"Damned ogres!"

"Fight beside me! Don't wait in your cells for them to come kill you. Swear to fight, and I will release you."

"I swear it on the Claw of the Khan-Ur," growled the one-eyed charr, spitting on the floor.

Logan jabbed the key into the lock and turned it, hauling the gate open.

The charr strode from the cell and snorted, "I'm Flinteye. And you don't stink as much as most humans."

"Greetings, Flinteye. You don't stink as much as most charr." Logan flashed him a smile. "You think any of these others want to fight ogres?"

"Let's find out."

Logan turned to the other cells in the corridor. "All right, listen up! You can sit in here and rot and wait for the ogres to break in and kill you, or you can come with me and get weapons and fight these monsters. Who wants to kill some ogres?"

30

KRALKATORRIK

Big Zojja kicked her way down into the sands. Great plumes of grit flew out of the trench she was digging, curving in a wide semicircle from one side of the northern archway all the way to the other side.

Eir waited beside the trench, clutching a burnoose full of enspelled dragon-blood jewels. "Looks like ten feet deep, Zojja. That should do it."

Big Zojja looked at her, and from within the golem came the metallic voice of Little Zojja. "I don't want anything to jump out."

"Me, neither," Eir said. "But you've got to be able to *climb* out. We need you to guard the east entrance."

The golem stared at the sandy ground up to her waist, nodded, and then began her less-than-graceful climb from the trench. Meanwhile, Eir walked along it, pouring the dragon-blood crystals into the bottom. Those stones were enspelled to cling to the dragon's minions, to embed in the flesh and root deep.

At last, Big Zojja had extricated herself from the trench and clambered to her feet. "One more to dig," said Zojja within.

"No. I got Glint to do it."

Big Zojja's head slumped dejectedly.

Eir shrugged. "We just ran out of time. Don't worry. You've contributed tremendously here, Zojja. These stones at the bottom of the trenches—they're the genius of this plan."

Big Zojja looked up at Eir to see if she was kidding.

"I'm serious. This is going to work," Eir said. "Now, go make sure Snaff is finished with the powerstone yoke, and make sure he's safe within his golem. This whole thing rests on him."

Big Zojja stood rooted before her. "You promise me he'll be safe."

"I promise," Eir replied, "as long as you get to your post."

Big Zojja nodded and tromped off through the archway, heading toward the central dome.

Eir meanwhile looked to the north, where the sky was darkening. At first, it seemed only a giant shadow, as if an eclipse were moving across the world. But then the shadow gained substance. It was a storm—a boiling cloud that grew on the horizon. In minutes, it spread across the whole northern desert. Then it came on, piling high in giant thunderheads.

A monster was in that storm.

She could see it now—the flash of a gigantic eye, the surge of a huge wing, the long lash of a scale-covered tail.

"He's coming!" shouted Eir. "Stations, everyone!"

From within the sanctum came the tromp of Bigs and the scratch of talons and the skitter of claws.

Garm bounded up beside Eir, pressing his muzzle to her hand as if to say this was the day she had always wanted—the day that she would destroy a dragon.

She patted him. "You're right, Garm. You're right."

The black presence now overspread the whole sky. Lightning crackled among the clouds. Golden beams of light stabbed down to bake the desert sands. The ground seemed to melt, to boil and twist. The golden fire seared a highway through the desert. It was heading straight toward Glint's sanctuary.

Eir hoisted her bow, nocked three explosive charges on the string, and drew back to sight the heart of the cloud. She took a deep breath and released.

Three long shafts vaulted skyward, carrying their powerstone payloads toward the beast. The shafts vanished into the murk, and three green flashes ignited within the cloud.

Then came the *boom! boom! boom!*

Shock waves shook the ground.

Already, Eir was lifting three more arrows.

But suddenly the belly of the cloud ripped open, and out of it dropped the dragon. Huge and jagged like cracked stone, it soared toward Eir. Its fangs gaped, its eyes blazed, its hackles spiked.

Eir held her breath and launched another salvo. The three arrows arched over the dragon's head and dropped to stab through the thing's back. Three more flashes, three more *booms!* and the creature shuddered.

Still, the explosions seemed only to enrage it. Its massive mouth dropped wide, and golden breath roared out. The plasma splashed down across the desert, melting sand to glass in a road that led toward Eir.

"Come on, Garm!" Eir shouted. She turned and ran through the archway of the stone sanctum, her wolf at her heels. Behind them, dragonbreath bathed the great arch, which crackled dangerously. "Take cover!" Eir leaped into a niche along one wall.

Garm, meanwhile, ran full out ahead of a flood of dragonbreath. It filled the air from floor to ceiling and gushed around every column and crystallized anything it didn't dissolve.

A moment later, the caustic cloud drew back as the dragon strafed over the top of the sanctuary. The stone ceiling boomed with a huge impact. Stones split, and the archway came to pieces. Another boom sounded farther down the corridor, and this time, the dragon's tail broke straight through. Blocks of stone plunged from the ceiling and bashed down columns and shattered the floor. The dragon's tail ripped on toward the crystal dome.

Just as Eir had planned.

Kralkatorrik struck the dome, and it shattered, hurling shards of glass outward.

And out of that shattered dome, Glint vaulted into battle.

For thousands upon thousands of years, Glint had waited for this moment. She spread her wings, grabbed the air, and rose above Kralkatorrik.

The Elder Dragon was gigantic, twenty times her size, but more sorcery than sinew.

How do you fight a hurricane?

The answer hung in her fangs—the dragon-blood yoke. It had to fit down tightly behind the horns of the giant beast, pressed against its stony skull.

But where was that skull in this tumbling sandstorm?

Glint knew her master—rapacious and ruthless. Its gold-beaming eyes would even now be raking the ground for her. The best way to bring its head around toward her was to draw its attention.

Glint soared down through the pelting crystals of the storm until she could see the beast's broad back. A blow between the wings would bring that massive head around.

Shrieking, Glint dived onto that back and smashed into Kralkatorrik. Talons tore off scales, and fangs ripped through muscle. Green blood sprayed from it, emerald droplets plunging through the air. Glint vaulted off its back, rose up, and dived again.

This time, though, there was nothing to strike. The Elder Dragon's flesh had melted into a sandstorm. She tore at it with claws and fangs, but Kralkatorrik was as insubstantial as a dream.

The dream turned on her. In midair, the Elder Dragon rolled to its back, talons reaching up. Glint tried to loft away, but those claws solidified and grasped her. They pierced her leg and flank and held on crushingly as Kralkatorrik rolled again.

She flailed but could not escape. She could little breathe. Her lung was punctured and bubbling.

Kralkatorrik climbed into the sky, hauling Glint away from her lair. Its hissing bulk merged with the storm.

Eir ran back to her post at the shattered northern archway and loosed three more shafts. They rose past the gutted sanctuary and buried themselves in the storm. Three more flashes bloomed from the cloud.

A skittering sound came behind Eir, and she turned to see Garm rush up beside her. He halted and stared up at the boiling cloud.

Within it, flashes of light illumined two draconic figures locked in a death match.

"She's overmatched," Eir said breathlessly, nocking and releasing three more shafts. "She's a wren, and it's a hawk."

The three charges blew within the cloud, illuminating the hackled back of the dragon.

"I only hope she can place the yoke."

Garm nudged Eir's leg. She glanced at him, but he was watching the horizon.

There, on the plains of the Crystal Desert, marched new figures—giant Gila monsters and tarantulas, gargantuan lizards and snakes and coyotes. All had been turned to living stone by the breath of Kralkatorrik.

Eir stepped back and cupped a hand to her mouth and shouted through the archway. "Man your posts! The minions approach! Let none of them through!"

The monsters came on rapidly. They bounded over the desert—stone jackals and hackled lions and hulking hyenas. All moved with the hunger of the dragon itself.

Eir nocked three more arrows and pointed them at the flood of beasts that approached. She didn't want to waste arrows meant for the dragon on his minions, but they came so quickly. Eir stepped back, and Garm with her.

A stone-skinned lion and a gibbering hyena arrived first, leaping over the trench works. Their claws were spread before them, their fangs gaping in mad grins—

But stones shot from the trench into their bellies.

The lion and the hyena tumbled in midair and crashed to the ground. Their translucent hides showed where the dragon-blood crystals had bedded within them. Thrashing in fury, the two beasts scrambled to their feet and turned on Eir.

She backed up another step, the powerstone arrows jutting before her.

But the lion and the hyena only turned away. Side by side, they bounded back over the trench and rushed into the oncoming wall of monsters.

"Snaff's got them," Eir said breathlessly. "He's got control."

The lion and the hyena tore apart a number of the beasts, but more slithered and pounded and bounded forward. Some dropped right into the trench, and others tried to leap over it, but all of them were brought down by dragon-blood stones. All of them turned from attackers to defenders.

"He's buying her time," Eir said, at last releasing the

three arrows to vault skyward and explode in the hide of the beast. "If only Glint can set the yoke."

Kralkatorrik held Glint in a death grip. It would never release her now. It wanted her dead, and to kill her, all it had to do was close its talons.

But then—*boom! boom! boom!*—three bright green blasts erupted across its belly. Pain ripped through it, and for a moment it was not thinking of the traitor clutched in its grip.

A moment was all Glint needed. She wrenched sideways, ripping the claws of the dragon from her side, and darted away from it on the wind. The dragon-blood yoke was still clutched in her fangs—this one slender hope for success.

Though her lungs were filling with blood, Glint labored skyward like a wounded dove. She would have but one chance this time. Kralkatorrik knew she was there in the storm, would be seeking her with all its focus. If only she could spot its head first.

And there it was, below her and to the left.

Glint tucked her wings and dived. She jutted her jaw so that the blood-stone yoke reached forward to take hold. She fell from the sky, millennia of vengeance packed into a moment.

The yoke stabbed down toward the dragon's horns and neck.

But it glimpsed her.

Its head darted up.

Before she could set the yoke, its fangs snapped onto her body.

Glint jolted, seized in the maw of the monster.

She could almost reach the back of Kralkatorrik's head, could almost put the yoke in place, but one more bite from him would kill her.

She lunged.

Kralkatorrik bit.

A dragon scream split the heavens.

Eir looked up. "Which one?"

The black cloud parted, and something plunged from it.

"No!" Eir cried.

The figure that fell was Glint. Broken wings streamed in the wind. Claws jutted stiffly. She fell like a comet, trailing smoke.

The other heroes saw it, too—staggering out into the sands.

She plunged toward the desert. Her body struck, hurling up a great plume of sand. Fire erupted around her, and she tumbled end over end across the ground.

Two seconds later came the sound of the impact— shattering stone, a mountain breaking. The ground trembled and reeled, and the dragon's broken body left a long furrow ending in a crater. A storm of sand rose into the heavens, and a rain of crystalline scales cascaded all around.

The dragon Glint was dead.

THE CHARR VANGUARD

Logan Thackeray and Flinteye Blazestone marched nearly a hundred charr warriors up from the bowels of Ebonhawke Keep. As they reached the ground floor, Logan gestured through a doorway: "Weapons in there, boys!"

The charr roared, piling through the door and greedily grabbing up swords, crossbows, axes, hammers, knives . . .

Logan strode to the banded-iron door and hoisted the beam. The door swung outward. "Whoever wants a fight, follow me!" He turned and bolted through the archway. "Charge!"

"Charge!" echoed Flinteye.

The charr vanguard rushed out past the ravaged body of Dylan Thackeray and into combat with the creatures that had slain him.

Crystalline hyenas ran rampant through the bailey and feasted on the fallen. The beasts looked up from their meals, jowls spattered in red. One loped away from its kill, and two more joined it. The pack formed up and came on. Stone hackles spiked across their backs, and they broke into a run toward the charr.

Logan and his allies lifted their weapons and charged. Logan's hammer crashed into a canine head, splitting the rocky carapace and smashing through to bone and brain. The beast was dead, but its momentum carried it forward so that Logan had to spin aside and let the hyena smash to the flagstones. The move brought his hammer wheeling up and bashing into the head of another beast.

Flinteye meanwhile brought his elbow down to break the back of a hyena. With a roar, the charr lunged at another, seized its crystalline throat in his teeth, and ripped it out.

Two crystalline creatures leaped at Flinteye. He sidestepped one and ducked down to head-butt the other. Horned brow crashed into stone brow. One skull cracked. The hyena yelped and fell to the ground, whining. Flinteye reeled back and grabbed his forehead. Even as he did so, though, he stomped on the hyena's neck and broke it.

Logan, meanwhile, slung his hammer overhead and shattered the hackles of the other beast. Enraged, the hyena crashed into him, knocking Logan back. Stony teeth clamped on his breastplate, digging in to gouge Logan's chest. He slammed his hammerhead into the creature's jaw but couldn't break free.

Flinteye kicked it in the throat, and when the hyena staggered back, he grasped its head and twisted to snap its neck.

"Thanks," Logan said.

"Whatever," replied Flinteye, spinning to attack another hyena.

Logan and his charr allies waded through the pack of hyenas. They fanned out through the courtyard and bashed every beast in sight. Hyena cackles gave way to yips and barks and whines. The pack was calling for help. Every last hyena within the fortress converged on the killing ground. Fangs and claws met maces and mauls. Soon, in the bloody midst, only Logan and the charr remained.

Logan sighed, swinging his hammer in long loops to stretch out his shoulders. "Nothing like a good fight to get the cricks out."

"That was nothing like a good fight." Flinteye nodded ahead, where a band of ogres had just staggered into the courtyard. "*This* will be a good fight."

Logan pivoted toward the ogres and brought his bloodied hammerhead to bounce on his hand.

The ogres' eyes lit with rage, and they thundered forward.

Flinteye roared and charged. He ducked beneath the moaning hammerhead of one ogre and ripped his claws through the back of the monster's thigh. Two loud *pops* sounded, and the ogre's leg collapsed.

"Look out!" Logan shouted as the ogre toppled toward Flinteye.

The charr rolled away just as the beast crashed down, driving flagstones deeper into the ground.

Logan brought his hammer down to stave in the forehead of the ogre. "That's one for me."

"This is no game, mouse!" Flinteye roared, thumping his chest.

Logan laughed. "You're no Rytlock Brimstone."

"And you're no Blood Legion warrior!"

Logan leaped back as a charr slumped down dead before him. The ogre that had killed the charr reached for Logan.

He wheeled around, his hammer shattering the wrist of the monster.

The ogre staggered back, shaking its hand, and nearly tromped on Flinteye.

Roaring, Flinteye hamstrung the ogre. It fell to its backside, and Flinteye leaped on its chest and ripped out its throat. Clutching the grisly trophy in his claws, he scowled at Logan. "Don't make me clean up after you."

"Look out!" Logan shouted, pointing.

Flinteye never saw the massive cudgel that struck him in the stomach and hurled him through the air. He tumbled across the courtyard, crashed into the wall, and slid down in a heap.

Logan charged the ogre and hammered its left leg. Bones broke, sending the creature to its knees. Then Logan smashed the ogre's jaw. Down it went, rolling belly to face.

Dodging beyond it, Logan ran to the place where Flinteye lay. The old charr's legs and arms were shattered by the impact, but his chest still moved.

"Flinteye!" Logan said.

The charr stared back, blood gurgling from his mouth. "Tell Rytlock . . . tell him I died fighting." His last breath rattled out of his lungs.

A roar of incoherent rage shook the walls of Ebonhawke. Humans clutched their heads and charr and ogres winced back from battle.

The cry came from Chief Kronon, who stood above the bloodbath with arms outstretched and head thrown back—bellowing. As he brought his head back down, an eerie light shone from his eyes.

"This can't be good," Logan muttered.

Chief Kronon howled again, an otherworldly sound like the cry of the Elder Dragon itself.

That cry was answered by another ogre, and a third and a fourth. All of them were throwing their heads back and bellowing to the sky. Their voices rattled the stones of the keep and made humans and charr drop to their knees. The ogres shuffled toward their chieftain and stood beside him, wailing their lament. The remaining hyenas loped up beside them as well, adding their peculiar cackles to the cacophony.

As the ogres and hyenas filled one side of the courtyard, the humans and charr gathered on the other, all around Logan.

Suddenly, the howling ceased. The crystalline monsters lowered their heads, and their gold-glowing eyes stared levelly across the courtyard. Then they broke into a charge.

Logan raised his hammer and roared, "Charge!" He swept forward, surrounded by humans and charr.

The tide of ogres crashed on the defenders, trampling some, kicking others through the air, crushing more in titanic claws.

A man on one side of Logan fell beneath a stomping foot.

A charr on the other side had his head bitten off.

The clamor of combat, the groans and screams—it was the same as that battle in the Blazeridge Mountains, as Logan and Rytlock fought side by side against ogres.

This time, though, there would be no survivors.

32

BATTLE OF THE CRYSTAL DESERT

At the center of Glint's sanctuary, Big Snaff stood alone, so there was no one to hear the tinny shout of joy that came from Little Snaff: "She did it! Glint did it! She got the yoke on Kralkatorrik!"

The powerstone laurel on Snaff's head flashed, bathing the cockpit in an eerie glow. Those stones cast an even stranger light into Snaff's mind.

Everything went green—solid green, as if he was staring into an emerald. He could even see his own reflection in a facet of the stone. His face looked intent, squinting, trying to peer into the heart of the gem.

Snaff backed away.

This jewel had *many* facets, all reflecting his curious gaze.

But it wasn't a jewel. It was an eye—a huge compound eye.

The true eye of Kralkatorrik.

The dragon was *staring* at him, seeing him in a

thousand facets. Its gaze was cold and calculating, inexpressibly cruel.

Then every reflection of Snaff in every facet began to crystallize.

"No!" Snaff yelled.

His flesh hardened, grew rigid and angular.

He was becoming a minion of the Elder Dragon!

Panicked, Snaff thrashed to get away, but the dragon saw all.

Snaff was dying.

Tap . . . tap . . . tap . . . !

What was that sound?

Tap, tap, tap—

Was it the stony heart of the dragon, mesmerizing his mind with its monotonous beat?

"Did you call for me?"

His eyes flashed open, and he ripped the emerald laurel from his head. The cockpit was plunged into darkness. Through the windscreen, Snaff saw the concerned face of Big Zojja.

She crouched beside Big Snaff, tapping her finger on the glass. "Helloooooo? You in there?"

"Yes, I'm in here!" Snaff blurted. "Of course I'm in here. There's not an escape hatch." He blinked in sudden alarm. "Why isn't there an escape hatch?"

Big Zojja straightened up, and Little Zojja's voice rang from within. "I thought I heard you shout something, and I wanted to make sure everything was all right."

"I'm trying to wrestle a dragon's mind! Of course everything's not all right!"

"Don't get testy. I was just checking on you."

"Go guard." Snaff said, waving his hand vaguely toward the eastern colonnade. "I'll be safe. I'll be fine."

"Better be," she said, and Big Zojja pivoted away, her foot grinding grit into the floor.

Snaff watched that miracle in steel and silver—that genius apprentice of his—jog away through the sanctum. "You be safe, too."

And then Snaff closed his eyes and lifted the emerald laurel to his head and sought out the mind of the dragon.

It was not hard to find.

The dragon's eye was seeking *him*.

Its mind was in every facet.

As Big Zojja stood in the eastern colonnade, inside the cockpit, Little Zojja wondered if she or any of her friends would survive this day. They had fought dragon champions, yes, but never dragons, let alone *Elder Dragons*. And nobody in the history of *history* had ever tried to take hold of an Elder Dragon's mind.

But Snaff would succeed—wouldn't he?—if only so that he could brag about it afterward: "Did I ever tell you about the time I single-handedly wrestled Kralkatorrik to the ground? Or I should say, single-*mindedly*?" How annoying would *that* be?

Yet Zojja hoped against hope that Snaff would live to tell that tale—and that she would live to hear it.

The fact was, Snaff really was a real genius. No one could build golems the way he could. No one understood mind auras the way he did. He could think circles around anyone. That was what was so annoying and inspiring about him.

If anyone could take hold of an Elder Dragon's mind and drive it to the ground, Snaff could.

But not if those giant devourers reached him.

Ahead, a line of massive, two-tailed scorpions scuttled through the eastern gate and swarmed among fallen hunks of ceiling.

They'd never come close to her master.

Big Zojja's left hand splayed, and fire roared from her fingertips and engulfed a group of devourers, sizzling their joints until they couldn't move. It baked their innards until they burst like popcorn.

Pure genius. Snaff had stocked the water reservoirs with oil.

Big Zojja's right hand crashed into another batch of devourers. The rock drills cracked through stony carapace and ground the meat within.

Big Zojja cleared the hall, baking half of the monsters and grinding through the other half. In mere moments, she had cleansed the whole colonnade and stood, shiny and spectacular, in the sanctum's eastern entrance.

Let the dragon minions come. None would get past her.

Snaff stared at his reflection in the compound eye of the beast—stared so long that he passed *through* the reflection and found himself on the other side . . .

Within the dragon's mind.

It was like standing in the eye of a cyclone. All

around, a great storm raged, tearing down the heavens and churning up the sands and whirling all in primordial chaos. Tortured coils of cloud mixed with dissolving seas of silt. The winds scoured away rock and rill, tree and blade, flesh and bone—and tossed them all in a crystalline tempest.

All things were fuel to that storm.

Everything was a feast to Kralkatorrik.

How does one fight a hurricane?

Snaff suddenly knew. The insight came from an offhand conversation he had had with Master Klab, the icebox genius. He was speaking about temperature differentials—how the air in the icebox was cold and dense, and the air in Rata Sum was hot and light, how opening the door of an icebox created a vortex of frost, where the dense, cold air sought to spiral into the light, warm air "like water swirling down a drain!" Klab had proclaimed this idea in his grating way, and Snaff had curled his nose and said that he had "gotten it."

But only *now* did he understand.

The center of every vortex is a great emptiness—a hollow longing. The storm tries to fill the emptiness, but the more it hungers, the deeper the emptiness becomes.

And Kralkatorrik's hunger was insatiable.

To draw the dragon, Snaff had to become the eye of the storm—to *be* what Kralkatorrik was not.

Where the dragon was fury, Snaff had to become bliss.

Where the dragon was rage, Snaff had to be delight.

Where the dragon was ancient and bloodthirsty and voracious, Snaff had to be new and altruistic and quite content, thank you very much.

Snaff thought of mathematics, the infinite beauty of numbers.

The dragon's mind whirled tighter around the intruder.

Snaff thought of the smile on Zojja's face when she invented a new ankle joint for her Big.

Around Snaff, the fury of the storm redoubled. The eye squeezed around this still center.

Snaff remembered the look of shock and betrayal on Klab's face when he became the director of pest control.

Enraged, the dragon sought this delighted mind, this maddening contentment. The eye of the dragon shifted, fixing on the ruined sanctuary far below.

That was where it lurked.

But not for long.

The minions of Kralkatorrik would root out this intruder.

At the south gate of Glint's sanctuary, a thousand-ton snake reared up, searching for Snaff.

"To get to him, you'll have to get past us," Rytlock growled. He leaned his crystalline lance toward the looming beast, daring it to attack.

The snake's gigantic head swayed from side to side. Blinking eyes the size of bucklers, the snake lunged past the lance and snapped down on the charr—or tried to. Rytlock leaped aside as the fangs buried themselves in sand.

Caithe meanwhile vaulted onto the creature's back and jammed its scales up and rammed her white-bladed stiletto into its spine.

The giant snake arched to snap at the sylvari, but she clung just out of reach. Each jolt only drove her dagger deeper into the beast's neck. It flailed back and forth upon the sands, trying to hurl its attacker away, but Caithe held on. At last, the snake slumped to the ground and twitched to stillness.

"Nicely done," Rytlock remarked as Caithe vaulted from the serpent's back.

"Like old times," Caithe said.

"Not like old times," Rytlock growled. "Logan's not here."

An enormous Gila monster charged the entryway. The charr rammed the lance into its neck. The crystalline spear cleaved through one side of the creature's jowl, spilling stony darts to the ground. The blade delved deeper until it bit through the spine, sending the huge lizard to its belly.

"Doesn't seem we need Logan," Caithe said.

Rytlock shot her an amazed look. "It should be the *three* of us guarding this gate, just like Eir planned. What happens when I go to attack the dragon? Can you hold this gate alone?"

Caithe stared unblinking at him. "I'll have to."

"Yeah, you will."

Just then, a giant spider rushed the two. Rytlock drove the lance into its mandibles and deep into its throat. Impaled though it was, the spider swarmed over Rytlock, knocking him to the ground and clutching him with spiny legs. Its swollen abdomen twitched as a dripping stinger slid forth.

Caithe stung first, plunging her dagger into the narrow joint that connected the spider's abdomen to its body. The spider shrieked. Caithe twisted the blade, cutting the abdomen free. It fell to the ground, its stinger gushing. The creature convulsed, and its legs seized up around Rytlock.

"Damnit!" Rytlock growled. Sohothin flared free of its stone scabbard and blazed through the tangle of legs. Rytlock climbed through the smoldering mess and strode to the front of the monster. He yanked out the crystalline lance. "Can't kill a bug. How's it going to kill a dragon?"

"It will," Caithe assured. "You have the strength."

"Yeah," Rytlock said as a pack of crystalline coyotes loped toward them. "The question is, does *Snaff* have the strength?"

If its minions could not reach the intruder, the dragon could.

"There it is!" shouted Eir, lifting her bow skyward.

The clouds burst open, and Kralkatorrik dropped out of them. Its wings reached from horizon to horizon, and its blazing eyes poured ravening power on the ground below.

Eir loosed three blood-stone arrows. They climbed the sky and smashed into the belly of the beast and lit up bright green. Three more shafts rose as the dragon plunged. The arrows exploded on the dragon's shoulders and back, embedding more powerstones. Three more. Six. Each bolt gave Snaff that much more hold on the dragon's mind.

But Kralkatorrik soared down toward Eir, opening its cavernous mouth.

"Get under cover!" Eir yelled to Garm. She glanced back at the sanctum, torn open from end to end, and then forward at a giant Gila monster. A blow from her mallet brought it down, and she dived beneath it. Garm crowded in beside her.

Plasma roared down from the cloud, and crystals erupted across the army. The dragon's first breath had turned these creatures to living stone, but this second breath made them dead monuments.

In hatred for all mortal flesh, Kralkatorrik destroyed the monsters it had made.

Scabrous backs bristled into heaps of stone. Heads shriveled to black nubs. Flesh melted, and creatures died, and the dragon winged on.

Eir and Garm crawled from beneath the stone beasts.

The world had been transformed. From the northern horizon to the place where Eir stood, the land had been blasted and fused and crystallized. Hundreds of minions of the great beast now stood as statues.

Eir hoped that Caithe and Rytlock and Zojja had found cover, but of course, the most important question was—had Snaff survived?

The dragon's ravening power had roared through the whole of the sanctum, crystallizing everything. Even Big Snaff had turned to stone.

But within the belly of the golem, Little Snaff hung unharmed. Gemstones flashed around his head.

Snaff was deep within the dragon's mind now. He had sunk past its consciousness and delved into the recesses of the lizard brain. This was the reptilian place beneath all that crystalline thought. It was a place of breath and blood, hunger and lust.

Here, Snaff was not just a maddening idea. He was an irresistible itch bedded deep in the spine of the beast.

Lungs, forget to breathe.

Heart, forget to beat.

Wings, fold.

Eyes, close.

The lizard brain battled back. It struggled to regain control.

Dragon, fall.

Eir drew more exploding arrows from her quiver, nocked them, and drew back her bow as Kralkatorrik approached for another pass.

But something was different this time. The dark center of the storm where it flew had begun to twist. Sand and wind and blackness knotted themselves around it in a churning ball. Lightning raked out from it and split the sky and lashed the ground. The crackling thunder gave way to an omnipresent roar.

Still, the wyrm turned, twisting the storm tighter and tighter around it. Here, a wing tip slashed through the black shroud; there, a claw raked free before being swallowed again. Golden beams of ravening light flashed all around that whirling core.

Then the Elder Dragon seemed to ignite. Fire roared

out from it, the heat melting the sands, destroying the minions that raced along below.

Eir fell back into the archway, shielding herself.

Kralkatorrik shot by overhead, eating up the air. Its flaming form caused the stone walls of Glint's sanctuary to explode with heat.

A moment later, the burning dragon plunged toward the desert beyond.

Kralkatorrik fell like the fist of a god.

It smoked.

It roared.

It plunged into the sands.

A white-hot shock wave swept out, leveling any beast it struck. From the point of impact, a vast plume of sand hurled skyward, the particles catching fire as they flew. Still, the massive beast plowed through the ground, ripping a long furrow in the desert. Pyroclasts rolled out all around it. The world shuddered as the beast tore it open.

Then, at long last, the shaking stopped, and the fires flared out, and the cloud of debris lifted. It revealed a deep crater torn through the desert floor, a black and smoldering scar. At its farthest point thrashed an Elder Dragon. It was on its back, giant wings pounding the tortured ground, but it could not right itself, could not rise.

"Kralkatorrik is down!" shouted Eir. "Kralkatorrik is within reach!"

"I've got to go!" Rytlock said, lifting the crystalline lance.

"Then go!" Caithe replied. "The dragon has thinned the ranks for me."

Hundreds of dragon minions had been turned to stone, but dozens more clambered across the desert toward the south gate.

"You can't guard the gate alone!" Rytlock said.

Caithe's eyes blazed. "I have to! Go!"

The charr nodded and ran. In his claws, he carried the crystalline lance.

Before him, the glassy ground sloped away into a great black crater, wide and deep. Rytlock bounded into it and ran down the ragged rift. Crystals cracked beneath his claws as he went. Ahead, at the terminus of the great scar in the ground, lay the mountainous monster.

Kralkatorrik was upside down, thrashing with his breast bared.

Rytlock ran on, lifting the crystalline lance. The rift seemed impossibly long. He only hoped he could reach the dragon before the dragon's minions reached Caithe.

Caithe stood alone in the south gate as dozens of beasts came her way.

First was a crystalline coyote, enormous and whooping. Its rocklike teeth snapped at Caithe.

She feinted back and grasped one stony whisker and flung herself onto the coyote's back. She plunged her white-bladed stiletto into the creature's neck and twisted, ripping through its spine. The coyote's whoop devolved into a ragged gasp of pain, and it collapsed.

Caithe leaped free, only to see more of the dragon's

minions pour past her. Horned lizards and giant rats
and geckos and tarantulas and jackals and snakes all
thundered by, heading for Big Snaff in the center of the
sanctum.

Caithe rushed after the bounding horde. She jumped
from beast to beast, ripping out their throats and pounding their skulls into the ground as she leaped away,
squealing, but still the others ran on.

They converged on Big Snaff.

Snaff lay embedded in the deepest layers of the dragon's
mind, choking off breath and pulse. The dragon could
not find him here, could not root him out. It could not
even right itself.

But its minions found Snaff elsewhere.

There came a crash—stone shattering—and the
rumble of claws.

Claws dug, and jaws gibbered.

Snaff opened his eyes.

Big Snaff had toppled and shattered, and the monsters were on him.

Fangs snapped.

Muzzles bled.

Hungry. Angry. Insatiable.

Teeth clamped on Snaff. They bit through him.
There was blunt pain and the sudden certainty that he
was dying.

More teeth seized him.

Bones broke.

Breath burst through his wounds.

Blood foamed out.

Fangs met in his stomach.

Rytlock was galloping toward the downed dragon when it suddenly rolled over and righted itself. Its holocaustal eyes glared down the length of the crater at the running charr, a stone lance in his claws. Then Kralkatorrik spread massive wings and beat them against the air and rose from what should have been its grave.

"*No!*" roared Rytlock.

The dragon lifted easily away and climbed into the sky.

"*No!*" Rytlock bellowed, hurling the spear.

It arced up, cracked off the shoulder of the beast, bounding away. The lance fell, useless, in the crater.

Already, Kralkatorrik was out of reach. Its mile-long wings thrummed the air, blasting flat every creature on the desert below.

Rytlock Brimstone fell to his knees.

Winds buffeted.

The dragon retreated, unhearing, uncaring. Its wings boiled the clouds as it climbed. It ripped through them and rose, leaving only a troubled wake across the heavens.

SUNDERING

Logan's hammer shattered the knee of an ogre. It toppled like a tree and smashed into one of its comrades, which crashed on top of a charr. A second charr vaulted onto the fallen ogre and ripped out its throat—only to be cleaved by a great axe.

It was a bloodbath in the courtyard of Ebonhawke. Seraph and Vanguard, Blood Legion and Iron Legion, ogre and hyena, fought and fell. The battle roared like a ravenous monster that would not rest until it had eaten them all. At the heart of that maelstrom, Logan Thackeray held the line by sheer force of will and rallied the defenders for one last, desperate surge.

Then, above the fortress city, a greater monster arrived. Its wings blackened the sky, and the beat of those wings pounded down on the warriors below. Ogres and hyenas looked up and wailed in glee. Humans and charr groaned in dread.

Kralkatorrik had returned.

It shrieked, a sound bigger than the sky.

Every mortal creature dropped to its knees.

Kralkatorrik's eyes lit, and twin beams of ravening power raked down upon the warriors. Charr hackles hardened to spikes. Human muscles clenched to stone.

The ogres grinned to see their enemies transformed. It turned them to rock but left them puny—punishment for their resistance. The beams blazed through the courtyard, catching every last human and charr.

The battle of Ebonhawke was done.

Kralkatorrik had declared the victors.

The last outpost of humans in Ascalon would now be a dragon fortress.

The Elder Dragon screamed, and its ogre minions bellowed in joyful reply.

Then the dragon's wings pulsed, and it pivoted massively above the fortress. Another stroke of those wings, and Kralkatorrik banked away, heading south.

The ogres and hyenas watched in grief as their master left them. Their faces fell, and they stared at the pathetic dragon minions all around. With looks of disgust, the ogres turned away and loped toward the shattered southern wall. They clambered through, their hyenas leaping at their heels.

The once-humans and once-charr did not move from their spots, as if rooted in place.

Still, the ogres followed their master. Let these puny minions hold Ebonhawke. The ogres would serve their lord directly.

Through the wall they went, and down upon the rocky lands beyond—southward, ever southward into the Crystal Desert. With bellows and cackles, they followed their ancient lord.

Kralkatorrik already was impossibly distant, and it flew at terrific speed. Soon, it would be lost to sight, but the ogres would follow until they were in the presence of their master.

Logan stood unmoving in the courtyard of Ebonhawke. He had been transfigured like all the rest—not transformed, but *transfigured*. When the dragon's eyes stared down upon him, his outer semblance became something new—stony and strange. It was as if every muscle seized up, and he had become a living statue.

But his mind still turned, still told him that his friends had failed. They had failed because he had abandoned them. And now, Kralkatorrik held him.

As the last of the ogres climbed through the wall and lumbered away across the rocky hills, the glamour that gripped Logan and the others faded away.

Logan panted, only then realizing he had forgotten to breathe.

A Vanguard warrior nearby staggered and clutched his knees.

A charr legionnaire whipped his head back and forth, eyes blazing. "What sort of sorcery was that?"

"My type of sorcery," came a voice high above, "mesmerism."

Logan and the others looked up to see, on the highest balcony of the keep, Queen Jennah. From that lofty spot, she had cast the illusion of the dragon in the sky. She had poured down golden light to lave the warriors below, had made them seem creatures of stone. Her spell had been so powerful, they had not known they could still breathe.

"I've deceived them, the minions of Kralkatorrik," Queen Jennah called. "I have saved you, human and charr alike. We have been enemies these many centuries, but now there is a new enemy for us both.

"This is a dark day, the first of many. This is a day of dragons. We must stand together against them, or we will all fall beneath. And so I am releasing these charr prisoners." She gestured down at the group of charr standing beside the fortress's portcullis. "They have fought beside us, and they are free."

Logan strode toward the line of charr. "Did you hear that? You're free."

One of the warriors said, "We fought beside humans. We will be outcasts."

"No," Logan said. "I've spent the last year fighting beside a charr. Am I an outcast?"

The charr looked him in the eye. "I will tell them I fought beside Logan Thackeray."

"Yes. Tell them that."

Zojja ripped away the straps that bound her into the cockpit and pounded the button that made the blast shield slide down. Vaulting from her golem, she landed achingly on the floor of the sanctum and ran to Big Snaff.

It lay where it had fallen, shattered stone and smoking servos.

Zojja stared hopelessly into the gutted belly of the golem. There, amid torqued stanchions, lay a limp figure, pierced in many places and bloodless.

He was dead.

Snaff was dead.

"No!" Zojja screamed.

Running feet approached—Eir arriving to grip the fuselage of the golem and stare within. "You can't die!"

"He's dead already!"

Eir reached into the cockpit, hands fumbling. "You can't die." Eir pulled Snaff's broken body from the wreckage and cradled him.

"Put him down!" Zojja yelled. "You have no right! Your plan failed. You *killed him!*"

Eir's green eyes opened wide. "*I* killed him?"

"Put him back!"

Eir stood for a long while, holding the asura genius. Then slowly, reverently, she lowered his body back into the ruined golem.

"Now, get out of here!" Zojja snapped. "I have to cremate him."

Numbly, Eir turned and wandered away through the shattered sanctum.

Zojja waited until the norn was gone. Then, with tears streaming down her face, she said, "Good-bye, Master."

She lowered her hands into the shattered cockpit of Big Snaff and called forth cremating fire.

"Pointless," Rytlock muttered as he stared out at the battlefield.

Before him, the sands had fused to green glass, entrapping a thousand stone creatures. To his right lay Glint, destroyed in combat against her master. To his left lay her ruined sanctuary—once a haven in the Crystal Desert and now a ragged memorial.

"Pointless."

Especially because they had been so close. Just a few moments more and the lance would have pierced the dragon's heart, and Kralkatorrik would have died, and Snaff would have lived.

A few moments that Logan could have given them.

"Logan!" Rytlock roared, ripping Sohothin from its sheath and ramming it into the ground. "It's your fault!"

The shout rang false. It wasn't Logan's fault. It was Rytlock's, for trusting a human. For letting a human's softness make him . . . weak.

"I'm a fool," Rytlock said.

"You're a hero," said Caithe, stepping up to him. "We can't wallow in grief."

"Wallow!" Rytlock growled. "Two of our companions are dead."

"And more will be if we don't join together," she insisted. Her strange white face, so small and intense, stared at his own. "We have to regroup, come up with a new plan."

"There's no more group. There's no more plan."

"But we haven't finished—"

"*I* have." Rytlock crouched to pull his flaming sword from the ground, slung it in its sheath, and strode away.

"What does that mean?" she shouted after him.

Rytlock continued to walk.

"Rytlock, what does that mean?"

He made no reply.

Caithe strode through the ruined sanctum of Glint, heading toward the fallen golem.

Zojja was within. She had removed one of Big Snaff's epaulets and was using it as an urn to gather her master's ashes.

Caithe spoke softly. "Rytlock is leaving."

"Just like Logan."

"We have to stop him, or go with him."

Zojja smiled sadly. "I don't have to do anything."

"Don't be irrational," Caithe said.

Zojja's eyes clouded with anger. "Who are you to tell me anything? You're not my master. My master is dead."

Caithe said sincerely, "This could be the death of the whole world."

"*My* world *is* dead."

Eir stood stunned on the battlefield.

Logan was gone. Snaff was dead. Glint was dead. And Kralkatorrik lived.

She staggered toward the broken hulk that had once

been Glint. Her wings had been sheared off on impact, and her body was bashed, her neck broken. . . . But her head lay on the sands as if she only slept. Those ferocious horns, those wide and wise eyes, that noble muzzle all mantled in whiskers—

"Forgive me," Eir said. "I was sure we could keep him safe. With Logan, we could have. But now . . ." Eir looked away across the desert. "The plan went wrong. *My* plan."

Glint lay unmoving.

Eir leaned against the jowl of the beast and whispered into her torn ear, "Forgive me."

Only silence answered.

Caithe approached and said, "Rytlock is leaving and Zojja won't move."

Eir clung to the dead dragon.

"Kralkatorrik will be back. We have to regroup."

"Who?" Eir asked, infinitely weary. "You, me, and Garm?"

Caithe tried a different approach. "We can't stay here. There's nothing to eat or drink."

Eir didn't answer.

"So, we have to go somewhere, and we might as well go the same way that Rytlock is going." Caithe took a deep breath. "We have to take Zojja with us, but she won't go."

"Neither will I."

"Come along, Zojja," Caithe said. "We have to go."

The asura looked up from the gutted shell of Big Snaff. Her eyes were empty.

"We have to catch up to Rytlock," Caithe went on.

"There's only one thing I have to do: take his ashes back to Rata Sum."

Caithe nodded. "I will help you. Hand me the urn so you can climb out."

Zojja blinked. "All right." She lifted the metal casing with its precious cargo.

Caithe held it while Zojja climbed out of the wreckage.

Then, side by side, the asura and the sylvari walked.

Rytlock got smaller and smaller on the horizon. In time, he was only a black spot. When night fell, he was gone altogether.

"We should probably stop," Caithe said, setting down the urn that held Snaff.

"I'm cold," Zojja said bleakly. "We need a fire."

"There's nothing to burn," Caithe said.

"I'm going to look."

Zojja spent the next half hour picking across the dunes around them, returning with only a few creosote twigs and the skeleton of a lizard. "Not even enough to keep us warm."

The two women sat side by side beneath the wheeling stars.

"We never caught up to Rytlock," Caithe noted.

Zojja nodded. "We never will."

The sun shone brightly from the white walls of Divinity's Reach and from the white robes of the Seraph.

They filled the street, marching to the slow cadence of tight-strung drums. The snares crackled, and the bass boomed.

It was a funeral march. Each Seraph held one end of a pallet on which lay their fallen friends. One hundred thirty-three Seraph had died in the Ogre Revolt. One of them was Dylan Thackeray.

Logan helped carry his pallet. It was light. The hyenas had been thorough.

But Logan marched beneath a heavy weight. He had returned, but they were gone. All that was left was smashed crystals. He had failed his brother, and he had failed his friends.

At least he hadn't failed his queen.

Even so, the mirror-bright armor he wore—the plate mail of a captain of the Seraph—weighed heavily on Logan, as did the weapon at his belt.

He'd given up his war hammer to wield his fallen brother's sword.

The procession turned down the main avenue between high walls. The people of Divinity's Reach lined the way. Little girls solemnly cast flowers into the lane.

How quiet this parade was.

At least Logan was in Divinity's Reach now. At least he could defend his queen. And maybe in this city, he would never have to fight a charr again.

Legionnaire Rytlock Brimstone stood guard on the curtain wall of the Black Citadel. It was not glamorous duty, but at least he was fighting for the right side again.

When first he returned to the Blood Legion, he was stripped of rank and assigned menial work. An overseer called him a traitor, and Rytlock killed him. That's how he became an overseer. Later, a legionnaire called him a deserter, and Rytlock killed him as well. That's how he became a legionnaire.

Let a centurion call him a friend to humans, and Rytlock would rise again.

He was no longer a friend to humans, especially not to Logan Thackeray.

Rytlock spit from the top of the wall and watched the gobbet fall a hundred feet down before smearing.

Logan, who was now Queen Jennah's lapdog . . .

Logan, who had corrupted a dungeon full of charr . . .

Logan, who had made a fool out of Rytlock . . .

"He'd better hope the Seraph never fight the Blood Legion."

At last, Zojja was back in Rata Sum.

She descended the stairs into Snaff's laboratory. Her gaze fell longingly on the half-finished golems lying there, the projects her master had left undone.

Reaching the floor of the lab, Zojja set down the jar of ashes and lifted a pry bar. She levered up one of the large paving stones and used a shovel to dig into the ground beneath it. An hour of sweat and grit later, his grave was ready.

"You'll always be here," she said to the jar.

Then she lowered the ashes into the ground and shoveled dirt on top.

Soon, she slid the stone back into place. It boomed, the sound echoing from the wide walls.

It was no longer Snaff's laboratory. It was hers, now: genius.

At last.

But she would never build golems the way Snaff had. No one ever would. They would try, of course, but they would fail. Snaff had been a one-of-a-kind genius, and he had taken the secrets of powerstones to the grave with him.

It didn't matter.

Nothing mattered anymore.

"Don't move!"

Garm snapped his head upright, eyes blazing ferociously.

"Stay exactly like that."

He and Eir had returned to Hoelbrak, to her long-disused workshop. Just now, Eir was working on the wolf statue she had abandoned long ago. But she hadn't set a single chisel to the sculpture. She only stood there, holding her tools and staring at the thing.

That's why it was so hard to stay still.

Eir sighed, shaking her head. "I can't see it."

Garm lifted his eyebrows questioningly, but then tried to look straight ahead.

"It's not in there. The statue isn't in there anymore."

Eir laid down her chisels and mallet and stepped up and shoved the rock over, smashing it to the workshop floor.

•   •   •

Caithe walked along the Dragonbrand—the wide swath of destruction laid down by Kralkatorrik. Every once in a while, she would bend down and pull a large green crystal from the sands.

"Dragon blood," she said, staring gladly at one such stone before sliding it into her pack.

It was lonely work, wandering these desolate places, searching for the secrets of Kralkatorrik and the Elder Dragons. But it was even lonelier when she traveled to Hoelbrak or Rata Sum or Divinity's Reach or the Black Citadel only to find that her onetime friends had become strangers.

But they would be friends again. Someday, they would join her. Someday, they would fight the dragons again.

Someday.

About the Author

J. ROBERT KING has written over twenty published novels. In addition to *Guild Wars: Edge of Destiny*, Rob has recently published *Angel of Death* and *Death's Disciples* with Angry Robot Books. Rob also authored the *Mad Merlin* trilogy with Tor, and the Holmes novel *The Shadow of Reichenbach Falls* with Forge.

Rob is very pleased to be collaborating with the ArenaNet team, many of whom he has worked with before. About a decade ago, Jeff Grubb taught Rob to play *Magic: The Gathering*, and Rob went on to write eight Magic novels, including the *Onslaught* and *Invasion* trilogies. He also got to write *The Thran*, which told the origin story of Yawgmoth and the Phyrexians. During that same period, Rob wrote three short stories for *The Duelist* magazine for Will McDermott, who became his point person on all things *Guild Wars*. Rob also edited the first *Legend of the Five Rings* novels, including a couple fine entries from Ree Soesbee, who has been instrumental in developing *Edge of Destiny*. Rob could not have hoped for a finer team of creatives to work with.

Rob lives and works in Wisconsin, where he is editor-in-chief at Write Source and UpWrite Press, imprints that produce writing-instructional materials for kindergarten through graduate school. He has three brilliant sons—writers as well—and a beautiful, multitalented wife. A pair of guinea pigs, two rabbits, two cats, a gecko, and a salamander consider Rob their food god, though he has not had the courage to claim them as dependents on his tax forms.

You can find Rob on Twitter @jrobertking.